"May I rest now?" William said. "Or have you some other torture designed for me?"

"No. Lie still." Rose pulled his boots and stockings off, leaving him only in his trews. She considered removing those, too, but decided to wait until she'd given something to help him sleep. She didn't know if she could strip him with those brilliant blue eyes peering at her.

Rose wiped the rag over his swollen throat, then over his shoulders and chest, wiping down his arms and hands. Though she tried to remain detached from what she was doing, her body grew warm from touching him so freely. He was even more compelling out of clothes than he was in. His bones were long and elegant, layered thickly with smooth slopes of muscle and crisp black hair. No scars or imperfections blemished his smooth, dusky skin. He was a wholly beautiful man and she was not immune. Neither was he, it seemed, for when she reached the hard flat muscles of his belly, she noticed the thick bulge in his trews and was grateful she'd left them on.

Without thinking, she glanced up at his face. Dark, hazy eyes regarded her.

At her look he quirked an eyebrow. "I'm sick," he said. "Not dead."

available as an eBook

ACCLAIM FOR JEN HOLLING'S

BRIDES OF THE BLOODSTONE TRILOGY

CAPTURED BY YOUR KISS

"Passionate, engrossing. . . . *Captured by Your Kiss* is a book to lose yourself in, falling into the intense emotions of the characters and the harshness of the setting and time period, and letting the complex threads of the plot hold your attention until the last page."

—The RomanceReader.com

"Great depth, drama and action. . . . A very strong novel that will satisfy readers of the series. You'll be captivated and completely engaged with the myth, the magic, and the romance Ms. Holling has so beautifully created."

—*Romantic Times*

"Sure to captivate. . . . A trilogy full of love and adventure. All three [are] sure to thrill those who enjoy a medieval tale."

—*Romance Reviews Today*

"Ms. Holling creates a romantic tale with characters who stay in your heart long after their story is over. *Captured by Your Kiss* is a gem of a book, and not to be missed. Get your copy today."

—TheWordonRomance.com

"It was hard to catch my breath as I galloped through the pages of *Captured by Your Kiss*. Ms. Holling's plots are so skillfully written that each book of the trilogy seems to melt into the other. The readers feel right at home in the period, enjoying the company of friends, some old, some new."

—*Rendezvous*

"*Captured by Your Kiss* is a fantastic conclusion of this fascinating trilogy. There is adventure, danger, and a beautiful love story."

—ReadertoReader.com

TAMED BY YOUR DESIRE

"Time stands still as the reader is caught up in the conflict and experiences the excitement of this romantic tale."

—*Rendezvous*

"The clash of wills and biting and dynamic repartee are reminiscent of Shannon Drake's Scottish romances."

—*Romantic Times*

TEMPTED BY YOUR TOUCH

"A tender triumph that tempted me to keep reading all night long."

—Teresa Medeiros, author of *A Kiss to Remember*

ALSO BY JEN HOLLING

My Devilish Scotsman

My Wicked Highlander

Captured by Your Kiss

Tamed by Your Desire

Tempted by Your Touch

Available from Pocket Books

JEN HOLLING

My Shadow Warrior

THE MACDONELL BRIDES TRILOGY

POCKET BOOKS

New York   London   Toronto   Sydney

An *Original* Publication of POCKET BOOKS

POCKET BOOKS, a division of Simon & Schuster, Inc.
1230 Avenue of the Americas, New York, NY 10020

ISBN-13: 978-0-7434-7108-4
ISBN-10:   0-7434-7108-3

First Pocket Books printing August 2005

10   9   8   7   6   5   4

Cover design by Min Choi; cover art by Alan Ayers; type lettering by David Gatti

Manufactured in the United States of America

For information regarding special discounts for bulk purchases, please contact Simon & Schuster Special Sales at 1-800-456-6798 or business@simonandschuster.com

To Jennie Patterson,
For always coming through in a pinch,
long emails and phone calls, and most of all, friendship
You've taught me more about storytelling than anyone else.
Thank you.

My
Shadow
Warrior

Chapter 1

To the right and noble William MacKay, Lord Strathwick,

My deepest wishes that your health and prosperity continue in this most difficult time. Your lack of response to my previous correspondence signifies that this might not be so. If I am mistaken, please take care to correct this misconception. As I explained in my previous missives, my father is still very unwell. It is my greatest wish that you should grace our humble home with a visit. Your miraculous skill in the arts of healing is spoken of throughout the land and I fear you are his last hope. I pray you to remember that these gifts you are blessed with were given to you by the Almighty, to use as He wills. Alan MacDonell is a good and honorable man. He has been a just chieftain to his people and a good servant to His Majesty and God. It cannot but be God's will that you do this. So why do you ignore my pleas?

We have much to offer in the way of compensation and reward, and we will endeavor to meet any request you might make for sustenance or comfort. I pray you, my dear lord, do as God wills you and come to Lochlaire with haste. You are our only hope.

Thus indebted to the great pains you shall
take on our behalf,

your good and humble servant,
Rose MacDonell
From the House of Lochlaire on xv July
The year of our Lord 1597

Rose read the letter over again with a critical eye. It was the tenth letter she'd written him in so many weeks. Her gaze strayed to the window. A gray pall lay over Glen Laire. Soon it would be harvest, then it would turn cold and there would be snow. William MacKay lived in the far, wild north, where the weather and terrain—as well as the inhabitants—were brutal. It would be foolish to attempt the journey in the winter. Time was running out.

It would take at least a week for the letter to reach him. An unspecified amount of time for him to respond. And again, another week or more to receive his answer. A month? Winter was months away. The journey was still possible. Perhaps there was time.

Her shoulders sagged at the futility of these calculations. She'd been writing to the MacKay chief for months. He'd yet to respond to a single plea. What made her think this one was any different? And when the weather turned ugly, it was certain he would not come.

She looked over her shoulder to the still figure on the bed. Alan MacDonell had been clinging to life for months now. He was horribly thin and weak but no worse. In fact, there had been some improvement over the past month. That should encourage her, but it didn't. Rose feared he'd given up the good fight, and without the will to live, all was for naught.

She'd tried, over the past two months, to convince her

family members to help her bring Lord Strathwick to Glen Laire. Uncle Roderick thought it was a bad idea to bring a hunted wizard to Glen Laire and had forbade her to continue writing him. She'd ignored this edict, of course. Hagan, her father's guard, also thought it too dangerous, what with the current state of matters in Scotland. He felt that the wizard's healing powers were too mythic to be true. He feared that Rose only opened herself to disappointment. And though her sisters and brothers-in-law agreed with both Uncle Roderick and Hagan, the earl of Kincreag, Gillian's new husband, had sent a man to fetch the Wizard of the North. To humor her, certainly, but it was something, and Rose was grateful to him.

It was past time Kincreag's man returned, and yet there was no sign of him. Lord Kincreag feared he'd had a mishap on the journey and wouldn't return until the spring. If ever.

All of this merely frustrated Rose. If only she could talk to Lord Strathwick. If only he would answer her letters. She stared down at the parchment before her, wondering what she could do to make this letter somehow different, more convincing than the previous ones.

She rose from the writing table and crossed to her father's bed. Unfortunately her ability to heal was not sufficient to save Alan MacDonell. His sleep was restless. She watched as his gaunt face twitched beneath the full gray beard. He frowned in his sleep, shook his head slightly.

Rose placed a hand against her father's forehead. It was cool. She exhaled, her hand closing into a fist. If he were feverish, then at least she'd know what to do. She closed her eyes, sliding her hand over his head and body, fingers almost touching him, but not quite, seeing the shape of his body in her mind, glowing softly with color.

This was her magic. With concentration, when she passed her hands over a body, she could *see* the ailment. A fever was an angry red glow suffusing the body. The area causing the fever—often internal—was a dark, textured color. Her magic was a great help in diagnosing and treating all sorts of ailments, but it was of no use if she could not see what was wrong.

With her father, she saw nothing. Every person possessed their own color when healthy, and Rose could see that, too, when she passed her hands over them. Alan MacDonell's color was green. Normally a lovely shade like spring grass, it had faded so that she could barely see it. As if the light—and life—were being drained from him. Rose could pinpoint no source, no darkness. Nothing. He was just fading away before her eyes, and there was not a thing she could do to stop it.

The door opened, and Rose's hands fell to her sides.

"How is he?" Uncle Roderick asked softly, moving to the other side of the bed to look down at his brother. Roderick was a big man, with powerful shoulders and lustrous copper hair tied at his nape. His handsome face creased with worry and sadness—and resignation. Everyone else had accepted the inevitable, that Alan MacDonell would soon die. Rose could not accept it. After twelve years apart, it could not end like this. There was more to do. More to say. He *could not* die.

She gazed down at her father. His sleep had calmed.

"He's the same." She clenched her useless hands. Energy still coiled tight in her chest, making her restless and confused. It was always this way, as if there was more to do—but what, she couldn't fathom. "The nightmares are fewer and less severe. No bruising." For a time he'd suffered from horrible nightmares that he'd been unable to remember. And when he'd woken, he'd been covered with odd bruises, as if he'd been beaten. It had been nearly a month since the last incident.

Rose rubbed her eyes wearily. "How is Tira?"

Tira was Roderick's third wife. The MacDonells seemed to be cursed. Rose's father had managed to have three healthy daughters with his wife, Lillian, who had been burned at the stake for witchcraft. He'd wed again, but his second wife had died in childbirth. Uncle Roderick had married three times in the past twelve years. The first two wives had died in childbirth as well. He had no children. His current wife, Tira, was heavily pregnant and due to give birth in a few weeks.

It was a very important baby Tira carried. Alan had no sons, so his lands and leadership of the Glen Laire MacDonells would pass to his younger half brother when he died. If Roderick died without issue, it would all revert back to Alan's children. As Isobel was the oldest, it would go to her husband, Sir Philip Kilpatrick. Rose could think of worse things than Sir Philip being chieftain of the MacDonells, but then Roderick was a strong leader, too, and the MacDonells knew him and trusted him.

And more importantly, it was a son that Tira carried. Many MacDonells were fey. Rose's mother, Lillian, had been a powerful witch. Rose and both of her sisters were witches. And Alan had a shine. One of his powers was the ability to determine the sex of the child a woman carried. He'd never been wrong. Before he'd fallen ill, women had come from miles around so he could touch their bellies. He'd once confided to Rose that he didn't actually have to touch the women to do it, but they'd always offered their bellies up, and it had seemed to make them more confident when he'd laid hands on them.

"Poor Tira. She's tired and has been a bit achy," Roderick said. "Mayhap you could come look at her when ye're done here?"

Rose sighed. She was forever tending Tira for every little twinge. It wasn't Tira who was difficult; it was her doting husband. He panicked at every little pain she had. Though Tira could still get around fine, Roderick had confined her to bed for the past two months.

"If ye're not busy, that is . . ." His gaze moved behind her to the table, where she'd been composing her letter to the Wizard of the North. Rose froze, her gaze darting from the parchment lying innocently on the tabletop back to her uncle. He moved fast. He was around the bed and at the table before her.

Rose tried to snatch the letter, but he grabbed it first. She ended up ripping it, and in the end, she had nothing to show for it but a ruined letter, which her uncle was now reading. Rose watched him, sullen, as he scanned it, his brow furrowed, and resigned herself to the impending tongue-lashing.

When he looked up from the letter his face was grim. "What did I tell you? Did I not warn you to cease writing this man?"

"You're not my chief yet."

Red suffused his neck. "But I *am* your uncle."

Rose had never been one to back down from a fight, especially when it came to one of her patients, and this was no exception. She did not fear her uncle. Beneath it all she knew he loved her and her sisters, but of late, he'd been especially hard on her.

She took a step forward so they were nearly toe to toe. Though a big man, Roderick was not tall. He stood but an inch or two above Rose's height.

"I am a healer—healing is what I do." She gestured helplessly at the bed. "But I can do nothing for my own father. This man can help. I will not stop writing him because you are afraid of witches."

Though Roderick tried to remain stern, his blue eyes were merry with the effort to contain a smile. Finally it burst forth and he shook his head, chuckling. "Afraid, aye? And here I am, surrounded by them." His smile faded and his eyes grew serious again. "It's not the wizard I'm afraid of, but the trouble he'll bring."

"I don't care about that."

Rose turned away, but Roderick grabbed her shoulder and forced her to face him again.

"You should. He is a hunted man. His own clan has turned against him. They say he can change forms—turn into wolves and such, and has familiars. It's said he goes nowhere without a demon rat."

Rose made a dismissive sound and rolled her eyes.

Roderick's fingers tightened on her shoulder. "Nonsense it might be, but the fact remains people are talking, and they are frightened of him. It takes less than that for a burning. He's too dangerous. I have heard, too, there is a witchpricker traveling the Highlands, searching for work. If he gets word the Wizard of the North is here at Glen Laire, where do you think he will travel next, aye? Would you really bring this upon your family in these times?"

Her jaw tightened. *These times*. They were bad times. Burning times. At one time, only the king could burn a witch—legally, but witches were often lynched and burned anyway. Rose's mother was the perfect example of such a transgression gone unpunished. Five years ago, the king had granted commissions to any body of men in any village, giving them the power to try and burn witches. Churchmen and villagers had wasted no time rooting out suspects and singeing the air with pitch and fire. There was still no end in sight.

And that was exactly why there was no time to lose. What if Lord Strathwick were lynched as her mother had been? The urgency of the situation descended on Rose with renewed force. She could take care of herself, and her sisters had able husbands. Bringing the wizard here was an acceptable risk. This traveling witchpricker need never know a thing. But there was no convincing her uncle of this.

She let out a defeated sigh and nodded, eyes averted.

Despite twelve years apart, in the few months they'd been back together her uncle had gotten to know her relatively well.

"I mean it, Rose. Ye'll not convince me so easily. No more letters, understand?"

She glared at him, which seemed to be what he expected from her. He nodded and went to the door. He turned back, his hand on the latch, and asked pleasantly, "Ye'll be up to tend my Tira, aye?"

Rose managed a curt nod.

When he was gone, her father's guard, Hagan, entered, his heavy brow creased apologetically. "I'm sorry, lass. Roderick just told me I was not to aid you anymore."

The enormous Irishman had been helping her smuggle the missives to Lord Strathwick out of the castle so they could be given to travelers heading north. Hagan stood at the door, dark head lowered, thoroughly sheepish.

It seemed there was nothing left to do but fetch the wizard herself.

Rose found her sisters in the great hall. They were both seated near the largest fireplace at the west end. Isobel's gloved hands were extended out before her, draped with wool yarn. Gillian rolled the red yarn from Isobel's hands into a ball, gray eyes on something in the corner that only she could see.

"Well, dear, what *is* the last thing you remember?" Gillian asked the empty air.

Isobel watched the corner avidly, as if she might see something materialize.

"Any luck with the bairns?" Rose asked, sitting on the bench beside Isobel.

The ghosts of two wee lassies haunted this hall. They'd been spotted on occasion by servants, laughing and playing, but when someone got close they always disappeared. Gillian not only saw them all the time but spoke to them, too. It hadn't always been this way for

Rose's sister. Someone had cursed Gillian after their mother was burned, and she'd only recently regained her ability to communicate with the dead.

Gillian ignored Rose for a moment, soft gray eyes intent on the corner, apparently attending to something the ghost children said to her. She was as lovely and perfect as always, in a green silk gown draped with a red-and-green arisaid. Thick sable hair was pulled away from her face, the glossy curls packed into a jeweled caul. The perfect countess.

Isobel's pale green eyes turned toward Rose, and she whispered, "They don't understand they're dead." She shook her head sadly, her thick copper-gold braid slipping over her shoulder. It, too, was kinked from curls. Rose was the only one of the three with impossibly straight auburn hair.

Isobel continued in a low voice, "It's making it most difficult for Gillian to help them move on."

Gillian smiled ruefully. "All they want to do is play."

"And what's wrong with that?" Rose asked. "I think I'd like to be a bairn forever and have nothing better to do than play."

Gillian's eyes softened and her smile faded. "You never did play much, did you? Always healing, even when you were a wee thing."

"Aye, well," Rose said, feeling guilty for expressing such feelings. Her mother had worked very hard to teach her, even though Lillian herself had not been a healer. She'd had such faith in her youngest daughter, and Rose had failed her. She'd been barely competent when Lillian had died. Rebellious and complaining, she'd given her mother fits. Rose gave a small shake of her head, putting it from her mind. She couldn't change it now, so there was no value in dwelling on it. Instead she worked hard to be the healer her mother had always believed she could be.

Rose nodded to the corner. "Why can't they just stay here and play?"

Gillian sighed and gazed at the empty air thoughtfully. "I suppose they can for now. But they should move on. Others are there, waiting for them. They'll be happier."

"It sounds as if they're happy now."

"They keep asking about their mother," Gillian said. "They understand that she's dead, but they don't understand *they're* dead. If they'd move on, they'd be with their mother again."

"Unless she went to the other place," Rose said.

Gillian shook her head firmly. "She didn't."

"How do you know?" Rose asked, skeptical. Her sister could see ghosts, but so far there'd been no mention of an afterlife.

"Because there is no hell."

Isobel looked around the hall nervously, but no one was close enough to overhear. "Hush, Gillian. That's blasphemy you speak."

Gillian shrugged. "It's the truth—or so it seems to me. Hell is of our own making, if we're afraid to move on."

"So the wee lassies are in hell?" Rose asked.

"That's not what I said. They've not made it into a hell. They don't even understand they *can* move on. They're just children. It's the ones that tie themselves to a place and haunt it. Those are the ones in hell."

Rose considered this while Isobel glanced around nervously.

"Can we speak of something else?" Isobel whispered. After nearly being burned herself for witchcraft, Isobel had become quite cautious about such things.

"Aye," Rose said. "I've something to tell you, but you must not breathe a word to anyone—especially Uncle Roderick." Rose scanned the hall. It was deserted except for a few hounds lazing in the rushes. She leaned closer to her sisters. "I'm leaving at first light. I'm going to bring Lord Strathwick here."

They both stared at her as if she'd gone mad. And perhaps she had, to undertake this alone, but she could see no other alternatives.

"Tell Da for me, but give me as much of a head start as possible in case he tries to send someone after me. Two days would be good."

Isobel reacted first, shaking her head in bewilderment. "You're going north—*alone?*"

Before Rose could respond, Gillian gripped her arm. "You *cannot* go alone."

"And who should I take? Who can I trust here?"

Isobel and Gillian exchanged an uneasy glance.

"Fash not. I will disguise myself as a man."

Gillian grabbed her hand and squeezed it. "Rose—think! Broken men roam the Highlands. Even lone men are in danger."

"You and Isobel traveled alone, and not disguised as men either. You came to no ill."

"We were fortunate."

"As will I be."

Her sisters still looked uneasy, and Rose couldn't risk them doing something foolish, like telling their husbands. That might end her journey before it began. She stared down at the rush-strewn floor for a long moment, then inhaled deeply through her nose. "I'm not a fool. I know that some of the stories about this wizard might be just that—fables. But I can't help hoping . . ." Rose's heart raced at the thought, her voice catching momentarily. "If he is real, then I'll bring him back if I have to tie him to my horse. But if he's not . . ." She didn't want to consider that. "I *have* to know."

Gillian's lips thinned, and she gazed at Rose with worried gray eyes. "But are you sure it's wise? Nicholas's man never returned . . . we don't know what happened to him. The journey north is harsh and dangerous."

"Aye, but they haven't burned nearly as many witches up north. It's far safer than what you two did a few months back, traveling into the heart of the witch hunt to save Sir Philip."

"Aye," Isobel conceded, "but there are other dangers in the north."

"It'll be fine. I promise. I lived on Skye, remember? I can't imagine a bigger band of hempies then the MacLeans. I'm well used to such men."

They both still looked so worried. Rose sighed and held her arm out to Isobel. "Have a look—see what happens."

Isobel frowned uncertainly. She had visions when she touched some things. Sometimes she saw the past, sometimes the present, sometimes the future. She'd been working hard to gain greater control of the gift, and she was having some success. She removed her gloves and gripped Rose's sleeve. After a moment she shut her eyes, her smooth brow creasing.

Rose and Gillian watched her closely. When her sage green eyes drifted open, they were empty, sightless. The troubled lines in her forehead became more pronounced, and her hand tightened on Rose's arm. She shook her head slightly, as if trying to shake off something disturbing, then her shoulders relaxed and a smile spread across her face. She released Rose's arm.

"What is it?" Rose asked impatiently.

"Oh, you'll be back—and in time to deliver Tira of a large son."

"You saw this?" Gillian asked, eyes wide.

"Aye, I did. It will be a difficult birth—you'll nearly lose both mother and child. There is a strange man there I don't recognize. He has gray hair. I think he's your wizard. He helps with the birth."

A surge of excitement and determined hope shot through Rose. Isobel's visions weren't always accurate, but they were often enough to make Rose confident her mission would be a success. "You see? There is naught to fash on. I'll be back with the wizard within the month."

Isobel grew serious. She seemed to be mulling something over, then she blurted out, "I saw something else, Rose, before the birthing. Something from your past."

Rose's gut clenched. "Aye?"

Isobel bit her lip hesitantly. "Would you like to talk about what happened on Skye?"

"No, I wouldn't." Rose tried to keep her face expressionless, though it felt stiff and unnatural from the effort, but she was determined to discourage further questions.

Gillian, of course, had no clue what they were talking about, and she looked between the two of them curiously. Rose was certain Isobel would fill Gillian in later, and that made resentment simmer, but not enough to discuss it. Let them think what they would. She had other things to fash on.

"What about Jamie MacPherson?" Gillian asked.

Rose's hand went to the ribbon around her neck, drawing the locket from her bodice where it lay against her heart. Jamie MacPherson was her betrothed. He'd been writing letters to her for months now. They'd known each other as children, and she remembered him with great fondness. She longed to wed him, but she'd written him, telling him she could not in good conscience marry him so long as her father was so ill. He'd written back assuring her that he understood and would wait.

She opened the locket and gazed down into her betrothed's cerulean eyes, his handsome face framed by golden hair. She shut the locket abruptly and tucked it back into her bodice. "He doesn't have to know . . . besides, if he ever finds out, he would understand. He is a good man, like Sir Philip and Lord Kincreag."

Her sisters had been most fortunate in their husbands—fine men both, who adored their wives.

Rose stood. "I need to have a look at Tira so Uncle Roderick doesn't suspect anything." She gave them both a penetrating look. "Not a word to anyone. If someone comes looking for me tomorrow, tell them I've the bloody flux and cannot leave my chambers."

Isobel and Gillian stood, giving Rose swift, firm hugs

and wishing her Godspeed. Filled with hope and resolve, she left to begin her preparations.

From his tower window he watched her leave under shadow of darkness and fog. She thought she was being clever—she always thought she was being clever. But in truth, she was doing exactly what he wanted. She'd interfered for the last time. The demon-raising ceremony was a lengthy one, consisting of days of fasting and prayer, and he could not do it with her present. Her sisters might cause some problems, but not nearly the delays Rose had caused him. Besides, he could charm the sisters into anything. Rose did not respond to charm or scolding or anything.

How she had become such a hard woman, he didn't know—her time on Skye with the MacLeans, no doubt—nor did he care. Not anymore. He looked to the sky. The moon was waxing. Soon it would be full and he could finally begin.

Chapter 2

◈

Strathwick Castle, Northern Highlands, a fortnight later.

"My lord? She's still out there. In the rain."

William flicked a disinterested glance at the large, scarred man-at-arms standing in the doorway, wringing his hands. The rather incongruous sight gave him a brief prick of amusement.

When he made no response, Wallace went on, "She'll catch her death, she will. At least let me show her to the stables."

William's brother Drake made a rude noise. He lounged in William's chair before the fire, a leg slung over the carved arm, jet-black hair gleaming in the firelight. "Serves her right if she does catch her death. It's not my lord's fault if she's stupid enough to stand out in the rain like a coof."

"She's not stupid," William said. The carved wooden box on his desk drew his gaze. "She'll get out of the rain eventually." His gaze swept the room. "Leave me."

Drake stood and stretched but didn't leave. When the others were gone, he gave William a keen look. "You're acting strange."

"Rumor has it I *am* strange."

Drake lifted a shoulder and palm to acknowledge that. "Aye, well, more so than usual. You seem preoccupied since the MacDonell lass arrived."

That was true, but William didn't mean to discuss it with Drake. "I'm well enough."

Drake hesitated, as if there was more he wanted to say, but finally left. Alone at last, William crossed the room to his desk. He rested a hand on the wooden box, pensive. Why had he kept that letter? He'd burned all her others. He tapped the lid of the box. The musing question repeated itself with each tap of his fingers against the wood. *Why? Why? Why?*

He removed the letter and held it in his hand, still folded, still bearing the broken red wax and her bold scrawl: *Deliver to Lord William MacKay of Strathwick.*

He had known immediately something was wrong when he'd received this letter. All her letters were full of desperation and pleading—and authority. Her father was dying. He was her only hope. God commanded it of him. Her audacity made him smile. But still, he'd burned all the others. It had never occurred to him to reply.

This letter, however, had been different. His name across the front was uneven, scrawled, lacking the brazen confidence of the others. He strolled to the fireplace, fingers caressing the parchment. He stared down at the folded letter. *Feed it to the flames.*

Instead he sat, leaning back in his chair, and unfolded it for perhaps the hundredth time since receiving it.

My dearest Lord Strathwick,

Why do you ignore me? I know you must be used to such requests. You must receive scores of them with regularity, and I ken I'm just another hopeful petitioner. It is impossible on parchment to convey my earnest need for you. I can only tell you that I, too, am a healer, and every soul I lose is a burden to my conscience. At first, I didn't suppose a man possessing the miracle of healing by touch could understand that, but then recalled that even the Saints endured trials. You are a man with a divine gift, but you are still a man. I know that at times you must feel helpless and alone as I do now. I cannot tell you the circumstances that separated my family for twelve years, but I have only just regained them, and I am now losing my father to a mysterious ailment. The loss of my mother was the catalyst for the events that tore my sisters and I from my father and each other. That is all I can say of that. I cannot bear to lose my father now when there's still so much unfinished. I feel so impotent when it seems as if there must be something I could do. Why would God give me this gift, then make it impossible to help those I loved the most? It vexes me terribly. Surely you can understand this and as a fellow healer will grant me this boon?

My hand has run away with me. I plead like a fool and make little sense. I think to tear this letter to shreds and start anew, but I fear, you do not read them anyway, so what matter?

> *Your friend eternally,*
> *Rose MacDonell*
> *From the House of Lochlaire on x June*
> *The year of our Lord 1597*

William inhaled deeply, carefully refolding the parchment and tapping it against his thigh. He had replied to this letter. Twice. He'd burned both versions. That was the only reason he'd saved this letter, he told himself, and not very convincingly. Because the rawness of it—as if she'd opened a vein and bled onto the parchment for him alone—deserved an answer. And yet everything he wrote in response was inadequate, mere dressing to cushion the force of his reply. No. He would not help her. And she would not accept that answer.

He lifted the letter so that firelight reflected off the smooth surface of the parchment, smudged now from his many readings. She was here now, outside his walls. Would he really send her away without even talking to her? Without looking upon the face that had written these words? It seemed wrong to invite her in, to give her hope, and yet he needed to see her. It was a physical pull, a hole that somehow wanted filling.

He rubbed the corner of the letter thoughtfully against his chin. Perhaps there was a way.

Rose's clothes were soaked through so that she shivered violently, her teeth chattering, but still she sat in the meager protection of the gatehouse, rainwater pooling about her feet and bottom. She could see faint lights from the village, but the rain and fog obscured the cottages. Logic told her to get to her feet, walk to the village, and seek shelter. Her horse stood over her, head down, the rain beating onto her back.

Rose had told the porter to inform Lord Strathwick that she wasn't leaving until he spoke with her. The porter had warned her she would drown first, but she waited stubbornly. Her mother had always said she was obstinate, that when she got an idea in her head, she refused to let loose of it.

She buried her face in her cold, wet hands as another violent shiver racked her. It had taken a fortnight to get here, and not through easy terrain. It had been long and grueling and she'd done it alone, disguised as a lad. She'd looked forward to company on the return trip, eagerly anticipated long conversations with Strathwick about healing. Perhaps he'd even have been willing to teach her something.

Fool!

And still she sat, stubborn as an ass. She'd said she wouldn't leave until she spoke to him, and by God, she'd drown before she left this spot. Judging by the puddle forming around her, it appeared that might actually occur. Laughter rippled through her unexpectedly.

"Miss? Are you unwell?"

The deep, masculine voice startled her, and a jolt went through her. She dropped her hands and squinted upward, pushing back the sopping brim of her hat. A man towered over her, his plaid pulled over his head, shielding him from the rain and her scrutiny. His face was but a dark shadow, the features indistinct, leaving her only with the impression of great height and breadth.

"Just drowning," she said, then bit back a foolish smile.

He said nothing for a long moment, staring down at her. Though the dark and the plaid hid his expression, she sensed he frowned at her. Probably thought she was mad. Perhaps she was.

"Come," he said, his deep voice kind but impersonal. "You must get out of the rain."

His sudden presence and concern sparked hope. "Inside the castle?"

"No, I know someone in the village who will give you a place before their fire."

Rose sighed. "My thanks, but I'm not moving." She frowned up at him thoughtfully. "Are you from the castle? I didn't see anyone cross the bridge."

He hesitated, then nodded. "Aye, I work in the stables."

"Tell your master he can throw my bloated corpse in the moat when I drown. I'm not moving."

"I doubt he'll want your body floating in his moat, making the place smell, but make no mistake, you will die out here before he'll see you."

Rose's heart sank, and she found herself perilously close to tears for the first time in weeks. She'd held out such hope that Strathwick was the answer to her prayers, had traveled so far, for it to come to this. There was nothing more to do. Her father's cause was lost.

She held out her hand, resigned that she'd lost another battle. He stared at it for a moment, then grasped it. He was solid and warm, and again she felt a wave of despair, along with the urge to sob her story on this nice groom's shoulder. He pulled her to her feet and abruptly dropped her hand.

She turned and gazed up at the tall walls, at the black clouds boiling above.

"Can you tell me why he won't answer my letters? Why he won't even speak to me?"

The man had taken her horse's reins and had already

turned Moireach around, ready to lead her across the bridge to the village.

"I know not, miss. I just work in the stables."

Rose turned to get a good look at her new friend. He was very tall, a head taller than her at least. His hair was dark, but that was all she could discern with his plaid covering it. He was a fine-looking man, clean-shaven, with a strong, unsmiling mouth. He had the broad, thick shoulders of someone used to hard work. His trews and boots were faded, though well made.

"What is your name, sir, so I might thank you for your kindness?" She slanted a poisonous glance at the castle. "You are far kinder than your master."

"Dumhnull."

"Well met, Dumhnull. My name is Rose, and you can tell your master that I will be back on the morrow." She looked upward and grimaced. "But for tonight, I think you're right. He cannot speak to a dead woman, can he?"

Dumhnull had yet to smile at her, and though he didn't now she thought perhaps there was a softening to his stern mouth. His lips parted as if he meant to speak, then shut on an exhalation. Finally he raised his dark brows and said, "No, miss, I suppose he cannot." There was a curious note of forbearance in his voice, but before she could question it, he inclined his head for her to follow him.

She trudged after him, keeping her head down. The brim of her floppy hat bobbed with each step. It had long ceased protecting her from the deluge. Her hair was thoroughly soaked beneath the hat, plastered to her head and streaming in rivulets down the sides of her face and neck. She shivered convulsively, eagerly anticipating dry clothes and a warm fire.

They crossed the bridge and passed several cottages before he stopped near one. Fresh thatching repelled the rain so it flowed down to shower on the ground. Bags of sand pressed up against the base of the dark stones, preventing the rain from seeping underneath.

He nodded at it. "The blacksmith and his wife live there. They'll feed you and give you a place to sleep."

"My thanks, friend." Rose reached for the reins, but when her fingers closed over the leather, he didn't release them. She stood rather close to him. She tilted her head back to meet his eyes. Blue, brilliant as a sapphire and just as startling. She stared for a long moment, and he stared back. His gaze moved over her face in a manner overbold for a mere groom. Rose felt a moment of panic, her sisters' warnings echoing through her mind. He knew she was alone and unprotected. She held his gaze without wavering and tugged on the reins.

He released them and averted his eyes to scan the sky. "You really should be on your way in the morn, if the rain clears."

"I thank you for your warnings, but I cannot." She gave him a speculative look from beneath her lashes. "Would you be willing to help me, Dumhnull?"

"How?"

"Sneak me in?"

He appeared scandalized at the suggestion. "Nay— you'd not want to do that, miss. Have you not heard the tales? He's a wizard, he's evil."

"Idle gossip spread by ignorant rustics. I pay it no heed."

He glanced around cautiously, then leaned in closer. She resisted the urge to step back. An uncomfortable fluttering had begun in her belly. He was so very large, and she was very much alone. Though he'd shown her nothing but kindness, his proximity unnerved her. But if he had any inappropriate intentions, it did not behoove her to show fear. She knew from experience that to men with mischief in mind, fear was oft an aphrodisiac, whereas courage nearly always discouraged them.

"The villagers have tried to capture him several times. He doesn't dare leave the castle."

Rose's mouth opened on an exhalation as she gazed up at her new friend. "But I mean him no harm. I—I know about that, about persecution. Not myself," she hastened to add when he drew back from her warily. "I—well, someone I knew."

He shook his head firmly. "Your sympathy is wasted, lass. Go home."

She gazed helplessly at him, but he just backed away. "Ask the blacksmith. He knows. He'll tell you true. But do not mention that anyone from the castle sent you. They hate us all."

She frowned at the cozy cottage, beckoning to her as she shivered in the rain. When she turned back, Dumhnull was gone.

She was welcomed by the blacksmith and his wife. The blacksmith was an enormous redhead named Tadhg, and he was beside himself with excitement when he learned Rose was a healer.

"Ack—my tooth, it aches and throbs. I cannot sleep, I

cannot think of aught anymore but the tooth. It's my whole life." He sat, his brawny frame slumped in his chair, his thick-fingered hand cupping his copper-bearded cheek, looking thoroughly pathetic.

His short, stout wife placed a bowl of a thin broth and a chunk of dark bread before Rose, then stopped behind her husband, putting her hands on his shoulder. Her dark hair was caught back in a severe bun and her round face was dour, but she gazed at her husband with affection, kneading his shoulders.

"He moans so terribly at night, I cannot sleep at all, either. Is there aught you can do for him?"

"Do you not have a barber?" Rose asked, gratefully sipping the stew. The goodwife had loaned her a homespun shift that was too large but clean and warm. She sat huddled on the bench under a thick wool plaid while her clothes dried before the fire.

Tadhg shook his head. "Plague got him."

He gazed at Rose with such pained hope, his big hand rubbing his copper-bearded cheek.

She smiled reassuringly. "I'm sure there's something I can do. But tell me, why do you not go to your chief? I've heard he is a great healer."

Tadhg's face darkened. His wife turned away abruptly, returning to the hearth.

"He is not a healer. He is a sorcerer. He doesn't heal people, he gives them to the devil. I'd not let him touch me if he begged."

His wife turned from the cauldron she stirred, her cheeks ruddy with affronted passion and her eyes dark slits in her doughy face. "Not that my lord would beg.

Not him. He'd let us all die afore he'd soil his hands with any real healing, mind you."

Taken aback by their fervor, Rose said, "But the stories I've heard—"

"Och, there's stories all right," the older woman said.

Rose's shoulders slumped. "They're not true then."

"Oh, it's all true." Tadhg nodded sagely. "I've seen him do it myself."

He leaned back in his chair, the pain in his face easing at the prospect of a story. "It was about a year ago. Allister, my apprentice, was out cutting wood. His wee wife came by to bring him some dinner. He didn't know she was there, so he was startled. The ax slipped, and he cut her in the leg. He brought her here. We bound it up, but it festered and she fell into a fever. We knew the end was near. Allister had sent word to Lord Strathwick, but our chief never came. Allister was sore grieving there at the end, and went up to the castle himself, carrying on about how if the chief didn't save his Betty he'd have the MacKay's heart."

Rose leaned across her stew, listening with breathless interest. "Did that work?"

"Aye, it did. He came down, though you could tell just by looking at him he'd rather be any place else. He had a look at Betty's leg, then told her not to fear." Tadhg extended his thick, rough hands in front of him, his expression reverent. "He lay his hands on her leg. It took but a minute. When he lifted his hands, Betty's leg was as smooth as if the accident never happened. She was awake, too, blinking at us like an owl, asking what happened."

Rose sat back on the bench. "So that's it? He touched

her leg and the wound disappeared? Did he say anything afterward?"

Tadhg dropped his hands to his knees. "Nay, he never stays after a healing. His brother comes with him, and they leave immediately. Never around long enough for a thank-ee sir."

Rose frowned, confused. "Why do you feel so ill about him? It sounds as if he could heal your tooth better than I could. I have no such magic."

Tadhg's bearded face distorted into a sneer of hatred. "Nay, I'll not let him mark me for the devil."

"What about Betty? He healed her. That is a miracle and you saw it. "

"No miracle—the devil's work. He made her into a witch."

"Really?" Rose said, skeptical. "How do you know? What did she do?"

"She told old Gannon that if the weather turned, his chickens would die. Sure enough, when it got cold last winter, two chickens did die. Allister also said that sometimes he saw her staring at his arm, or his foot, and the next day, he'd have cramps in the limb she'd been staring at. 'She be giving you the evil eye,' I said to him. So he turned her out, and several others drove her into the woods. But did she leave? No, she's with *him* now. A married woman, living in sin with the chief."

Rose raised her brows but didn't respond. Married or not, they'd exiled poor Betty. Rose couldn't blame her for going to her chief for succor. It was a terrible pass they'd come to if a wife could no longer look at her husband without being suspected of witchcraft.

They finished eating, and Rose had a look in Tadhg's mouth. His breath was foul, and no wonder—he had a rotting tooth. She extracted it for him and packed the socket with a poultice, giving him instructions to bite down and not talk until the morning, when she would have another look. She waved away his wife's profuse thanks, glad she was able to repay the couple's kindness.

Rose bedded down before the fire with several chickens, a pig, and a large goose. She found she could not sleep, in spite of the comfortable bed and full belly. She was besieged by thoughts of Lord Strathwick and Dumhnull and all Tadhg had said. She remembered Isobel's vision and was more convinced than ever that if she could only speak to the MacKay chief face-to-face she could convince him to aid her. He was not without mercy or kindness, otherwise he'd have left Betty to her fate—both times.

When Tadhg's peaceful snores joined the general snuffling, scratching, and rooting of the animals, Rose slid out from beneath the warmth of her blanket. The rain had stopped. She'd brought a clean shift and gown and had kept them dry by wrapping them in oiled canvas.

She dressed quietly before the fire, putting her boy's boots on and carrying her finer slippers. She brushed her hair until it shone, then twisted it behind her head. She had no looking glass, so she smoothed her hands over her hair to be certain it was presentable. She had scrubbed her face and hands before she'd lain down. She felt like a warrior donning his armor before a great battle, except her armor was the trappings of femininity. She could only hope he would find her pleasing and feel pity for her plight.

She left coins on the blacksmith's table, gathered her things, and left the cottage. Moireach was stabled behind the cottage with the blacksmith's mule and goats. Rose decided to leave her there for now. She was determined to find a way in to Strathwick and it would be easier without a horse in tow.

She hurried along in the dark. She wore a dark plaid wrapped around her to aid in blending into the misty darkness. At the bridge leading to Strathwick she crouched low to the ground. Torches lit the ramparts, and two men-at-arms made a slow circuit of the walls. She tracked their path, and when they disappeared, she sprinted, racing across the bridge and up the path, stopping only when she was in the shelter of the wall. She pressed herself against it, breathing hard, her breath pluming out before her in a cloud. She clapped a plaid-covered hand over her mouth to hide it.

Her heart hammered in her ears as she waited. When she was certain she'd not been sighted, she crept along the berm, staying close to the wall. Dumhnull had left the castle somehow, and not through the gatehouse, as she'd been sitting by it and would have seen him.

She glanced upward. The sky was thick and hazy, the air close with moisture. It would rain again soon, and if she didn't get inside, her good gown would be ruined. Then how would she look presenting herself to Lord Strathwick?

She walked for some time, circling the castle and passing two drum towers before arriving at a postern door. There was no porter window on this door, so they'd have to open it if they wanted to see who was there.

She stood there for several minutes, heart racing, considering what she would say when they opened the door. What more could she utter that she hadn't already? Not a single plea had moved them. She would have to use force. She pressed her palm to her forehead. She was not a short woman, but she was thin, always had been. That did not mean she was weak, but still, she was no match for a man-at-arms. She bolstered herself. Speed and surprise would be her ally. She could do this. For her father.

She drew her dirk from her boot and set her bundle aside. She took a deep breath, preparing herself, and hid the dirk in the folds of her skirt. She hammered on the door purposefully.

It opened almost immediately, as if someone waited on the other side. She rushed in the open door. A woman stood on the other side, her mouth opened in almost comical surprise.

She came at Rose, frantically trying to push her back out the open doorway. Rose quickly sidestepped, pressing herself against the wall just inside the door.

"Oh, no! You must go!" The woman grabbed Rose's arm and tried dragging her.

The woman was shorter than Rose was, but stouter. Still, when Rose dug in her heels, the woman could not budge her.

"I'm going nowhere until I speak with Lord Strathwick."

The woman ran away, shouting for help. Rose panicked. Men-at-arms would come, prepared to deal with an intruder, and she would be thrown out or worse. Rose sprinted after the woman, fear spurring her to recklessness.

The woman was easily caught but not so easily restrained. She fought, arms flailing, screaming and scratching. Rose grappled desperately with her as two men appeared, afraid she might inadvertently stab the woman or herself in the battle.

The men were wrapped in green-and-brown wool plaids, bristling with weapons, their expressions forbidding. One seemed vaguely familiar. He had pale blond hair thinning at the crown and a ragged scar on his cheek. Rose's heart surged. She grabbed the woman's hair, yanking her head back. The woman screeched in pain. Rose pressed the dirk to her throat.

"Be still, woman, before I cut you," Rose hissed in her ear. Even to her own ears she sounded dangerously unstable.

The woman finally grew still, though she trembled and moaned.

The men stopped in their tracks, hands out in a calming gesture. The other man was younger, a comely man, with thick black hair and dark, angry eyes. He had drawn his sword and looked ready to hack her in two. So much for looking pitiful.

Rose looked from one man to the other, her hand shaking so violently that she feared she would nick the woman inadvertently. She glared at the men. "Take me to Lord Strathwick or I slit her gullet." Rose would never do such a thing, but it sounded sufficiently threatening, and she was desperate.

Apparently some of that desperation showed in her eyes. The men exchanged an alarmed look. The dark man lowered his sword but did not sheath it.

The blond man took a deep breath, his hands still out in a calming gesture. "Put it down, Mistress MacDonell. No need to hurt anyone."

Rose nearly dropped her dirk in astonishment. He knew her name! But there was no time to ask how he knew her. She pulled the woman's hair back, exposing more neck. "Bring me to him, damnit, or she dies!"

The woman whimpered and snuffled, and the men just stood there, watching Rose as if she were a wild animal, which she supposed she was at the moment. She *felt* wild—capable of nearly anything—which was both frightening and exhilarating.

"Now!" she bellowed to emphasize her point. The woman she held flinched and let out a squeak of terror.

But still the men made no move to comply with her demands. Rose was scrambling for her next course of action when she noted the blond man's gaze dart to something behind her.

Rose tried to jerk around, but she wasn't quick enough. Her wrist was seized and her dirk yanked downward, away from the woman's throat. Another arm snaked around her waist and hauled her off her feet. The woman ran, throwing herself into the blond man's arms. Rose fought her captor, frenzied with fear and confusion, legs kicking gracelessly in the air, her free arm flailing. The hand holding her wrist squeezed until she dropped the dirk.

Her captor dropped her abruptly. She fell hard on her posterior, knocking the air from her lungs. She scrambled around, gasping for air and wincing at the pain in her backside.

"Dumhnull!" she gasped, then shut her mouth tightly. She didn't want to cause him trouble, but she feared it was too late. She glanced at the other men. The black-haired one frowned severely at Dumhnull.

The groom leaned over to pick up her dirk, avoiding her gaze. His head was uncovered now, and she saw that he was older than she'd initially thought. Gray streaked his black hair, and though his face was unlined, the set of his jaw was rigid, and his beautiful eyes were hard and flat.

He was angry with her for her brutal entrance after his kindness. She couldn't blame him. She wondered if he would help her still, or even if he could, as a mere groom. She continued to gaze at him, her heart still racing, but he refused to look at her. She was caught now, at their mercy, without a single ally. She closed her eyes, rejecting the urge to capitulate. She was here, in Strathwick. She couldn't give up yet.

She turned her attention to the other men. "I'm here to see Lord Strathwick. I'll not leave until I see him." Her bravado elicited some amused glances and an exclamation of disbelief from the black-haired man, but she rose to her knees and raised her chin.

The comely black-haired man stepped forward, his mouth curved into a sneer of contempt. "*I'm* Lord Strathwick."

A jolt of surprise went through Rose. She closed her eyes in horror. This was worse than she'd thought. It would have been bad enough having him hear about what she'd done secondhand; she still might have been able to talk her way out of it, charm him. But he'd witnessed her chasing one of his people down and holding a dirk to her throat.

Against her will and pride, she looked back at Dumhnull, unable to hide the blind panic building inside her. He still would not look at her. He tapped her dirk thoughtfully against his thigh, staring at his chief with an odd intensity.

Rose turned back to Strathwick. She spread her hands before her, trying to appear submissive and contrite—not difficult, as she still knelt in the dirt. "I pray you, my lord, just hear me out. If you still refuse me after speaking to me, I vow to leave you in peace."

Lord Strathwick approached her slowly, his slashing black brows lowered over dark blue eyes. He circled her, looking her up and down. Finally he stood before her, his expression scornful, but he said, "Very well, then. Follow me." His gaze jerked behind her. "You, too, *Dumhnull.*" He turned abruptly and stalked toward the castle.

Rose let out an astonished breath, weakness flooding her limbs.

Dumhnull grasped her arm and pulled her to her feet. "Looks as if you've gotten your way, miss."

From his grim expression, she wasn't at all certain that was a good thing.

Chapter 3

Rose's heart beat furiously as Dumhnull led her through the castle. "Forgive me for speaking your name," Rose whispered, looking up at him anxiously. "I hope I didn't cause you any trouble."

He kept his gaze fixed straight ahead, the sapphire color of his eyes hidden by thick, sooty lashes. He was dressed finer today, in close-fitting trews that accentuated his long, muscular legs, a leather doublet and a red-and-black plaid mantle slung over his wide shoulders. She wondered if he was really a groom.

"No trouble," he said without sparing her a glance.

Rose slanted another look at him as she hurried to keep up with his brisk pace. "You are vexed with me."

He finally looked at her, arching a dark brow. "Why should I be vexed?"

"Because you warned me away and I did not take your advice."

"I didn't think you would."

"Really?" she said, surprised by this revelation. "Then why did you bother?"

The look he gave her was enigmatic and dark, sending a strange thrill through her that centered somewhere in the pit of her belly. She quickly averted her eyes from that gaze, unnerved to find herself responding to it, and instead studied the room they'd just entered.

They were in a dark, cavernous hall. Swords and shields adorned the walls. An enormous wooden candelabrum hung from the rafters, the candles cold, but a large fireplace at the end of the hall blazed. Trestle tables and benches lined the walls, leaving the center of the hall clear and sprinkled with fragrant rushes. The MacKay chief sprawled into his chair before the fire. He snapped his fingers at Dumhnull. "Get me a drink."

Dumhnull stiffened, and his eyes narrowed slightly. He bowed. "And what do you wish to drink, my lord?"

Lord Strathwick regarded the groom keenly, a small, strange smile about his mouth. "Mulled wine." When Dumhnull inclined his head, Strathwick added, "Mull it yourself."

Dumhnull hesitated, glaring at his master before stalking to the kitchens. Rose watched his retreating back before returning her attention to the MacKay chief.

Strathwick's face grew serious as he regarded Rose steadily beneath thick black brows. He was younger than Rose had expected, not much older than herself, it seemed. She was twenty. He couldn't be over five and twenty. He was tall and well formed—not as pleasing to look upon as the groom, though some would argue, she suspected. He was dressed carelessly, a once-fine plaid slung about his shoulders. His trews were worn, and his quilted leather vest had a tear in it.

"Now, woman. What is so important that you threaten to murder one of my people?"

Rose swallowed convulsively at the reminder of her earlier debacle. She glanced quickly and longingly toward the kitchens, wishing for Dumhnull's sympathetic presence, then squared her shoulders, passing a hand over her hair. She was dirty and mussed now, but there was no help for it.

"My lord, I meant her no harm, truly. I was desperate. I had to see you. I've been writing to you for months—have you not received my letters?"

He gazed thoughtfully at the screen that blocked the kitchen from view. Rose leaned toward him slightly to recapture his flagging attention.

"I wrote you every week. We sent a man, too. I *know* he arrived." She pointed to the balding blond man who stood near the entrance. She knew he'd looked familiar. "*He* is the earl of Kincreag's man. We sent him to fetch you back to Glen Laire, but he never returned." She sent the blond man a disapproving look. "We were worried he'd been hurt."

Lord Strathwick's harsh countenance did not ease. "And my lack of response to your missives . . . to what did you attribute that?"

Rose hesitated. "I . . . I didn't know." She felt foolish suddenly. Because she had written him so often and had once sent a terribly personal letter, she'd felt certain that when she spoke with him, was able to look into his eyes, there would be some recognition there. Some kinship—healer to healer. But there was nothing of friendship in this man's eyes. He seemed confused and annoyed.

She moistened her dry mouth. "You read none of my letters?"

Dumhnull returned with two pewter tankards, fragrant steam rising from them. He handed one to Strathwick. "Tasted, of course," he said, a mocking tone to his voice. Strathwick gave him a strange look, but Dumhnull had already turned to offer Rose the second tankard.

She took the warm tankard between her palms and smiled gratefully at him. He studied her briefly, his eyes slightly narrowed, before returning to his position behind her. She felt his presence there, as warm and reassuring as the mulled wine spreading through her.

Strathwick sipped from his tankard, swinging the foot that dangled over the side of the chair. Then, as if he'd forgotten she stood before him, his gaze lighted on her. "What were you saying?"

Rose made a small sound of disbelief. In all her imaginings she'd never supposed the MacKay chief would be so incredibly rude. But she was the supplicant here.

"I pray you, my lord. I ken my actions were harsh, but I vow my intent was never to harm. I, too, am a healer. But I'm desperate. My father is dying. Nothing helps. No one can fathom what is wrong with him." Her throat constricted, her vision blurred. "I pray you to aid him. The reward will be great."

The chief's expression remained aloof. "There is nothing you have that I want."

Rose spread her hands, taking a hesitant step forward. "There must be something? The resources of the MacDonells are not insignificant. The earl of Kincreag offers rewards, as does my betrothed."

Lord Strathwick waved this away. "I have no need of money."

"There are . . . other things."

His gaze slid behind her, then back to her. He raised a sardonic brow for her to continue.

She sipped nervously at her wine. For some odd reason she was compelled to glance over her shoulder at Dumhnull. He stared back at her impassively. She didn't want to say this in front of him, but there was no help for it. Besides, his master was a wizard. Surely such things would not trouble him.

She turned back to the chief. "My sisters are powerful witches. One can divine the past or future, the other speaks with the dead. Their gifts are at your disposal."

Strathwick considered her thoughtfully. "Dumhnull. What think you? Have we any need for divining? Any ghosts who need exorcising?"

"You ask me, my lord? What could my humble opinion matter?"

Rose cringed at the sarcasm in the groom's voice and looked warily to the chief. But he only seemed amused.

"It matters a great deal to me, as she appears to know you, and yet I cannot fathom when you might have met."

Rose's eyes widened. "My lord, I beg you not to punish him. He showed me naught but kindness and warned me away from petitioning you."

Strathwick looked at Dumhnull with mock astonishment. He swung his foot from the chair arm and leaned forward, gazing at her with new interest. "He did? Pray tell when this occurred."

Rose glanced apologetically at the groom. He stared at the ground, his broad chest rising in a deep sigh. She was causing him trouble and she'd not meant to. She supposed it was partly his own fault, too. If he only sounded a bit more contrite and a bit less recalcitrant, he might save himself worse punishment.

"Uhm . . . last night. He took me to the blacksmith for food and shelter."

Strathwick steepled his hands beneath his chin and smiled with malicious glee at the groom. "He did! And here I thought he was busy with other matters."

Rose's unease increased as she watched this bizarre byplay between the chief and his groom. "I pray you not to punish him, my lord."

"Punish him?" Strathwick said, then laughed. "That's an idea!"

Rose groaned inwardly. Was she giving him ideas? This was not going as she'd hoped. "My lord," she said firmly, bringing his attention back to her. "I beg you, come to Lochlaire and heal my father."

He stood decisively. "No. There was a reason I didn't answer your letters, Mistress MacDonell. I receive so many requests that I haven't time to read them all, and I certainly cannot go hieing off to heal strangers when people I know are in need. You may rest here if you wish, but I expect you to leave on the morrow—as you vowed you would. Wallace will show you a place where you can rest. I do not wish to be bothered with this anymore. No more letters. No more visits. And the next time you threaten someone under my protection I will not be so merciful."

He started to walk away, then stopped, pinning Dumhnull with a dark stare. "Don't you have something to do?"

"Aye, and I'll be doing it soon enough, don't you fash."

Strathwick glanced at Rose again, then turned away with a small shake of his head.

Rose stared blankly at the fire, the bright orange flames blurring and running together. She didn't understand. How could Isobel's vision have been so wrong? Or had it? Rose closed her eyes, shoulders slumping. The man Isobel had assumed was Strathwick had been an old man. Her vision wasn't wrong—just misinterpreted.

Someone approached. "Miss?" Wallace said, touching her arm.

"Go on," Dumhnull said. "I'll show her."

"Aye, m—er . . . aye."

Rose didn't know how long she stood there. Dumhnull stayed with her, not urging her to leave nor speaking, a solid, comforting presence. Her chest felt hollowed out, her mind empty. She didn't know what to do now. *Her father would die.* Everyone died. Rose knew that, but she needed her father alive and well. There were things she needed to say to him but could not when he was so ill, could not in good conscience tell him when he was so close to death. And now it appeared she might never have the chance.

"I must go," she said numbly, handing the tankard to Dumhnull and turning away from the fire. "My father needs me."

"You should rest before undertaking another such journey so soon after the last. I cannot believe you came here alone." He exhaled loudly. "Wallace will return with you."

Rose swiped a hand across her eyes and gave a strangled laugh. "Aren't you in enough trouble over me? I'll be fine."

He stared down at her, brow creased with intense concern, as if she'd somehow become his responsibility and he was in a conundrum as to what to do with her.

"You tried to warn me," she reassured him. "I didn't listen. Thank you for your kindness, but you've done enough. I can take care of myself."

This did nothing to alleviate his disquiet. He looked so troubled that she forced a quavery smile.

"You worry too much." She raised a hand and touched his hair, threaded liberally with silver. "You have too much gray for one so young."

He grew very still. When she met his gaze, it had changed. His face was taut, his brilliant eyes intense as they stared into hers. She was momentarily frozen, held breathless by his eyes. She dropped her hand abruptly. Why would she touch a man she barely knew in such a familiar manner? She turned away, shaken by the way he still stared at her and her own urge to lay hands on him.

"I must go. Thank you." She turned and hurried toward the end of the hall.

She was crossing the courtyard when she heard his swift steps behind her. "Where are you going? The gatehouse is that way."

"I know, but I left my things outside the postern door."

He did not reply to that but stayed beside her, so she could only conclude he meant to make certain she did leave. But once outside the door, a guard closed and bolted it behind them both. Rose held her bundle in her arms and frowned up at Dumhnull.

"You are unlike any groom I've ever known."

"Have you known a great many?"

"I'm a healer, remember? Grooms have a nasty habit of getting kicked and stepped on and sometimes even bitten by their charges."

"Ah," he said, and she thought she detected a hint of a smile. He took her bundle from her and began to walk. The berm was wide enough for two, so Rose fell into step beside him.

"I suppose I don't seem like a groom because . . . I'm not really one."

She looked at him cautiously, putting more space between them. "You're not?"

He lifted a shoulder. "I am . . . sometimes. I'm related to Strathwick . . . and we're friends."

"Oh," Rose breathed, nodding. "I knew there was something more there. You don't have the . . . *presence* of a servant. So you're not in terrible trouble." She looked up at him. "I'm glad."

He looked away, his mouth a stern, hard line. Did this man ever smile? She studied him as they walked. He kept the pace sedate, unlike when he'd led her through the castle. She inhaled the scent of rain and earth, strong after the storm. They walked for several minutes in silence but for the muted sound of their footsteps and a distant dripping. His presence calmed and comforted her. Was he a bastard son? She saw the resemblance to the MacKay chief in the black hair, the eyes, the fine, strong bones of his face, but the resemblance ended there. Dumhnull was clearly older, but it was more than silvered hair. It was something about him, world-weary and wise. Something that drew her dangerously.

"Why do you keep trying to help me, Dumhnull?"

He shook his head, seemingly perplexed by his own actions. "I know not."

Rose thought she knew but didn't offer up her opinions. Though she'd only met the groom the night before, she'd liked him immediately, and a bit more than was wise for a woman betrothed. Not only that, but he was a groom, and a bastard if she read his meaning correctly, and she thought she did. A hopeless attraction, nevertheless strong and undeniable. She'd indulged in such a doomed affair once before, and had learned her lesson; there would be no repeat of that folly here.

He stopped at the bridge, staring out at the gray, misty morning and the villagers emerging from their cottages.

"I can take you no further." He did not hand over her bundle.

She looked up at him expectantly. It seemed as if he couldn't look at her. He stared hard at the village with penetrating blue eyes that seemed to pierce the stone cottage walls and see the inhabitants within.

"I'm sorry you came all this way for naught," he said.

She shrugged. "It's not your fault."

He exhaled impatiently, looking skyward for a moment. "I feel as if I should have been able to do more."

Rose placed her hand on his arm, drawing his gaze to her. "I always feel that way. That's why I'm here. All for naught it seems. Wasted time away from my father when his time is so short." She sighed. "But I don't suppose I would have done anything different had Lord Strathwick written back and said no. For some reason I felt that if I could just speak to him he would say aye. But he's not the man I thought he'd be—or hoped he'd be. But I had to know, and now I do."

He stared down at her, his beautiful gaze moving over her upturned face. "You're so much bonnier than I expected."

Rose started to smile, but it quickly turned to a frown. "What do you mean?"

He shook his head and looked away, thrusting her bundle at her. "From the letters. He read them to me sometimes. You were different in most of them."

Rose clasped the bundle to her chest, her mouth falling open. "He *read* them to you? So he could mock me?" Her face flushed as she turned an evil glare on the castle. "I cannot believe he mocked my letters!"

His brows flew upward in bewilderment. "Did I say he mocked you?"

"Why else would he read them aloud? I met him—I know what he's like!" She closed her eyes, mortified, trying to remember all the things she'd written, but her mind fixated on one letter, the one she'd poured her heart into and still had not managed to move him. "How many others did he entertain with my folly?" she muttered, face aflame. She didn't wait for his answer. "I must go!" She whirled away, running across the bridge, not stopping until she reached the blacksmith's cottage.

At the door she looked back. He still stood at the bridge, staring after her.

*   *   *

That had not gone at all as he'd planned. Not that he'd had any sort of plan in regards to Rose MacDonell. She'd just barged her way into his life and wouldn't seem to go away. Even when she *was* away. He stared at the cottage she'd disappeared into, his irritation increasing. Irritation because in his own lands he could not risk crossing the damn bridge to go after her. Why he had an itch to do that was simply beyond logic.

He was already eliciting curious stares from villagers going about their business. He spotted a tall man with a thick blond beard. Allister. He exhaled grimly and returned to the castle. His people watched him hesitantly, clearly uncertain at this point how to address him. He did not spend time enlightening them. Once in his own chambers, he still found no peace. His brother sat behind the desk, letter in hand. The wooden box sat open.

Drake smiled guiltily. "The mulled wine was very good, thank you. I'd never guess you'd never made it before."

"I didn't make it then, either."

William crossed the room and snatched the letter from Drake's hand. He folded it carefully, glowering at his brother.

Drake gazed up at him, amused and entirely unabashed. This only further irritated William. He was inordinately vexed, but in truth, he did not know what he was vexed about, could not pinpoint any one thing. The way that woman had violated his home was enough to enrage anyone. But that was not it. Not at all. He was not angry about what she'd done. Indeed, he understood it. He understood her. Perhaps that was it—a sense of helplessness at his inability to help her. That was closer to what vexed him but not it exactly, either. He wanted to help her, but damnit, he *couldn't*. Could he?

Drake leaned back in William's chair, regarding his brother thoughtfully. "She's bonny, I'll give you that. But a damn shrew."

"She's not a shrew. She's desperate. I was her last hope."

Drake scratched beneath his chin, still regarding William thoughtfully. "I suppose. She's a wildcat, though, aye? Too bad she thinks I'm you."

"Why is that?"

Drake leaned back further, propping his feet on William's desk and crossing them at the ankle. "We never go anywhere anymore, and no one ever comes here—well, at least we don't allow anyone in."

"That was your idea," William pointed out.

"And a fine one it is—things have been far more peaceful around here since we've become recluses. But I grow bored of this place. Of these women."

"I thought you'd set your eye on Betty."

Drake rolled his eyes. "She insists she's still married, despite the fact Allister had her driven from the village with stones." He shook his head, helpless. "Naught I say will loosen her laces."

William snorted, amused. Good for Betty. "Well, no doubt she knows what you're about and wants none of it."

Drake arched a brow incredulously, clearly doubting such a thing was even possible.

William laughed aloud, feeling better. Trust Drake to lighten his mood. He patted his brother's shoulder. "Methinks that's for the best. We need no more trouble with Allister."

"I say we kill him. I don't care who he is."

William shook his head. "That's not the answer, brother. Don't even think it." He held Rose's letter up before replacing it in his wooden box. "Stay away from this one."

Drake gave him a slow, sly smile. "Oh, she's all yours."

William scowled and shoved his brother's feet off his desk. They hit the ground with a thump, startling a laugh out of Drake. "Oh, this one has you in a chuff all right, *Dumhnull.*" Drake left the room, chuckling to himself over William's foolishness.

And foolishness it was. William sat in the chair his brother had vacated. He'd left her moments ago, but already he longed to seek her out again. But on what pretense? Neither Dumhnull nor Lord Strathwick had any reason to trouble the bonny healer any longer. And perhaps that's what vexed him most of all.

Rose had first thought to leave immediately. Get on her horse and never look back. She was humiliated and depressed and wanted to be away from this place. But there was no wisdom in that. It was noon. She was tired and needed rest. Tomorrow morning she would start fresh, putting this whole unpleasant incident behind her.

Though she'd hoped for rest, it was not her fate. It rarely was. Excluding the elusive Lord Strathwick, the village had not had the benefit of a healer in some time. Rose spent the day helping the blacksmith's wife make lard candles, interrupted with the odd ailment from a villager who'd heard there was a healer present. The news traveled quickly, so that by evening she'd tended festering wounds, boils, rotting teeth, coughs, and aching bellies. It was good work, and she threw herself into it. It made her forget, for a time, how she'd failed.

She was in the blacksmith's cottage, rebreaking and setting a lad's leg, when she noticed Wallace through the window. He sat on a stump on the village side of the bridge, his bay hobbled nearby. When she had a moment, she joined him. He stood, spitting out the blade of grass he'd been chewing.

She pushed back a hank of sweaty, disheveled hair that had come loose from her plait. "What are you doing?"

"Waiting, miss. When you're ready to return to Lochlaire, I'll accompany you."

"I made it here without your help, I'll make it back."

"You shouldn't be traveling alone." Disapproval laced his words. "My lord Kincreag wouldn't like it at all."

She shot him a cutting look. "I might not have come at all if you'd returned." She doubted that was true. She'd needed to speak to the wizard herself. "Why did you stay? Have you so little loyalty to the earl of Kincreag?"

"Nay, miss," he said hastily, his brown eyes panicked. The scar on his cheek reddened. "That's not it at all! It's Lord Strathwick . . . he healed me. I was attacked by broken men not far from here. They left me for dead. I lay there for two days, the buzzards circling, waiting. Two of Strathwick's knights found me and brought me here. I should have died . . . but he brought me back. I owe him my life. The debt is far from paid."

Rose's jaw hardened as her gaze was drawn to the castle. The resentment boiled up inside her. Strathwick had helped Wallace but would not help her. Wallace had been a stranger to him, just as Rose was. Why did he deny her, when she'd come so far? Would it have been different if she'd brought her father with her? But her father could not survive such a journey, and Lord Strathwick refused to come to Lochlaire. She wanted to scream her frustration.

Instead she pinned Wallace with a hateful glare. "Then stay here and pay your debt. I don't need you."

It was dusk when Rose trudged out to the shelter that was the blacksmith's stable, gratefully tired from her long day of work. The more tasks she had to accomplish, the less her mind turned and turned. And she did not want to think of all that had passed this day. The pain of Strathwick's rejection was still raw, still there, waiting for examination, but she could not. She had a long ride ahead of her on the morrow. She would not be able to escape from it then.

The leather bag containing oats rested atop her saddle. Rose picked it up and turned to feed her horse—and yelped with surprise. Dumhnull leaned against Moireach's stall.

Rose put her hand to her chest and let out the breath still strangling in her throat. "You frightened me." Then she frowned and looked around cautiously. They were alone. "I thought you said you couldn't come to the village."

"I don't, usually. Not during the day, at least. And not where everyone can see me."

He was dressed again in old and faded garments,

though it did nothing to mask his height and breadth, singular so far as she'd seen in Strathwick. It would be difficult for him to disguise himself. He possessed a presence that couldn't be hidden simply with rough clothes.

She remembered their last conversation at the bridge, where he'd shared the fact that Lord Strathwick had read her letters aloud, and her face grew hot. She brushed by him, pouring oats into Moireach's trough. Rose scratched the mare between the ears as she ate.

"Why are you here?" she asked, still avoiding his gaze.

"I heard you were tending the villagers' ailments." He hesitated, then continued diffidently, "I . . . have a problem with my elbow. I was hoping there was something you could do for it?"

Her eyes narrowed, skeptical. "Why not have Strathwick heal you?"

"Go to Strathwick? For a strained elbow?"

She leaned an arm on the top slat of the stall and turned to face Dumhnull. "He doesn't heal elbows?"

He looked momentarily bewildered, then lifted a shoulder. "No. It's . . . fatiguing for him to heal. One does not ask him to do it for such minor complaints."

She thought grimly about the day she'd just spent, the ailments she'd tended, the exquisite effort it had taken to break and reset the leg—her muscles still ached from the strain—and glowered at Dumhnull.

"Well then," he said, straightening from where he leaned against the stall. "I suppose not—"

"How did you hurt it?"

He paused, then leaned against the stall again, eyeing her cautiously. "I was kicked."

"In the elbow?"

He nodded, straightening and folding his arm experimentally. "It hurts."

Rose sighed. "Very well. I suppose I owe you." She straightened from the stall, wincing and rubbing at the small of her back. "Let's have a look."

He shrugged out of his doublet, untied the points at his right wrist, and pushed his sleeve up. Rose took the arm he offered, giving it a cursory inspection before she used her magic. It was a very fine forearm, thick with muscle and dusted with black hair. The wrist in her hand was strong-boned and wide, the palm broad, the fingers long. She could smell him, standing this close. He smelled clean, of wool and soap, as if he'd recently washed. For her? A quick glance upward revealed slightly damp combed hair. She smiled inwardly, and when she called on her magic, passing her hand over his elbow, she saw nothing, only his color—strong and healthy blue. She frowned and did it again, spending more time with her palm hovering over his elbow. If there was damage of any sort she would see it—dark red streaks, or a gray film or dark blobs.

"What was that?" he asked sharply, his arm tensing beneath her hand.

She looked up at him, surprised. "What was what?"

"What you did with your hand there?"

Rose dropped her hands and stepped back, flustered. No one ever seemed to pay any mind to what she did during an examination. All thought she healed through skill alone. He was the first to notice anything different.

"Nothing," she lied. "I don't know what you mean."

He continued to frown at her for a moment, then looked back down at his bare arm. Rose debated what to do. There was nothing wrong with this man's elbow. Even without the benefit of her magic she could see it was functional—no bruising, swelling, or discoloration. This must be a ploy to spend time with her again, and she was flattered. She enjoyed his company and felt no small amount of attraction for him. She'd grown somewhat jaded over the past few years, so although she was no stranger to flirtations—especially from her male patients—she rarely returned the interest. This felt different somehow, wicked and unsafe, but darkly alluring. She decided to play along, refusing to deny herself the pleasure of his presence, however unwise the decision.

She gestured to an overturned bucket. "Have a seat and I'll put some liniment on it. It should feel better in the morning. I'll be right back."

She hurried out of the stable, returning to the blacksmith's cottage and retrieving her pot of liniment. She found herself sprinting back to the stable, as if she feared he would leave if she was gone too long. She stopped herself just outside and caught her breath, not wanting him to notice how she'd exerted herself. She knew her behavior was unconscionable. She was betrothed. He was a bastard and a stable hand, for heaven's sake. And yet for this moment, she didn't particularly care about any of that. She was enjoying herself, and she couldn't recall the last time she'd found real enjoyment in anything.

Inside the stable Dumhnull waited on the bucket, his shirtsleeve rolled up to his muscled biceps. Rose stared at him in the gloaming, her breathing disturbed by the sight of him. He was so very large—he seemed to fill the small stable, even crouched on a bucket. Such a fine-looking man. No wonder he was overbold for one of his station—she doubted even a princess would be offended by his interest. He looked up at her, shadowed eyes fringed with such thick lashes, set deep beneath thick black brows.

She realized she stared rudely and came briskly forward, kneeling beside him. "Give me your arm."

He gave it to her. As she rubbed the strong-scented liniment into his elbow, she felt his gaze on her, weighty, nearly a physical thing, as if he touched her. Her skin reacted all over, warm and prickly.

He said, "We did not mock you."

Rose looked up at him quizzically, then immediately realized her mistake. Their faces were inches apart. She returned her gaze to her work, to the strong bulge of muscle above the bend of his elbow. She could see the veins in it, protruding slightly, dark blue. The skin in the crease of his elbow was soft and tender, such a contrast to the rough, muscular man before her.

"What are you talking about?" she mumbled.

"Your letters. You were wroth earlier, thinking we mocked you. I want you to know that is not what happened at all."

"You're still worried about that? I'm not," she lied blithely. "It doesn't matter what Lord Strathwick thought, does it? He won't help me. It's behind me now. Let him laugh his arse off at my letters."

He let out an irritated breath. "He did not laugh, and I certainly didn't either."

She gave him a perceptive smile, amused by his attempts to flatter her. She was leaving tomorrow and he knew it. She couldn't imagine what he hoped to accomplish here tonight. A roll in the hay? He wouldn't succeed, but she enjoyed his attempt.

He was silent for a moment. "You are a courageous woman, to come all this way alone."

Again, she made the mistake of glancing up and being caught in his darkly beautiful gaze. Her heart already raced from touching him so freely, savoring it, in fact, her fingers kneading into his supple skin. It struck her that she was being far too nonchalant about this game, pretending she could control it. She'd played it before and lost—and this time she had a betrothed. Had she no wits?

She stood and backed away, wiping her fingers on her skirts. "That should help."

He stood, too, looking at his arm for a moment before rolling his sleeve back down and snagging his doublet from where he'd dropped it on the ground. "My thanks, Mistress MacDonell. You're a fine healer."

She nodded, finding it suddenly difficult to meet his gaze. The room seemed stuffy and close, her skin overwarm. She crossed her arms beneath her breasts and stood aside to let him pass, but he didn't pass. He stopped in front of her.

One of his long fingers touched her beneath her chin, tilting her face upward so she was forced to look at him. She should not allow him to touch her with such familiarity. She should demand he remove his hand and leave. But she did nothing of the sort. Her skin beneath his fingers tingled, her heart trembled in anticipation.

She met his gaze as it swept over her upturned face, and waited for him to kiss her, knowing she would let him, knowing she'd walked into this trap willingly, knowingly—eagerly.

But he didn't kiss her; he just gazed down at her, his expression dark and unfathomable. Then he sighed deeply and regretfully. "I wish the world were different, Mistress MacDonell. I really do." He dragged his fingers along her jaw, let them drop to his side.

And then he left her standing there, blinking in disbelief and disappointment, her heart still stuttering against her ribs, skin burning where he'd touched her.

Chapter 4

       ~ひ〜や~

A frantic pounding ripped Rose from the grips of another nightmare. Rain chattered on the thatching. She inhaled sharply, peat smoke choking her. The small smoke hole in the thatching had been stopped up to keep the rain out and the warmth in.

The blacksmith stumbled out of bed and threw the door open.

"Is the healer still here?" a desperate voice asked.

Rose pushed herself up. "Aye, I am."

A boy darted under the blacksmith's arm. "You must come! My sister is dying!"

Rose had not bothered to undress, so she slipped on her shoes, threw her arisaid over her head, grabbed her wooden box, and followed the boy into the rain. He led her to a cottage at the edge of the small village. The door opened immediately at their knock. A painfully thin woman stood there, her damp, hollowed eyes passing over Rose and the boy, scanning the emptiness behind them. Her face fell when she realized they were alone.

"Where's the MacKay?" she asked.

"He won't come," the boy said.

Rose gritted her teeth. *Some healer*. Had he not said to

her, *I certainly cannot go hieing off to heal strangers when people I know are in need?* And here, one of his own people was dying and he couldn't trouble himself. For the first time she began to believe that perhaps his miraculous healing was nothing more than fakery.

She put her anger aside and placed her hands on the woman's shoulders. "Lord Strathwick might not be here, but *I* will do my best for your child."

The woman shook her head, hands over her mouth, as if holding back a scream. She pulled away from Rose and dashed out into the storm.

The boy looked after his mother morosely. Water dripped from the dark hair plastered to his head, making tracks down his cheeks. "She'll be back."

"Where is she going?"

"To stand outside the castle and scream. We all do that."

"Does it work?" Rose remembered Tadhg's story about Betty's husband, how he'd stood outside the castle and threatened to murder Strathwick if he didn't come heal his wife.

"Sometimes." The boy took Rose's hand and led her to the back of the cottage. A small child lay upon the large bed, plaids and furs smothering her. He gazed at his sister with large, worried eyes. "Her name is Ailis. She's six."

Rose pulled most of the coverings off and tossed them aside. Ailis was a small girl with a mop of dirty blond hair curling around her face. She was very red, her skin alarmingly hot to the touch, and clear fluid drained from her nostrils. Every inhalation rattled through her narrow chest.

Rose sat on the bed, closed her eyes, and took several deep breaths. Her heart twisted with the knowledge that this was most likely an ailment she could not help, but she refused to dwell on that until she knew for certain. She forced everything else from her mind—the rain, her father, Strathwick, Dumhnull—and the calm settled over her. Sometimes it was difficult to do, but when the situation was urgent, as this was, no matter how upset or anxious she was, she could always focus quickly.

The magic curled inside her, twisting and turning like a serpent. She opened her eyes and the world was different. She placed her hands just over the child's head, cupping it but not touching it. The color around her hands was a pale yellow overlaid with a vivid angry red from the child's fever. She continued over the face to the throat, where she paused. A blackness clouded the throat. She continued down the rest of the body and saw nothing else.

She returned to the throat to examine it now with her eyes, rather than magic. The throat was swollen beneath the jaw. Rose pressed on it and the child moaned fretfully. Rose motioned the hovering boy to fetch her box. He moved quickly, setting it on the bed beside her. She found her glass and a candle. She bade him to light it at the fireplace.

"I need you to hold this near her mouth so I can see."

He nodded and did as she bid. Rose opened the child's mouth. When she moved close, a sickly sweet odor assailed her, sending her back to her box to tie a handkerchief around her face and nose. Thus protected, she peered inside the child's mouth, motioning to the boy several times to move the candle about so she could view it from different angles. Then she took her glass and peered through it, using the base of a spoon to depress Ailis's tongue. She saw it then, the thick gray membrane spanning the back of the swollen throat. Her heart contracted with the knowledge that this small, sweet girl would probably die and there was little she could do to prevent that eventuality.

She composed her expression, then shooed the boy away. "Stay back, lad. No need for you to get ill, too."

"My name is Lucas and I want to help my sister."

Rose forced a smile and squeezed his thin wrist. "You've been a great help to us both, but I need you to stay away now, aye?"

He nodded, large dark eyes grave, and backed away to crouch in the shadows and ashes beside the hearth.

Rose sat on the bed, gazing at the child. Bull throat. She quickly scanned her memory for possible remedies, but defeat settled hard on her shoulders as she realized there was nothing she could do but attempt to make the child comfortable. It was the curse of her hands, to show her what was wrong, even when she could do nothing. If it was a cancer or a wound—even a festering one—there was much Rose could do, but with an illness like Ailis's Rose was as helpless as any other healer. She could try to bring the fever down and ease her patient's discomfort, but beyond that, it was in God's hands. The magic still constricted her chest, curling down to knot uselessly in the pit of her belly. She closed her eyes and willed it away before it made her sick and weak.

When the mother returned Rose was boiling water at

the fireplace for an infusion. The mother was filthy, mud splattered her skirts, her coarse gown soaked, her hair straggling around her face. Her eyes were empty. She sat on the edge of the bed, staring at her child.

"How long has she been like this?" Rose asked softly.

"Last night she said her throat hurt, but she seemed fine today. Then . . . then this . . ." The woman's voice was dull. Her empty gaze met Rose's. "What's wrong with her?"

Rose licked her lips. "Morbus suffocus—bull throat. I've seen it before."

"Bull throat . . ." The woman looked back at her daughter, her eyes wide with horror. "Will she die?"

Rose bit her lip. "I don't know." It was a lie, but Rose couldn't take away the mother's hope, especially when in some part of her heart she had not yet released hope. But the fact was, Ailis would most likely die. Certainly people pulled through even the direst illnesses, but rarely children as small and frail as Ailis. The last person she'd seen with bull throat had suffocated—a man, hale and strong. His throat had swollen, and a black, leathery membrane had formed, closing his throat off. When Rose had removed the membrane, he'd bled, almost drowning in his own blood. The membrane had re-formed, and he'd died a horrible death.

Rose rubbed a trembling hand over her mouth at the memory, chilled by a deep reluctance to relive it through this small child. She pushed it away and fisted her hands to ward off the shaking. This was what she did. She was all Ailis had now, and she would do her best for the child, however paltry that aid might be.

"My lord is not coming, is he?" the woman said, her voice empty, resigned. "He's punishing us for hunting him." Tears tracked her face.

Rose knelt beside the woman and took her hands, squeezing them firmly. "Aye, I'm sorry to say it looks that way. There's naught we can do about that now, though. We cannot force him to do what he doesn't wish to—and it would be foolish to sit about and wait for a miracle. We must act now to help your daughter. I need your help. Will you help me?" She gave the woman's hands another hard squeeze. "What is your name?"

She was a few years older than Rose's twenty years. She looked so lost and empty, but her gaze focused on Rose. "I am Iona, and I will do anything you ask, cut out my own heart if it means saving Ailis."

Rose choked back her emotion, putting it firmly where it belonged—deep in the recesses of her heart, to be examined later, when this was over. But not now. "Well met, Iona. Let's get busy."

Rose stayed with Ailis through the night. She wiped the child's small, delicate limbs with rags dipped in cool water and gave her infusions of willow bark for the fever, cantharis for the swelling, and monkshood to assuage her pain and help her sleep. When the moon rose, hope filled Rose that this time she'd made a difference. The child's fevered skin had cooled and the swelling was reduced. But around midnight, Ailis began to wheeze. Rose opened the child's mouth and peered inside. The membrane nearly covered the throat.

She checked Ailis's fingernails. Pale blue. She turned

to her box as if in a dream, her heart beating slow and calm. This time she would do it. She couldn't watch Ailis suffer a horribly painful death, would not force Iona through it. She took out the bottle of laudanum, stared at it for a long moment.

"What is it? What's wrong with her?" Iona asked, her voice still hopeful, still believing Rose could make a difference.

Rose replaced the laudanum in the box, choosing instead a small probe.

"I need your help again," Rose said. "What I must do will hurt and frighten her, but it will help her breathe again. Please hold her down."

Iona's eyes widened, looking from the gleaming probe to the resolve in Rose's eyes, and she nodded slowly, grasping her child's limbs. She trusted Rose and would do anything Rose asked now.

Ailis struggled against her mother. Tears streamed down their faces. With Iona's help Rose managed to push back part of the membrane, widening the opening. In the short term it caused Ailis to choke and cough terribly, but when the spasm passed, she breathed easier. For the moment.

Lucas still huddled in the corner, his face buried in his knees, thin arms wrapped tightly about his legs, as if trying to block out the horror of it. Iona lay close to Ailis, whispering how sorry she was. She looked up, meeting Rose's eyes, and mouthed her thanks. For what? Rose wondered. For prolonging her daughter's suffering? She had to look away from Iona's grateful eyes, wondering why she still tried.

She sat by the bed all night, alternately pouring infusions down Ailis's throat and battling the membrane. By morning it became impossible. Her efforts caused the child's throat to bleed. A tracery of veins webbed her red cheeks, and a thin line of blood trickled from her nose. Ailis had not even struggled the last time Rose had attempted to remove the black and putrid membrane, so Rose had not needed Iona's help. A blessing, that, as the odor had become so foul that it had sent the mother heaving in the chamber pot afterward.

Iona was asleep on the mattress beside her daughter. Rose wondered if she should wake her, for the end was surely near. Rose watched helplessly as Ailis's small body strained to take in each breath, the fever burning her alive. Wallace had come a short time ago, peered in the door, then left with Lucas before Rose could give him a tongue lashing to take back to his master. How could Strathwick allow this child to suffer? Heartless, he was. Either that or a charlatan even more useless than she was. Even so, Rose was grateful the boy was gone. He should not have to witness his sister's painful death.

Rose was for all purposes alone. Reluctantly, she took the bottle of laudanum in her hands. Enough of the dark poppy juice would give Ailis a painless death, a deep dark sleep from which she would never wake. Rose should have given it to her earlier, not made her and her mother suffer. A wave of hopelessness washed over Rose. *Useless.* She was useless to everyone. She wanted to help people live, not help them to an easier death, but what else could she do for the child?

She rarely gave in to self-indulgent bouts of despair,

instead choosing to channel her frustration into working harder to heal the next person. But this . . . after all that had gone on before, her disappointment in Strathwick, the hopelessness of her father's illness . . . it was too much. Her useless hands clutched the small bottle, pressing it hard into her stomach, trying to alleviate the hollow ache, shutting her eyes against the burning, clenching her teeth against the scream that threatened to rip from her throat.

She was leaning forward, making a keening sound, tears squeezing from her tightly closed eyes, when she felt a hand on her shoulder. She jerked away, tumbling from her stool beside the bed. She looked up from where she sprawled on the packed dirt floor.

Dumhnull stood above her, his face grim and taut, as if facing a terrible foe alone and unarmed but resigned to the necessity of it. Rose put a hand to her chest and let out the breath he'd startled out of her.

"What are you doing here?" she whispered. She started to get to her feet, but he squatted beside her.

He didn't speak, studying her with grave eyes. He reached his hand out and took hers, pulling her fingers open and staring down at the vial of laudanum she held. He met her gaze again.

Tears welled in her eyes. "I didn't know what else to do," she heard herself saying. "I tried. I feel as if I should be able to do more, but I'm useless when it matters."

He frowned slightly and made a soft sound to hush her. She quieted immediately, staring up at him, confused by his presence and yet comforted by it.

"It's clear," someone said at the door.

Dumhnull sat back on his heels and looked over his shoulder. Rose followed his gaze. Wallace peered out the door, and Strathwick stood at the window across the room, peeking out a crack in the shutters, dag drawn.

"He came," Rose breathed, clutching Dumhnull's arm. "He came."

The groom turned back to her, his face dark, withdrawn. "Aye, he came."

A strange feeling overcame Rose as she gazed up at him, a swelling in her chest, a mixture of fear and confusion and wonder.

The bed trembled, and Rose jumped to her feet. Ailis convulsed, her tiny body rigid. Iona woke immediately in hysterics, trying to grab her daughter, as if her arms could absorb the child's pain.

"Hush," Dumhnull said. He put a hand out, urging the mother to move back.

"My lord," Iona said, her voice soft and awed, her eyes wide. She moved away from her daughter.

Rose looked to the window. Strathwick still stood there, peering outward, glancing quickly back at the groom but keeping his attention on whatever was outside the window.

She turned slowly back to the bed, her heart beating hard and fast with slow understanding. Dumhnull—or the man she'd known as Dumhnull—sat on the bed beside Ailis. She was rooted in place, unable to speak or move, only stare. His hands passed over Ailis's head, just as Rose's had earlier. They came to rest on the throat. Then, instead of hovering over it, his hands closed around her throat, as if he meant to strangle her. His head bent. The convulsions stilled. A moment later, he released the child with one hand. It moved down to her chest and stayed there.

The man she'd thought was Strathwick came away from the window to stand behind the "groom." When Dumhnull finally released Ailis, he bent over the bed, his breathing labored.

The fake Strathwick took his arm. "Come on," he said softly, his voice gentle but insistent.

Wallace turned from the door, eyes hard. "They're coming."

Dumhnull stood and walked slowly toward the door, wheezing and struggling for air. He stopped at the door to the cottage and leaned heavily against the frame, coughing violently. It was a horrible cough, a metallic rattle deep in his chest.

"We must go now," the fake Strathwick urged.

Heart-wrenching sobs distracted Rose. She turned to find Ailis awake, her skin pale and clear, large brown eyes blinking dazedly. Her mother held her in her arms, weeping.

Rose sat on the bed beside the child. "Open your mouth, sweetheart."

The child complied. Her throat was pink and healthy. No signs of swelling or a membrane, or even the bleeding from Rose's attempts to open the passageway. Dumbfounded, Rose stared at the child for a long moment. She summoned her magic again, passing her hands over the child, seeing nothing but the child's pale yellow color, pulsing with health.

Rose's hands went to her mouth as her heart seemed

to rise in it, her vision blurring. "Dear Lord," she whispered. Her gaze went to Iona. "That man . . . *that* was Lord Strathwick." It was a statement, but still the mother nodded.

Her Dumhnull was really the Wizard of the North. Of course. She should have known. There had been a compassion in him, lacking in the imposter. And his presence was like no other; he filled a room with authority even when told to fetch mulled ale. But why had he still refused her? Her mind instantly turned to his condition after healing Ailis. He was unwell. What had he said to her in the stable? *It's fatiguing for him to heal. One does not ask him to do it for such minor complaints.* She saw it all with such clarity that it brought her to her feet, propelled her toward the door.

Before she reached it, the door burst open and men poured in, bearing weapons of their trade. Hoes, hammers, scythes, pitchforks, axes, butchering and tanning knives. The leader was a huge man with a blond beard like a tangled bush.

"Where is he?" he bellowed.

When Rose just stared up at him, he grabbed her arm and shook her. "You saw him! Where did he go?"

"Who?" Rose heard herself ask. She seemed numb, as if she watched everything from outside her body.

The blond man bared his teeth at her and thrust her away, turning on Ailis and her mother.

"He was here—Strathwick was here!"

Iona shook her head, her face defiant. "You're wrong, Allister! Only this healer and my family."

The man grabbed Ailis's chin and pushed her head

up, peering at her throat. He twisted his neck to peer at one of the men crowded inside the cottage. "You said your daughter's throat was swollen, did you not? That she was dying."

A man with long wet hair streaming down his back nodded hesitantly.

"Pol?" Iona whispered, her voice full of helpless betrayal.

"I healed this child," Rose said, finally regaining her wits. "And not with magic." She waved her hand at her wooden box. "I did it with herbs. I spent the night feeding her physiks, and as you can see, they were exceedingly effective."

The men murmured amongst themselves. The blond man growled, and his dark blue eyes narrowed. "I know he was here! I can smell him!"

Rose sniffed delicately. "Indeed? And of what does he smell? For I can detect little above the stench of wet men and wool. And I've been told my sense of smell is exceptional."

Allister turned on her with a torpid frown. "He smells like evil."

Rose cocked her head in mock interest. "The scent of evil. Hmm. Could you describe that in more specific terms? I'm not familiar with it. I hope it doesn't reek of sweat and livestock, for I fear you detect something on your person."

Allister stared at her with slowly dawning insult. He looked quickly at the men behind him as if for support, then turned back to Rose. "Did you just say I stink?"

Rose gathered her things together and replaced them

in her box. "No, I don't think I did. I simply urged you to have a care. The stench you perceive could very well be coming from yourself."

His mouth gaped, a dark hole in his tangled beard.

Rose went to the open door. "The rain has stopped."

The morning sun burned away the fog. Droplets of rain clung to blades of grass and dripped from the thatching. Rose inhaled the scent of rain-washed earth deep into her body, then turned and smiled at the blank faces gazing back at her.

"I think this will be a fine day after all."

And she left them, skipping over, and sometimes through, puddles on her way to Strathwick Castle.

Her mood quickly darkened when she could not gain entrance to the castle. She pounded on the door in the gate with her dirk hilt, but the porter didn't even open his window. She circled around to the postern door and pounded on it for what seemed an eternity, but again drew no response.

She returned to the gatehouse and started over. She had to see him. Now that she knew Dumhnull was Strathwick, and had seen him perform a miracle, she would not go away without speaking to him. And she knew that if she pushed hard enough, he would see her—her friend Dumhnull would. And maybe, just maybe, he would help her. Besides, he was ill. That had been obvious when he'd left the cottage.

She stepped back, gazing up at the ramparts, hoping to catch a man-at-arm's eye, but when they passed they didn't look down at her. She shouted at them, and still they pretended she didn't exist. She was pacing irritably outside the gatehouse when the door beside the gate opened.

It was Strathwick—or the man who'd pretended to be Strathwick.

"Come quick," he said. He had discarded his plaid and his vest hung open, unhooked. His hair was disheveled, and his eyes were wide with fear, replaced immediately with relief when he spotted her.

Rose hurried to the door, wary of this strange man but anxious to be inside the castle walls. He held it open for her, scanning the area behind her cautiously, then quickly shut and bolted it behind her.

Before she could ask him a single question, he took her arm and dragged her across the courtyard. "There's something wrong with Will. He cannot breathe."

"Will? You mean Strathwick?"

"Aye."

Rose dug in her heels, forcing the man to stop. "Wait! I don't understand what's happening! Why did he pretend to be someone else?"

His hold on her arm became punishing, and he yanked her hard so she stumbled, forcing her to move. "There is no time for explanations now. He is dying."

Rose's heart leapt at this information. He was right—this was not the time. Strathwick's life was in danger. Her stomach dipped. She could not be responsible for the life of such a great man. But she couldn't say that to the man hauling her through the castle. His face was set in rigid, uncompromising lines as he pulled her into the great hall. He finally released her arm. Blood flowed again, but he immediately pushed her ahead of him, as if he feared she'd attempt escape.

"At least tell me who you are!"

"His brother."

He shoved her down a hallway, and then into a large, dimly lit room. A fire blazed in the deep fireplace and two candelabras flanked the bed, but otherwise the room was shrouded in darkness. An enormous bed sat on a dais in the center of the room. A choking, gagging sound came from the bed, as well as a little girl shrieking, "Da! Da!"

The brother propelled Rose toward the bed. "Christ, he cannot breathe! Do something!" He snatched the child off the bed and set her aside. She grabbed at his leg, burying her face in his plaid.

Rose didn't have to use her magic to see that Strathwick suffered from the same thing Ailis had. He lay on his back, struggling to breathe. His throat had swollen, and his skin was on fire. Blood trickled from his nose.

She didn't have time to dig through her box for her probe, and the brother grew increasingly frantic, urging her to do something *now*, making it difficult for her to think. Finally, she climbed on the bed, took Strathwick's face between her hands, and looked hard into the burning blue eyes.

"Open your mouth if you want to live."

He complied slowly, as his jaw was swollen and tender. The membrane was there, and she used her finger to open his airway. He gagged and bit her.

She jerked her hand away as he rolled onto his side,

putting his back to her, coughing violently and retching. The brother pushed her aside and climbed onto the bed with Strathwick. The little girl crawled onto the bed, whimpering, tears streaking her pale face. "Da? What's wrong?"

"Will?" the brother asked urgently, leaning over to peer into Strathwick's face.

"I'm fine," came the rasping voice. "Get her out of here."

The girl threw herself on Strathwick. "No! I'm not leaving." She buried her face in her father's plaid, her small shoulders shaking. Strathwick made a vain attempt to sit up, only to fall back onto the pillow and lay unnaturally still. The child's hands clutched at him as she cried, pulling at him.

The brother sat back on his knees and met Rose's eyes. His shoulders slumped wearily. He ran a shaking hand over his pale face, shoving his fingers through his already unruly black hair so it stood up all over his head. His throat worked, and though he said nothing, there was deep gratitude in his look.

Strathwick muttered something unintelligible, but his hand cupped the child's head, stroking the mop of black, unruly curls. Her cries quieted. He still lay with his back to Rose, broad shoulders hunched and inky black, silvered hair a stark contrast to the snowy linen of his sheets.

The brother climbed off the bed. He covered his mouth with both hands, as if trying to gather his thoughts, and took a deep breath. He dropped his hands to his narrow hips and looked back at the little girl, whose head lay on Strathwick's leg. Her father's limp hand had fallen away, and she took it and placed it back on her head.

"Come, Deidra. Let your father rest and this woman tend to him."

The little girl didn't move but turned her head to observe Rose gravely. She was a chubby thing, with round cheeks and large blue eyes. She looked seven or eight years old.

"Who is she?" Deidra asked her uncle.

"Her name is Rose MacDonell, and she's a healer."

Rose nodded politely. "Pleased to meet you, Mistress Deidra." Then she directed an inquiring gaze at the brother. "And your name?"

"Drake." His thick black hair had fallen flat, so he shoved a weary hand through it so it stood on end again. "Sorry I gave you such a difficult time before, pretending to be Strathwick and all. It's just that . . ." He shook his head. His face was haggard, and there were more important matters to attend to.

"We'll discuss all that later," Rose nodded to the child. "You really should get her out of the room. Yourself as well. The ailment he has is contagious. I will look after him."

Drake nodded. "We just have to get him through the worst of it, aye? Then he'll be fine. He always is. Come on, Dede."

Deidra's face set into stubborn lines, her brow lowering and her mouth puckering. She shook her head and held onto her father tighter.

Drake put a knee on the bed and reached for her. "Do you want to be getting sick? Then your father has to heal you and he's sick like this all over again. Let Mistress MacDonell do her mending, aye? You know he'll be all better tomorrow."

Deidra still looked mutinous, but she let her uncle draw her off the bed and lead her from the room.

Rose set to boiling water in a small pot in the fireplace. The room was sparsely furnished, though the furniture was well made and solid. The walls were bare of ornamentation, as were the tops of the cupboards and chests. A desk sat at the opposite end of the room, and its top showed the only signs of habitation outside the bed—papers scattered across the top, a large, misshapen rock with eyes clumsily painted on it holding them down, a carved wooden box, writing implements, a tankard.

Cautiously, she approached the large, sturdy bed draped with thick wool plaids. Her patient's coughing had calmed, though he still wheezed. She climbed partially onto the bed and rolled him onto his back. His eyes opened, bleary and dazed, and fixed on her. Though it made sense, she still had a hard time reconciling that *this* was Lord Strathwick. It made her uneasy, but she set that aside, determined to care for him the best she could.

She murmured calming nonsense to him, as she did to all her patients. He didn't respond; he only stared at her, his expression enigmatic. She passed her hands over him, and though what she saw was similar to what she'd seen with Ailis, there was something different—odd. The blackness encompassed his throat, streaked with the angry red of the fever—but a blue-white pulsing light underlaid it all. It was so strong that she didn't just see it— she felt it, tingling against her palms, ebbing and flowing like the tide. She curled her hands into fists and stared down at him, a strange fluttering sensation in the pit of her stomach.

He tried to speak but instead dissolved into a fit of coughing. His thick shoulders shook with it. He turned his head into the pillow, his face creased with pain. Blood stained the linen.

"Come on, sit up." She gathered his numerous pillows and crammed them behind him. He was too weak to aid her, but she was accustomed to shifting large weights around all by herself. Before he'd died, her foster father, Fagan MacLean, had weighed at least twenty stone of fat, and no one but Rose had tended to him.

A small bowl with a rag in it rested on the floor beside the bed. Rose wrung out the rag, then sat on the edge of the bed. She smoothed the rag over the strong bones of his face, the day's growth of black and silver stubble on his chin and jaw, and she wiped the blood from the stern line of his mouth. Her Dumhnull was the Wizard of the North. It still filled her with awe, made her chest flutter in a strange, anxious manner, both exciting and frightening.

She reached for the hooks on his doublet, and the fluttering increased. His eyes opened, narrowing on her.

"I'm cooling you down. Then I'll make you something for the fever and to soothe your cough."

She unhooked the doublet, then her hands moved to the ties of the linen shirt he wore. His big hand came up to catch hers. "My daughter? . . . Dede? . . ."

Rose hushed him, speaking soothingly, "Drake took her away. You should rest now. I'll bring her back later."

His hand fell away and his eyes closed again.

Rose struggled to remove his doublet and shirt. He seemed a bit more cognizant, and he helped as best as he could, pushing himself up on one arm and finally falling into his pillows. "May I rest now? Or have you some other torture designed for me?"

"No. Lie still." She pulled his boots and stockings off, leaving him only in his trews. She considered removing those, too, but decided to wait until she'd given him something to help him sleep. She didn't know if she could strip him with those brilliant blue eyes peering at her. Rose wiped the rag over his swollen throat, then over his shoulders and chest, wiping down his arms and hands. Though she tried to remain detached from what she was doing, her body grew warm from touching him so freely. He was even more compelling out of clothes than he was in them. His bones were long and elegant, layered thickly with smooth slopes of muscle and crisp black hair. No scars or imperfections blemished his smooth, dusky skin. He was a wholly beautiful man, and she was not immune. Either was he, it seemed, for when she reached the hard flat muscles of his belly, she noticed the thick bulge in his trews and was grateful she'd left them on.

Without thinking, she glanced up at his face. Dark, hazy eyes regarded her. At her look he quirked an eyebrow. "I'm sick, not dead."

Though flustered, she retreated into the brisk manner of a healer, which served her well with recalcitrant or randy patients. She grabbed the edge of the plaid blanket and yanked it up, covering him to his chest. "I'll get you something for that cough."

She brewed the same infusion she'd poured down Ailis's throat all night, then propped him on the bed so she was behind him, his head against her shoulder. His bare skin burned her everywhere they touched.

"Drink this," she said, pressing the cup to his lips.

He'd drifted off. He seemed confused when she woke him, though he drank the infusion readily enough.

"You aren't angry?" he rasped between sips. His hands came up to hold hers steady around the cup. She resisted the urge to snatch her hand away.

"Oh, I'm angry. But I'll not harangue a sick man. When you're well enough, you shall get an earful."

He finished drinking and groaned softly, turning his face into her neck. Rose panicked momentarily but calmed quickly. He meant her no harm. She set the cup aside and looked down at the thick black hair below her nose. It gleamed in the weak light, threaded through with coarser silver hair. His hand, broad and hot, lay against her ribs, below her breasts. She could feet the heat from each long finger imprinting itself on her body. Her own hands hovered uselessly, suddenly afraid to touch him. Finally she let one hand drop to the arm that lay across her, stroking over the muscle, feeling the latent strength coiled in him, and wondering about him, hungry to know more.

She was a ninny perhaps, but she felt as if she already knew him. She should not. He had lied about his name and who he was, but she still felt that he'd been honest in all else. She knew inherently he had good reason for his ruse and hoped he would tell her in time. And he *had* wanted to help her—he'd said as much when he'd pretended to be Dumhnull, though she'd not understood then. His hot breath stirred her hair, and an odd trembling shivered through her.

"I'll be fine. This is naught."

She was startled by his voice, by the way his breath felt against her neck when he spoke. She'd thought he was asleep. "Naught! Ailis nearly died from this."

"But she didn't, aye? And neither will I." The black lashes rose, and he peered up at her. "Trust me."

She did trust him. He was the real healer, after all. What she did was mere child's play compared to his power. She slid out from under him and stood beside the bed. He turned his head on the pillow so he could watch her.

She placed a hand on his brow. "Rest, my lord."

He inhaled deeply, then let it out in a heavy sigh. "I never imagined you'd be so damn pretty."

Her heart tripped on itself and she smiled. "You're delirious."

"Perhaps."

She moved her hand over his hair, fingering a lock of silver, then pushing it behind his ear. His hair . . . silvered black hair. He *was* the man in Isobel's vision—not an old man, but a man with graying hair. He *would* help her. He must.

"Was I wrong to come here, my lord? Was I wrong about you?" She watched her fingers as she spoke, unable to look into his eyes.

His hand caught hers, enfolding it with heat. She stared at their joined hands, afraid of what she'd see in his face. If he said no to her now, it would somehow be worse. A no from Drake had been terrible, but a no from this man would devastate her.

"Please," she said softly. "Don't let me be wrong."

His hand tightened briefly on hers, then fell away. "Aye, I'll go to your father."

Rose sucked in a shaky breath, her hand covering her mouth. When she finally dared to look at him, his eyes were closed. She took his fevered hand in hers and pressed a reverent kiss to his knuckles. His lashes fluttered slightly but did not rise.

"I am in your debt, my lord."

Chapter 5

When William woke, it was dark again. He'd spent the entire day in a fevered haze, hovering on the edge of delirium. The only thing that kept him from giving in to it was his lovely healer. She was a lodestone, drawing him back with the cool touch of her hands and her soothing voice when the world grew confusing and hazy. For the first time since he lay hands on Ailis, the blinding pain in his head was gone and he could breathe deeply. His hand went to his throat. The swelling was gone and his skin was cool. His hand dropped back to the bed in relief. It could have been worse.

Rose lay on a rush mat before the fire. He stared through the gloom, wondering if she was awake. When had she last slept? He felt odd—restless and discontented. And all because of her. He started to throw back the bedding and was surprised to find himself undressed. He looked again to his little healer. He must have been very ill to forget that.

Something else pricked at his memory. Her hands passing over him, not touching him. She'd done that in the stable as well. She was no mere healer, but something more.

He slung a plaid about his hips and crossed to where she slept by the fire. Only the firelight illuminated her, casting shadows over her face and lighting deep copper fires in her hair. She was an exceptionally beautiful woman. Dark auburn hair, pale skin, midnight eyes, fine cheekbones, a strong chin and straight nose. She appeared slender and delicate, and yet she was clearly capable of great things. What was he going to do with her? He was loath to send her away, and yet what else could he do?

He crouched beside her and touched a loose lock of hair, pushing it away from her face, as she had done to him the night before. She was a skilled healer to have kept Ailis alive as long as she did. And she'd known just what to do when he'd been choking.

Her eyes flew open. Wild eyes. Terrified eyes.

He drew his hand away slowly. "It's all right. You're safe."

She pushed herself to sitting, then backed away, her arisaid sliding from her shoulders. She looked at him as if she feared him. He did not touch her, only watched her silently, waiting. Her gaze scanned the room, confused, before returning to him, this time with recognition. The fear in her eyes disappeared, replaced with weariness and relief. She flexed her shoulders in a small stretch, twisting and grimacing as her back cracked.

"You are much improved," she said, her gaze still on him, cautious.

He did not stand, remaining at her level. "Aye. It's only bad in the beginning. Illnesses never tarry in my body."

Her gaze roved over his chest and lower, then skittered away. "My lord . . . I'll leave you so you can dress."

She started to stand, but he put out a hand. She froze before he touched her, so he drew back. She had not been so wary of him when she'd thought him a mere groom. He didn't like it, wanted their prior rapport back.

"I wanted to thank you for coming as you did, and clearing my throat and staying with me. I did not deserve your kindness after deceiving you."

She lifted her midnight eyes to him. They were slightly slanted like a cat's, with a thick sweep of cinnamon lashes. "It is I who should be thanking you. You are forgiven everything."

He tapped a thumb to his mouth, frowning at her. This was not right. He was forgetting something. A strange tightness gripped his chest.

"What mean you?"

"You said you would come to Lochlaire and heal my father. What I did for you is paltry payment for such a gift, my lord. Do not for a moment believe I consider my debt paid—"

He stood abruptly. "What did you say? I agreed to heal your father?"

She gazed up at him, her eyes narrowing slightly. "Aye, you did."

He paced away from her, arms crossed over his chest. "I was feverish, delirious. Why would you take aught I said seriously?"

When she didn't answer, he turned back. She gazed up at him with such a look of betrayal that he stopped short.

"Because you said you would."

Of course she'd believed him. She'd come all this way; she would latch onto anything he'd said in support of her mission, no matter the state he'd been in at the time he'd said it.

He closed his eyes and scraped his hand over the whiskers on his jaw. "Bloody hell." He opened his eyes and pinned her with a hard stare. "You are nothing but trouble, do you know that?"

Her gaze had grown sharp, her full lips compressed into a line of suppressed anger. "You *said* you would."

"I was ill. I knew not what I sputtered on about."

She got to her feet, hands fisted at her sides. "I saved your life! Or have you forgotten that now, too?"

He crossed to the carved wooden chest against the wall and lifted the lid, grabbing a clean shirt. "I haven't."

"And have you forgotten that I did it *after* you deceived me? How you and your brother must have laughed at me! Mocking my letters, then pretending to be some ridiculous groom. And a poor bit of acting it was."

He pulled the shirt over his head. "I told you—I never mocked your letters."

She smirked. "And you're such an honest man, I should believe you, aye?" Her gaze hardened. "You *owe* me."

"Ah," he said, a grim smile curving his mouth. "Now you're beginning to sound like the virago in the letters."

Her mouth dropped open in insult. "Virago! I see." Her tone was biting, her skin flushing with fury. "Well, I think you are a knave. No! A blackguard." Though she didn't smile, she stood straighter and lifted her chin a notch, obviously well pleased with her insult.

He held back the smile threatening to surface and crossed the room to stand before her. "Anything else? Now that you've had time to think on it?"

She raised a scathing brow. "A son of a—"

He raised a finger. "I wouldn't if I were you."

"But you're not me, and if you were you'd know that healing my father is the most important thing in the world to me."

William didn't like the tightness forming in his chest. "How old is your father?"

"What does that matter?"

He raised his brows expectantly.

She sighed. "Eight and forty."

"Not ancient, but neither is he young. Everyone must die, Rose. I know you love your father, but I cannot heal the infirmities of old age."

"He is not infirm, and it is not old age that is killing him!"

William inhaled deeply and decided to try another tack. "When a person begins to age, this makes them susceptible to many illnesses. I suppose I could keep healing them, one after the other, but I cannot make the body stronger or younger and so they will continue to deteriorate—"

Her eyes flashed. "Do you think me daft, to speak to me in this manner? I, too, am a healer. I cannot perform miracles, but I am competent, I assure you."

William rubbed the bridge of his nose. "No, I do not think you daft. I do, however, think you cannot see this clearly. You said in one of your letters that your family had only recently been reunited after a long separation. Could this be clouding your judgement as a healer?"

She gazed up at him with such pleading, such disappointment in her lovely eyes that he found himself wavering, being led by something far baser than intellect.

"But you said you would." Her voice was soft with defeat. She lowered her gaze and turned away, folding her arms beneath her breasts and gripping her elbows.

He couldn't remember saying it, and yet it was likely he had. He did not make a practice of trailing after lasses like lost puppies, but he'd done it with this one. In fact, since Deidra's birth, he'd left women alone entirely. But since Rose MacDonell had forced her way into his life, he'd said and done things he knew he should not.

"What else did I say in my fever?" he asked grudgingly.

She looked at him over her shoulder, from beneath a fan of cinnamon lashes. His body responded immediately to the look, tightening and growing warm.

"You said I was pretty."

"I suppose I wasn't too far out of my head then, was I?" he muttered dryly. He still could think of little but how damned appealing she was and how he wanted to tumble her on the bed behind him.

She lifted a shoulder with elaborately feigned disinterest. "I wouldn't know, my lord, as you've been naught but dishonest with me."

"Shaming me into it now, are we?"

She just gazed back at him, unblinking.

He rubbed his forehead, then sighed again. "Very well. I will go to your Lochlaire and try to heal your father."

She let out a gasping breath and clasped her hands together in stunned disbelief, then jumped at him, grabbing his hands in hers. "Oh, thank you, Dumhnull—I mean, my lord! You will not be sorry, I vow it! I will take care of you afterward, just as I did today. And you will be paid, of course. And anything else you wish that we can provide is yours. You only have to name it."

"A kiss," he said, surprising himself, but once the words were out, he did not take them back; in fact, everything in him was suddenly focused on her mouth, the soft, plump swell of her bottom lip that he wanted to taste. Since he'd met her he'd wanted to kiss her, touch her, bed her, with a single-minded intensity that startled and troubled him.

She stopped her excited rambling and stared up at him, her throat working, but no words issued forth. Her hands stiffened in his and she tried to pull away, but he held firm.

He leaned toward her, using his hold on her hands to pull her closer. He could feel the whisper of her skirts along his lower body, the prelude to something soft and yielding igniting sharp lust in his blood.

"That's hardly adequate payment," she said, her gaze dropping to his mouth, then darting back to his eyes.

"Nevertheless," he said softly, "it's the payment I demand."

She parted her lips to make another protest, but he silenced her with his mouth.

She was stiff, her fingers digging into his. He coaxed her mouth to softness, tasting the salty sweetness of her, running his tongue lightly along the generous curve of her lower lip. Her breath exhaled on a sigh, her lips opening to him, kissing him back. He released her hands to put his arms around her, to press her closer. Her hands came up to his shoulders, as if to push him away, but she didn't. She was warm and soft in his arms, and tasted like heaven. He didn't know what demon had prodded him into demanding a kiss, but he was glad for it.

"My lord," she breathed, exerting the slightest pressure against his chest. "I—"

He took advantage of her open mouth to kiss her deeper, sliding his tongue between her lips. Her tongue met his with no hesitation, and need closed around him like a fist, hot and urgent. He wanted more. He wanted her in his bed.

Her hands slid up to his shoulders, where they clutched the fabric of his shirt near his collar. Her breath came fast and fluttery, her skin gloriously warm and flushed to his palms. He was quickly descending into the realm of mindless lust, and she offered him no resistance.

What was he planning? To bed her, obviously, but then? She was no village whore, or even a widow in need of companionship. This was a gentlewoman betrothed to someone else. He was asking for trouble. These thoughts were like a trickle of freezing water down his spine, returning him to sanity. He set her away while he still could. She blinked up at him with wide-eyed confusion. He made himself cross the room to put some distance between them, then he grabbed his trews off the bench beside the bed. All his clothes from the day before were folded and neat.

"We'll leave tonight, after dark. I suggest you get some sleep." His voice was gruff, making him sound badtempered—which in fact he was. He was damned uncomfortable now. He threw off the plaid he'd wrapped around himself and pulled on his trews, grimacing in discomfort as he laced them. When he turned back to her, she looked away quickly, staring into the fire with intense interest.

"Come, let's find you somewhere to sleep."

Rose's heart still thundered against her ribs as she stood alone in the cold room William had deposited her in. She gazed around her. The room was sparsely furnished, but the bed was sturdy and soft, and the woolen blankets and furs would keep her warm. She had a large fireplace, cold now, and a tall clothespress. A brass chamber pot peeked out from under the bed.

She propelled herself to the chest at the end of the bed and sank down onto it, folding her body over her legs so her forehead pressed into her knees. With great clarity she could recall the last time she'd been so shaken. It had been an unrest of a very different sort, but it had still left her both numb and strangely sensitive. She put that from her mind. She was closer than ever to resolving what had happened all those years ago—at least as best as it ever could be. Time to focus on the present.

The wizard of Strathwick had agreed to heal her father. And then he had kissed her senseless. And then shown her to a bedchamber as if nothing had happened. It was all very strange. Had it been Dumhnull who'd kissed her, she would have felt differently, she realized—which was absurd. Dumhnull and Strathwick were the same person. But it was a matter of birth. What could

Strathwick have meant by kissing her in such a manner?—for it had not been chaste at all. It had been slow and hot, his hands, his body . . . She covered her flushed cheeks with her palms. It had been a very long time since a man had roused such a passion in her.

But she was older now, smarter. She could handle Strathwick and his advances. She was no silly outraged female. It was just a kiss. It wasn't as if she hadn't been kissed before. The important thing was that he'd finally said yes, he would come to Lochlaire and heal her father.

Someone knocked at the door. Rose gripped the sides of the chest, wondering if it was Strathwick, come back to finish what they'd started in his chambers. Her heart resumed its frenzied pace.

"Aye?" she called cautiously.

The door opened and, to Rose's embarrassment, the woman she'd held hostage in the courtyard entered, shoulders hunched, as if she expected to be bludgeoned. A young man bearing an armful of peat blocks followed, staring threateningly at her, as if daring her to attack the woman now. As Rose sat in mortified silence, her fingers digging into the wooden chest, the lad arranged the peat in the fireplace and the woman set a pitcher and ewer on the hearth.

"Miss?" Rose said, when the woman would not look at her.

She glanced suspiciously at Rose and moved closer to the lad. She was a very pretty lass, with big blue eyes and bright blond hair pulled back into a thick braid.

"What is your name?" Rose asked, smiling politely.

"Betty."

"Betty—forgive me for what happened earlier. I vow I would not have hurt you . . . but I was desperate." When the woman only stared at her, wide-eyed, Rose stood and took a step toward her. Betty backed away, and the lad at the fireplace straightened to give Rose a warning look.

"My father is dying . . . I've been writing Lord Strathwick letters. Then I came here and he wouldn't see me. I didn't know what else to do. Please forgive me?"

Betty's suspicion softened as Rose spoke. She smiled slightly, showing good teeth. "Aye. I ken how it is. People come all the time and yell and scream for Strathwick to aid them. But they've never made it in—and it was all my fault."

"I hope I didn't cause you any trouble?"

Betty shook her head, and the lad returned to his work.

Rose took a step closer, and this time the servant didn't retreat. "Your name is Betty? Are you from the village? Allister's wife?"

Her face fell and she looked at the floor, nodding. "They told you about me?"

"Tadhg did."

Betty looked up, her expression fierce. "They're wrong, all of them. Lord Strathwick is not evil. And I am not a witch."

"I know," Rose said gently. "But this is a bad time, and people frighten easily. What happened? Lord Strathwick healed you?"

"Oh, aye, miss, he did. I don't remember it, ken? But I remember Allister axing me. I remember the pain and the fever when it began to fester. Then I remember naught else but nightmares. I would have died. Then it was all gone. I opened my eyes, and there was my lord's fair face, gazing down at me."

"Did he say anything?"

She shook her head. "No. When Allister saw I was awake, he grabbed me and started bawling like a bairn. When I was able to breathe again, my lord was gone." She smiled shyly, looking down at her feet. "I've been able to thank him since I've been here, though."

I'm sure you have. The thought pricked her when it shouldn't have. She didn't like imagining Strathwick embracing Betty as he had her—but it was good that she did imagine it, she told herself firmly. That was the way of things. He wasn't Dumhnull, and he hadn't kissed her for any reason but lust and that she'd been available. Rose wondered if he was married. Not that it mattered; lords and chiefs accosted female servants with or without a spouse.

"What happened in the village?" she asked, as much to stop the troubling direction of her thoughts as from curiosity. "Tadhg seems to believe you killed someone's chickens."

Betty shook her head, her shoulders slumping dejectedly. "I didn't! Gannon left those poor beasts out in all sorts of weather. All I said was, 'Gannon, you must let those poor chickens in your house when it snows, or build them a shelter. Otherwise they're going to die come winter.' When the snow came, most of the chickens managed to get under the cottage, but two couldn't fit and they froze. He said I killed them with the evil eye."

The story chilled Rose, so similar to others she'd heard. It took so little to incite people these days.

"Do you believe me, miss?" Betty asked anxiously, her hands twisting in her skirt.

Rose gave her a reassuring smile. "Oh, aye."

The lad finished with the fire. Rose moved closer to the blaze. Pale smoke wafted from the fireplace, and the sweet, acrid scent of burning peat filled the air. Rose coughed, but she welcomed the warmth, rubbing her hands over her arms.

"Your leave?" the lad asked, kinder now that Rose and Betty had made amends.

Rose nodded, and Betty followed him out.

Rose sat before the fire, warming herself and thinking about Betty's tale and the caution with which Strathwick left his castle. Men had come for him, to lynch him, and that had been after he'd healed a child—brought her back from the edge of death. She unbraided her hair and combed her fingers through it, thinking about Strathwick, the miracle he'd performed, and how it had debilitated him afterward. That was why they were leaving at night, to avoid being seen and mobbed. What a dismal existence, to be hated and hunted by your own people. Even when her life on Skye had been naught but misery, she'd never feared for her life.

Her mood low, she lay in bed unable to put all the thoughts from her mind. Sleep would not come, and her stomach growled sullenly. She threw back the covers, slipped on her shoes, threw her arisaid around her shoulders, and left her room in search of food. The cavernous stone corridor was deserted and silent. Torches sputtered at intervals, casting strange, fluid shadows along the walls. Rose stole through the castle, feeling the intruder still.

There was no one in the great hall, not even the dogs. She went behind the screen, into the kitchen. The vast room was redolent of stew and bread, but it too was empty. She considered just helping herself to the larder but decided against it. On Skye, the punishment for pilfering from the larder was harsh. It was probably locked anyway. Surely someone was nearby. The stew bubbled merrily over the fire. Partially chopped vegetables lay on the table, knives beside them, as if something had caused the servants to drop what they were doing and leave. With a last, longing look to the loaves lined up along the table, Rose returned to the hall. It was then that she noticed the double doors leading to the courtyard standing open.

A breeze blew through the open door, setting the rushes to swirling and disturbing the hem of her nightrail, sending currents of chill air up around her ankles. She pulled her arisaid closer around her shoulders and stepped outside in time to see Lord Strathwick climbing the battlements, his long, lean-muscled body moving with quick grace that belied the many hours he'd spent wasted with illness. Her heart sped. Something was wrong. Half the household lined the torch-lit battlements staring at something over the wall. Rose climbed the ladder to follow. The wind caught her loose hair, wrapping it around her body and arms.

It was still dark out, being the early hours of dawn, but the battlements were alight. Strathwick immediately drew her gaze. Like the rest, he leaned forward, hands braced on the wall, peering at something below.

"Keep your witches!" someone shouted below.

The wall came to Rose's chest, but raised blocks rose from the ground at intervals against the wall. She stepped onto one and leaned forward to see over the side of the thick stone. A group of men bearing torches and weapons had gathered on the other side of the wooden bridge. One man crossed it, dragging something behind him. Rose inhaled sharply. It was a person. The flickering of his torch revealed skirts—torn and stained. The face seemed strange, distorted, but it could have been the fire-light; the hair, however, was loose and wild, matted with a dark, glistening substance. He hauled the body a few feet from the portcullis and dumped it next to another, smaller bundle in the same appalling shape.

These were the witches? A woman and child? They were dead, whoever they were. The man spotted Strath-wick on the wall and shook his fist at him. "We don't want your sorcery! Keep your hands off our women!"

With sick horror, Rose recognized the man and real-ized who the bloodied lumps were. Ailis and her mother. "No!" she cried. She whirled, to descend the ladder and examine their bodies for herself. They couldn't be dead. She'd just seen them! Just seen Strathwick breathe life into Ailis's wee body.

Wallace caught her at the top of the ladder. "No, you cannot go out there." She tried to pull away from him, but he grabbed both her arms and shook her slightly. "Don't you see? Look at yourself—you spent the night in these walls and you show up on the wall with your hair down. You go down there and try to intervene, and they'll burn you as his witch, too."

"But I helped them . . . I tended them—"

"It doesn't matter."

He was right; she knew how it was. A sense of numb unreality descended on her, as if she were trapped in a nightmare. She turned away from the ladder, returning to the wall to stare down at the poor broken bodies.

The man had jogged back across the bridge. He had long dark hair. He'd been at Ailis's house after Strathwick had left. The man with the blond beard, Allister, had called Ailis this man's daughter. Rose's hand went to her mouth and clamped down hard to hold back her cry of horror and disgust. The man returned with a bucket, still holding his torch high. Drake appeared beside Rose, a crossbow tucked into his shoulder, his face hard with fury. "The bastard had them stoned," he hissed at no one in particular as he nocked an arrow in his crossbow. "Unfortunately they didn't get away, like our Betty."

Rose looked on her other side to Betty, whose face was bloodless, her gaze riveted on the grisly events playing out below. She'd been down there once, been the object of the stones.

"I'll kill him," Drake muttered. He raised the crossbow to take aim, but Strathwick was there, his hand on the arrow, pushing it down.

His eyes were narrowed, his mouth a hard uncompromising line. "Death is too good for him." He was still unshaven, black and silver stubble hugging his chin and jaw, making him look malevolent, a dark, angry wizard bent on mayhem.

The man emptied the bucket—pitch—on the broken figures, then dropped the torch on them. It burst into flames. He backed away, hand held before his face to shield himself. He looked upward, to the people lining the battlements. "You cannot have them, do you hear? You cannot!"

Strathwick uttered a vile curse and grabbed the crossbow from his brother. He sighted on the man shouting up at him. The instant the man saw what his chief intended, his eyes widened. Before he could turn to run, the arrow slammed into his shoulder, sending him sprawling in the dirt.

Strathwick shoved the crossbow at his brother and flew to the ladder, shoving past Rose and the others, his eyes wild with fury. He shouted to his men. "Stop him! Don't let him cross!"

Rose stayed on the battlements. As the man tried to gain his feet, the thick wooden door below opened. Strathwick's men poured from the castle walls to surround him. The villagers shouted and screamed, but no one dared challenge the heavily armed men.

"Why would he do such a thing?" Rose asked Betty, her voice hushed, transfixed by the gruesome events. She wanted to hide her face, yet she could not look away. Her mother had been lynched and burned alive. Rose had not been there, of course; she'd seen nothing. And though witches had been burned on Skye, she'd never witnessed such an event. It twisted her gut with fear and nausea.

The pale blond woman beside Rose didn't take her eyes off the wounded man in the dirt. "That's Pol, Ailis's father." Her voice was a thin, thready whisper. "When the MacKay healed me, they ran me out of the village, believing me a witch. I know Allister was furious when he heard the MacKay took me in. I guess Pol wanted to make certain my lord didn't take his women, too."

Strathwick exited the castle, striding purposefully into the circle of guards, his hands fisted at his side. Across the bridge, the villagers' yelling abruptly ceased. No one attempted to cross to give Pol aid. The tension inside Rose wound tighter, and she realized she was holding her breath. Strathwick approached Pol, who was still sprawled on the ground, his hand gripping the base of the arrow that pierced his shoulder. He spit at Strathwick, though the spittle went wide, landing in the dirt. "You can kill me, but you'll not make my women into the devil's whores!"

Strathwick stared down at Pol, circling him slowly, balefully, a devil wolf surveying his next victim. His words, almost gleeful, carried to Rose on the wind. "Oh, I'm not going to kill you." He gripped the arrow shaft and yanked it from Pol's shoulder. Pol screamed and writhed in the dirt. Strathwick dropped to one knee in the dirt beside him and put his hands on the man's shoulder.

Pol yelled and fought. Strathwick dropped a knee in his chest, pinning him to the ground. The sour, acrid scent of burning pitch and hair filled Rose's lungs and singed her nostrils, making her eyes tear. She pulled her arisaid closer around her. Strathwick was healing him. He'd shot Pol and now he healed him. It made no sense. It made her angry.

It was over in a minute. Strathwick stood, yanking the

man up with him. He dragged Pol toward the bridge, then ripped the man's shirt from his shoulder and used it to scrub away the blood, exposing smooth, unblemished skin. Drake raised the loaded crossbow, training it on the men across the bridge. The men-at-arms on the battlements did the same.

"You saw the arrow pierce him," Strathwick yelled to the assembled villagers. "I have healed him. Either you believe he is a witch now too, or else you stoned an innocent woman and bairn."

The villagers were silent, motionless, staring at Strathwick and Pol.

Strathwick shoved Pol toward the bridge and said, his voice laced with contempt, "You're not welcome at Strathwick. Let's hope you're shown more mercy than you showed your wife and daughter."

Strathwick strode back into the castle, his men closing ranks around him. Pol did not cross the bridge. The village men stood on the other side, staring back at him as if he were something unnatural, to be feared. Pol turned and looked frantically up at the castle, then his gaze fell to the burning bodies. He dropped to his knees beside them, burying his face in his hands.

Rose left the wall. She knew, from the long day and night she'd spent nursing Strathwick, that he wasn't as unaffected as he'd appeared. She raced through the castle. The members of the household slowly returned to their duties, their manner subdued. Strathwick was nowhere in sight. Rose went to his chambers and knocked on his door. There was no answer, but he must be in there. The door was locked, and he was nowhere else. She had to see him, to help him if he was hurt. She knocked until her knuckles hurt.

"Let me in, my lord! Your shoulder must be tended!"

She heard the scrape of a boot and turned.

"He won't let you in," Drake said, leaning against the wall, arms crossed over his chest and his face grim.

"Then you must get me in. You saw him before. He cannot be left alone."

"Oh, aye, he can." When she just stared at him, bewildered, he continued, "The wound was not fatal. Pol would have lived through it—unless it festered. Course, Will's shoulder hurts like hell, but it will be much improved by tonight. We'll leave on time, fash not."

"But . . . he shouldn't be alone after that."

Drake pushed off the wall, his grim gaze on his brother's door. "Aye, he shouldn't. But he will." He gestured for her to move along. "Get some sleep. We'll be riding all night."

"Does he have a wife?" she blurted out. When Drake turned back to regard her curiously, she added, "To be with him now, that is."

He quirked a mocking brow. "I would hope, had he a wife, she would have wished to be with him before as well. When you tended him, that is."

Rose's cheeks flushed, and she nodded stupidly. "Of course, I wasn't thinking. But he has a daughter? . . ."

"Aye, he was married once. She died." He looked back at the closed door, then at Rose, his gaze thoughtful. He gave her a reassuring smile and wink. "It will be fine, you'll see. Get some sleep."

Rose left reluctantly. It troubled her that Strathwick

was alone. She'd only known him a short time, but she had not witnessed a large circle of friends. He had his brother and his daughter and servants. No wife to comfort him. But she was not his wife, she reminded herself, and it was not her place. But she was a healer, and as a healer she tried to provide comfort.

It didn't matter either way; he didn't want her aid or comfort. She was passing through the great hall, feeling disheartened by all that had happened, when she spied a small form huddled with the dogs near the hearth.

As she approached it, surprised recognition sped her pace. "Lucas?" she said, kneeling before Ailis's brother.

He raised his head from where it was buried in the mastiff's neck. Blood ran from a split in his swollen lip, and his eye was mottled black and purple.

"Oh, Lucas," she breathed, touching his chin delicately. His eyes were vacant.

"Who did this?" Her voice was tight as she tried to control the fury boiling through her. She had no wish to frighten the lad.

His gaze remained downcast, his voice emotionless. "My da."

"For bringing Lord Strathwick to heal your sister?"

He nodded, finally meeting her gaze. Anger animated his face suddenly, and tears overflowed, spilling down his dirty cheeks. His hands clenched into fists, and he shook beneath her hands. "I'm not going back. I'm staying here. Master Drake said I could."

Rose stroked a hand over his hair. "Of course you can. Come with me." She took his hand and raised him to his feet. He followed along after her like a poppet, mute.

In her own chambers, she opened her wooden box. She cleaned his lip with garlic water and began making a plaster of woundwort. As she crushed the leaves in the mortar, she watched the boy. He huddled on her hearth, skinny arms wrapped around his legs, chin on knobby knees, staring starkly into space. He was in shock, that much was obvious, but when it wore off, what then? Would every person who supported Strathwick be killed or forced to take shelter in the castle?

"Does everyone in the village hate Lord Strathwick?" she asked.

Lucas shook his head.

"How many?"

Lucas frowned slightly, then said, "Some of the men . . . mostly Allister. Sometimes people forget . . . or don't care as much. But Allister won't let anyone forget." A tear escaped to track his cheek. "I hate him. When I'm big enough, I will stone and burn him . . . And my father, too."

Rose set her pestle aside and knelt in front of the boy. She knew such hate, had felt it once. She took his hands, meaning to say something comforting or supportive, but compassion and empathy swelled in her chest. She pulled the boy close, hugging him tightly. Nothing could make it better, she knew. Nothing.

Great, shuddering sobs wracked his small body. She held him until he lay limply against her shoulder, then settled him on a rush mat before her fire. She applied the plaster to his wounds, wishing woundwort could heal the deep rends in his heart as well as it would the cuts on his face. She stroked his hair until his face relaxed in slumber, then she drew away quietly.

With a heavy heart, she packed her few things back in her satchel and lay on the bed. But sleep did not come. Though she tried, she could not erase from her mind the images of the night, of William MacKay standing on the battlements, staring down at the dead, broken body of the child he'd healed at such great cost to himself. All for naught.

Chapter 6

It was full dark when they set out. They were a grim, silent party of five—Drake, Wallace, Strathwick, and, to Rose's surprise, Strathwick's daughter. Deidra rode a small, docile mare that appeared oblivious to her bouncing and chattering and was perfectly happy to have its mane braided and laced with ribbons. Rose supposed it wasn't so strange for him to want his child close. Ailis had been only a year or two younger than Deidra. Had she a child, Rose wouldn't have left her in that place either.

Rose surreptitiously observed the MacKay chief as he rode, to see if he suffered any discomfort in his shoulder. He looked well enough. The dark whiskers had been shaved from his jaw, and his eyes were clear, his face unlined. He didn't appear to be in any pain. He sat straight in the saddle and kept watch over his daughter, who was very excited by the adventure and had to be warned repeatedly to keep her voice down.

Dawn drove away the darkness and with it the tension of the night. Rose did not know the boundaries of Strathwick's lands, but she assumed that by now they were out of immediate danger from his people. They traveled a mist-shrouded mountain trail. It was wide enough to ride three abreast, but the way was littered with jagged rocks that had fallen from above. Wild scrub grew along the sides in places, threatening to overtake the road.

Rose was considerably calmer on this journey than she'd been on the previous one. She'd been alone then and disguised. This time she was surrounded by three brawny men; she enjoyed the feeling of safety and the opportunity to survey her surroundings without constant, watchful fear.

She had been riding beside Wallace, with Strathwick and Drake behind, Deidra between them. With a brief gesture Strathwick sent Wallace and Drake ahead to scout the trail. Rose took Drake's place, flanking Deidra. The child looked at her with sleepy blue eyes.

"Good morn, Mistress Deidra," Rose said, smiling. "Are you still anxious for an adventure?"

Deidra's mouth opened wide on a yawn. "I'm tired."

Strathwick leaned toward his daughter and plucked her from her saddle, settling her across his lap. "Rest your eyes then, my wee squirrel."

Rose caught the reins of Deidra's mare and tethered them to her saddle. Deidra snuggled against her father but didn't close her eyes, instead fixing them on Rose.

She returned the child's solemn stare. "Why does your father call you squirrel?"

Deidra smiled, showing dark gaps on either side of her large front teeth, making her look very much like a chubby rodent. "Because I like nuts!"

Rose put a hand to her mouth and laughed, glancing up at Strathwick to see that he grinned down at his daughter. Her heart snagged. She had thought he was incomparably handsome before, but when he smiled, he was devastating. She stared until his gaze met hers, then she quickly averted her eyes. She longed to be the one coaxing forth his smiles; it bloomed inside her, the want, unnerving in its sudden, unexpected force.

They rode in silence until Deidra's thick black lashes drifted shut. She was so very young and vulnerable. Rose had been about Deidra's age when Alan MacDonell had sent her to Skye, away from everyone she knew and loved, to be raised by strangers. She watched the peacefully sleeping child for a long while before raising her gaze to Strathwick. He stared straight ahead, his jaw rigid and grim now, all traces of his earlier smile gone.

"Why did you bring your daughter?" Rose asked, doubting her own father would have taken her or her sisters on such a journey. "Is it because of what happened to Ailis and Iona?"

He sighed, gazing down at his daughter, his brow creased in a slight frown. "Aye. I can't leave her at Strathwick. I can't trust anyone to protect her but myself and Drake."

A thread of anger twisted in Rose. Not at him, but at her own father, who'd sent his children away rather than protect them himself. Shame immediately followed the thought, sending her into the state of restless unhappiness that seemed to plague her of late. She'd thought it had to do with her inability to heal her father, but now she had the Wizard of the North and still she felt vaguely unhappy. She supposed it wouldn't go away until her father was well and she was able to confront him.

She glanced back at William, cradling his sleeping daughter, and knew this was a great thing he did for her, uprooting his family. All for some woman he hardly knew—a woman who'd forced her way into his home and threatened one of his people, all to honor a promise he'd made in the throws of fever. She felt slightly ashamed of herself and said, "Thank you again for doing this for me."

He lifted a shoulder slightly. "Perhaps it's best if I leave Strathwick for a time."

"Is it always like that?"

His throat worked as he swallowed, the firm line of his mouth flattening. "No. They've hunted me, and run a few people that I've healed out of the village, but they've never killed anyone before."

"Do you have somewhere you can go? Another castle?"

"Aye, but then they'd win—driving me out like they did Betty." A muscle bulged in his jaw. "No. Strathwick is mine and the instigators will be dealt with." The glance he gave her was grim and rueful, his eyes dark. "I'm sorry you witnessed what happened to Ailis and her mother."

Anger tightened Rose's throat, making it difficult for her to speak immediately. When she could, her voice was low with suppressed passion. "It was so very wrong, what they did. It makes me ill to think on it. And if it makes me ill, I can only imagine how it makes you feel." When he didn't respond, she continued, "You must wonder what the purpose is, to put yourself through such danger and pain to save one life, and then lose two because of your trouble. I want you to know, my lord, such horrors will never occur at Lochlaire."

One black cynical brow arched. "It sounds as if Lochlaire is a haven."

"It was."

His gaze sharpened, studying her. "Was?"

Rose looked away from his perceptive eyes and stared down at the reins grasped loosely in her leather-clad hands. "Things have changed a great deal. My father is dying. When he's well, everything will be right again."

A thoughtful silence followed, then he said, "You were not specific in your letters about this thing that tore your family apart."

Rose scanned the road ahead, wishing now she'd kept quiet. But there was no distraction in sight. The road was empty, no sign of Drake and Wallace. When she looked back at Strathwick, he still waited for her answer.

"My mother was a witch. She was attacked by a mob and burned. To protect us, my father sent us away to foster with people he trusted, separately, so I didn't see my sisters for twelve years."

Strathwick's brow furrowed in disbelief. "He sent you away?" He looked down at his daughter, his expression growing darker. "How convenient for him, relieving himself of the responsibility."

"He thought he was doing the right thing," Rose said defensively. "It's what my mother wanted."

He met her gaze, a brow slightly arched. "But you don't agree."

It was not a question. Rose's gaze dropped to the child nestled in his arms, a plump hand beneath her cheek and her mouth open in innocent slumber. She was so young. . . .

"No. . . . I don't know."

"Why did he send you to Skye?"

"Because Crisdean Beaton was there. My mother wanted him to tutor me. He was Fagan MacLean's personal physician. A very fine healer."

He frowned as he studied her expression. Rose tried to appear indifferent. She didn't want to discuss this any longer—she'd never meant for their conversation to take this turn. She very much wanted to discourage any further probing, but she did not want to call attention to the fact that it upset her. She judged herself successful when his frown smoothed and he said, his voice bland, "And you learned well from him. What was that thing you did to me with your hands?"

Relieved, Rose raised a slightly amused brow. "You mean like that thing you did to Ailis with *your* hands, before you healed her?"

The corners of his mouth deepened, and a very slight dimple indented his right cheek. "Aye, that's it."

Rose was powerless to do aught but smile in return, inexplicably thrilled she'd coaxed the grudging half-smile from him.

"I see colors," she said. "They direct me to what ails someone, but naught else. You saw that I was helpless to heal Ailis."

Strathwick nodded, his eyes lit with surprise and pleasure. "Ailis was pale yellow, aye? The fever a dark red—like merlot? The sickness in her throat was black. It had substance, too, it felt—"

"No, I felt nothing," Rose said regretfully, and strangely she did regret it. For a moment, he'd seemed so pleased, as if discovering a kindred spirit. "The rest, though, aye, I saw that."

He frowned. "You only see the colors? You don't feel them?"

"That's right. You *feel* the colors?"

He shook his head. "Not exactly . . . or not the colors. But the ailments. They have form and substance." He squinted at the terrain before them thoughtfully, then asked, his tone casual, "Have you ever been ill?"

"Not that I recall. Why?"

"As a healer, you are surrounded by illness. It would seem to follow that at times you become ill yourself."

Rose had thought about that herself sometimes, but the truth was, she'd never even had the sniffles. She shrugged. "I've been fortunate."

He slanted her a mysterious look, dark and full of unfathomable meaning, then looked away. "I've never been ill either," he mused. "Outside of healing, that is."

Rose waited for him to say more, but he only continued to meditate on the mountains. She rolled her lips, biting them, then finally gave in to the urge to ask him a question that had been nagging at her.

"I was wondering, my lord . . . how is your elbow complaint?"

He gave her a sour look. She tried to hide her smile but couldn't. She laughed.

"Since you see the colors, you must also know there was naught wrong with my elbow. Ah, well."

She had suspected but was inordinately pleased to hear him say it. "I thought it very sweet." She looked down at her gloved hands. "I was growing rather fond of

Dumhnull. I should have guessed he—er, *you* were not a groom. You neither looked nor acted like one. In fact, I don't think you even tried. Maybe you wanted me to discover you?"

The breeze rustled his silvered black hair as his blue eyes burned a slow trail over her. "Mayhap I did," he murmured, his gaze resting on her mouth.

Her breath grew short and she looked away, to her horse's mane. The way he looked at her made her burn inside, calling forth memories of his mouth on hers, his arms enfolding her. She gripped the pommel of her saddle to help ground herself. Did she want to do this again, entangle herself in another hopeless flirtation? No, not if it was hopeless. But was it? Her blood rushed, remembering how pleased he'd been to discover that she also saw the colors. Perhaps not hopeless.

She was betrothed, she reminded herself. She belonged to another man. Contracts had been signed, promises made. She shook her head at her wayward thoughts. So stupid to worry about these things, when he'd done nothing more than kiss her. She resolved to put it from her mind unless he gave her good reason not to.

By nightfall they had descended into a narrow forested glen, where they camped for the night. As the only other female present, Rose led Deidra to a nearby stream to wash. She combed the tangles out of the child's hair while Deidra squirmed and protested until Rose produced a blue ribbon and held it enticingly in front of her face. The child's eyes crossed trying to focus on it, her mouth a small O of wonder.

Rose laughed. "I'll put it in your hair and you'll be the prettiest lass your father has ever seen."

Deidra grew rigid as a board, staring straight ahead as if made of stone. Rose smiled to herself and resumed combing the thousand knots from the black curls.

"Who combs your hair every night and morning?" Rose asked.

"I do!"

Rose paused in her ministrations, mildly shocked. "Who dresses you?"

"Me!"

There was a great deal of pride in Deidra's answers. Rose didn't want to diminish that, but the girl's bodice was hooked askew, and the points were so knotted that Rose couldn't fathom how the child took her sleeves or kirtle off.

"You certainly are a big lassie, combing your own hair and dressing yourself."

"That's what my da says. Ouch!" She winced as the comb caught on a snarl of black curls, then immediately straightened her shoulders. "Sorry."

"That's fine. You may say ouch, but you must not pull away or I might hurt you worse."

"Aye, Mistress MacDonell."

The formal address was quite a mouthful for the child, and though Rose was pleased that Strathwick had not neglected his daughter's manners, she said, "You may call me Rose, if I might call you Deidra."

Deidra nodded, black curls bobbing. "Or you can call me Dede."

"What about Wee Squirrel?"

"If you like."

The combing grew easier, and Dede's stiff spine softened.

"What do you prefer?" Rose asked.

"Only da calls me Wee Squirrel." There was a note of reservation in Deidra's voice that made Rose smile wistfully. As a child, she'd adored her father, and he had been fond of her, but there had never been any special nicknames, or the closeness Rose witnessed between Deidra and her father.

"Then I shall call you Dede—or is that your uncle's special name for you?"

"No. Uncle Drake calls me other names, but they're secret."

The statement startled Rose, and she dropped the comb. It clattered onto a stone beside them. Rose grabbed clumsily at it, her heart somewhere in her throat, her belly queasy. Surely she'd misunderstood.

"What do you mean?" Rose asked, her voice strange. She continued combing the black curls mindlessly, although all the tangles were gone. Deidra didn't protest. She leaned back against Rose's legs.

"I cannot tell! It's a secret."

Rose's stomach turned hard. "A secret from who, Dede? From strangers, like me? Or from everyone. Including your father?"

"You're not a stranger, silly! And aye, from everyone—most especially my da."

Rose's fists dropped to her thighs, pressing hard into them. "Will you tell me your secret?"

Dede shook her head firmly, curls bobbling. "Can't

tell." She twisted around, peering into Rose's lap. "Is the ribbon in my hair now?"

As if in a dream, Rose pulled the front of Dede's hair back and tied the ribbon in it, making a small bow so the tails hung down to mingle with her curls. Dede patted it, fingering the ribbon tails reverently.

She jumped to her feet and raced away, back to camp. Rose slowly gathered up their things, her mind searching frantically for a solution to the frightful thing she'd just heard. What kind of secret would Drake ask a child to keep from her own father? The worst kind, she feared, the kind she couldn't bring herself to contemplate, to re-member. But she must, for Dede's sake. She could not stroll into camp and begin flinging accusations about. She knew from experience that an outsider making such accusations would not be believed but reviled.

She pressed at her stomach, the sickness in her rising until she took several quick steps away and threw up. She dropped to her knees, rubbing her hands over her face, forcing the heels of her hands into her eyes, driving back the images trying to insinuate themselves into her mind. Memories. Things she'd worked so hard to forget.

Corpulent, sweating Fagan MacLean, leering at her, lying to her. Her innocent, stupid trust. It sickened her, humiliated her. Her vision blurred, but she fought it, dig-ging her fingernails into her palms. Stupid, stupid to be so upset still, when it was long over. There was nothing that could change what had occurred, and she knew it. Stupid to be so angry still. It took time and effort, but she managed to push it away.

She splashed water on her face and straightened her

arisaid. There was nothing for it but to protect Deidra herself. The decision calmed her, infused her with sudden strength and determination. She had been denied a champion when she'd needed one most, but by God, Deidra would have one.

Deidra raced into camp with a dark blue ribbon in her hair, dancing about to make her curls and ribbon bounce to maximum effect. After receiving exclamations of how bonny she looked from all present, she settled down against William's knee to eat. Her freshly scrubbed cheeks glowed, and her hair had been combed to a glossy sheen. He could thank Rose for that—he was haphazard at best when it came to such things, trusting the servants to see to such matters. He ran a hand over the thick curls, and Deidra tipped her head back to smile at him upside down.

He smiled back. "What's become of Mistress Mac-Donell, Squirrel? Did you frighten her away?"

Deidra's attention returned to her meal of cold bannocks and dried beef. "No, she's still at the burn."

His gaze strayed again to the stand of bushes through which Rose and Deidra had disappeared earlier, and he wondered what detained Rose. He thought about her more than was wise. Pretty lasses were one thing, but she was a bit more. He found the woman a great deal like the letter he'd kept and read countless times. Compelling. Beautiful. *Known*. He'd sensed a similarity in her letter, that was why he'd kept it, he understood that now. He'd finally stumbled upon someone who saw what he was and understood it. But it didn't matter. It couldn't matter.

She finally emerged from the bushes and sat near him, taking the food Wallace offered. She seemed troubled; her face was unnaturally pale in the moonlight and her auburn brows drawn together, forming a line of concentration between them. William wondered what troubled her. Her father? Or was it something he'd said to her when they'd ridden together earlier? She had withdrawn from him rather abruptly, relieved when Drake and Wallace had returned.

He pondered this in silence as he ate, annoyed at his preoccupation. Their modest meal was punctuated with conversation about the journey on the morrow, whose lands they would be passing through, some broken men they'd sighted, where they might be heading and how best to avoid them. Rose contributed nothing to the conversation, though her gaze strayed repeatedly to Deidra or across the fire to Drake.

William found her silence vexing, especially when he could not draw her into conversation—a singular experience since he'd met her. She always seemed eager to share her opinion.

"You came all this way alone, Mistress MacDonell?" William asked.

She nodded, eyes fixed on her meal.

"And you encountered no broken men? No trouble along the way?"

"I disguised myself as a lad and hid at night." Her reply was distracted, her gaze on Deidra, who nodded off against William's knee. "Are you tired, Dede?" she asked.

Deidra sat up straight and shook her head vigorously, then rubbed her eyes and yawned.

"Good." Rose held out a hand. "Come here and I'll show you something."

Deidra scrambled up, taking Rose's hand eagerly. Rose settled Deidra between her legs, then set her wooden box between Deidra's. William watched, puzzled, as Rose painstakingly showed Deidra everything in the box—herbs, needles, probes, and many other interesting little things. He didn't know what to make of Rose's sudden interest in his daughter. On the one hand, he was pleased—Deidra clearly enjoyed it. She examined the items in the box as if it were a treasure chest, asking questions, eyes widening with awe over some unfamiliar instrument. But eventually her lids grew too heavy, and she fell asleep against her new friend's chest.

Rose then lay down, pulling Deidra down beside her and covering them both with a plaid. William watched all this with a sort of painful uneasiness. Rose was a woman, after all, and it made sense she wanted to take care of Deidra. Besides, she seemed so very comfortable with it, and Deidra obviously liked Rose. Yet it bothered William inexplicably. He felt he should not allow it. What if Deidra became attached? Grew accustomed to Rose? But he hadn't a clue what to do about it, or even if he should do anything.

William doused the fire and took the first watch. As the moon rose, he sat back against a stone and, for the first time that day, let himself think about Ailis and her mother. Somehow he'd known such a day would come. He'd done too many terrible things, and no amount of good could take it all back. Was it God's voice screaming at him in the dirt? Throwing pitch on the stoned bodies of the child he'd touched and the woman who'd allowed it? Was it God's judgement on him? For it couldn't be judgement on Ailis. She was but a child. He lowered his head to his hands but quickly straightened. He could not indulge in melancholy when he had a watch to keep.

He gazed at his companions sleeping around him, at his daughter nestled safely against Rose. A shadow seemed to pass over him, a responsibility unwanted, and yet darkly alluring. What was Rose? She could not heal as he could, but she saw the colors. He'd seen the colors for years before he'd healed anyone, and he'd discovered that accidentally when he was thirteen. Could it be she hadn't discovered her true magic yet?

He rubbed his eyes wearily with a self-deprecating groan. And would he be the one to show her? Open a whole world of misery to her? Of course he would not. This was his hell, to suffer alone. He would condemn no one else to it.

A soft moan made him straighten. Rose thrashed about beneath the plaid. William quickly crossed the short distance between them, shaking her gently awake before she disturbed Deidra.

Her eyes opened, wide and terrified.

"Quiet—you'll wake the others," William whispered.

She swallowed several times, then nodded, fear fading to confusion then to embarrassment.

William sat on his heels, staring down at her charmingly mussed state. Wisps of hair had come loose from her braid to float about her head on the breeze. The right side of her face was flushed and lined from sleeping on her hand. His gaze seemed to disconcert her. She patted at her hair, then sat up, adjusting her bodice and kirtle, and glancing at him warily.

"I'm sorry I woke you," she said.

"I wasn't asleep. I was keeping watch."

"Oh. Well, I'm awake now, I'll keep watch so you can sleep."

He waved the offer away. Considering the hour, it seemed inappropriate for him to remain beside her, but he was reluctant to return to his stone. "You had a nightmare?"

She grew still, gazing back at him, then gave a curt nod.

"Do you want to tell me?"

Her brows shot upward. "Surely you can't be interested."

"I *am* interested. I have very strange dreams. I even write them down sometimes, so I don't forget."

She blinked at him, her mouth softening slightly in surprise. "Really? I don't want to remember mine."

He lifted a shoulder and sighed. "Then don't tell me."

He moved back to the stone and she followed, rather than lying back down. This pleased him absurdly. She settled down opposite him, crossing her legs and smoothing her kirtle over them, tucking the edges beneath her knees and feet. She glanced around at the others, then leaned toward him and whispered, "Tell me about one of your dreams."

He settled back against the stone and crossed his arms over his chest. "Why should I tell you one of mine when you will not tell me one of yours?"

"Because mine are nightmares. You said yours were dreams, and those are not so terrible to recollect."

A smile pulled at his mouth from her logic. "Have you only nightmares, Rose? No dreams?"

Her dark lashes lowered thoughtfully, and when she raised them again, he could see a memory there. "Aye, there is a dream I have sometimes. It's silly, or though it will seem to someone like you."

"Someone like me?"

"Aye, a great healer."

He snorted softly at her praise. *Great healer*. If she only knew. But she would never know. "Tell me anyway. I vow I will not laugh."

She took a deep breath, her gaze unfocused in recollection. "Very well. It never starts the same. I will be dreaming of what I did that day. Some healing—setting a bone, stitching a wound—then someone yells at me to stop, that I'm doing it wrong. When I turn to look at the person, it's me." She frowned, her gaze far away. "The dreams change then. The patient is gone and I am swimming. This is where they are all the same. It's raining, and I am in a great, dark body of water." Her voice grew hush, her brow furrowed. "There is something beneath the water, something I'm afraid of. I cannot see land, so I just swim and swim." She swallowed convulsively and licked her lips before continuing. "Sometimes I go under, and I'm drowning, but there's no pain. I float downward, my arms out." Her arms opened as if to embrace someone. Then her gaze cleared and fixed on him. She lowered her arms. "And that's it."

"That sounds like a nightmare to me. The second part at least."

She gave him a small, humorless smile. "Not really. At

least, not compared to my other dreams." Her mouth curved a bit more, into something genuine. "You have to tell me one of yours now."

"Very well. But remember, I never said they made sense."

He couldn't believe he sat in the moonlight talking to this woman about dreams. He'd only spoken to his daughter of dreams, and only then some of the more fantastic ones that he thought she might find entertaining. It was an unusual experience, whispering in the dark with Rose, at once utterly right and terribly wrong.

"I recently dreamed I was a boy again. I was at Strathwick, but it was different. It was filthy and run-down. The well was fouled. Everyone was gone, even the animals. I saw feathers and dung but no living thing. I searched all over the castle but couldn't find a soul." He paused, trying to translate the elusive images of the dream into words. "I was standing in the courtyard when it suddenly occurred to me to look up." He tilted his head back, blind to the starlit sky, still looking within. "There, coiled all along the battlements, was an enormous serpent. It drew back its head and hissed at me."

He returned his gaze to Rose, who leaned forward, eyes wide and lips parted.

"I couldn't move at first," he continued. "It swayed toward me—its head did, that is—as if it wanted to eat me, but I just stood there, staring at it. Then Deidra ran by—I know not where she came from, as I vow the castle was deserted when I searched it before. I tried to yell, to warn her, but I couldn't speak. The serpent saw her and moved as if to strike. I was finally able to move, so I reached for my sword, but when I drew it, it was not a sword but a goose."

He leaned back against the stone, signaling the dream's end, and looked at her expectantly.

She'd been watching him with wide, rapt eyes, and when he fell silent, she blinked. "That's all? You don't know what happened to Deidra?"

He shook his head. "I woke up."

"That *is* very strange." Then she covered her mouth and laughed softly. "Your sword was a goose? How did it fit in the scabbard?"

He laughed, too, and shrugged. "I know not. And it was a large goose."

"Cooked or alive?"

"Alive and honking."

Rose felt as if she were dreaming now, sitting in the dark, laughing with the wizard of Strathwick. He was an exceedingly handsome man when he laughed—when he made her laugh. She had not felt so lighthearted in months. When was the last time she'd forgotten, for just a moment, her father and his illness? But Strathwick made her forget all that and made her recall, all too vividly, how he'd kissed her.

She bent her knees beneath her kirtle, wrapping her arms around her legs and resting her chin on her knees. She bit her lip thoughtfully. "May I ask you a question?"

"Aye."

"Why did you pretend to be a groom?"

He leaned his head back and gazed up at the sky, his lips still curved in a slight smile that made her heart flutter and race.

"You're not going to let me forget about that, are you?" He sighed. "Very well. More than once someone has attempted to kill me. I have guards, but if I'm severely wounded, there is little I can do. Drake and the others will fight, of course, but if they're also hurt, I cannot help anyone until I am better. So it only makes sense. An assassin will strike their intended target—me, or the person they *think* is me. If Drake is hurt, I subdue the assassin and am still able to heal Drake."

"What if someone were to kill Drake? Surely you cannot raise the dead."

His expression sobered, his jaw tightening. "No, I cannot. There is always that possibility. This is our best chance." When she didn't respond, Strathwick gazed steadily at her. "Does that answer your question?"

"No. Not at all."

He raised a brow with mild, mocking surprise. "Then I suppose I don't understand the question."

Rose gripped her legs harder. "I was not even in the castle. A threat to no one, sitting wet outside your walls. And no one but you was present, alone and unguarded. Why did you come out in the rain alone, pretending to be a groom?"

He'd looked away from her halfway through her speech, staring off to his right with unusual intensity.

"My lord?"

"I know not." He paused, then said, his words somewhat more hesitant than before, "I had to see the author of the letters, I suppose."

And now that he'd seen her, what did he think, beyond that she was "bonny"? She wanted to ask him that but could not. She lowered her chin so her mouth pressed against her knees, and she stared at the ground, acutely aware of the sudden silence between them. She supposed she knew what he thought. The kiss said it all. A man with honorable intentions did not kiss a woman like that without stating those intentions. Strathwick had stated nothing but that he found her bonny. He wanted to bed her, and God help her, but her body wanted to let him. Even now she trembled, sitting this close to him in the dark, being the recipient of his smiles and laughter. *Stop it!* She was being foolishly hopeful again, seeing castles in the air where there were only dunghills.

After a time she chanced looking at him again. He still contemplated the darkness, his mouth flat, jaw hard. The soft wind stirred his hair, so black it melted into the night, except for the silver, dull and indistinct in the darkness. He seemed so alone that her heart ached.

"You should sleep, my lord," she whispered. "You've kept watch long enough. I will finish out the night."

He shook his head. "Nay, I could not sleep now."

She hesitated, knowing sleep would elude her as well. But he did not look at her; he'd forgotten she was there. She returned to the bed she'd made for herself and Deidra, and curled beneath the plaid. Sleep did not come, but she did not return to his side, though he sat through the night, unmoving in the moonlight. She wanted to go to him, to talk to him and see him laugh again, but he made her uneasy. She made herself uneasy. Who was this man who dreamed of empty castles surrounded by serpents? She wanted to know him, far more than was wise for a woman betrothed.

Chapter 7

The next day of travel was as uneventful as the first, though near dusk, William began to suspect they were being followed. They were on a deserted moor, with naught but the occasional dead tree and the distant mountains as far as the eye could see.

They rode on, pushing the horses to exhaustion, until finally they came upon a ruined cottage. It was the best shelter they would find, and William took it. They had a cold, silent meal, and Rose bedded down with Deidra in the lee of the wall while William, Drake, and Wallace situated themselves around the ruined cottage, keeping watch on the empty moor around them. William knew Rose was aware something was amiss; her sharp gaze had followed him throughout the day, marking his watchfulness, but she'd said nothing. She did not sleep now either; she still watched him and the others as she lay with Deidra. When the child dozed off, she crept across the floor to the empty doorway where he crouched.

"Something is wrong," she whispered, peering into the night.

"I think we're being followed. Probably the broken

men Drake spotted yesterday. They must have caught our trail and are hoping for easy prey."

She crept back to where she'd lain down, grabbed her bag, and returned to settle beside him. She didn't speak and he tried to ignore her, but her presence beside him was highly distracting. She never sought out Drake or Wallace as she did him, and he took note of it. Though he tried, he could not long ignore the sudden industry of the woman beside him, so he finally looked to see what she was doing.

She was cleaning her gun. He watched silently as she swabbed the barrel, then pushed down wadding and an iron ball with the short ramrod. Everything was gray in the moonlit darkness—her hair and skin and eyes shades of gray. But his imagination painted her in the vivid colors he observed in the daylight: her hair, a sleek fall of amber and roan; her skin, glowing, a faint sprinkling of freckles across the bridge of her narrow nose; her midnight gaze, focused intently on her work, cinnamon lashes hiding her catlike eyes. Bracing the gun barrel between her knees, she poured gunpowder into the pan, inserted the spanner, and cranked the wheel until it caught, primed and ready to be fired. She set it carefully aside.

She looked up to find him watching, and she smiled. His heart skittered against his ribs.

"I'm ready now," she declared, her eyes glinting.

He made a soft snort of amusement and shook his head.

"What? You don't think me capable?"

"You are rather small."

"Compared to you, perhaps," she said tartly, lifting her chin and squaring her shoulders. "It doesn't take size to aim and fire a dag."

He laughed softly. "That it doesn't. Just be certain your aim is true and you don't shoot one of us."

She scowled prettily at him, but before she could retort, Drake hissed his name.

William pivoted in his crouching position to peer across the ruin at his brother. Drake pointed to something in the darkness.

"Stay here," William said to Rose. He crossed to his brother. When he glanced back, Rose had assumed his position, staring out into the night, dag in her lap.

"What is it?"

"Watch there and wait," Drake said, his voice hushed. They sat motionless for several minutes, William frowning into the dark where Drake had indicated.

"There." Drake pointed.

William saw it—a shifting of the darkness near a sparse stand of distant trees. And the harder he stared, the more he realized there was an unnatural mass to the trees.

"Bloody hell," William breathed. "What are they waiting for?"

"They probably hope to catch us all asleep."

William looked over his shoulder to his daughter, sleeping peacefully, oblivious of the danger laying in wait. *Damn.*

"Well," William said, removing his dag from his belt and checking the charge. "Let's get this over with."

Drake looked at him in disbelief, then scanned the

dark, deserted moor around them pointedly. "Until they attack, what are we to do?"

"Rose," William called in a loud whisper.

She turned and came when he gestured for her, then squatted down beside him.

"I want you to take Deidra and ride southwest, as fast as you can."

"What? Why?"

"The broken men outnumber us," Drake said.

"Aye. If we don't overtake you by morn, keep going. Take her to your home and send word to my sister, Maggie Munroe. She's married to Paden Munroe of Norcreiffe. She will take Deidra."

William felt Drake staring at him, but he didn't look at his brother.

Rose shook her head, confused. "If we're outnumbered, you cannot send me away. I can shoot."

"You've one shot in your dag and no time to reload. Even if we prevail, I cannot hope to keep you both from harm when they outnumber us. You *must* ride to safety."

Rose nodded, her face pale. "Very well. Maggie. Paden Munroe of Norcreiffe."

He placed a hand on her shoulder and squeezed. "Get the horse ready—and hurry."

She did as he bid while William crept to the wall and picked his daughter up. Deidra stirred as he carried her to the horses hobbled at the other end of the cottage. They'd not unsaddled them in preparation for this eventuality.

Rose was beside him. "Let's all go. Why are you staying here if they outnumber us?"

"Because they'll keep following, and we must stop sometime. Best to do this when we're prepared, rather than be ambushed later."

"But you said you knew some Rosses near Strath Ben that were friends. Could we not ride there for help?"

"That's another two days' ride at least." He smiled grimly. "Fash not—we're not so bad with a sword."

She exhaled loudly and stared at him, tight-lipped. She shook her head slightly as if she meant to say more, but finally she mounted. He passed Deidra up to her, then caught her hand, pressing on her cool, slender fingers.

"Remember what I said. Keep riding. Don't turn back."

Rose clasped his fingers back, gazing down at him with worry and fear.

Deidra blinked awake and stared at William, who was at eye level with her, then she glanced up at Rose.

Her confused gaze flew back to him. "Da?"

"You must go with Rose now, Squirrel. I'll be seeing you soon." He released Rose's fingers and took his daughter's hand, squeezing it and pressing a kiss to the back of her small, soft palm. He met Rose's gaze, still fixed unhappily on him, and tried to convey to her with a look the importance of the trust he'd just placed in her. Until tonight, he'd trusted no one but Drake with his daughter's safety.

"Go," he said before he changed his mind.

Rose spurred her mount and raced into the night. As expected, this was a beacon to the waiting broken men. They broke from the trees and charged the cottage.

"Make haste," William said, swinging into the saddle. His horse, sensing impending danger, pawed and snorted nervously. Drake and Wallace mounted beside him, and, with swords drawn, they burst from the cottage, bellowing their battle cry.

Rose struggled to keep a grip on the wildly thrashing child. "No! No! Da! Uncle Drake!" she cried.

Rose held her tightly, dropping the reins once when Dede would have slithered from her arms to the ground.

"Dede! Listen to me!"

Dede shrieked and kicked. Rose was forced to slow Moireach to a walk.

Dede abruptly went still. Before Rose could reason with the child, the mare veered to the right and reared. Rose's heart leapt in panic. She sawed on the reins, but the horse was determined to turn.

"Moireach! No, damnit!"

Rose pulled and yanked, but a demon possessed the horse. Moireach pawed at the ground and screamed furiously—then bolted forward, back to the cottage.

"No! Stop!" Rose cried, pulling on the reins. Dede clutched her waist.

Lights burst ahead of them, followed by three loud *pops*. Rose pulled her dag from the saddle holster, her heart hammering in her throat. As they drew nearer the cottage, the clouds shadowing the moon scudded aside, and she could see the fighting. Bodies littered the ground around the structure. Six men still battled. Three were on horseback, and another three had been unhorsed. They fought savagely, two against one. Rose still had no control of the horse. It raced toward the men on the ground. Rose recognized Strathwick, sword in one hand and a dirk in the other, fighting off two men. He slashed at them with a fury she'd never guess of the taciturn man, single-handedly driving both men back.

Moireach ran at one of the marauders, surprising him so he had no time to react before her hooves drove him to the ground. She pounded him for good measure before wheeling away and turning back.

One of the horsed bandits appeared beside Rose. She tried to block his blow, but his fist struck her arm. She cried out and, clutching Deidra to her, toppled back. She landed on her back, knocking the wind from her lungs. Deidra sprawled across her chest. The dag skidded away.

Pain radiated through Rose's back. She fought to catch her breath and clear her vision. Lights exploded before her, and a great weight still pressed into her.

Deidra screamed and the crushing weight disappeared, replaced with a burning on Rose's scalp as someone pulled her to her knees using a handful of her hair.

"Two pretty ones," a rough voice rasped gleefully. "No wonder they sent you away."

Rose's vision cleared enough to see the ragged plaid at eye level and Deidra screeching and struggling in the man's other hand. Fury and fear twisted inside Rose. She drove her fist into the man's groin. He pitched over and back, releasing Rose, but dragging Deidra down with him. Rose stumbled to her feet, pain radiating through her back. She ignored the pain and kicked the villain. "Let her go!" she screamed, then she kicked him in the head and stomped on the arm trapping Deidra.

He howled and cursed but released the child.

"Deidra, run!" Rose yelled.

Deidra sprinted toward the cottage. Rose started after her, but the man was on his feet already, furious.

Blood poured from his nose. "Stupid bitch!" he yelled, his voice strange and nasal. He lurched at Rose.

Rose ran in the opposite direction, praying Deidra found a safe place to hide rather than more trouble. Her breath wheezed in her chest, burning. The pain in her back seized at her, making her stumble. Her pursuer tackled her, dragging at her hair and arisaid. She slammed into the ground, bringing her hands up to break her fall. Stones cut her palms, and the impact jarred her shoulders. His hot, stinking body covered her, suffocating her. She bucked crazily, blind terror gripping her. The back of her head slammed into his face and he gasped, his weight easing enough for her to crawl forward on her elbows. A glint of metal caught her eye, and she scrabbled for it. The man snatched at her skirts, seizing her ankle and yanking. He laughed wickedly, his grip punishing. Rose fell, twisting so she landed on her bottom and kicked wildly at him with her free leg. She heard a feral growling and moaning and realized it was herself. She drove her heel hard into his face with a grunt of effort and was rewarded with a crunch.

He roared his fury and pain but didn't release her. Still, she gained the few inches she needed to grab her dag. She rolled onto her back and swung the gun around, the hilt gripped hard in both hands. He lumbered up, bloodied teeth bared, hands already reaching for her. He paused only a moment when he saw the gun barrel aimed at his face, then he threw himself at her, his bearded, misshapen face distorted with rage. Rose pulled hard on the trigger. The wheel lock spun, scratching pyrite. Sparks showered around her as the gun discharged with a deafening blast. The force of it sent her reeling back, knocking her head into the ground.

A cloud of smoke surrounded her. She dropped the gun, useless now, and coughed, scooting backward. Her attacker lay in a heap on the ground, part of his head gone. Rose closed her eyes and tried to catch her breath, her stinging hands pressed to her chest. Her heart raced, and she felt nauseated.

A sharp twinge in her back reminded her of Deidra. She scanned the moor around her. The fighting was over. The wind whispered over the moor, disturbing the tufts of grass. Horses meandered about, two of them cantering together playfully. Where was everyone? Her heart raced again as she limped hurriedly to the ruined cottage. She counted four bodies of broken men and spotted several more dark mounds further away.

She found Wallace on the ground inside the cottage, leaning against a wall, grasping his side. His hand was dark and wet.

Rose dropped to the ground beside him. "What happened?"

He spoke through gritted teeth. "Sword wound. Not bad."

"Let me see." She pulled his fingers away and pushed his plaid off his shoulder, then removed his leather vest. The linen shirt beneath was crimson with blood.

Against his feeble protests, Rose peeled the shirt off. "I need some water," she murmured, scanning the interior for their supplies. A water flask was near and she grabbed it, returning to her patient. She pulled the cork out and held it to Wallace's mouth so he could drink.

"My thanks," he gasped.

Rose poured water over the wound. Wallace hissed, and the muscles along his side contracted. The gash was deep but not mortal, slicing him along his ribs.

Rose let out the breath she'd been holding. "It will be fine. I just need to stitch it up. Let me find the others first."

She stood and through a gaping hole in the wall, she saw Drake approaching. Strathwick followed, holding his daughter by the hand. Rose finally allowed herself to truly breathe, putting a trembling hand to her mouth. Everyone was safe, and, it appeared, the broken men vanquished.

As soon as they entered the cottage, Strathwick growled, "I told you to keep riding! Why did you come back?"

His gruff tone brought her up short, and she snapped, "I didn't mean to! It was Moireach—I lost control of her. She went mad."

"That cow went mad?" He pointed.

Moireach had wandered to the hole in the wall and gazed in blandly. Deidra giggled.

Rose had no explanation for the mare's behavior. Her back ached and a wounded man needed her help. She had no time to argue.

"My box," she said wearily and left the cottage to fetch it off the horse, chastising Moireach all the while for being such a naughty beast. When she returned, Strathwick was kneeling beside Wallace, inspecting the wound in his side.

Annoyed, Rose hurried to join them, edging Strathwick out of the way. "What are you doing?"

"I thought I might heal him," he said dryly.

"No—it's not bad." She brushed his hands away. "I'll stitch it and it will heal normally. Waste not your magic on something I can easily tend."

"And if it festers?"

Rose turned to look at him, her mouth tight with doubt.

"I do it now," Strathwick said patiently, "and cause myself mild discomfort, or I do it later and am laid up for a whole day at least. I choose now."

"It might not fester."

"Let her sew me up, my lord," Wallace gasped. "I owe you my life, I can ask for naught more than to give fate her chance with me. Mistress MacDonell is a fine healer; it will be fine."

Strathwick gripped Wallace's shoulder and gazed at him with grim affection. "And that is why I want to do it." He turned to his brother. "Gather up the rest of the horses. Take Deidra with you."

"No!" The word exploded out of Rose without warning, surprising even herself.

Everyone stared at her in astonishment.

She hesitated, her mind racing for an explanation but drawing a blank. Nevertheless, she could not allow Deidra to go off alone with her uncle. She said, "I'd like Deidra to stay here."

Strathwick shook his head decisively. "Nay, I never allow her to witness a healing." He nodded to his brother. "Go."

Drake extended his hand for Deidra to take. "No," Rose said, standing and grabbing Deidra's arm, pulling the child close. "It's not safe. What if there are more broken men?"

Strathwick stood, too, his patience clearly wearing thin. "There aren't—and if there were, she'd be safer with Drake than with you, lass. At least he follows my orders."

"Does he?" she bit out, her eyes narrowed on the dark-haired young man now gaping at her.

Strathwick's brows drew together in confusion and annoyance.

Drake stepped forward, indignant. "What mean you?"

She glowered at him and said in a low voice, "You *know* what I mean."

His eyes narrowed and his face grew hard. His words were clipped with anger. "No, I don't."

"Since no one seems to know but you," Strathwick said, his voice rife with barely controlled irritation, "I beg your indulgence on this. What are you accusing my brother of doing?"

Rose should have kept her mouth shut. The timing was not right, but after the night's harrowing events, her emotions were raw and close to the surface. She thought of telling them to forget about it, asking pardon for her insinuations, but she knew that wouldn't do now. They would not forget. And besides, she wasn't sorry. There was something empowering about saying it aloud after all the years she'd suffered her own pain and humiliation in silence.

Rose pinned Drake with an accusatory look. "Why don't you tell your brother about the secret you and Deidra are keeping from him?"

Drake shook his head in confusion, then abruptly his eyes widened in surprise. He turned to his brother guiltily. "Oh . . . that."

Rose nodded in cold triumph. "Aye, *that*."

Strathwick spoke through clenched teeth, hands braced on his hips as he glared at the two of them. "Someone prithee explain to me what '*that*' is."

Drake shoved a hand through his hair. "Now? Can you not tend Wallace first while Dede and I see to the horses?"

"Why?" Rose said angrily, taking a step toward him and pushing Deidra behind her. "So you can take Deidra outside and get your stories straight? So you can threaten her?"

"What the hell?" Drake cried, his face darkening with furious indignation.

Rose whirled to face Strathwick. "He has been doing things to your daughter. Making her touch him."

Strathwick turned on his brother, his eyes icy. His voice was low and menacing. "What is she saying?"

Drake sprang at her suddenly, grabbing her arms, giving her a hard shake that rattled her teeth. "Are you mad?" he sputtered. "You vile bitch—I would never—"

Rose pushed at him, clawing at his face with her nails. Strathwick was between them, shoving them violently apart. They glared at each other over Strathwick's arms, panting.

"She told me!" Rose pointed at Deidra, who stared at the adults around her with wide, frightened eyes.

Strathwick frowned at Rose, worry creasing his brow. He gave his brother a long look, then pushed his shoulder lightly and pointed to him to stay where he was. Strathwick squatted in front of his daughter. "Squirrel?" he said with forced calm. "Has Uncle Drake made you keep secrets?"

Deidra swallowed and started to turn, to look up at her uncle, but Strathwick grasped her arms, bringing her gaze back to him. "Don't look at him, sweetheart, look at me."

"Uncle Drake said you'd be upset."

Strathwick's jaw hardened, and he exhaled hard through his nose. Rose could see he fought for control, not wanting to frighten Deidra.

"You know there is naught you could do that would upset me. Just tell me, love. You don't keep secrets from me."

Deidra bit her bottom lip, looking torn and woeful. Rose gave Drake a look of disgust. She wanted to geld him—had ever since Deidra had first said the words to her. But now, seeing the child so miserable, holding so much trust in the man who mistreated her, made Rose livid with rage.

Deidra gazed at her father with wide, unhappy eyes. "Uncle Drake said you have enough worries, that we should not add to them."

Strathwick shot his brother a look of barely suppressed fury. "I am your father. I gladly shoulder all your worries."

Deidra nodded hesitantly, then said, "I can hear the animals. They talk to me."

The tension abruptly released from the set of Strathwick's shoulders as he frowned at his daughter. Rose gave Drake a wary glance, but his gaze was fixed on brother and niece.

"What do you mean?" Strathwick asked gently.

"I'm a witch—just like you, but I can talk to animals. See—" She turned to the hole in the wall. Moireach's entire head hung through the hole now, but she promptly pulled back. Her hoofbeats could be heard around the side of the cottage until she appeared in the ruined doorway and stepped delicately inside. She came to Deidra and nuzzled her head.

"She wants an apple," Deidra said, smiling. "Watch." Deidra said nothing to the horse, but Moireach turned and walked over to Strathwick's bag and pulled at it with her lips and teeth.

"She'll tear it," Deidra said. "She can't untie things with hooves."

Drake walked over to the bag and untied it. Moireach buried her nose in it and came out munching an apple. When she finished, she lowered her head back to the bag, then stopped and walked away, going to the horse's end of the cottage, where she stood expectantly, tail swishing.

Everyone turned to stare at Deidra. She said, "I told her she could only have one." She looked up at her father hopefully. "Are you very angry?"

Strathwick let out a nervous and clearly fake laugh. "Of course not. I think that is a splendid trick." He grew serious and intense. He gripped Deidra's shoulders again. "Uncle Drake has the right of it, though. We should keep it a secret—just not from me. We'll talk more about this when I've had time to think on it, aye?"

He stood, gazing about the cottage, thoroughly confounded.

Rose knelt in front of Deidra. "*This* was your secret?"

Deidra nodded.

"And it was nothing else?"

Deidra shook her head. Rose's stomach dropped sickeningly. Drake's shadow fell over her in the moonlight, threatening and furious.

"What did you think it was?" Drake asked, his tone scathing. "Because it sounded vile to me."

Rose flushed, confused and embarrassed. "I made a mistake . . . I'm so sorry . . . forgive me." She couldn't look at him, couldn't bear the revulsion she'd see in his face. She pivoted and stood, trying to move away, but he caught her arm roughly and turned her to face him.

"No—you've dishonored me to my family and it was just a 'mistake'? I think not! I've done naught to deserve this. For God's sake, why would you accuse me of such a thing?"

Rose could not tell them why, and it sickened her and humiliated her. She wanted it to all go away. Her palms were damp with clammy sweat; it trickled between her breasts. Why had she opened her mouth? Why had she not handled it better? And why, oh why had she assumed such a thing? An image of Fagan MacLean flashed through her head, leering at her in his beard, throwing back his plaid. She gritted her teeth and forced the image away. She knew why, and she *would not* share that. She looked wildly at Strathwick, pleading silently for intervention, but he still frowned at his daughter, looking befuddled and a bit ill himself.

Drake shook Rose. "Answer me!"

Rose yanked her arm away from Drake's punishing

hold. "I made a mistake and I apologized! Leave me alone!"

Drake's brow lowered and he stepped toward her again, but Strathwick put a hand on his shoulder and pushed him. "Leave her! Wallace must be tended." He looked angry again. He leaned close to his brother. "You and I will talk later. Take Deidra."

Drake gave Rose a final, baleful glare and left, pulling a wide-eyed Deidra along with him. Strathwick sighed and rubbed at his forehead. Rose waited for him to demand that she explain why she thought Drake had done something so horrible to his daughter, but he didn't.

He knelt in front of Wallace and gestured to her. "Come here."

On watery legs, Rose did as he bid. She wanted to curl into a ball and shut it all out, but she couldn't. Work was the next best thing.

"How are you?" Rose asked Wallace, embarrassed that he'd witnessed her outburst, horrified she'd completely forgotten him in the midst of her stupidity.

He gave her a tight grin. "Fine."

Strathwick touched her arm. "You told me before you only see the colors. That you cannot feel them."

"That's right."

He placed a hand on Wallace's shoulder. "A moment of indulgence, friend?"

"Of course," Wallace said, though pain had etched lines beside his mouth and the scar on his cheek was dark.

Strathwick gestured to the wound on Wallace's side. "Tell me what you see here."

Rose took a deep, shaky breath and closed her eyes, summoning the magic. It took a moment to focus, but she welcomed the distraction and the opportunity to forget, for at least a brief moment, what had just happened. She opened her eyes and passed one hand over the wound. "I see gold . . . that's his color. But at the wound site there are black and burgundy streaks—I always see that on this type of wound. There are also splotches of gray. Normally, I would clean the wound until those splotches faded, then sew it up."

"Good. That is also what I see. But I want you to try something new." He placed his hand over hers. "The magic isn't here, but here." He tapped her breastbone. "Your hands are just the instruments."

Rose nodded. She took a deep breath, trying to assimilate Strathwick's instructions into something that she could understand. It was true that she felt the magic in her chest and gut, not her hands. But she never saw the auras around others unless her hands hovered over them, so she'd assumed her hands did the magic.

"Close your eyes and see it," Strathwick instructed.

She clenched her hands in fists and did as he bid, closing her eyes and trying to envision the magic inside her.

"It's a dark blue," Strathwick said softly. "And it pulses with life. See it as such, a throbbing cloud in your chest."

Rose imagined it, a pulsing, shimmering ball of midnight blue.

"It's all in your mind. It's yours to command if you wish. Now shift it, send it up, to your shoulders, down your arms—"

Rose gasped. She'd done just as he said and felt something warm and tingling rush down her arms. Her eyes sprang open, and she gazed at Strathwick warily.

He stared back at her, his face grim. "You feel it, don't you?"

She nodded, speechless with disbelief and wonder. He was teaching her, yet he didn't seem pleased.

"Now don't lose it." He nodded to Wallace's wound again. "Tell me what you feel."

"Very well." The magic inside her pulsed in her breast, stronger now than it had ever been before, twisting and turning on itself, eager for an outlet.

"Send it to your hands," Strathwick said, as if he could see it in her mind.

Again, Rose imagined it moving down her arms, and she felt the corresponding tingle and warm rush down to her fingers.

"Now feel it."

Rose placed her hands just over Wallace's wound. She saw the sharp black and burgundy streaks again.

"Stop looking and start feeling," Strathwick urged.

Rose bit her lip and willed her hands to feel something. She was startled by Strathwick's hands over hers, his fingers sliding between hers and holding her lightly. His hands glowed sapphire blue all around hers. She felt a deep throb up her arms.

"Do you feel it?"

Rose nodded. Wallace's pain radiated up through her palm like heat from a fire, washing over her in pricks and aches. Rose resisted the urge to flinch away from it. Strathwick released her hand, but when she would have drawn back, he said, "No. Place your hands over mine."

She slid her hands over his, her fingers curling gently between his. Her hands were so pale and delicate next to his large ones.

He turned his head toward her, his face so close that she could feel his breath against her cheek. She looked at him, waiting, her breath short with the mingled excitement of what they were doing.

"Are you ready?"

"Aye."

He turned his head away and Rose focused on their hands. He placed them over Wallace's wound. She felt the slick blood on the backs of her fingers where she held onto Strathwick's hands. She gasped when she saw it, so different from what she'd been imagining. The sapphire blue washed down his arms like a dam breaking, pouring over her hands. Power flowed through her fingers and palms, sending energy and warmth up her arms. His magic surrounded the dark, angry colors of Wallace's wound. Then she felt a change in his magic, like a line being reeled in, and it washed back over her, taking the pain with it.

It was over quickly. Rose struggled to catch her breath, the strength of his power leaving her breathless and stunned. A faint blue glow lingered around their hands when Strathwick pulled away. Rose disentangled her fingers from his. Blood stained their hands and Wallace's skin, but when Strathwick used the discarded shirt to wipe Wallace's side, it was clear, the wound gone. Only a slight redness remained as proof anything had once been there.

Wallace moved gingerly at first, then leaned forward,

gaping down at his midsection. "A saint, you are. This is twice you've healed me. How can I ever repay you?"

Strathwick stood, grimacing as he did, his hand over his ribs. "You repay me tenfold with your loyalty and friendship." He walked stiffly to the cottage wall and sank down against it. Wallace fussed around him, bringing a plaid and food, wanting to know what else he could do.

"A fire," Strathwick said, and Wallace was gone, off to gather what kindling could be found on the moor.

Rose knelt beside Strathwick. "When the fire is built, I'll make you a physik for the pain and to help you sleep."

"That would be fine."

Rose stayed with him, unable to make herself move. He had shown her something wondrous on this night, something only she could see because of her magic. She felt bound to him somehow and was confused by it, wondering if he felt this new connection or if it was just her. The wind blew across them and she shivered, then noticed his hair. He kept it short and neat, like a warrior's. She'd just been admiring it the night before, and so she noticed the change. She touched a lock at his temple. He drew back slightly, but when her fingers followed, he let her touch him.

"This wasn't all gray yesterday. And now it is." She fingered it a moment more, perhaps longer than necessary. She dropped her hand and gazed at him. He returned her look, solemn and silent. She whispered, "You *are* a saint."

He shook his head. "No."

"How can you say that? You perform miracles."

His mouth twisted bitterly. He gripped her wrist suddenly, tightly, and pulled it up between them. "Miracle, you say? What would you say if you knew the danger you were in right now? If you knew how I could hurt you with a single touch."

She looked into his eyes, then put her other hand over his, where it gripped her wrist. "Your touch does not hurt me."

His gaze moved over her face, to her mouth, and Rose's heart sped, wondering if he would kiss her. Hoping he would.

But he only dropped his hand and turned his face away, shutting her out.

Chapter 8

The next few days of travel were comparatively uneventful. They crossed bog and heather-clad moor, dark forests and mountains. The harsh, unrelenting mountains were occasionally relieved by the discovery of hidden waterfalls pouring into crystal pools. Otters poked their heads out to observe their party, then disappeared, their slick bodies shining in the weak sunlight. They were able to wash, catch fish, and refill their leather water flasks almost daily. Rose collected watercress to supplement their meals.

Not that anyone noticed. Communications were strained with all except Deidra, and Strathwick spent a great deal of time riding alone with his daughter, no doubt lecturing her about being a witch. When he wasn't talking to Deidra, he was invariably brooding and unapproachable, snapping at Drake and answering Rose and Wallace more politely but just as succinctly.

Rose thought that perhaps she understood why Drake had wanted to keep Deidra's magic from her father. He was a man with many burdens, and here was yet another. Being a witch was dangerous business; better to teach Deidra to hide it. Drake obviously cared deeply about his brother and niece, and, however wrongheaded, he'd been trying to help.

But there was no telling him that. Drake would not speak to her, and though she was still appalled at having made such an assumption about him, she didn't know what more she could say. She'd tried repeatedly to apologize, but he only responded with biting sarcasm. So they traveled single file, with wide gaps between them. At night, Strathwick shielded himself with his daughter, making it impossible for Rose or Drake to speak to him on any matter of importance or sensitivity—or to even get close to him. Rose worried that he, too, was angry at her vile assumptions. It vexed her terribly.

On the afternoon of the fifth day they came upon a castle high on a rugged mountaintop. Rose didn't see it until they drew closer. Its gray stone blended into the craggy mountains and heavy clouds gathering overhead. Wallace informed her that Lord Strathwick knew the inhabitants and that they would shelter from the coming storm there.

A stout man with a black graying beard and his equally stout wife greeted them in the castle's hall— Comyn Fraser and his wife, Grainne. Rose thought their reception a trifle cool, though very polite. She discovered why over dinner, when Strathwick informed Deidra that Comyn was her grandsire. These were Strathwick's in-laws. Deidra was full of questions after that, which at first seemed to disconcert, then delight, Grainne.

During the remainder of the meal, Rose learned far more than she'd ever wanted to about Strathwick's beautiful, kind, and generous late wife. She'd been a real lady, who'd made exquisite embroideries and tapestries. She'd been delicate as a flower. A pious woman, she'd never missed kirk services and had always given alms. A paragon of beauty; ballads were still composed in her honor.

Rose could not fathom why hearing this depressed her. The woman meant nothing to her, and besides, she was dead! Deidra, however, was in awe of it all, and when Grainne offered to show her some of her mother's tapestries, she jumped to her feet and clasped the old woman's hand.

Comyn got to his feet, too. "We'll see to the lassie tonight, aye? Roy will show you to your chambers."

Strathwick hesitated, standing, then nodded. "Of course. Enjoy her. If she's any trouble—"

"Oh, no trouble, no trouble . . ." And Comyn wandered away in the direction of his wife and granddaughter, leaving Rose, Drake, Wallace, and Strathwick at the table, with Roy standing patiently and unobtrusively behind Strathwick's chair.

When they all stood at the same time, Strathwick gestured to Wallace and Drake to sit. "Roy, see Mistress Mac-Donell to her chambers first." He inclined his head coolly. "Good e'en, Rose."

Wallace also bid her good evening, but Drake refused to even look at her, drawing his brother's dark stare. Drake did not appear to care, gazing blandly back.

Her chambers were small but comfortable—a single room with a bed, chest, and fireplace. Rain tapped against the shutters and chill fingers slid along the floor, wrapping about her ankles. Rose built up the fire to drive back the cold. She washed her face and unbraided her hair, combing it until it was free of tangles. Then she sat before the fire and tried to bolster herself, as she always had when she'd lived on Skye with the MacLeans, reminding herself of all the good things in her life. She had no good reason to feel so despondent. She'd succeeded in convincing Strathwick to come to Lochlaire to heal her father. She had her sisters near again. Isobel's vision had confirmed she would soon be an aunt. She was no longer on Skye—that was a big thing to give thanks for. And her betrothed, of course. Jamie MacPherson.

She removed the locket from her bodice and gazed down at the man she was to marry. He was a stranger to her now, though once they'd been great friends. But that had been so very long ago. When she was a child at Lochlaire she would sneak away from her lessons to catch toads and rats with him. He'd kept them as pets. She frowned at the angelic face gazing back at her, hoping he'd stopped that practice, then she laughed at herself. Of course he had. He'd only been two years older than her. He'd grown up, too.

She closed the locket, her mood improved, and decided to write him a letter. She searched the room, but there was no paper or anything to write with. She tied a quick knot in her hair and left her chambers in search of Roy or some other servant to ask after writing implements.

She was passing a gallery when movement caught her eye. A single candelabra lit the long, high-ceilinged room, casting the rest in shadows. She stepped in the doorway.

"Hello?" she called out.

"Hello, Rose."

The disembodied voice startled Rose, coming from the depths of shadows. She entered the room, peering into the darkness until she located the source of the voice.

Strathwick sat on one of the benches that lined the wall, his hands on his thighs, his face in shadow. The wall was lined with long windows, most shuttered up tight like dark eyes. In the center were two stained-glass windows, casting wavery red and blue light over the floor.

"I was looking for Roy."

"He's not here."

"Are you all right?" she asked, moving closer.

He inhaled deeply and, after a pause, let the breath out. "Aye, of course."

Such an obvious lie.

She took another step closer. "This is the first time the Frasers have seen Deidra?"

"Aye. I invited them to Strathwick when she was a wean, but they would not come."

"Why?"

"They think I'm responsible for their daughter's death."

"Surely not," Rose said, aghast, unable to believe anyone would think such a thing about him. Her death must have occurred in some situation in which he could not have saved her—difficult for a man like him to live with, surely.

When he didn't respond, she asked diffidently, "Do you miss her? Your wife?"

"I hardly knew her."

"How did she die?"

"In childbirth." His voice was cool, emotionless.

"Oh." Rose bit her lip and tried again to draw him out. "Are you troubled about Deidra?"

He remained silent. She probably should not have reminded him of what had happened on the moor. He was obviously angry with her. Her heart sank, and she cursed herself again for her stupid mistake.

She started to turn away when he said, his voice no longer cold but thick with repressed betrayal, "I cannot believe he didn't tell me. That he thought to keep it a secret. I still can't look at him without wanting to choke him."

Rose closed the distance between them and sat beside him on the bench. "Forgive me. It was so thoughtless of me to blurt that out."

"No, I'm glad you did."

"Did he tell you why he kept it from you?"

"Aye. Deidra only recently discovered she was an animal charmer—within the past year. Drake was with her the first time it happened. Considering the witch hunts and what is happening in the village . . . well, he thought he should wait a bit, until everything died down."

"He did it because he loves you."

Strathwick glowered into the dark. "He is an ass."

Rose sighed and looked down at the stone floor. "He hates me."

"He doesn't hate you."

Rose looked up at his profile in the dim light. So strong and handsome, yet so remote. Dark brows shadowed his eyes, his nose was blade straight over full lips, his jaw flexed with some internal tension.

"You're worried about Deidra."

"Aye, it was danger enough for her, being my spawn. But now she's a monster, too."

"She's *not* a monster."

"Of course not. But think you anyone else will see that?"

Rose looked down at her hands, fingers twisted together in her lap. "This is why Drake didn't tell you, you know. He wished to spare you this worry."

Strathwick grunted dubiously, then bit out, "It's not his place."

"Someone must help you with this burden."

His mouth flattened, but he did not respond. Rose wished there were something she could say that would ease his mind, but there was nothing. Witches or anyone remotely resembling a witch were not tolerated in Scotland. As a healer, Rose was somewhat more tolerable, but even her situation had become precarious from time to time. And Strathwick was proof that things could go terribly wrong should someone develop a grudge.

"Why do they hate you—your villagers?" Rose asked.

"Because I am a monster."

"You're not," Rose said with a depth of feeling that unnerved her. She couldn't bear to hear him say such things.

He turned his gaze on her, half his face shrouded in darkness, the other illuminated from the candelabra across the room. "You don't know me. You don't even know yourself."

His words made her uneasy, and she looked away. She stared at the cold fireplace at the end of the long room, wondering what she could say to him. He was in a strange mood. She should probably leave him to brood alone, but she didn't. Instead, she pondered the enormous portraits on the wall in front of them as she tried to think of something to say to him, something to ease whatever troubled him. Weak, dappled light from the colored glass fell across the portraits, lending strange mobility to the faces. Gleaming, watery colors wavered across the large swords and elaborate shields mounted between each of the portraits.

The silence was not uncomfortable, and yet she feared that if she didn't speak, he would leave. She stared down at her cold hands clasped tightly in her lap. "I am grateful for what you showed me when you healed Wallace. I cannot yet see the uses, beyond what I already know, but I'm sure that with time and practice, I will."

She felt his gaze on her again and slanted a look at him from beneath her lashes. One hand slid from his thigh to press into the bench between them. His shadowed eyes bore into her, making it suddenly difficult to breathe, as if the air had grown close around her. Her scalp prickled, but she couldn't look away.

"You cannot see the uses?"

"No. I learned nothing more than what the colors show me. But I felt better afterwards, and that's always a good thing. I'm a better healer if I'm well."

He tilted his head quizzically. "How did you feel unwell, before?"

Rose pressed a hand to her stomach. "A sort of tension here, as if I had worms writhing about. But it always fades."

He inhaled deeply and turned his gaze forward again. "*Why* did you show me? I've wondered that."

He closed his eyes and leaned his head back. "You don't know?"

"No."

"Then I don't know that I should tell you."

She shook her head, sighing. So cryptic. Perhaps that's what drew her to him—the mystery, the fascination. "So many secrets," she said, her voice hushed. "How does anyone ever know you, my lord?"

"They don't, and that's for the best, methinks."

She didn't believe that, didn't believe he truly believed it. Perhaps he thought he did, but no one wanted to be so alone. She placed her hand over his, where it rested on the bench between them. She didn't know why she did it; she'd put no thought whatsoever into the action. She was all impulse, her blood rushing, her heart drumming in her ears.

He raised his head to stare down at her, his gaze unfathomable, and though his hand tensed beneath hers, he didn't pull it away. It was a large, strong hand, the fingers long and supple, smooth except for the dark hair at his wrist. It did strange things to her body to touch him so freely, made her warm and fluttery, shortened her breath.

Her throat grew tight as she returned his stare, the words sticking, tangling with the furious hammering of her heart. When she spoke, her voice was strange, thick and breathless. "I cannot see the benefit in being so alone."

"And that, too, is for the best." But still he didn't pull

his hand away, didn't look away from her gaze, didn't even blink.

She felt as if she were in her dream, drowning, but without pain. She moved her hand over his, sliding her fingers between his as she'd done when he'd healed Wallace, except gentler, meant to soothe. "I want to know you."

His gaze dropped to their joined hands and he lifted them, curling his hand closed to trap her fingers and bringing her hand to his mouth. He pressed his lips to the back of her palm in a warm, lingering kiss that sent waves of heat and weakness all the way to her toes. He watched her over their hands, his eyes so dark in the candlelight that they seemed black, intense, obscure.

He bent toward her and she leaned forward, meeting his mouth. His lips were warm and firm and tasted of whisky and man and secrets she longed to uncover. His hand was at the back of her neck, guiding, tilting her head so he could kiss her fully, openmouthed, their breath mingling. It was all dizziness and heat, and Rose sank into it, her heart thudding in her ears. When his tongue slid between her lips, she opened to him, welcoming him.

His kiss changed from gentle exploration to fierce demand, his whiskers scraping her skin. He turned on the bench, his other arm circling her waist to pull her closer. She wrapped her arms around his waist, pressing into his warmth, inhaling the scent of him, spicy and male.

He caught her face between both his hands and drew back. His breathing was uneven as he stared down at her. "What am I doing?" he murmured, his hungry gaze roving over her face, his thumb stroking over her damp mouth.

Rose's breath shivered between her lips. She was unable to keep her eyes open under his sensuous caresses. She didn't want to talk about what they were doing or even think about it, she just wanted him to keep kissing her. When his thumb moved over her mouth again, she touched it with her tongue. He inhaled sharply.

Her lashes rose. He stared down at her with dark desire. His gazed roamed over her face and lower, to her bodice. Rose's breath caught with anticipation, her blood surging fast and thick. But he did nothing. He grew so still as he stared down at her body that Rose was compelled to look downward herself.

His gaze was riveted on Jamie's locket. She usually tucked it in her bodice, but as she'd been looking at it earlier, she'd left it out. The clasp must not have caught either when she'd closed it. It lay open, Jamie's pale face and cerulean eyes gazing up at them.

Rain tapped against the shutters, and the cold swirled around Rose's ankles again, chilling her. She pulled free of William's arms. He released her readily enough, but his hand lifted the locket, his gaze still fixed on the miniature. The longer he stared, the hotter Rose's face became.

"Your betrothed?" he asked quietly, flicking her a quick, quizzical look before ruminating on the miniature again.

Rose swallowed the bile threatening to rise in her throat. "Aye."

"So you're marrying young Jamie."

A small jolt of surprise went through her. "You know him?"

He closed the locket and let it drop back to her chest. "You could say that." There was an edge to his musing tone, a tautness around his eyes and mouth.

Rose was mortified, imagining what he must think of her, and she spoke in a great rush. "You must think I'm a loose woman. I'm not . . . I haven't seen him since we were children, though we've been writing. And I don't go about kissing men I hardly know—"

"I kissed you."

"I let you."

He smiled slightly, causing Rose's heart to flutter madly, then he stood, extending his hand to her. Rose let him pull her to her feet. He laid her hand over his arm, tucked it into his side, and led her from the gallery. She glanced up at him several times. He seemed distracted, thoughtful.

Her heart still raced with excitement and fear. "Where are we going?"

"To your chambers."

She should not. She knew she should not, but she said nothing, letting him lead her along like a faithful hound. What was she doing? What was she thinking? She wasn't thinking, and that was the bliss of it. There was something about him that drew her powerfully. Time disappeared in his company. Before she was ready, they stood before her chamber.

He pushed the door open and released her. Rose went into the room but turned quickly at the door. He didn't step over the threshold, leaning instead against the door-frame, his hands behind his back. He looked enormous, his broad shoulders filling the width of her doorway, his silvered hair nearly brushing the top of the frame. He glanced idly about the small chamber before his gaze rested on her again.

No longer touching him, her senses slowly returned. What *was* she doing? She was betrothed! And he knew it—therefore nothing he wanted from her was honorable. She put a hand on the door and closed it partway.

"Goodnight, my lord."

"You may call me William."

"I don't think that's wise."

He raised a brow, straightening from the doorframe. "Came to your senses, I see." He lifted a shoulder and heaved a regretful sigh. "You're right, I expect."

His easy acquiescence disappointed her. It was strange to feel so torn between what she desired and what she knew was right. There was nothing right about what she wanted. It was pure folly. She was a fool for being disappointed. She should be grateful he had the honor not to push the matter, for she feared her resolve was a flimsy thing, easily set aside.

"My lord?" she called after him when he turned to leave.

He turned back, wearing a mildly hopeful expression that made her smile.

"Would you convey my apologies to Drake?"

He returned to the door, a small frown appearing between his black brows. "You've apologized to him several times already, lass. I heard you. Fine, sincere apologies. There's no need to keep at it."

Rose shrugged, staring at his boots, her chest tight

with the memory of that night on the moor. "I just thought, coming from you, he might listen. I don't know why I thought such a thing of him. . . ."

His finger touched her chin, raising her face so she looked in his eyes. "Aye, ye do. And so do I. You've no more apologies to make, Rose. You've done naught wrong—just drawn the same conclusions anyone would, considering."

A heavy weight sank to the bottom of her belly. She nodded stiffly. "Goodnight," she murmured through wooden lips. She shut the door and leaned against it, her body rigid, as if tensed for flight. *He knew.*

How did he know? Her skin crawled at the thought of him *knowing*, imagining. No. *No!* She wanted to scratch her own skin off at the thought. Instead she hurried across the room to her wooden box. It needed to be cleaned.

For the next hour she stood over the ewer and basin and scrubbed every instrument in her box until each one gleamed. But still her mind turned and turned, remembering that even after William had been reminded of her betrothed, he'd still thought she might let him into her bed. And why wouldn't he think such a thing? She'd acted the wanton, and besides, he *knew*. Was it so obvious? Just from looking at her or speaking to her? Was it something in her manner? Did others know and say nothing?

She pulled out the mortar and pestle and began frantically grinding herbs, reciting receipts for physiks in her mind, anything, anything to shove back the horrible thoughts, the terrible memories.

*   *   *

William returned to his own chambers but found he wasn't tired. He should be, considering the grueling pace they'd set after being attacked by the broken men. That and the weary sense of guilt that had descended on him at dinner as he'd listened to Comyn and Grainne extol his late wife's many virtues, wishing he remembered them and sickened that he didn't. All he remembered was a small, frightened girl, begging him to save their baby.

But his interlude with Rose had washed all that away, leaving him restless and unsatisfied. He paced for a while, drinking some of the fine whisky Comyn had left for him. After his second dram he set the cup down decisively and left his chambers. He strode down the hall and up the curved stairs, pounding on the door at the top.

There was some muffled cursing, and after William's repeated pounding, the door finally swung open. Drake stood there, disheveled and naked except for the plaid wrapped around his waist.

"What the— Will, wait—"

William pushed his way into the room only to find his brother wasn't alone. A pretty blond servant was in his bed. She made a small sound of surprise and pulled the sheets over her head.

Drake raised his brows meaningfully. "Can't this wait?"

"No, it cannot. You, in the bed—get out."

Drake scowled at his brother, then hurried over to the upheaval of bedding, picking women's garments off the floor on his way, then apologizing profusely to his bed partner as he helped her dress. William paced the room impatiently, pouring himself wine and standing near the fireplace with his back to them.

When Drake finally ushered the woman out with promises to come for her as soon as he was done, William turned. Drake had thrown on a shirt and turned from the door, black brows drawn together in profound irritation.

"What was so damn important it couldn't wait until morning, aye?"

"Mistress MacDonell wishes to extend her apologies to you for her false assumptions the other night."

Drake paused in the act of pouring himself wine and blinked at him, his mouth slightly agape. "You jest."

"No. I am very serious."

"You came here for that? That damn shrew! Tell her to take her apology and—"

"And what?" William asked darkly, eyes narrowing.

Drake's mouth snapped shut. He stared at William with incredulous betrayal. "You cannot expect me to accept her apologies after she believed such revolting things of me. I would never harm Deidra. It makes me sick to think on it—"

"I know, I know." William waved this away. "However, you are being very small-minded, Drake, and it wounds Rose."

Drake shook his head in disbelief. "Wounds Rose? What about me?" He pounded his chest with his open palm. "She wounds *me!* She dishonors *me!* But what care you of that? You are so smitten you care for nothing else."

"Smitten?" William rolled his eyes. "Don't be absurd."

"Ah—you lie!" Drake grinned widely. "You adore her.

I can tell. That Dumhnull farce was my first clue, but you make us all travel to Glen Laire—for a skirt!"

"It's not for a skirt and you know it. She saved my life. Magic or no, I'd have choked to death from whatever Ailis had. She was the only one who knew what to do."

Drake sighed and drained his cup. "I am grateful to her for that, of course, but damn it, Will!"

"And we still haven't addressed your deception. Colluding with my daughter, teaching her to deceive me and keep secrets." William shook his head grimly as Drake averted his gaze. "You will do this for me. You will accept her apology, and you will treat her with courtesy and respect."

Drake's jaw hardened mutinously, but he said, "Fine."

William put a hand on his brother's shoulder. "You know I never believed it of you. If such a thing had been true, it would have killed me."

"You mean *you* would have killed *me.*"

"Aye," William agreed dryly. "But it would have killed me to be forced to murder you."

Drake tried not to smile at the ridiculous turn of the conversation, but he couldn't stop himself, which made William feel better about the whole thing. William squeezed his brother's shoulder and gave him a small, affectionate shake before turning for the door.

"Why not marry her, aye?" Drake asked, examining the bottom of his empty cup.

William paused, his hand gripping the door latch. The question caused a strange leaping sensation in his chest. "Who?"

"Grainne—after you murder Comyn and hide the body. Who do you think, neephead? Rose MacDonell!"

"I'll not marry again. You know that."

"You need an heir."

"I have an heir," William said grandly and made a sweeping gesture, encompassing Drake, who was standing barelegged in his shirt.

"I told you, I'll not wed until you do."

"I don't think that will be necessary. Surely you have a bastard or two running around we could leave Strathwick to."

Drake didn't rise to the bait. He raised his brows. "It's been eight years, Will. *Eight years.* Don't you think it's time?"

A mantle of loneliness descended on William. "And in those eight years, I have not been forced to make another such choice, have I?" He shook his head firmly. "I won't do it again." He started to leave, but he paused before closing the door behind him. "Remember what I said. Courtesy and respect."

"For you, brother. I do it only for you."

William returned to his chambers, his conversation with his brother still circling his mind. He *was not* smitten. He liked Rose—and he lusted after her as well—but that was the extent of it. He was certainly not smitten.

He thought back to the night on the moor and thanked God only Wallace had been hurt, and that it had been minor. He liked Wallace but kept the man at a distance, just as he did everyone else except Drake and Deidra. Until Rose. He could not seem to keep her at arm's length, and it was as much his fault as hers. A most vexing situation.

No, he definitely could not be smitten. He'd worked too hard to keep the circle of those dear to him small. He couldn't risk letting her in and one day being forced to make another soul-rending choice.

Of course, all of this was speculation. She might feel something for him now, but that would be over soon enough. He'd known that the moment he looked down and recognized the pale blue eyes staring up at him from the locket. She was betrothed to Jamie MacPherson, which meant she would discover the truth about him eventually. It also meant that whatever suspicions he had about her ability to heal must never be more than that. He couldn't guess what MacPherson would do to her, but it was guaranteed to be something ugly.

Chapter 9

❧

They arrived at Glen Laire around noon on the eighth day of their travel. William's first sight of Rose's home was of a lush green valley, surrounded by mountains and guarded to the north by a thick forest. About half of the land was cultivated, striped with oats and barley; the other half was dedicated to grazing beasts. A river twined through the valley, emptying into a large loch. Lochlaire sat in the center of it, as impenetrable a stronghold as the glen was.

Their small party gathered on the wide ledge just inside the mountain pass.

"The trail is difficult," Rose cautioned. "Deidra should ride with someone."

"I can do it!" Deidra cried and tapped her mare's sides, bobbing in the saddle.

William caught her reins and swung her off her horse, plopping her onto the back of Drake's. "Hold onto your uncle."

She scowled at being thwarted but quickly got over it, wrapping her arms as far around Drake's waist as she could reach and craning her neck to see in front of him.

Rose started down the trail first, effectively hiding her

expression from William, but he'd noticed that the closer they got to Glen Laire, the more tense she seemed. He'd expected her to be happy or excited to finally be here, so close to healing her father, but she seemed almost reluctant. Perhaps she worried that her father had not made it, and that was very likely, considering how ill he'd been when she'd left.

All of this, however, was mere conjecture. Since they'd left the Fraser stronghold, they'd hardly spoken. And though William had resolved to keep her at arm's length from here on out, he'd been more than a little disappointed to find that effort on his part was unnecessary. She had apparently come completely to her senses, and, excepting excessive politeness, she spoke only to Wallace and Deidra.

William brooded at the slim, auburn-haired woman carefully leading them down the mountain. He did not consider himself a happy sort of man, but he'd been content enough until Rose had come along, making him restless and unsatisfied with the life he'd made. The prospect of returning to Strathwick and the bleak, rutted track of his life held no appeal, and it was her fault, for forcing him out of a life he had not even realized was unsatisfactory.

They descended the mountain in single file without incident, though Drake's horse became irritable halfway down from Deidra's bobbing on its haunches, but a few sharp words from her uncle and she reluctantly sat still. As they cantered down the dirt road that led from the base of the mountain to the loch, crofters left their dwellings or stopped their work in the fields to wave at

Rose. Children came out to run beside them. One boy skipped along beside Rose's stirrup, asking if she would come tend his grandsire. She promised to visit soon.

Deidra was wide-eyed at it all. She'd never left Strathwick, so everything was a novelty to her. When she saw Lochlaire she gasped and pointed, eyes wide. "Look, Da! It floats!"

William laughed softly. "Nay, Squirrel, it's not floating. It's built on an island."

She cocked her head, regarding the island castle quizzically. "How are we to go to it, then?"

"By boat, I imagine."

They arrived at the stables near the loch, and Rose dismounted, handing her reins to a bearded man who waited for them.

"My father?" she said, her voice breathless, her dark eyes fearful.

He smiled kindly, gathering all the reins in a thick-fingered hand as the rest of them dismounted. "He's still fighting, lass—too mean to die."

She took a deep, shuddering breath, smiling slightly. "Thank you, Gowan."

She led them to the shore, where several boats were moored. They all clambered into one, and William and Drake took the oars. Drake looked ill at ease, surveying their surroundings with a tense, watchful eye. The Mac-Donells were neither enemy nor ally, and William knew nothing about the Glen Laire MacDonells past what Rose had told him.

William rowed, his gaze lingering on the woman facing him. The sun glistened on the copper strands of her hair.

She still seemed troubled, in spite of the good news that her father was alive. Her mouth compressed into a thin line as she stared blankly at the approaching castle. Her hands gripped the wooden slat beneath her, white-knuckled. William's curiosity was well and truly piqued now.

He pulled at the oars, eyeing the open portcullis ahead of them. Why the hell did he even care? It irritated him that he dwelt on it. He tried to focus on other things, but his mind circled back to her when he was unawares.

The boat slid through the water, passing through the arched gateway and into the cavernous chamber. William's eyes adjusted to the gloom, and he noted the welcoming party. It consisted of two men and a woman. The woman was very pretty, with dark hair and a very shapely form. Drake sat up straighter at the sight of her. But she was spoken for, it seemed—there was a proprietary air about the tall, swarthy man beside her. He was dressed simply, but there was no mistaking the quality of his garments—all black, a black-and-red plaid mantle secured across wide, heavy shoulders with an obscenely large ruby. The second man was substantially shorter than the dark man but by no means small. He was broad-chested and muscular—the calves below his plaid bulged as he stood on the quay, stone-faced. This one was clearly a relation to Rose—the fiery copper hair told all.

Rose stiffened further as they neared the quay. They let the boat drift to the flight of stone steps descending into the water. Drake tied the boat off using one of the iron rings driven into the stone.

The red-haired man suddenly came alive, taking the

stairs two at a time. William stood to help Rose from the boat, but the man beat him to it, grabbing Rose's arm and hauling her onto the damp stone steps. He clasped her to his chest in a smothering hug.

"Jesus God, ye gave us a scare!"

He closed his eyes, overcome with emotion, but when he opened them they were a startlingly vivid blue. Rose struggled, gasping for air, so he released her from his punishing embrace but held her shoulders at arm's length, glaring down at her.

"What were you thinking, lass?"

"I was thinking of my father—"

He gave her a shake, his expression hardening. "Were you truly? Your father was worried frantic. How could you do this to him? Did ye want to kill him?"

William was still trapped in the skiff with the others, but at the red-haired man's sudden violence he pushed his way onto the steps, enabling Rose to escape his hold.

She glared at the man. "I am trying to save him—and besides, what I do or do not do is not for you to say. You are not my father, my laird, nor my husband. And I would think if you loved your brother at all you would understand why I had to do it."

He looked her over with mock amazement, then his gaze tipped up to view William disdainfully. "We should be pleased you brought this . . . this man to Glen Laire? That you put the entire clan in danger for your caprice?"

Rose looked close to exploding. Before she could speak, William put a hand on her shoulder, drawing her closer to his side. "I understand there is a very sick man that needs my attention. This is wasting his time."

The man looked from Rose to William distastefully. William didn't care what he thought; he wasn't going to let the man accost Rose for trying to do a good deed.

"Uncle Roderick," Rose said, her voice still full of resentment, "this is William MacKay of Strathwick. Lord Strathwick, this is my uncle, Roderick MacDonell."

Rather than exchange greetings, Roderick turned on his heel and climbed the steps. The tall, swarthy man descended the steps, giving Roderick a look of quizzical irritation as he passed him. He scanned the occupants of the boat and stopped short, his black brows raised in surprise. "Wallace, man! What happened to you?"

Wallace stood abruptly, causing the skiff to wallow precariously. William caught Deidra and pulled her onto the steps beside him before she toppled into the water.

"Well, my lord Kincreag," Wallace said, his scar reddening, "What happened, is—"

All the conversation thus far had been carried out in Scots rather than the Gaelic William was accustomed to, so he answered in the same. "It is a verra long story, my lord, better told o'er a dram and meal."

The dark man—apparently the earl of Kincreag, or the Devil Earl, from the stories William had heard of him—nodded and said, "Of course—aye, come out of there. It will wait."

The earl retreated to the top of the quay where Roderick stood, arms folded hard over his chest. Rose paused, waiting for William and the others to follow. William raised his brows at Drake as his brother hopped onto the steps, and Drake nodded back, sighing. The uncle would be trouble—they'd seen it before. They each grabbed one of Deidra's hands and swung her up the steps. She did not shriek and giggle as William had expected, and when Drake released her, she clutched William's hand with both of hers.

At the top of the quay Rose hugged the pretty, dark-haired woman, murmuring to her, then broke away and came to stand beside William.

"My lord, this is the earl of Kincreag, and my sister, Gillian, his lady wife." She introduced Drake and Deidra, the uncle's thunderous expression not changing the whole time. The earl greeted William courteously enough but studied him with such an obscure intensity that William couldn't be certain what he thought.

"Come," the earl said, taking charge. "I'll take you to Alan."

Deidra remained leeched onto William's hand, and Rose stayed close to William, for his protection or her own from her uncle, he didn't know but found it endearing.

They could only walk two abreast up the stone steps leading into the castle, so Rose fell behind. William heard Roderick say to her in a low voice, "Your betrothed wrote."

There was a sharp intake of breath, then Rose hissed, "Wrote who? Have you been reading my correspondence?"

"No. He wrote your father, worried because he hadn't received a letter from you in some time. So I wrote to him and told him what you'd done."

Rose let out a long, angry breath. Dread sunk like a stone in William's gut. He knew what was coming next.

"He wrote back immediately," Roderick said. "He should be here any day now."

They entered the great hall, but Rose did not return to William's side, hanging back to walk with her uncle. "Why? You knew where I was. There was no reason to send for him."

Wallace separated from their party, heading for the kitchen, and William took that opportunity to glance over his shoulder at Rose and her uncle. Roderick shrugged innocently. "I didn't tell him to come. His reply was verra short. Methinks you've angered him."

Rose's eyes were narrowed, her mouth a thin, angry line. "No, *you've* angered him. He didn't need to know."

"He's to be your husband. Methinks he needs to know the trouble he's buying."

They gathered before a door, and Roderick left off haranguing Rose. Her face had drained of color, but when she caught William's look, she smiled encouragingly. He was no more pleased to hear of MacPherson's impending arrival than she was, but for vastly different reasons.

Before the earl could knock on the door, William touched Rose's arm. "Will you see to Deidra? I don't want her to watch."

"Gillian?" Rose said, trying to take Deidra's hand. "Will you take Miss Deidra to her chambers?"

"No, Da," Deidra said under her breath, hugging his arm and shaking her head vigorously at Rose, curls bobbling.

William knelt before her and put his hands on her arms. "It's been a long trip," he said gently. "The countess will see that you're washed, fed, and given a nap. Rose and Drake will come to see you soon."

Deidra's eyes widened with panic, and she threw her

arms around his neck. "No, Da, no! There are bad things here! Please—the animals are afraid, they say there is a bad man here."

William looked quickly at the earl and Roderick, his heart skipping a fearful beat. The earl merely raised a curious brow at Deidra's ravings, but Roderick's brows lowered in irritation. "What is this rubbish? Bad men?"

"It's nothing." William took his daughter by the shoulders and stared into her eyes. "Remember what we spoke of, Squirrel?"

She swallowed and nodded, her eyes swimming with tears.

The countess knelt beside them, touching Deidra's curls gently. "What bonny hair you have! I have a poppet with curls like yours. Would you like to see it?"

Deidra looked from William to the strange woman, then nodded.

She took possession of Deidra's clammy hand and gave William a reassuring smile. "She'll be fine."

When they were gone, the earl pushed the door open. They all filed in, William and Drake last. Thick Turkish carpets covered the floor of the large room. Fires blazed in both fireplaces, and candles were lit all over the room, making it brighter and warmer than the hall they'd just left. The smell of sickness was strong beneath the masking fragrance of lavender.

A fur-covered bed was central to it all, set on a raised dais. William studied the room's occupants. Another woman and three men. One of the men was enormous, black-haired, heavy-browed and burly. Rose introduced him as Hagan Irish. The woman was Rose's eldest sister,

Isobel—another lovely woman, this one with a mass of red-gold curls secured at her nape. She inspected him with narrowed pale-green eyes. Her husband was Sir Philip Kilpatrick, another large man who was cordial enough, if a bit suspicious. And last was a young blond man, Stephen Ross. He limped over, using a shiny black cane to aid him, and pumped William's hand enthusiastically.

"It's pleased I am to meet you, my lord! Been praying Rose would be bringing you back."

William was sure he was—and that he no doubt expected William to heal whatever ailed him. William gave the lad a grim nod and turned his attention to the bed.

Rose leaned over the bed's occupant, giving her father a kiss and murmuring something to him. William could not understand the MacDonell's reply, but it sounded gently reproving: No doubt he chastised her for running off like a little fool and frightening everyone. She straightened and beckoned for William to join her.

The man on the bed was painfully thin, enveloped in a mass of furs and plaids. His long gray beard flowed around him, freshly brushed, and his gray-streaked auburn hair was secured at his nape. Dull green eyes sunk deep in the sockets stared back at William above hollowed cheeks. He looked close to death.

Rose leaned close to her father. "Da, this is the man I told you about, William MacKay of Strathwick. He is a great healer. I've seen him perform miracles with my own eyes." She smiled up at William with watery midnight eyes. "Lord Strathwick, this is my father, Alan Mac-Donell."

William inclined his head in greeting. Alan said nothing at first, scrutinizing William as he absently stroked a silver Skye terrier sprawled on the bed beside him. The door shut loudly, and when William quickly scanned the room, he noted that Roderick had left.

"So, you think you can fix whatever ails me, aye?" Alan said, his voice weak and rough.

"If you permit me, we'll see, shall we?" William replied mildly.

Alan glanced at his daughter, then back at William. He sighed, resigned. "Aye, go on."

The poor man was likely weary of all the poking and prodding, yet he must be of extremely strong mettle to still be alive. Rose had said the illness had disabled him for months now, and despite his decrepit appearance, he survived.

"It won't take long," William said, touching Rose's shoulder. She moved to stand on his other side, watching her father anxiously. Drake moved closer, always near to protect William when healing debilitated him. Isobel came to stand on the opposite side of the bed, staring at William with troubled eyes. Rose had yet to even notice her sister's strange expression, but Sir Philip had, and he put a protective arm around his wife as he watched William warily.

"Is something amiss, Dame Isobel?" William asked.

Rose looked up at her sister then, frowning. "What is it, Isobel?"

Isobel shook her head slowly, then turned away. "It's naught. Forgive me."

Rose stared after her sister, then shrugged up at

William, but he could tell by the line between her eyes that she only shrugged it off for his benefit. Had she not said one of her sisters had visions? Had he not seen the light of recognition in Isobel's eyes when she'd looked at him?

He took a deep, bracing breath and rested one knee on the bed. The Skye terrier bared its teeth and gave a nasty, warbling growl.

"Hush now, Conan," Alan said, stroking the dog.

"Father?" Rose chided him. "I told you no more dogs."

"Oh, this is just a wee one. Let me keep him."

The "wee one" snarled like a feral wolf, its black lips peeled back to reveal needle-sharp teeth and a mobile, curling tongue.

"Be nice," Alan reprimanded, feebly trying to push Conan away, but he was not strong enough to even move the small dog.

Conan got to his feet and barked hysterically at William. When Sir Philip tried to remove the dog, it snapped at him.

Alan scolded Conan, but the dog would not calm. The earl approached the bed with a plaid and threw it over the snarling beast, then swiftly wrapped it up. The bundle convulsed harmlessly in his arms.

"Shall I add a stone and toss it in the loch?" the earl asked.

"Aye," Sir Philip said testily, examining his hand for wounds.

Alan laughed at the jest. "He's just trying to protect me. Let him out."

The earl left the chamber, only to return seconds later, closing the door quickly on the vicious wee beast.

William returned to the bed, Rose at his side. He took a deep cleansing breath, calling on the healing magic and focusing it on the man on the bed. A pale green light shimmered faintly around Alan, weak, as if something drained him. When William saw nothing else, he used his hands, feeling his way, but could find no source to heal.

He'd seen this twice before. Once was from a slow poison, the other something he didn't wish to contemplate. Unfortunately he saw none of the other signs of poison—such as a brackish film over areas of the body indicating that the poison had attacked certain organs and they were dying. William could heal that, though it was quite painful for him and took longer to recover from.

He passed his hands over Alan's body again, frowning with deepening concentration. A sharp pounding began in his temples. The door opened, and Roderick reentered the room. Conan shot in between his legs, snarling viciously, and went straight for William.

"Uncle Roderick!" Rose cried helplessly, hands on hips. "No dogs! I told you that before."

Drake intercepted the dog, trying to shove it back with a boot, but the dog only latched onto it. Drake yelped in surprise and tried to shake the dog off. The earl attempted to recapture it with the same plaid, but Conan had grown savvy to this ploy and darted under the bed.

"Confounded dog!" Alan said, the lines in his forehead deepening. "I've never seen him behave in such a manner."

William stepped away from the bed so the others

could attempt to recapture the dog. He rubbed his hands together, squinting slightly from the pain in his temples. He had a very bad feeling about what ailed Alan Mac-Donell. When he looked at Rose, she kept her gaze averted, her face and throat taut. If she hadn't already guessed that William could not heal her father, she was beginning to suspect.

Roderick came to stand beside him. He lifted his chin at his brother. "So . . . is he healed?"

William looked down at the man for a long moment. "No, he's not."

"Canna do it, aye?"

"No, it seems not. You don't sound surprised."

Roderick's smile was sharp and humorless. "I'm not. I've seen your kind before. Now you'll insist on some elaborate and expensive ritual, eh? One that keeps you here leeching off our goodwill for months."

The dog was finally recaptured, but William did not return to the bed. He'd been accused of being a charlatan before. In the past he'd either proven himself or shrugged it off. He was not one to care overmuch what others thought. But this man's words sent a sharp stab of anger through his chest—especially since what he said was partially true.

When he did not reply, Roderick arched sardonic brows. "Hmm? Have you an answer for me, man?"

William had an answer for him, but since ladies were present and he was a guest, he kept his mouth shut.

Rose was beside him, her hand on his arm, her auburn brows drawn together. "What is it?"

Roderick looked from Rose's face, to her hand, to

William. His sneer became knowing. "Is that the way of it, now? Because if this is all to get a fine MacDonell dowry, we dinna give our lassies to cummerwalds."

Rose's mouth dropped open in astonished horror. "Uncle Roderick! What are you saying?"

William's pulse pounded painfully in his temples. "Nothing I've not heard before." He gave Roderick a dark look. "It will interest me greatly if he'll have so much to say when we discuss this later. Alone."

Roderick snorted. "We have naught to discuss, charlatan. Finish your business tonight and get gone."

"He will not," Rose said, the high blades of her cheeks stained red. "You *will not* speak to him in such a manner."

"God damn it, Rose—he's duped you! Dinna be his gawpy."

Next to William, Rose shook, hands fisted at her sides. He recognized the moment she was about to lunge at her uncle, and he put a hand on her shoulder to stay her. "Later, lass." He turned her so she could accompany him to the bed.

Summoning the magic again, he moved his hands over Alan's body. And again he felt nothing on his first pass. Frowning deeply, he did a second, slower pass. Nothing. He fisted his hands against his thighs, staring hard at the man on the bed.

William's healings were not always successful: Sometimes more than one person needed his help, and he could not heal more than one or two people at a time, as a major ailment laid him up for a day or more, making him useless if anyone else needed him. There were two other reasons he could not heal someone. A wound that had healed—however incorrectly—was healed. He could not undo that. He suspected that would be the case with young Stephen Ross.

The last reason was witchcraft. A witch he might be, but he could not undo black magic. He'd seen it once before, though it had been far different from this, the person bocking up nails and hair and such, shuddering and convulsing and acting like a madman. William had been at a loss, and the man had died.

"Let me guess," Alan said dryly. "You can find nothing wrong."

William did not want to admit it. He did not want to let Rose down—had not known how much it had meant to him to do this for her, to make her happy. It was so important to her, it seemed, as if her life were stagnant, waiting for her father to live or die. He'd been her last hope. She'd written that to him again and again until it had made him angry and he'd burned the letters. It made him angry now, but a different sort of anger. At himself. At her ill-tempered uncle for making it worse with his badgering.

"No," William admitted reluctantly. "I canna find anything wrong."

Alan shrugged, fatigue etched in every line of his face, the tilt of his head. "Didn't think you would. I've been seen by every healer in Scotland, methinks, and some without. None can find a damn thing wrong with me. But all agree I'm dying." William read the words he left unsaid—that he wished to get on with the dying part.

William heard Rose's quick intake of breath beside him, as if she fought to control her emotions. A band tightened around his chest, urging him not to give up.

"I'm going to touch you," he said. Though he'd never attempted to heal an ailment he couldn't see, it was worth a try.

Alan nodded his consent. William placed his palms on the man's sunken chest, aware of all the eyes watching him intently, hopefully. He closed his eyes, and the magic washed down his arms and into Alan. The older man gasped, but there was nothing there, nothing for William to latch onto, and it quickly surged back up inside him.

He removed his hands and straightened from the bed, shaking his head slowly. "I canna find aught wrong with you."

Alan raised a skeptical brow. "It certainly *feels* as if something is amiss."

William took a deep breath. "Well, I suspect something is very much amiss, and if you've a moment alone, I'll tell you what I think."

"Alone?" Roderick said, trying to shove William away so he could stand at Alan's bedside. William didn't move, giving the unpleasant man a warning glare.

But Roderick didn't seem to notice, sneering at him. "Why do ye need to speak to him alone? So you can feed him lies and squeeze more payment out of him?"

"He has asked for no payment!" Rose cried, pushing to stand in front of William and confront her uncle. William stepped back for her.

"Rose will stay," he said. "To make certain I cozen no one."

Roderick grunted rudely. "She is completely besotted with this man. He has her in thrall."

Alan grasped his daughter's hand and gazed up at her, his thick auburn-and-white brows drawn together. "Is this true, Rose?"

Rose hesitated for the merest second, then shook her head. "No, Da."

Isobel had begun to cry, and Sir Philip put an arm around her, pressing her head into his shoulder. Alan looked at the gloomy faces surrounding him.

"Come now," he said with false cheer. "Let's not be so fiddle-faced. What of Stephen, aye? Come here, lad."

The young blond man stumped forward.

Alan gazed up at William hopefully. "Mayhap Lord Strathwick can heal Stephen?"

William rubbed his fingers hard into his closed eyes. The pain was nearly blinding now, compounded by the fact that he *knew* he could not heal Stephen.

He sighed and dropped his hand. "I cannot help the lad."

At this revelation everyone began to talk at once.

"What do you mean?"

"How do you know?"

"You haven't even looked at his back!"

"You won't even try?"

"Do you even know what ails him?"

The lad himself said nothing; he only stood there, staring down at his hands braced over the top of his cane. William gritted his teeth, feeling like an ass and a fraud.

Rose gazed up at William, studying him with a small, worried frown. "You are unwell."

He thought to deny it, but in truth, he wanted out of this room and away from these people, so he nodded.

"Lord Strathwick is unwell," Rose announced, her hand on his arm, propelling him toward the door. "We'll continue this on the morrow."

"How convenient," Roderick said, shaking his head contemptuously. "Well, on the morrow I will have many questions, *healer*."

Drake bumped into him rather violently and unnecessarily on the way to the door. Roderick went for his dirk, but Sir Philip's hand was on his shoulder, his back to them. He lowered his head to speak to Roderick in a low voice. Planning the lynching, no doubt.

The door closed behind William, Drake, and Rose.

"I am going to kill your uncle," William said mildly.

Rose's shoulders slumped. "What would you think if you were him?"

William's jaw tightened. "That I was a fake."

"I would, too, if I hadn't seen you heal." She started walking, and William and Drake followed. Her words made William's head pound harder. He *felt* like a fake, which was absurd and made him even angrier. He glanced at Drake, who glowered at her back. William elbowed him, and he directed his scowl elsewhere.

She led them up two curving stone stairways, then down a short hall to a door. "You'll have to share. The earl and all his retainers take up a lot of room when they visit."

Drake crossed the chamber and threw himself face-down on the bed, giving William a moment alone with Rose.

He leaned against the wall beside the door. "I am sorry."

And he was sorrier than he'd ever been for not being able to help someone he didn't know. He knew nothing of Alan MacDonell but what Rose had told him. Whether the man lived or died was nothing to him. But it mattered to Rose, and so now it mattered to him.

"Why can't you heal him? I don't understand." There was a faint note of accusation in her voice, though she tried to hide it from him.

"But you do, if you'll think on it. What did you see when you looked with your hands?"

She looked down at her open palms. "His light . . . it is weak. Growing weaker."

"But nothing else. No sign of illness, aye?"

She shook her head, still staring at her hands as she clenched them into fists.

"That is what I saw. I cannot heal what is not there."

She crossed her slender arms beneath her breasts, her brow furrowed. "I don't understand. What is killing him?"

"I think I know what ails him but not how to fight it."

Her head came up, hopeful eyes on him. "You do? What is it?"

"Witchcraft, Rose. Someone is murdering your father with magic."

The hope evaporated from her expression. She shook her head. "That's what I thought at first, too. But who? Why? It doesn't make sense."

"I know not, but I've seen it before. What else could it be? Have you ever seen aught like that before?"

She raised her brows and her shoulders simultaneously. "No . . . but that doesn't mean we have to act like hysterical elders, crying witchcraft."

He arched a brow, taken aback by her sarcasm. How could she be incredulous about this? Her sisters were both witches. *She* was a witch. And she couldn't fathom someone using witchcraft to murder her father?

She held up a hand for peace. "I understand why you think it's witchcraft, but I've already examined that possibility. I've been through every grimoire I own and have found nothing. Gillian has consulted with ghosts. Isobel has searched for visions. But more important—who would do such a thing? No other witches besides my sisters and I have been near my father. And besides, he became ill before he brought us home. Who would do this?"

William nodded, seeing her point, but he was not ready to give up his theory until he tested it. "Humor me, aye? Not everyone wields magic as we do. Some use spellcraft."

"Spellcraft." She rolled her eyes. "I have tried this *spellcraft* and find it useless. A person either has magic or they don't. No amount of words will make it so. You make no spells when you heal, do you?"

He couldn't deny that. "I have not studied spellcraft, but there are . . . wizards, magicians, who can makes curses and evil spells."

Rose sighed. "Very well. Perhaps it *is* witchcraft. How are we to counter it?"

He shook his head slowly. "I don't know."

After a moment of silent thought she reached her hand out to him, and he took it. She squeezed it as she gazed up at him. "I know you tried. I know if you could have, you would have healed him, and I welcome any help you are willing to give. I thank you for everything you've done for me."

He held onto her hand when she would have pulled away, stroking the soft skin on the back with his thumb. His heart thudded, his blood running thick. He wanted to kiss her again, and this time do far more than kiss her. She did not protest or even speak; she just gazed up at him with wide eyes. A flush stole up her neck, igniting a fire in his blood. He tugged at her hand, drawing her closer.

A loud throat-clearing destroyed the moment. She yanked her hand away and abruptly bid him goodnight.

William turned to the bed and scowled at his brother.

Drake pushed himself up on his elbow and grinned lecherously. "I guess we're staying for a bit, aye?"

"Aye, we are."

Drake dropped onto his back and stared at the ceiling. "The uncle will be a problem."

William didn't argue, though it wasn't the uncle he was worried about but the soon-to-be-arriving betrothed.

Chapter 10

He climbed the stairs to his chambers, excitement rushing his blood. Finally, Rose had returned with the healer. Everything was in place. When Alan expired under the Wizard of the North's watch, no one would even think to look elsewhere. Not that they did now. No one suspected what really ailed Alan—all believed it was some illness that could be cured if they could just find the right healer.

He closed himself up in his chambers and threw back the heavy rug. He kept his instruments beneath the floor. He drew out a bowl containing naught but a blob of wax. He lit a fire beneath it and waited for it to melt. As he waited, he withdrew the strands of curly black hair he'd retrieved from Gillian and the earl's chambers after the bairn had returned to her father. Deidra was her name. The name meant *sorrow*. But the sorrow she brought would not be his. He would make certain of that. She was the one kink in his plan, the one thing he'd not anticipated.

There are bad things here . . . the animals are afraid, they say there is a bad man here. Childish fancies, most likely, but he had to be certain. He couldn't have her messing things up for him. Her father might be useful, but she could be cause for concern.

The wax bubbled and swirled in the bowl. He dropped a few of the hairs in, saving the rest to place on top. He drew a razor across his thumb and watched the blood ooze and drop, mixing in with the wax. He added the rest of the ingredients and said the words. He removed the wax from the fire to cool. When it became malleable like dough he would give it form. Then she would be his puppet. No longer a threat but useful.

Peace settled over him as he waited. Events were unfolding exactly as he'd planned. Soon it would be over, and another witch would burn.

By the next morning, William had formed a plan. Perhaps not a great plan, but it was the best he could cobble together. It had been the countess's idea, really, or at least she had been the inspiration for it. She had brought Deidra to him the evening before after feeding her and giving her a poppet.

Deidra had chattered on and on about the countess's wonderful deerhound and how much fun she'd had with the countess, her earlier fears—to William's relief—completely forgotten.

"She was so wonderful with Broc," the countess said, smiling fondly at the child. "He is a difficult hound yet he responded so well to her, as if they understood each other."

William gave her a strained smile and slid his daughter a sidelong look. She was oblivious, playing with her poppet's curling hair. How many times had he heard those same words and thought not a thing about them? How blind he'd been.

"Forgive me," Lady Kincreag said. "You must be tired. I ken she is."

Deidra yawned, as if on cue.

But the countess did not leave. She tilted her head and asked, "I heard the healing did not go well."

William shook his head regretfully. "I'm sorry I could not help your father."

"Prithee accept our thanks for your effort. You came a very long way, and we do appreciate that."

William inclined his head.

"I wonder if I shall see him after he passes," she mused, her large gray eyes distant, and William had surmised she was the necromancer.

"Are there many restless spirits here at Lochlaire?"

"Not many that I'm aware of. But then, I've learned spirits are territorial, and I haven't been all over Lochlaire since I regained my ability. So there may be more."

That had been the seed of the idea. Isobel and Gillian were wasted resources, and with their permission, he planned to make use of them.

When Rose came to fetch him, he told her of his plan. "Whoever is responsible has surely covered their tracks well. Your sisters are privy to information no one else is. With their help we might see what is otherwise hidden."

"I told you we've already tried that."

"Aye, but did you send Dame Isobel to sort the dirty laundry?" From the look on Rose's face, sending her delicate sister to do such a lowly task hadn't occurred to her. "Has she touched the dirty dishes? And the countess told me she's not yet been all over the Lochlaire in search of ghosts. There might be more to discover yet."

Rose nodded thoughtfully. She looked tired, her skin pale, a soft bruising beneath her eyes. She'd withdrawn from him days ago, but it had been a studied, deliberate withdrawal, likely done for the same reasons he'd withdrawn from her. This was different.

William caught her arm outside her father's door. "What is it, Rose? You did not sleep last night? Nightmares again?"

She looked down and to the side, then nodded.

His jaw hardened, wondering if her nightmares had been brought on by his failure to heal her father. He longed to heal whatever caused her such distress, to make it all go away so that she smiled again.

"I promise, Rose, if I can help your father, I will."

"I know."

Her smile was small and sad as she opened the door to her father's chambers, hollowing out his heart. She didn't believe there was anything he could do. She'd given up.

The room was dim and quiet except for the crackling fire. Alan MacDonell was asleep; his dog was curled up beside him. Hagan sat in a chair nearby, darning his hose. He looked up when Rose entered and nodded a greeting.

"Hagan," Rose said in a harsh whisper, crossing to the bed and picking up the sleeping terrier. It didn't stir. "What did I tell you about this?"

Hagan looked abashed and didn't reply until Rose put the dog outside and closed the door behind it.

"He loves the wee thing. I see no harm in allowing him his favorite pets, aye? It gives him peace."

Rose planted her hands on her hips. "After he gave Broc to Gillian, he did not have any pets. Why did you allow him another?"

"It was a gift from his brother."

A muscle ticked in Rose's jaw. She seemed on edge, ready to explode at someone or something. "I told Uncle Roderick no more dogs, too. What is so hard for everyone to understand about that?"

Hagan looked at her helplessly, beefy hands spread before him. "I just don't understand, Rose. You say you fear that the dog's fur affects his breathing, but I don't see it. He breathes no different with or without the dogs. And besides," Hagan's voice lowered, "the man is dying and the dogs comfort him. Can you not allow him that?"

Rose was definitely on the verge of some explosion, so William placed a hand on her shoulder. "Should we come back?" he asked Hagan, nodding to the sleeping figure on the bed.

Hagan shook his head, returning to his darning. "Nay, he had a bad night but has slept most of the morn. He's well enough I reckon, and his birse will be up if he finds out I didn't wake him for your visit."

"Och—he's a gift for exaggeration," came the gruff voice from the bed.

Hagan smiled to himself. "See you there? He's already awake and in a chuff."

"You'll see me in a chuff if I don't have some food posthaste."

Hagan stood, setting his hose on the chair, and left Rose and William alone with Alan.

As William approached the bed, he saw that the Mac-

Donell's show of spirit was for the guard's benefit. He looked worse than he had the night before; his face was gaunt, and a gray pallor tinged his skin. The arm that rested atop his blanket was bruised.

William leaned forward to inspect the marks. "How did this happen?"

Alan shrugged and sighed. "I know not."

Rose stared at the bruise, her face slack with disbelief. "They've begun again, the nightmares?"

Alan reached for his daughter's hand. "Aye, they have. Worry not for me, love. I've told you, I remember nothing of them when I wake."

But William could see she was more than worried. She was grief-stricken and unable to adequately hide it anymore. However, William found the bruises encouraging—at least in light of his theory.

"Rose, these bruises, they reinforce what I mentioned to you last night." William passed his finger over it, outlining the crescent shape. "An odd thing to appear while one is asleep—and in such a shape. This is nothing natural."

Alan studied him with weary green eyes. "What is your opinion?"

"Witchcraft. I believe there is a spell or curse on you."

Alan glanced at Rose, who tried to smile encouragingly but failed, her mouth a wobbling line, eyes bleak.

"And if this were a spell," Alan asked slowly, "what could be done about it?"

William sighed. "I know not. I do not deal in spells. I think our first task should be to discover who is behind it. Only they can undo it—or mayhap, with some *persuasion*, tell us how. Rose can think of no one, but what of you? I understand your family has been apart for a dozen years. Perhaps there are things your daughter doesn't know."

Alan frowned thoughtfully. "Another witch wishing me ill? Aye, there is one."

Rose blinked and stepped forward, her eyes finally showing some life. "Who?"

Alan reached a hand out to his daughter, and she grasped his fingers. "Your late stepmother. You never knew her. She died in childbirth. She was a bit of a witch, but she's dead, aye? So it cannot be her. Her father is the person I speak of—Sir Donnan. He lives still and blames me for his daughter's death. He used to send me terrible, evil letters with ill wishes inside."

Rose looked at William hopefully. "Could he cast such a curse from afar?"

"I know not. Perhaps if he had personal items—hair and nails—he could make an effigy."

Alan fingered the white hair of his beard. "But how would he get such things?"

"Perhaps he has paid someone in your employ."

Hagan returned with a tray of food, filling the room with the warm scent of pottage and honey.

"Fetch me Sir Philip," Alan said, and after setting the tray near the bed, the Irishman left again.

"Most importantly," William continued, "we need to discover if he has an accomplice. I think your other daughters could help with that. Dame Isobel could go through the castle and touch the inhabitants' things—laundry and dirty dishes and such-like. Perhaps her visions will reveal something. The countess said she doesn't know if there are more ghosts in Lochlaire. Perhaps there are, and they have observed something."

Alan nodded thoughtfully. He raised a gray brow at William. "You're a clever lad. How old are you?"

"Nine and twenty, sir," William said, though he couldn't imagine what his age had to do with anything. He smoothed his hair absently. "Most think me older because of the gray."

"Are you married?"

"My wife died in childbirth."

"Ah. It's sorry I am to hear that." Alan's eyelids drooped sadly. "My second wife passed that way, too. My brother has lost two wives in such a manner and is frightened for his Tira. We all are."

"When is she expecting?"

"Any day now," Rose answered. "She is great with child. It will be a big one. I fear for both her and the wean's life."

William could see the worry in the faint lines that creased her brow. So much she took on her lovely shoulders. He said, without a thought to the consequences, "I'll be present for the birth, if you wish. If aught goes wrong, I will help. But I must know first who is most important to your brother—the wean or the wife?"

Alan just stared at him, his brows furrowed. William felt the weight of Rose's gaze on him and glanced up at her. She regarded him with a sort of horrified surprise but quickly averted her eyes to contemplate the ground with unusual intensity.

William felt exposed suddenly, his shoulders tightening. Ridiculous. He'd said nothing revealing, had he?

He'd just asked a question—a very important one, to his way of thinking. He cleared his throat. "Perhaps one of you can ask Roderick, aye? I think he likes me not."

"He's just being protective," Rose murmured, gazing down at her father.

Alan snorted. "Smothering, you mean!"

Hagan returned with Sir Philip, and William retreated to the fireplace while Rose and Alan explained to the knight what they wanted him to do and why. He stole curious looks at William but agreed to do everything he was asked.

The sisters were summoned next and given their instructions. Isobel accepted her assignment with determination but little enthusiasm. Gillian, however, seemed excited.

William sat before the fire, apart from them, increasingly uncomfortable with his own actions. What was he thinking, becoming so friendly with this family? He wasn't thinking, that was the problem. Since he'd met Rose, he'd grown daft, operating at times purely from some base emotion. It was unlike him and highly disturbing. He'd been so careful for so long; why did he keep throwing caution away now?

He could not leave, of course, not when he'd set such a plan in motion. Not when he'd promised Rose. He'd even offered to assist a birthing. Again he wondered, in bemused astonishment, what ailed him, and as he wondered, his gaze lit on a gleam of copper and cinnamon hair. It was coiled in some sort of plaited roll on either side of her head, and the two sides came together into a thick, glistening plait that hung down her back, the end wrapped several times with her own hair.

Unlike Alan's, William's ailment had a name. *Rose.* He couldn't remember the last time he's sat mooning over a lass's hair. He closed his eyes, pressing his forefinger and thumb into the lids. He would make no more promises. He would spend no more time with these people than necessary. In the spirit of his new resolutions, he slipped surreptitiously from the room.

Chapter 11

❧⤸❦

Rose was so tired. She stood on the battlements, her head leaned against a merlon, too exhausted to even think. She'd spent the day watching over her father, poring through the books she'd accumulated over the years, searching again for something resembling her father's ailment but finding nothing. She'd reexamined him, bled him, fed him more physiks, and had finally been called away to tend a dislocated shoulder. She was of no use to either her father or William. She hoped he was right about what ailed her father and that when Sir Philip fetched Sir Donnan to Lochlaire, he would lift the curse. She hoped William and her sisters would discover an accomplice somewhere in Lochlaire. She hoped. But not as she once had. Hope was fading to resignation.

The air was thick with the threat of rain. Rose watched the moon rise between the scudding clouds. She ignored the sullen rumble of her stomach. A cool wind blew over her face, and she closed her eyes, her mind blissfully blank. She'd thought too much of late about things she could never change, things that should make no difference anymore but somehow did anyway. It made the nightmares come, made the anger rise. The only antidote she'd found was to work until she was too tired to think.

She heard the sound of others climbing the battlements several times, silent, to check on her, perhaps; she didn't know, as she didn't look at them or acknowledge them. The men-at-arms passed her on their circuits without a word.

The bailey below grew quiet as the castle settled in for the night. She slowly became aware that she was not alone in her empty vigil. Someone stood behind her. She didn't hear anything—she *felt* it. She turned quickly.

Strathwick leaned against a merlon, gazing through the embrasure, a tall, dark shadow. The wind stirred the gleaming silver in his hair. "You have been avoiding me," he said without preamble.

Rose was still a bit unnerved to find him behind her when she'd not heard him approach. How long had he been standing there? She turned back to the night, leaning her suddenly hot cheek against the cold stone. "I hadn't realized you noticed."

He was silent for a long moment, then said softly, "I notice everything about you."

Rose squeezed her eyes shut, pressed her hand into the stone wall.

He moved behind her; she felt him like a fire, warming her along her back. When he spoke, his voice was close to her ear. "What is wrong, Rose? You are different."

"I'm not."

"You are. Since the night at the Fraser stronghold you have avoided me."

Rose said nothing, willing him away with her mind while her body longed for something else entirely.

His hand touched her hair briefly, then fell away. "What did I say that made you turn away?"

Her stomach clenched. She whispered, "You knew. How did you know?"

"What do I know?"

She forced the words through her tight throat, her wooden lips. "About me. You said so, at the Fraser stronghold, you said you knew why I'd thought such horrid things of Drake. That anyone would, considering. Considering what?"

His hand went to her shoulder, and she pressed her cheek harder against the stone to keep from turning to him.

"When someone draws such a conclusion as you did about Drake, there is a reason for their way of thinking. Someone hurt you once, when you were young. A man you trusted? He asked you to keep secrets?"

Rose bit her lips and squeezed her eyes tightly, but still the burning tear slipped between her lashes. She swiped it angrily away. So stupid to let it rule her still. In truth, she hadn't thought it did until that night on the moor—but why else would she think such a thing, without at least exploring other possibilities? She'd lain herself open, showing everyone and herself the raw ugliness that still lived in her heart.

"I'm sorry, Rose."

She snorted. "Why? It's not your fault."

"It's not yours, either."

"I know that," she said, annoyed that her voice lacked conviction. "It's *his* fault."

"Whose?"

"My father's," she said through gritted teeth. "*He's* the one who sent me to Skye. *He's* the one who never noticed anything when he visited. And when I ran away—he sent me back."

"And you didn't tell him because it was a secret?"

She laughed softly, humorlessly, shaking her head against the stone. "I was stupid and young. And by the time I realized that, it was over and I was older, making other mistakes that were entirely my fault."

His hand on her shoulder tightened, then he drew her back, against his chest. She resisted at first, then gave in to him, leaning into his warmth, glad her face was hidden from him. She burned with shame and desire. She wanted him to hold her, didn't care what his reasons were, so long as he didn't let go tonight. He wrapped both arms around her, and she hugged the rounded muscle of his arm, turning her face into his shoulder, rubbing her cheek against the soft wool of his plaid.

They stood that way for a long while. Rose's heart grew calm, enveloped in the warmth and scent of him, his chin resting against the crown of her head. She closed her eyes and imagined herself wed to him. It would be a difficult life at Strathwick, but they suited well, she thought, and he liked her well enough. They were both healers. She could help him.

The locket seemed to burn into her breast. She already had a betrothed. But she hardly knew him, only remembered a dirty-faced boy with toads and rats. She wanted the man behind her, holding her until time stood still in his arms. But how did one ask for a man?

"Tell me about your wife," she said, then regretted the words immediately when he drew away from her.

She turned toward him, bereft and cold without his arms around her. He gazed steadily at her, his eyes black in the shadows of the battlement.

"Why?"

"Because I know so little about you and would know more, if you'd tell me."

"I told you before. There's nothing to tell. She was a girl—sixteen when we wed. I was one and twenty and not much interested in her. We'd been betrothed for several years, though. She was pretty; Deidra looks like her . . . in the eyes and mouth. . . ." He inhaled heavily, looking down at his hands, now fisted against the embrasure. "I hardly knew her. I didn't even try. And she was my wife."

Rose drew closer, studying his face, the tightness of his jaw. "You said she died in childbirth. Were you not there to heal her?"

He closed his eyes and shook his head. "I was there. Deidra was breech and wouldn't come out. The midwife said they both would die. I'd heard of babies being cut out of their mothers before . . . though the mothers do not survive. But I was not concerned with that, aye? I could heal her, right?" He slanted Rose a bitter look, his mouth curved into a humorless smile that did nothing to mask the pain this caused him. "Arrogant of me. Amber begged me to save her baby, so I ordered the midwife to cut it out. She refused." He looked away, his throat working. "So I did."

Rose put a hand over her mouth, eyes wide. She'd delivered many babies—and lost both mother and child before—and not once had she considered cutting them out. But then, she wasn't William MacKay either, able to heal with touch. Such arrogance could be excused.

"What happened?"

He shook his head slightly. "I don't know. I suppose we should have done it sooner, then mayhap there might have been a chance for Amber." He lifted a shoulder. "She . . . was bleeding everywhere . . . Deidra wasn't breathing. I thought I could heal them both. I chose to heal Deidra first. After, I was too weak to have healed again . . . but it didn't matter. Amber was dead."

Rose put her hand on his arm. "Listen to me. I have been in such a situation before, and both mother and child died. At least you saved one of them."

"I know that," he said, echoing her earlier words back at her with as little conviction as she'd stated them. Something fluttered deep in her chest.

She slid her hand up to his shoulder, wanting to comfort him as he'd comforted her earlier. "William." She said his name softly, her voice catching on the familiarity.

He turned his head slightly. Heat and want burned in the look he sent her, causing her breath to catch again. She wanted him, too. Her flesh hummed with it, her breath short, her body alive with the memory of his kisses.

He turned toward her and touched her, his hand cupping the side of her neck. His thumb stroked the sensitive skin of her jaw and the corner of her mouth, sending tingling sparks of anticipation through her. It was frightening to yearn so powerfully for a man's touch. A small part of her urged retreat, to think first, but her body and heart did not obey.

Her hand still rested on his shoulder. She slid it beneath the fold of his plaid, wishing there were no shirt beneath it, wishing . . .

His mouth came down on hers, forceful, demanding a response. Her thoughts skittered away in the mad rush of desire. She gave in to him gladly, opening her mouth and greeting his tongue, leaning into his hard body. The rough sweetness of his kiss pierced her. He was relentless, taking from her, consuming her. Blood rushed in her ears, fire blazed in her veins.

His hand gripped the back of her neck, commanding her, coaxing her. She gave in, her arms twining around his neck. This was oblivion of a different sort, and she ached for it, the thoughtless passion, the restless hands, the mating tongues.

William was mad, a raving lunatic to be kissing her again, to have sought her out this night—and that's what he'd done, though he'd lied to himself like a daft fool. Fresh air. That's what he'd wanted, though he'd wandered the grounds for nearly an hour earlier on the same pretext and found himself distinctly unrefreshed when he hadn't discovered Rose lurking in the gardens or the courtyard.

So he'd come up here and seen her standing there, sagging wearily against the battlements, and he knew she'd tried to work something out of her heart. He'd done it often enough himself to recognize it—the urge to forget the unforgettable. It never worked—it only delayed—but that had never stopped him, and it didn't stop her. It was a temporary fix to an impossible problem. She was an echo of his soul, calling to him, and he was mindless, unable to resist the siren song.

And then she'd said his name. *William.* Such a sweet sound. He'd never heard it from a woman's lips. His wife had called him Strathwick or my lord or Husband. But he was William to Rose. And so he'd kissed her, even though he'd vowed to himself he wouldn't. That he wouldn't be another man who stole her trust and left her with impossible shame. But here they were and she was warm in his arms, yielding, the skin of her neck and jaw soft beneath his hand. He was hard already, the sweet stroke of her tongue nearly sending him over the edge of sanity.

He pressed her into the stone wall, forcing his thigh between hers and lifting her higher, his arm around her waist. Her arms were tight around his neck and she pressed closer, as if they could somehow merge into one. With her anchored to the wall, he burrowed one hand beneath her skirts. The skin of her thigh was soft above her hose. Her breath hitched at his intimate touch, but she did not stop him. Her thighs tightened around him, her hips grinding into him, destroying his control. He pulled her into him, his hand on the supple, round flesh of her bottom. The pressure was exquisite; he felt as if he would shatter from her merest touch. He made a sound deep in his throat and renewed his assault on her mouth.

His blood pounded thickly in his ears so that he barely heard the throat-clearing nearby. When it happened again, louder this time, he tore his mouth away, peering into the dark. A man-at-arms tilted his head slightly in a mysterious gesture that William's lust-fogged mind could not grasp. Then the man moved away, giving them privacy. He would tell others what he'd seen. *Christ.*

Rose leaned against William, her face in his plaid, her hands curled into him. She trembled. He stroked his hand over her silky hair, closing his eyes and trying to gain mastery over his body. This black, mindless desire was like nothing he'd ever felt before, and he couldn't seem to control it; he didn't want to. He was in thrall to it, to her. He couldn't walk away.

She raised her head, gazing up at him with beautiful midnight eyes. "I want to be with you."

Bloody hell. His body responded instantly and forcefully. He made himself look away from her swollen lips and the naked desire on her face.

"Rose," he whispered when he could finally speak. His voice sounded rusty and harsh. He smoothed back the hair that had come loose from her plait. "You don't mean that."

"I do." She caressed him, touching his jaw and his neck, and he shuddered violently. He wanted to shove her skirts up and have her against the wall. He would pull out, he thought recklessly, there would be no bairns. He heard these fool thoughts and recognized his own folly, but he still didn't care. His muscles tightened as he fought to control himself.

And then in his mind he saw her with her betrothed, that pasty-faced scurr she was going to marry, and he couldn't stand it. When MacPherson arrived she would never look at him this way again. She would never say his name as though she cared. And when she learned how he knew MacPherson . . . she would turn away from him forever.

He kissed her again, hard, driving the image from his mind. His heart throbbed, urging him onward, perilously, thoughtlessly.

She slid her hand into his and pulled away from him. The eyes that gazed up at him were hazy with desire. She drew him along and he followed, telling himself he shouldn't, but his feet did not obey. She led him along the wall to the steps leading to the bailey. William caught sight of something over the walls and stopped, a cold stone settling in his belly. She tugged on his hand, and when he didn't come, she glanced up at him. She followed his gaze and grew very still.

"It's him, isn't it?" he said, emotionless, staring at the line of torches approaching. If they hadn't been kissing, they'd have seen the riders approach. As it was, they were nearly to the loch now. That had been what the man-at-arms had been warning them about.

Rose dropped his hand as if it were a hot brand. "Oh my God," she breathed, her hands covering her mouth.

A dark, relentless fury built in his chest. He'd been about to make an enormous mistake and was damned vexed at the interruption. He'd never have this chance again. Not now. He wanted to hit something in frustration—preferably the MacPherson lad.

But instead he smiled wryly. "Good thing I spotted them, or it might have been a wee bit awkward when they came looking for you, aye?"

Her eyes closed in horror at the thought. She opened

them and gazed at him, a slight frown between her brows. He wondered why she didn't leave, why she didn't ready herself to meet her betrothed. He was nearly unhinged with anger and thwarted lust. He didn't want her standing before him anymore, looking mussed and beautiful, tempting him.

"What's wrong, Rose?" he bit out, his calm façade crumbling. "Your future awaits."

She swallowed, her eyes bright with miserable hope. "Does it? Or is it here?"

His heart stuttered in his chest. Of course she thought that. *Of course.* Jesus God, he was a bloody fool. She was no tavern trull to be ravished on the battlements. Of course she expected something more from him.

He let out a slightly incredulous breath. "Rose . . ."

She drew back as if he'd slapped her.

He reached a placating hand toward her, but she just stared at it, brows drawn together in disbelief and horror. He could see the understanding dawning in her eyes before he said the words.

"I will not marry again. I . . . won't do that again, make that choice . . ."

"Aye. I understand." Her words were crisp, frozen. She still stared stiffly at his hand. "You will breathe not a word of this . . . considering."

"Of course." *Considering?* Considering what? What did she mean?

Before he could ask, she turned away from him, a dreamer caught in a nightmare of his creation. He stood in the dark for a time after she left, until his labored breathing calmed and a more calculated anger at the whims of fate smothered the flush of passion. He felt strangely hollow, detached from himself, as if he'd dreamed it all. He heard the approach of another man-at-arms, so he left, following her down to the hall.

The castle had come alive. The smell of cooking meat and bread being heated filled the great hall. Drake leaned against a wall, watching it all grimly. William joined him.

"It's a wee bit crowded here, aye?" Drake said. "Mayhap we should be on our way. You ken who has arrived? It will be ugly."

"I know, but I still have work here."

His brother knew him well enough to realize that arguing was futile, but still he sighed dramatically so that William was aware of his displeasure.

William scanned the hall. All the fireplaces blazed, and torches lit the walls. The great wooden candelabras that hung from the ceiling by chains were lit with hundreds of candles. Rose and her sisters were absent, as were their husbands. A lass with her arms piled high with clean sheets and bedding hurried across the hall, disappearing into a corridor. Two other lasses sprinkled sprigs of herbs onto the rush-strewn floor. Two lads dragged a brass tub across the floor.

"You'd think he was royalty," Drake murmured. He sent William a sidelong look. "You don't plan to be standing here when he arrives, do you?"

"Aye, I do."

Drake straightened from the wall to look at him incredulously. "You cannot be serious? Let him hear of it from someone else."

"No."

Drake swore and cajoled some more, but William remained adamant. Perhaps it was some penance he thought he deserved, but he had to see Rose's face when she discovered the truth about him. He did not want her to hear it from someone else.

It seemed like an eternity—but was probably only a few minutes—before Rose entered the hall, flanked by her sisters. William straightened from the wall, his mouth suddenly dry. She'd changed. The gown was sapphire and fit her body like a kid glove—the body he'd had his hands all over just moments before, which had flushed in passion and want. It was now wrapped coldly, beautifully, for another man. A single ribbon graced the delicate skin of her neck and chest, the silver locket resting against her rounded breasts. A blue-and-red arisaid swept over one shoulder, secured with a sapphire brooch. Her hair was down, cleverly braided at the sides with ribbons. It gleamed in the firelit hall, a long, sleek fall of amber and cinnamon. She was the most beautiful woman in the room—in any room that William had ever been in. He slumped back against the wall, his arms crossed over his chest, his melancholy mood taking a black turn.

He glowered at her visage, cool and beautiful and proud. She was solemn and stiff, chin held high, the skin of her neck tight with strain. Her head turned slightly toward the door leading to the quay.

The hall fell silent, and William heard what had captured her attention—the sound of heavy footsteps ascending the steps from the quay to the hall. The man who emerged from the doorway was tall, his shoulders wide and heavy with muscle. He had a strong, tanned face women no doubt tripped over themselves for. A golden god, his thick blond hair—not a gray streak in it—was pulled away from his face to hang in a lovelock.

Roderick emerged beside him, nattering on, but the big blond man did not listen. His gaze scanned the hall, then stopped, arrested. William looked at Rose. She stared at her betrothed with wide eyes, hands clasped hard before her. A hopeful bride. William's hand curled into a fist as the pointless anger rose again. It wouldn't be long now. Minutes, seconds even, before he was introduced to MacPherson and everyone knew the truth.

The people of Lochlaire crowded forward to better see the reunion of Rose and her childhood sweetheart, reminding William of how many people would witness the scene that was about to transpire. A sobering thought. Perhaps this *was* unwise. Drake was right. He should leave the hall. Let her hear it from someone else. William moved along the edge of the crowd, hoping to disappear in a room or corridor unnoticed.

Jamie MacPherson crossed the hall, his stride eating up ground, his gaze fixated on Rose. Then suddenly he glanced around, and his pale eyes fell on William. MacPherson stopped. He pivoted toward William, peering at him in the dim light. Rose and everyone else in the hall turned to see what had engaged MacPherson's attention.

William had wondered if the lad would even remember what he looked like. It had been a very long time ago, after all. But then, he supposed, one did not easily forget their father's murderer.

*   *   *

Rose watched her betrothed's approach, the whole while aware of William, standing against the wall. She did not want to be here, did not want to face Jamie tonight. She'd tried to plead illness and exhaustion, which wasn't so far from the truth, but her sisters had convinced her of the importance of this moment, and so she'd allowed them to dress her.

She'd thought, on the battlements when William had embraced her, when he'd said such fine things to her, that she'd been wrong about him, that he didn't think her a loose woman. That perhaps he too saw a future with the two of them together.

But she'd been wrong. He'd been ready to bed her, she'd seen it in his eyes, tasted it in his kiss. But he had no more use for her past that. Her humiliation and anger froze to hate. She hated him and men like him. Hated Fagan MacLean, hated his skinny wife and Fagan's son, who'd used her just as William had intended to. But most of all, at that moment she hated her father for sending her to Skye and leaving her there and, when she'd escaped, sending her back. And even now, when she should well and truly be free of the MacLeans, somehow they still trapped her.

All of this swirled inside her, making her sick with suppressed resentment and fury and disgust. She didn't want to marry and be touched by any man. They were all the same and she could not understand them, or how she could still ache for one of them so painfully.

Then Jamie had emerged from the doorway. She had not recognized him, had not seen in him the boy she'd once known. He didn't even look like the miniature she'd so faithfully worn. But he'd looked at her with a sort of wonderment that had lightened her spirit somewhat. He'd known her before she'd gone to Skye; perhaps he still saw in her the girl she'd once been, all innocence, knowing nothing of the vile nature of men, nothing of hate.

But then William had moved—she'd felt it, her body and mind, as always aware of him wherever he was—and Jamie had turned to gape at him. Who wouldn't? The tallest man in the room, the finest-looking man in the room—and the only one currently leaving.

They stared at one another for a long moment. Jamie looked as if he'd been kicked in the gut. William arched a black brow, and a thin, bitter smile curved his lips in greeting.

Rose's heart took a sickening plunge. She'd never asked him, never even wondered: *How did they know each other?*

Chapter 12

"You." The word exploded out of Jamie like a cannon blast, and he barreled across the room, hand on sword hilt, as if he'd been fired from one.

Drake drew his sword and moved to his brother's side, but William put out a staying hand. Rose lifted her skirts and ran, reaching them as Jamie's sword arced down.

"You bloody murderer!" Jamie raged, his handsome face distorted with hatred. "I'll kill you!"

"No!" Rose screamed.

William had already moved aside, his sword still sheathed, though his hand rested loosely on the hilt. Jamie's blade cut through empty air, clattering noisily against the wall.

"Not in front of your betrothed, surely," William said. He did not appear surprised or troubled by this attack. His fingers tapped the leather-wrapped sword hilt; his brow was cocked slightly in question.

Jamie straightened, his gaze flicking to Rose, then back to William, with murderous intent. But after a long, silent moment in which he breathed loudly through his nose and took in the horrified faces around him, he finally sheathed his sword.

His gaze narrowed on William. With both hands, he pushed back the golden hair that had come loose from his lovelock. "You and me. At dawn. In the courtyard."

Rose's heart thundered in her chest as William inclined his head in agreement to this.

She forced her way between the two men, pushing at their chests. Jamie took a step back, but William was granite, staring over her head, his eyes dark and inscrutable as he stared at Jamie.

Rose turned to glare up at Jamie. He was a stranger, a violent, angry stranger. "This man is a guest of the Mac-Donells. How dare you attack him in our hall."

Jamie didn't even look at her, still glowering over her head at William. "I would have killed him long ago if he wasn't such a crawdoun."

Rose inhaled sharply, insulted for William, though she heard not a word of protest behind her.

"Explain yourself," she demanded. Lord Kincreag had joined her, as well as several MacDonell men-at-arms.

Jamie's furious gaze finally moved to her and stuck. "This—this *wizard* murdered my father."

"Aye?" the earl of Kincreag said, raising a black brow skeptically. "Was it murder then, or just another petty blood feud? And how did it happen? During a raid? During a battle?"

"Witchcraft."

No. Rose didn't want to hear this. There was a slow sinking in her belly as she stared at her betrothed, shaking her head slowly. "How?"

"Ask him." Jamie jerked his chin at William. "Ask him how."

Rose was afraid to face William. Afraid to ask. His silence seemed to confirm the accusation.

Gillian, always the peacemaker, said, "Let us talk this over, friends. Mayhap it's just a misunderstanding—"

"There is no misunderstanding," William said. "But I do think Rose deserves to hear the truth in a different manner."

Roderick had been observing the conflict from a distance. He stepped forward now, his blue eyes creased with concern. "Come, come—let's take this somewhere private, aye?" He glanced meaningfully around the room at the curious faces of servants and various men-at-arms, then led the combatants from the hall.

Rose trailed behind, clutching Gillian's hand. Jamie seemed to have forgotten her presence. He stalked ahead of her, his gaze boring into the back of William's head. *You and me. At dawn. In the courtyard.* He meant to fight it out, to kill William. Her chest constricted with sick fear.

Roderick led them to a parlor her father had used for guests before his illness. Animal skins covered the floor, antlers and axes adorned the walls. The large fireplace was cold. Isobel summoned servants, and in no time a fire blazed, the candelabras were lit, and ale was served. But these pleasantries did nothing to dispel the chill atmosphere of the room.

Jamie stood near the carved fireplace, glowering across the room at William, who leaned negligently against the far wall, arms crossed over his chest, returning his stare with little emotion. Drake took up position beside William, hand on sword hilt, staring belligerently at the enemy. Between William and Jamie stood Roderick, the earl, Rose, and her sisters—a barrier against further physical conflict.

When the servants had finally vacated the room, Roderick moved to the center of the group. "Now, let us hear your grievance, MacPherson."

Jamie stepped forward, his pale blue eyes burning. He was enormous and threatening, thick biceps straining against the dun leather of his jack. "Why was my betrothed permitted to travel such a distance *alone?*"

Roderick made a soft sound of irritation. "My lord, I told you, no one *permitted* her. She just did it."

Jamie's pale, icy gaze cut to Rose. "Is this true? You fetched this man to heal your father? This is why you've delayed our marriage?"

"Aye," Rose said, meeting his gaze unapologetically. "He is a great healer. I knew if anyone could help my father, it was him."

"And did he heal Alan?"

Rose could tell by the look on his face that he already knew the answer, which made her belly turn again. "Nay."

He shook his head in disappointment. "Why did you not consult me on this, Rose?"

Rose let out an incredulous breath. "Why would I? He's my father. I don't even know you."

"I am to be your husband. We are betrothed. You should consult me about these matters. We've been writing for months—why did you never seek my counsel?"

Rose shrugged. It had never occurred to her to ask his counsel. In truth she hadn't asked anyone's counsel— she hadn't needed to. She'd known exactly what she'd wanted to do.

He waited expectantly for an answer.

"I know not," she finally said.

"I see." He crossed his substantial arms over his thick chest and frowned reproachfully. "If you had at least told me what you planned, I could have let you know the evil you've invited into your home." He turned to face the others, his gaze cutting to William, who seemed rather bored by the proceedings.

"I pray you," Rose said, "explain this grievance to us. How did Lord Strathwick use witchcraft to murder your father?"

"We have no direct feud with the Strathwick MacKays, but our friends the Sinclairs do." Jamie pointed to William. "This man's father and my father both wanted the same Sinclair woman for a bride." He dropped his arm. His gaze scanned his audience. "Since the Sinclairs would never give a woman of theirs to a MacKay, she married my father. Shortly after, she fell ill. When Strathwick got word of it, he and his wicked son disguised themselves to infiltrate our home. Once there, he killed my father and stole my stepmother."

Rose frowned at William, who unhelpfully maintained his air of ennui. She turned back to face her betrothed. "How do you know Lord Strathwick killed your father? Maybe *his* father did it."

Jamie sneered contemptuously at her. "I *saw* him. Go on—ask him if he did it."

William lifted a shoulder. "It's true."

Isobel, who had been listening quietly, with wide eyes, said, "This doesn't sound like witchcraft to me. Lord Strathwick had gone with his father to steal a woman—

such things happen all the time. No doubt your father offered resistance and he died. It is the way of things. You know this."

Rose nodded in agreement and asked Jamie, "How do you know it was witchcraft?"

"Because my father was hale as a horse then was suddenly felled with the same ailment that was killing my stepmother." He took a threatening step toward William, but the earl of Kincreag stepped casually into his path to intercept him. Jamie spun away, hands fisted at his sides.

Rose spread her hands in front of her in a placating manner. "My lord, many ailments are highly contagious."

He turned his irate gaze on Rose. "Including bleeding to death from a miscarriage?"

Rose's eyes widened. One look at William's grim expression confirmed the truth of this.

"That's not possible," the earl said, but he sent William a wary glance.

"Nevertheless it happened," Jamie said. "I told you— I *saw* it. I saw my stepmother, on the ground bleeding, clutching her belly. I saw him touch her, and she was well. I was yelling for my father to hurry, to stop them. When he came, Strathwick thrust his son at my father. The next thing I knew, my father was on the floor and the MacKays were leaving with my stepmother." He swallowed hard, his throat working with emotion, his eyes like blue fire. "We could find no wounds on my father, yet he suffered horribly . . . then he began to . . . bleed. From his orifices. Then he died." His gaze scanned the silent room, daring them to counter this story. "*Witchcraft.*"

The earl gave William a measuring look, then asked, "How long ago was this?"

"Eleven years," William said.

Rose felt weak—his answer was an admission. She remembered back to the moor, when he'd grabbed her wrist and told her he could hurt her with a touch. Gillian's hands covered her mouth, her gray eyes enormous above them. Isobel sat in a nearby chair, staring at William in horror. They all looked at him as if he were a monster. But he didn't notice them—his gaze was on Rose, and she could not hide her dismay. He saw it, and his lip curled slightly. He looked away, back to Jamie, as if he'd expected no better from her.

Drake stared hard at his brother, then his gaze swept the room angrily. "Since my brother will not tell his side of the story, I'll do it for him." He strode forward, his dark eyes fixed on Jamie. "My father was a wicked man, make no mistake, but the lassies liked him. Including Jean Sinclair. You didn't mention that Jean fancied herself in love with my father and ran away once to wed him. Her father caught her and forced her to marry your father—a vile man who beat and raped her repeatedly. You didn't mention why she miscarried? Because she was already ill and refused to rut with your father, so he beat her until she lost the wean."

"Lies!" Jamie cried, coming at Drake while drawing his sword. Drake leapt to meet him, lusting for a fight, but Lord Kincreag and Roderick stepped between them, forcing Jamie to resheath his blade.

"My father never laid a hand on her!" Jamie bellowed over Kincreag's restraining arm.

"My father came to rescue her," Drake continued, shrugging off Roderick's hold, "and brought my brother to heal her. At our father's order, William gave her ailment to your father, who unfortunately died from it, as *she* would have, if not for William."

Rose looked to William. "Who tells the truth?"

He shrugged. "Both. Neither."

Rose shook her head, exasperated. "What does that mean?"

"My father did lust after Jean Sinclair. The wean she was pregnant with was his. I know not if she was truly ill, or if it was a ploy to bring my father to MacPherson lands. It didn't matter. My father wanted her and what he wanted he took, even if it meant others must die. He could not have Jean so long as she was married to your father." His arms were crossed over his chest. He looked down, a muscle in his jaw twitching. "At the time I believed what my father told me, that the MacPherson beat his wife. It angered me, and so when he urged me to kill your father, I did so willingly. I was eighteen; a man, with my own mind. It is no one's fault but my own. I learned something later that made me believe that perhaps my father caused the miscarriage. She had no ailment for me to give MacPherson, and so he created one."

Drake looked at his brother in amazement. "That's not true."

"It *is* true. Our father did far worse than that in his life, and so have I. I don't know why you act so surprised."

"But you didn't know," Drake said angrily. "So it's not your fault."

One corner of William's mouth curled bitterly. "Oh, I

think I did know. I fooled myself about a lot of things back then."

"God damn it, Will, you didn't!"

The room fell silent for several moments. Drake glowered helplessly at his brother, who stared back apologetically.

Rose was shaken from all that she'd heard. She'd never suspected that such darkness lurked in William. Her mind rebelled against it. It had been a long time ago. He had been much younger then. He obviously did not do such things any longer. Or did he? If he had cause, perhaps he did. Just because she'd never witnessed any didn't mean he didn't do them. She really didn't know him at all.

She said, "I would like to speak with my betrothed alone."

William gave her a long, enigmatic look. She felt he must be disappointed in her but could read nothing in his dark gaze. She averted her eyes, unable to look at him, her throat tight. She was confused about him, about Jamie. But William didn't really matter anymore, and perhaps that was for the best. Even so, she could still try to set things right with Jamie. She owed William that at least.

She breathed easier when he finally left the room, freeing her of the intensity of his gaze. She watched the others file out after him, her hands clasped in front of her. She heard her betrothed move toward her, and turned quickly.

She'd paid scant attention to him with William present, but she gave him a closer perusal now. He was a very good-looking man. Long golden hair, deep-set cerulean eyes, tall and strong and well turned out in a fine plaid, leather doublet, and knee boots. She should be pleased by his appearance. Instead she thought how very young and angry he seemed compared to William.

"I am sorry our reunion was so . . . unpleasant," he said, taking her hands. His were sweaty. "I am pleased to finally see you again, Rose. You are as beautiful as I remember."

"I was beautiful at eight?" Rose said doubtfully.

He smiled. There was a dimple in his cheek. "To my ten-year-old eyes you were."

Rose smiled back, softening toward him. "You are kind. This story you tell troubles me. I don't believe Lord Strathwick is at fault."

Jamie dropped her hands. "You heard him. He admitted to it."

"Aye, I heard him. If we must all answer for our father's sins, I fear no one will make it to heaven."

"His father didn't kill mine," he growled. "*He* did! With his magic!"

"He did it at his father's—his *chief's*—insistence. And though he was a man, he was a young one, as you are. Are you never rash? Did you never believe the words of one you trusted? He should have been able to trust his father. We all should be able to trust the important elders in our lives. But they are men too, full of deceit and lies, just like everyone else."

"You defend him, and I like it not!" Jamie paced away from her. "Someone must pay for my father's murder. It has gone unanswered for too long."

Rose sighed. A few words from her were clearly not going to end this feud, so she settled for the next best thing. "There will be no fighting at dawn. Your retribution will not play out at Lochlaire."

He whirled toward her, his eyes blazing. "I *will* have vengeance."

"Then I will not marry you."

"What?" he cried incredulously. "You are bespelled." His face distorted with rage. "I *will* kill him now!"

Rose caught him at the door, latching onto his arm. "No! Listen to me!"

He turned around, his jaw jutting with fury, and glared down at her.

"He is helping us. He believes someone is using witchcraft to kill my father, and he is trying to undo it."

"He would know, the black-hearted wizard."

Rose reined in her temper. "We need his help if my father is to live. I pray you, don't do this to us. To me."

He stared mutinously over her head.

"Consider it a—a wedding gift."

His pale gaze fixed suspiciously on her. "Strathwick's life means so much to you?"

Aye! But she didn't dare admit such a thing. "There is nothing more important to me than healing my father." When he still didn't answer, she added, "I thought Alan MacDonell was your friend."

He sighed, some of the tension relaxing from his broad shoulders. "Very well. There will be no blood spilled at Lochlaire. That is all I will promise, aye?"

Rose managed a hesitant smile. "My thanks."

His gaze moved over her face. "I give you a man's life. I can think of a more fitting thanks from my betrothed."

Before Rose could ask him what he considered a more fitting thanks, he grabbed her, clasped her tightly against his chest, and kissed her. Rose clutched at his shoulders, fighting for air as his tongue thrust into her mouth. His teeth collided with hers with a sharp, uncomfortable *click*. Then it was over, and he set her away from him. She resisted the urge to wipe her mouth.

He gave her a self-satisfied grin.

Rose did not know what to say, so she gave him a wan smile. "Let me show you to your chambers."

After depositing her much calmer betrothed in his chambers, she returned to her own. A sensation of unreality had descended on her. She needed fresh air, but the thought of the battlements made her chest tight and her belly flutter. That the memory of William's touch and kiss could still affect her so, after how ill he'd used her, after all she'd learned this night, did not bode well for her. She'd gotten entangled with a scoundrel once before. She would not do so again—especially with her betrothed under the same roof.

She leaned against the closed door for several moments, trying to gather her wits about her again. Had William really killed Jamie's father with witchcraft? It was too horrible to contemplate, and yet it made sense. If he could take sickness away, he could give it to others, too. He did not have to suffer. He chose to.

She pushed away from the door, her heart heavy. Sudden movement startled her. She turned quickly and peered into the gloom. Only the low fire in the fireplace illuminated her chamber. A figure stood in the shadows near her window.

"Who's there?" she called.

William stepped forward, and her heart surged traitorously, angering her.

"What are you doing in my chambers?" she hissed, quickly latching the door lest someone walk in. "What can you be thinking?"

He crossed the room, bearing down on her relentlessly. "That you must have many questions and I'd rather you hear the answers from me than from someone else."

Rose resisted the urge to flee; instead she backed away until she was flush against the door. "What care you what I think?" Her voiced dripped with bitterness.

"I care." He stopped in front of her, staring down at her with such intensity that she could not hold his gaze.

His words inflamed her temper—and her desire. Her heart hammered. Memories of his mouth on hers, his hands beneath her skirt sent a flush over her skin, and shards of lust pierced her belly.

She slid along the wall, away from the door. "Get out."

He followed, bracing a hand on the wall by her head to halt her escape. "No—we're not finished, Rose."

"We *are* finished—you made that clear earlier." She tried to duck under his arm, but he blocked her with his body.

"I should not have touched you or kissed you in such a manner," he said as he touched her again, his hand on her face, tracing her jaw and temple.

Rose closed her eyes and swallowed hard, her muscles rigid as she willed herself not to turn into the caress. "Then why are you doing it now?"

"I know not." His voice was low, rumbling over her like thunder from a building storm. "Where you are concerned, I know not what I do anymore."

Rose was nearly shaking with fury and desire and despair, all twisted together in her heart. "Get out," she ground out between clenched teeth.

He took her face in both his hands, forcing her to meet his gaze. "Listen to me. I should have told you that I could hurt as well as heal. I should have told you the moment I saw MacPherson in your locket. But I couldn't."

"Why?"

"Because of the way you looked at me and talked to me."

She brought her hands up and shoved him. It was nothing to him, not moving him an inch. She wrenched her face from his grip, but when she tried to twist away from him, he caught her shoulders, pinning her to the wall.

"Let me go! You're no different than the others—than the MacLeans!"

His face was near her ear. "I am not like them. I would never intentionally hurt you."

Rose closed her burning eyes, hating herself for enjoying the feel of his arms around her, for wanting to give in to his soothing voice.

Her voice quavered when she spoke. "Then why are you here now?"

"I know not. I don't want to hurt you, and yet here I am. The logic seemed sound when I came here, but I see now it wasn't."

His breath was hot against her ear. She could feel his body against hers, erect, ready for her. Her body answered with a deep, throbbing ache. And then she felt his mouth, hot and wet beneath her ear.

"I pray you," she said, her voice catching. "Leave me now."

"I promised, and I'll not leave until your father is healed." He took her ear between his teeth, and her knees turned to water. She'd have sagged to the ground if not for his arms and the wall.

". . . and I'm ruined?" she whispered.

He stopped his wonderful kisses and stepped back from her, staring down at her, so dark and beautiful and frustrated.

His hands tightened on her arms, and he swore beneath his breath, his jaw bulging. "Dammit, Rose. You are not making this easy."

"Why should I?" she bit out. "It isn't easy for me, why should it be for you?"

He released her and paced away, rubbing a hand over his jaw. "You're right. I just wanted you to understand why. That's all. I shouldn't have come."

He went to the door and unlatched it. Rose did not move, pressing against the wall still, her body trying to hold onto the warm imprint of him thrust against her. He peered out the door for a moment, then closed it, tilting his head to gaze at her again.

They stared at each other for a long moment. She fought to keep her gaze hard, implacable. He started to open the door again, to leave this time. She said, "There will be no dawn meeting."

"I see." His mouth flattened grimly. "You mind if I verify that?"

"As you wish."

When he made to leave again, she blurted out, "Tira's baby has not turned. You will still help with the birthing?"

"You don't need me, Rose."

"I do." She didn't want to need him. She wanted to forget about him so she could get on with her life, but she doubted that would ever happen. *In time, perhaps.*

His mouth twisted wryly. "Of course. I said I would, didn't I?"

She could think of nothing further to detain him, and he finally left. The room seemed empty without him. She cursed herself for being a fool, but fool or not, now that he'd gone, she was lonely for his company and his kisses.

It had all seemed so simple before she'd actually met him. The Wizard of the North was to be the answer to her prayers. She'd imagined that if she could just bring him here, all of her problems would disappear, unhappiness would dissolve, and she could finally marry her Jamie and live a happy, fruitful life, the past finally behind her.

What a simpleton she'd been. It felt as if a lifetime had passed since then. Her father was still dying, and her reunion with Jamie had been nothing like she'd envisioned. She could no longer see the future she'd once imagined even if her father was somehow miraculously healed, an event she no longer had any faith would occur.

She thought of sleeping, as she was very tired and it was late, but thoughts and memories swirled through her head. She didn't want to think or feel anymore. She was raw from all that had happened. She needed distraction.

She crossed to the small connecting closet that she'd converted into a place to dry and store herbs. She'd had shelves installed from floor to ceiling along two walls; they were filled with racks of drying herbs, bottles, jars, and small sacks of the same. Several of the top shelves were full of books and manuscripts she'd acquired over the years. A sense of calm and comfort descended on her. *This* was her calling. The villagers of Glen Laire needed her. She would spend the next few days in the village tending the sick, so she must prepare.

After lighting candles, she checked on the drying herbs, then brought a selection to the table to grind into a fine powder. The industry of it soothed her. She recited the uses for each herb in her mind. There was no room for other thoughts beyond healing. Her eye caught on a glittering bottle that had tipped over on a nearby shelf. Sapphire dust. She set it upright, her fingers lingering, watching the way it sparkled in the candlelight, snagging something in her memory, something she'd once read. She turned to the books on the shelf behind her, running her finger over them until she found her mother's.

She took it back to the table with the sapphire dust. Her mother had not been a healer, so though Rose had occasionally perused her mother's diary, she'd never spent as much time studying it as she had the other healers' texts she'd accumulated. But she did remember something her mother had written down, a spell of protection against evil using the sapphire dust.

The sapphire dust had been Crisdean Beaton's. When he'd died, he'd left her all of his instruments and books and obscure ingredients. Though she'd made good use of most, she'd never had use for the sapphire dust, had never even opened the bottle. She pulled the cork free and sniffed, but it had no odor.

She set it aside and returned to the diary. It was full of

entries about her mother's visions. Rose carefully turned the sewn together vellum pages until she reached the back of the book. *Charm to hold back evil.* It involved reciting a lengthy spell over the person to be protected while sprinkling a powder made from sapphire dust and other ingredients over and around them. Rose found a sheet of paper, quill, and ink, and copied the charm. She'd attempted spellcraft several times with no success. That was not where her talents lay. Perhaps with the help of her sisters this spell would succeed.

She was closing the diary when a jagged piece of vellum caught her attention. It dangled from the stitching down the center of the book, as if a page had been cut out. The remaining pages were blank. She stared at the protective charm, written in her mother's flowing hand, for a long time. This was the last thing her mother had written . . . or was it? Had she written something else on the following page? Perhaps an explanation of why she'd needed a protective charm? How it had worked? Whatever it was, someone had removed it so no one else could read it.

The gray shadows of predawn lit the sky by the time she finished preparing the powder. She fetched Gillian, and together they crept through the castle, careful not to wake up the scores of men now sleeping in the hall, retinues of the earl of Kincreag, Sir Philip, and her betrothed. She knocked softly on her father's door, then pushed it open.

Hagan sat in her father's chair beside the bed, and Isobel slept in a chair near the fire. The dog was on the bed again. Rose gave Hagan a cross look, and he obligingly removed the dog from the room. Isobel was so much like their late mother, Lillian—they had the same gift of visions, and Isobel even looked like her, with her silver-green eyes and curly red-gold hair. Surely if anyone could make the spell a success, it was Isobel. Rose woke her sister, and together the three of them placed the protective charm on their slumbering father.

Afterward the sisters gathered in Rose's chambers. Rose flopped onto the bed while her sisters sat in chairs nearby. Rose knew why they'd followed her, what they wanted to talk about. She'd seen their speculative looks, but they waited for her to broach the subject. Rose didn't know what to say. She felt miserable and foolish. Surely her sisters had never been so stupid in love as she had. They wouldn't understand.

They spoke about trivialities until finally Isobel fixed her with a penetrating green stare and asked, "What are you going to do about Lord Strathwick?"

Rose kicked her shoes off and rubbed her aching feet. "Do? What do you mean?"

Gillian answered for Isobel. "The way he looks at you . . . the way you are with him. There is something more between you than you've told us."

Rose looked down at her hands, her jaw and throat tight. "I have a betrothed, remember?"

"Aye," Isobel said. "I had one, too, but then I met Philip. The heart doesn't read betrothal contracts, Rose. The heart wants without logic . . . and I think your heart is wanting."

Isobel saw too much. She always had. Rose rubbed her forehead with her fingers before meeting her sisters' eyes. "Aye, there is something more between us, but it matters not. He will never marry me—"

"You don't know that," Gillian said.

"Aye, I do. He told me." Rose closed her eyes and swallowed, her heart sinking at the memory, the freezing wretchedness washing over her afresh. "I . . . I practically propositioned him just before Jamie arrived. He was eager enough to lay with me but made it clear he wanted nothing more past that."

Gillian and Isobel exchanged dismayed looks. Gillian reached for Rose's hand and gripped it tightly. Rose squeezed her fingers back, comforted by the gesture and their concern.

"I'm sorry, Rose," Gillian said softly. "What of Lord MacPherson? Do you fancy him still? It's been so long since you've seen him."

When Rose didn't respond, Isobel said, "He's a very comely man."

Rose nodded. "Aye, he is." She wished that were enough.

"You don't have to marry him if you don't want," Gillian reminded her.

"I know that. I don't know what I want right now. I can't have William, and I don't know Jamie anymore." She shook her head firmly. "I don't want to call off the betrothal. I should at least try to get to know him. He's angry now, and who wouldn't be, considering what he believes of William. He's not himself. He deserves more from me."

Isobel searched Rose's face. "Can Strathwick do what MacPherson claims? Kill a person with a touch?"

"Aye. I didn't want to believe it, but it must be true."

Gillian's dark brows drew together with worry. "He's dangerous. What if he gets angry—"

Rose shook her head. "No, it's not that simple. When he heals someone, he takes their ailment inside himself. I've seen him do it. He can give that ailment to someone else. But if he has not healed, he's no different from you or me. And if the ailment is minor, it will not kill anyone."

"Do you think he killed MacPherson's father?" Gillian asked.

Rose nodded miserably. "And Jamie is determined to have revenge. And William . . . it seems almost as if he welcomes it. As if he thinks he deserves it." She covered her face and shook her head, despair rising in her heart. "I don't know what to do. I'm so confused."

Her sisters moved to the bed and sat on either side of her. They wrapped their arms around her, as if trying to absorb her troubles. Gillian spoke soothing words to her, rubbing her back. Isobel spoke more forcefully.

"It's not for you to fix, Rose, you know that. You're not responsible for everyone. You take on too much. Father, Strathwick, everyone else's problems. You must let some things go and live your life. I love Father, too, but he is dying and we must accept it. Maybe he still hangs on because we won't let go. He longs for release from his suffering, but how can he stop fighting when he knows how his death will destroy you?"

"I know," Rose whispered, and she did. But it was never as simple as knowing, and her sisters knew that as well. They huddled together on the bed, arms twined around each other, wishing they could set things right in their world and knowing fate had her own plans for them all.

Deidra sat in the sweet-smelling pile of hay, nibbling on her bread. She'd been told not to leave the room, but her father and Uncle Drake had still been asleep and she'd been hungry. There had been food in the hall. She'd grabbed some bread and a piece of sausage, then gone into the yard. So many people had been milling about that no one had seemed to notice her—except the other children. They'd stared but hadn't thrown stones at her like the ones at home did.

She had sought out the animals, since they always talked to her readily, and there was no awkwardness or staring—and they never threw things.

Moireach hung her head over the stall. *Sweet? Red? Good?* She wanted an apple. There had been plenty of those in the hall, too, and Deidra had been certain to grab one. She held it up to the mare, who took it delicately, expressing her gratitude.

The morning sunlight shining through the doorway disappeared suddenly. A man blocked the light. He stood there for a long moment, then entered, heading straight for where Deidra nestled in the hay. It was the red-haired man.

He squatted down in front of her, smiling. He had lots of square white teeth, and his hair was very pretty—long, like a lass's. He didn't plait it or do pretty things with it like lasses do; he just tied it back. His eyes were very blue, like her father's, but not as pretty. His lashes were pale, almost blond.

"Good morn, Miss Deidra," he said, smiling. He smiled so much that she thought his face must hurt from it. "Fancy finding you here. You ken it's dangerous to be in here by yourself, aye?"

"It's not."

His smile disappeared, though his eyes remained merry. He cocked his head slightly, as if her answer puzzled him. "It's not? Why is that? Horses bite and kick grown men. A wee thing like you could easily be trampled."

"They don't bite and kick me, and they don't trample if they don't have to."

"And why is that? Are you special, Miss Deidra?" He said it in a laughing manner, but there was a sudden hard shine to his eyes, and Deidra remembered what Da and Uncle Drake had said. *Tell no one.*

She shook her head.

"That's too bad. I've a secret to share but you must promise to tell no one."

"I can't keep secrets anymore."

"No? That's too bad. It's a good one."

Deidra wanted to hear his secret, and he looked so sad that he couldn't tell her. "Can I tell my Da? He said I have to tell him everything. He can keep a secret."

He frowned a bit in consternation, then said, "Forget about the secret. Tell me why you like the stables."

"I like the animals."

"Do ye? I like them, too. Sometimes I come here just to talk to them."

Deidra bit her bottom lip to keep from blurting out that she did, too. "What do you tell them?"

"All sorts of things."

"Do they talk back?"

He nodded sagely. "That they do."

Deidra narrowed her eyes at him. She'd never met anyone else who could talk to animals. She looked up at Moireach, who hung her head over the stall again and lipped at Deidra's hair. *Sweet? Red? More?* Deidra giggled and put her hand on the mare's velvet nose.

"What is she saying?" she challenged.

The man squinted his eyes and twisted his mouth, as if concentrating very hard on the horse. Then he said, "She wants to go riding."

Deidra laughed. "She does not!"

"She wants some oats."

"No!"

"Hay? Her blanket? To be brushed? A carrot?"

"No, silly! An apple!"

"Ah. Of course." He leaned his head back and smiled, rocking on his heels.

"You can't really speak to animals," Deidra said.

"No, I cannot." He looked toward the open door, then back at her, his head tilted slightly. "Would you like me to show you something, Miss Deidra?"

"What?"

"You'll have to come with me."

She struggled to get out of the hay as he straightened, extending a hand out to her.

Don't go!

Deidra dropped the hand she'd almost slipped into his and looked at Moireach in surprise.

The horse shook her head and whinnied. *Smells bad. Get away.*

Deidra backed away from the man. He gave the horse a narrow look, then smiled at Deidra again, his wide, white smile not so friendly anymore. "What's wrong, Miss Deidra?" He walked toward her.

She looked around for a place to hide. More men entered the stable, talking loudly, and the man turned away. Deidra ran past him, darting out the door. She didn't stop running until she was back in the room with her father and uncle. She crawled back under her blanket at the end of the bed just as her father sat up, rubbing his eyes.

"Squirrel? Where have you been?"

Her heart raced. She wasn't supposed to leave the room. "I had to go."

"Go where?"

She raised her brows and looked at the pretty painted screen that hid the closestool.

"Ah," he said. He never wanted to talk about things like that. He asked no more questions, and Deidra let out a sigh of relief, thankful she'd not gotten caught disobeying. Her father worried so much lately, and, just like Uncle Drake had warned, learning she was a witch made him worry even more. She wished she were better at keeping secrets. She didn't want to give him anything else to worry about.

Chapter 13

❦

Rose managed to avoid William by leaving Lochlaire the next day. He wandered the castle, Deidra and his brother trailing after him. He hadn't realized he was looking for her until he located her sisters. They were in the bailey with the laundresses, sorting through soon-to-be-washed garments. An enormous iron cauldron was set on a tripod, and servants piled faggots beneath it.

"Are you looking for Rose?" the countess of Kincreag called, shaking out a soiled shirt. "Because she's in the village."

In the village. His spirits sank abruptly, his prospects for the day diminished. He approached the women, nodding to the cauldron. "What are you doing?"

Dame Isobel sat on a low stool, her customary gloves removed. The countess passed garments to her, one after the other. Dame Isobel would hold them, pale green eyes glazing over momentarily, then she would pass them to a laundress with a shake of her head and take the next garment.

"We're looking for the witch's accomplice, as you suggested," Dame Isobel said as she took a kirtle from her sister. "So far I've had no luck."

"What about you?" William asked Lady Kincreag. "Have you seen any ghosts?"

"Aye, I did!" she said with a bright smile. "But he knows nothing."

"A ghost?" Deidra asked, her fist curled into William's plaid. She stared up at Lady Kincreag, awestruck.

The countess smiled and knelt delicately in front of Deidra. "Aye. There are ghosts, Dede, but you mustn't be afraid of them, do you understand?"

Deidra nodded but looked unconvinced. Her face was dirty, and her hair had not been combed. A blue ribbon was impossibly knotted into her curly hair. William was annoyed at himself for not noticing her dishevelment before. He and Drake were poor substitutes for Deidra's late mother. The child ran wild and refused to listen to the women he assigned to look after her and keep her clean. He was the only one—until Rose—who was able to do anything with the child's appearance, and it was such a trial for him that he generally "forgot." And Drake was no help. As far as he was concerned, Dede always looked just fine.

William caught her arm and scrubbed at her face with the corner of her arisaid while she twisted and whined. Finally she slipped from his grasp and came to stand beside the countess, who'd resumed her sorting.

"What do the ghosts look like?"

"Not so different from us," the countess said. "Not scary at all, really, once you get past the fact they're dead. Just remember they cannot hurt you and most are as frightened of you as you are of them."

Deidra cocked her head in surprise. "Really? Zounds!"

The countess laughed. "She is delightful! And look." She nodded to a gray deerhound bounding across the bailey. It leapt onto Deidra, who squealed with surprise, then giggled. They played for a minute, then both dog and child settled on the ground, facing each other. They proceeded to stare at each other, hardly moving, though occasionally an expression of happiness, or sympathy, or consternation would cross Deidra's face.

William exchanged a worried look with his brother, who just shrugged, undisturbed by this bizarre behavior. William glanced surreptitiously around the bailey, but no one else appeared to take note of child and dog obviously carrying on a conversation. To William's eyes it was obvious, but he tried to see it as the others might—just a wee lassie admiring a dog, perhaps even reluctant to touch it, though the deerhound was hardly a threat to anything but a soup bone. After a moment, Deidra began to pet the dog, which eased the tightness in his chest.

"Lord Strathwick," Dame Isobel said, distracting him from his daughter. "Why do you not aid Rose in the village?" She gave him a knowing smile. Had she seen something? A vision about him and Rose? That was a troubling thought.

"She didn't ask."

Dame Isobel raised a red-blond brow. "Need you an invitation? Aren't you a healer?"

"He's also a chief," the countess said mildly, giving her sister a frown. "Perhaps he doesn't fancy spending his days in such labor."

"Aye," Drake said. "He can't be wasting himself on minor ailments."

In truth William really wasn't much of a healer beyond what he accomplished through witchcraft. He *did* save himself for dire illnesses contracted by those he cared for. He would not be capable of carrying out his duties as chief of the MacKays otherwise.

"What of her betrothed?" William asked as casually as he could manage. "Is he not with her?"

"No," Dame Isobel said. "She left before dawn. I doubt Lord MacPherson is even out of bed at this hour."

William knew that Rose had spent very little time with MacPherson last night, as she'd returned to her room alone. And she wasn't with him this morning, either. He smiled, grimly pleased. "Perhaps I should go down to the village and aid Rose."

Dame Isobel smiled down at the garment the countess absently handed to her.

"She is a fine healer, though," William said thoughtfully. "It's doubtful there is much I can do to aid her. Still, a woman shouldn't be wandering the village alone."

The countess gazed at him speculatively. "You're quite right, my lord. She should have an escort. She goes about far too often without one."

"It's settled then." William was turning, eager to leave, when Roderick joined them, looking distinctly displeased. Deidra stood up and grabbed her uncle's hand, hiding behind him. The dog also retreated, crouching behind the countess's skirts.

"What is this?" Roderick cried, hands fisted on his hips. "My nieces doing laundry? A countess, no less! Gillian, mind your place. You're not a chieftain's daughter anymore but an earl's wife."

"We're not doing laundry, Uncle Roderick." The countess smiled, shaking out another stained shirt. "Isobel is trying to discover who wishes to harm Father."

Roderick scowled at William but said no more. After another sour look at his nieces, he turned on his heel and continued on his way.

"His milk must've been curdled this morn," the countess muttered to her sister.

Dame Isobel snorted. "Every morn, you mean."

The countess smiled at William and said, "Deidra can stay with us if you're going to the village."

William looked at Deidra to see what she wished, but she paid no attention, staring after Roderick.

Drake nodded his chin in the direction of the village. "Go on. I'll stay here with Dede—surely these ladies need an escort, too." He grinned and winked at the sisters, who looked at each other and laughed.

William leaned close to his brother and whispered, "They're married."

Drake merely shrugged at his droll warning, still grinning wickedly at the sisters.

"And their husbands are large," William added.

Drake raised sardonic brows. "Aye, you'd do well to remember that yourself."

William grunted and left them, not wanting to think about MacPherson, though in truth he'd thought of little else since the man had arrived the night before. That and how he'd almost had Rose on the battlements. The memory was still fresh, the taste of her mouth, the scent of her skin, the soft, supple flesh of her thighs. The thought of MacPherson touching her in such a manner set his teeth on edge and infused his step with fresh determination as he strode to the quay.

He rowed himself across the loch and wandered through the village until he found her stitching up a man's forearm. He waited just outside the doorway until she finished. The sight of her, even in an old, stained kirtle and bodice, the long, white sleeves of the shift rolled to her elbows, inflamed him with lust. She talked to the man as she stitched, asking after his wife and children. The man was so pleased by this question, and obviously so in awe of this intelligent, skillful beauty caring for him, that he stammered his answer, face red. William could empathize with the poor man.

When Rose finished, she gave him instructions on how to care for the wound and made him repeat them back to her as she packed her implements into her wooden box. So competent, so very thorough.

William knew the moment she spotted him. The hesitation in her step as she turned for the door, the surprise— and pleasure?—in her eyes that she quickly masked with a frown.

"What do you want?" she said, walking past him briskly, basket over one arm, box tucked under the other. A sleek auburn braid hung down her back. Wisps had come lose to float around her face. She tried to smooth them back irritably, and the basket banged against her ribs.

He tried to take it from her. "You need an escort."

She laughed sarcastically. "Here? In Glen Laire? Don't be absurd." She kept a firm hold on the basket handle.

"I also want to apologize."

"That's not necessary."

"Come, Rose," he cajoled, still exerting pull on the basket handle. "Let's call a truce."

That stopped her. She turned to him and gazed up at him warily. "A truce? Why?"

Because I cannot stomach the thought of you and MacPherson spending a second alone together. But of course he couldn't say that. He'd made his position clear to her on the battlements. He couldn't marry; he wouldn't do that again. And yet he couldn't seem to stay away from her, either.

"We were friends once, aye? Pretend I'm Dumhnull again, and I'll promise not to touch you."

"Dumhnull." She murmured the name sadly, staring across the loch at the castle. She looked up at him again, suspicious but clearly fancying the idea. "A truce." She looked down at her basket, then offered it to him. "Are you hungry? Morag gave me this for tending her bad toe."

He took the basket and folded back the linens covering it. Bread and cheese. He walked to the banks of the loch and sat. She followed a few seconds later, sitting beside him. She dug into the basket, then passed the food to him. He scanned the battlements, looking for the telltale golden head.

"So . . . where is MacPherson this morning? I'm surprised he allowed you out of his sight, what with a monster prowling the castle."

She gave him a narrow look. "Why do you say such things?"

"Because it's true, and you are well aware of it now."

She shrugged, popping a piece of cheese in her mouth and gazing back at him placidly, uncaring.

"It doesn't repulse you?"

Her brows drew together. "Repulsed? By what? I've seen you take the sickness into yourself and suffer with it. There is nothing repulsive in that."

"Aye, but I did not always do that."

She shook her head, rolled her eyes. "What do I care for what you once did? Do you do it now?" When he shook his head, she nodded, satisfied. "I didn't think so."

He had to look away from her direct midnight stare. *She did not care.* She was a fool. A sweet, beautiful fool. She should be terrified of him. Of what he could make her into with but a little more instruction. She had no idea. *His little fool.* But she was not his. She was MacPherson's. Sick anger stabbed at him, and he didn't trust himself to speak.

They ate in silence for a few minutes. He watched her, and she avoided his gaze. He wondered how long he had, how long before MacPherson discovered the wizard was with his woman.

"What will you do about Lucas?" Rose asked, breaking into his dark thoughts.

"Lucas?" He frowned thoughtfully, then remembered the small boy who'd taken refuge in his castle after his mother and sister had been stoned and burned. "Ailis's brother." He exhaled heavily. "I suppose he shall live at Strathwick for now. Why?"

She toyed with her bread, picking hunks out of it and tossing it into the water. Fish darted up, snatching at it. "Lucas told me Allister is to blame for everything. He seems to think the villagers would forget if not for Allister rubbing salt in the wounds." She hesitated, sending him a quick, sidelong look. "So I think you must deal with Allister."

He laughed incredulously. "You mean punish him? Make a martyr out of him? Wouldn't he love that! No, I think not."

She shook her head vigorously, leaning in closer. "No, no. Not death. He must be discredited somehow. Such as you did to Pol. Heal him publicly. That will take the wind from his sails, methinks."

William shook his head dismissively. "Unfortunately he is hale as a horse. The man nearly severed his own arm once and it didn't even fester."

Rose's shoulders slouched, and she frowned down at her food, picking at it again and worrying her bottom lip. He was amused by her effort to aid him and thought her idea a clever one—he'd thought of it himself. Unfortunately, Allister and he were too much alike. He knew he must do something about Allister and Pol and Tadhg—the instigators of all his trouble. He just hadn't decided what yet.

"There's a reason for that, you ken?"

His statement startled her from her thoughts. She blinked at him. "For what?"

"A reason Allister never ails." He slid her a speculative look, gauging her reaction.

"What is that?"

"He's our brother—Drake's and mine. Born on the wrong side of the sheets, of course." He smiled at the irony of it—it never failed to amuse him.

Her mouth dropped open in shock. "*Your brother?* Is he a witch?"

"I believe so."

She let out an incredulous breath. "Does he know it?"

William snorted. "Nay—he doesn't even know we share blood. His mum never told him."

Rose shook her head at him. "You find this humorous."

"Somewhat." He leaned toward her. "Think of it—he *is* what he seeks to destroy."

"Then you should tell him and let him destroy himself."

"I doubt he'd believe me."

She leaned closer, brows arched. "Make him."

The intensity of her expression riveted him, put him in mind of other, more salacious things. His gaze swept over her, noting the blush that stained her neck and cheeks as she gazed back. A strand of copper had come loose from her plait, and it lay against her cheek. He longed to brush it back, to twine it around his fingers, to . . .

She looked away abruptly, her breathing disturbed. "Stop it."

"Stop what?" he asked innocently.

"You *know*."

"I'm afraid I don't."

She shot him a furious look. "Aye, you do. Looking at me like that—like a hungry wolf. It's not *friendly* at all."

He felt like a wolf—ravenous, feral. And he didn't want to be her friend, regardless of what he'd said before. He gave her a hard smile. "Sorry. No more looks. I vow it."

The tight set of her shoulders relaxed slightly. "Good, because there is something I've thought long on, and until now I haven't had a single person with whom to discuss it."

"Aye?"

"The colors we see when we heal . . . what do you think they are?"

He slanted her a meditative look. "What do you think they are?"

She pursed her mouth and raised her brows. "I asked you first."

He lifted a shoulder. "I know not."

She sighed, pushing the loose hair behind her ear and giving him a challenging stare, daring him to call her foolish. "I think it's the soul."

He nodded thoughtfully. "Then it certainly follows why you think it is a gift from God. But to actually see a person's soul would make us more than human, don't you think? Like some sort of angel or saint."

She frowned at him, bewildered. "What are you talking about? 'Gift from God'? I didn't say that."

He suppressed a smile. "Your letters. My favorite phrase—repeated in nearly every letter—was how it was my duty to God and mankind to help your father. I had to wonder, however, that if God shared His great design with *you*, just when He planned to reveal it to *me*. I have wondered all these years and am now feeling rather left out. He seems to have forgotten me up in the mountains."

Her mouth dropped open. "You *did* mock my letters!"

He laughed aloud at her horror. "I didn't, Rose, I vow it. I loved your letters. Every one of them. I looked forward to them, in fact—with dreaded fascination."

She arched a glacial brow. "Really? Then why did you ignore them?"

He disregarded her question, perversely enjoying how agitated she was becoming. "I didn't just ignore them—I burned them, too."

She let out a huffed breath and began tossing food

and linens back in the basket, muttering to herself all the while.

As she stood, William reached a hand toward her, grasping a handful of kirtle and pulling her back down, laughing in earnest now. "All but one—all but one. I kept one."

She glared at him as she sat on her knees, still ready to flee. "Which one was that?"

"The one in which you shared something of yourself. I meant to answer that one . . . but I could never think of what to write."

She planted her hands on her hips and shook her head in bewilderment. "You mock the source of your healing, but who else but God would give you such a wondrous gift?"

He tried to look evil, raising a brow. "Many say the devil."

"A man's contemporaries can never perceive greatness. Look to the Bible for such stories."

His evil visage dissolved in pained laughter. "*Rose.* I am no saint. I have killed men with this gift. Your betrothed's father, for one. I *did* that."

She shook her head stubbornly. "No, I cannot believe it of you. You did what you thought was right at the time."

"I don't know that I thought it was right. Even at the time."

She did not reply to that. Her mouth was still set in a stubborn line. He sighed. Her refusal to think ill of him was sweet, if terribly misguided.

Continuing with their earlier conversation, she said, "So . . . you do not believe the colors we see are the soul?"

"I don't know what a soul is. Have you ever seen a ghost?"

"No, but my sister sees them."

He leaned back on the grassy bank and stared across the water at the castle. "I saw one once. It spoke to me . . . and it looked human. No light or color—I even tried to pass my hands over it. There was nothing there. What is a ghost if not the soul trapped here on earth?"

When he glanced over at her, he could see that the thought intrigued her. She arched a fine auburn brow at him. "Then what are we seeing?"

"When a person dies, the color leaves them. But they are the same as before. A bag of flesh, containing bone and blood and humors. The light and color is what animates them, what makes the heart pound, the blood rush. It is what warms the skin . . ." He shook his head helplessly. "It's as vital to life as the blood in our veins, but I still know not what it is."

She smiled ruefully at him.

"What?"

"You said you hadn't thought of it. That you didn't have any theories."

"That's not what I said. I said I know not. And I don't."

She shook her head, still smiling. Then her eyes brightened, and she leaned forward. "Can you see your own color?"

"No."

She closed her eyes for a moment, then opened them. She reached toward him, passing her hand over his. He could almost feel it, the heat of her, and his body tightened in response, the lightness of his mood falling away.

She smiled wistfully. "It's blue. Like your eyes. It's different from any I've seen before . . . more vibrant."

Arrested by the softness in her eyes, William didn't respond immediately. When he could speak, his voice was gruff. "I see the same in you."

"Really?" Her smile was like the sun on his face. "What color am I? Is it as I imagine? Dark blue?"

He nodded. "You're beautiful—a dark, vivid blue, indigo lightning."

She chewed her lip thoughtfully, pleased with the description. William stared at her profile, memorizing every line of her face, the sweep of her lashes, the bemused curve of her lips that he wanted to taste. . . . Her forehead creased into a frown. He followed her gaze.

MacPherson rowed across the loch, his face thunderous as he stared at William and Rose. William looked up at the sky and realized they'd been sitting there for hours. Afternoon had turned to evening. His bread was stale. He sighed and sat up, tossing his hard bread in the basket then stood. Rose stood too, nervously brushing the crumbs from her kirtle.

"Jamie," she said when he jumped into the shallows of the loch. "What are you doing?"

"I heard *he* was here." Jamie splashed through the water, never taking his eyes off William. Once out of the loch, he charged. William tensed but didn't retreat. MacPherson stopped in front of him, blowing like a bull. "Stay away from her, or I swear on my father's grave I will slice you open."

Rose took hold of MacPherson's arm, trying to pull him away. "You promised!"

"You can certainly try," William said, hating the man with a sudden, black intensity. MacPherson had every reason to hate William—but he had the one thing William wanted and couldn't have. *Rose*. And William loathed him for it.

At Rose's prodding MacPherson backed away, still glaring murder at William. The reckoning would come, William knew, regardless of the promises the lad had apparently made to Rose. William was ready for it.

She shepherded MacPherson back into the boat, her skirts sopping. William stood on the bank, watching as MacPherson rowed her across, his heart cankered with jealousy. In the middle of the loch, MacPherson stopped rowing and pulled the oars in. The skiff drifted. MacPherson gestured passionately as he spoke to Rose, while her gestures were placating. She touched him freely, her hands on his forearm, his shoulder. MacPherson's gaze sliced to William, who still stood on the bank, witnessing it all. MacPherson grabbed Rose's shoulders and kissed her. She let him.

William picked up the basket and box she'd left behind, and turned away.

Rose was relieved that her betrothed had finally calmed. She'd left her things on the bank, and when she twisted around, she saw they were gone. William was gone, too.

"What are you looking for?" Jamie asked, suspicious, scanning the bank himself.

"My box. I left it in the village." She smiled at him. "I'm going back tomorrow. I'll get it then."

"I'll go with you tomorrow."

"I'm afraid you'll find it terribly boring."

"Nonsense." He smiled at her. He'd been so furious with her, had felt so betrayed when he'd seen her sitting on the bank talking to William. She'd tried to explain herself, but he'd been implacable. She was his *betrothed*. Strathwick was his *enemy*. And never the two shall meet. Then he'd kissed her and she'd let him, and suddenly his anger had disappeared. Rose had been bewildered at first, until she'd noticed the way he stared at her—or more aptly leered at her. His gaze moved up and down her body, lingering on her breasts and mouth.

She worried now, wondering what to do about this. What to do? He was her betrothed! She'd let William kiss and touch her—surely she should let the man she meant to marry do the same and more. Trouble was, she didn't want Jamie to kiss her or touch her again. This did not speak well for their impending wedding night. What a tangle.

At the quay, Jamie assisted her from the boat, pulling her against his body and running his hands down her backside. Her heart beat furiously. She prepared to slap him if he tried anything else, but he did not. He took her hand and led her up the steps. All the while he stole lecherous looks at her, filled with promise and expectation. Oh, it was coming. It was just a matter of when.

The attack came outside her chambers. He kissed her again—abruptly, so she had no time to react. His mouth was over hers, tongue thrusting, his arms crushing her against him. She struggled, twisting her face away.

"Jamie! Hold, please! Wait! I can't breathe!"

His mouth was wet on her neck. Then he bit her, and she yelped. Reflexively, she rammed her knee into his groin.

The effect was instantaneous. He released her and bent over, groaning.

"Oh, no! Oh God, forgive me—I— I— You frightened me."

After a moment he straightened, his face red. "It's all right," he gasped when she continued her profuse apologies. He adjusted himself with a grimace, then fixed her with a stern look. "There's naught to be afraid of, lass. We're to be wed. It's expected that we do this. I ken you have no mother. Has anyone told you what happens on our wedding night?"

Rose managed—just barely—not to roll her eyes. Had anyone told her? Actually, no, come to think of it, no one had *told* her. Donald MacLean, fat Fagan's oldest son, had shown her in great detail. But she could not tell Jamie that. She planned to fake her virginity. She remembered losing it well enough and felt she could fake it with accuracy. She would procure a small bladder of blood and break it on the bed. He would never know.

As Jamie stared at her expectantly, Rose shook her head, deciding ignorance was the best defense against his advances tonight.

He gave her a gentle, superior smile and turned her toward her door. "Let's go inside and I'll tell you." His hand skimmed down her back to her bottom.

She turned quickly. "No—let me ask my sisters first, I pray you. I'm afraid. . . . This is strange, hearing it from you. I want to be better prepared." She gazed up at him pleadingly. "Please?"

He sighed, disappointed, then said, "Very well, though

it's naught to fear. Oh, it hurts the first time. After, it's not so terrible."

"Had a lot of virgins, have you?"

He started to nod, then frowned. "Why do you ask?"

She smiled sweetly. "No reason." He left her finally, and she locked herself in her chambers. How could she marry him? She wasn't even sure she liked him. Logically, she knew that most marriages were not based on friendship or love or even lust, but logic had nothing to do with it. She still wanted it. Friendship, at least. Lust was nice. She had those with William . . . Dumhnull . . . Her heart stumbled just to think of him. And love? . . .

It was useless to dwell on it! He'd made it clear he didn't want her that way. She *must* stop thinking about him. Irritated with herself, she retreated to the herb room to lose herself in the comfort of work, but for once it was no use. Though she spent an hour crushing dried herbs and studying her texts, she finally gave up. Frustrated and empty, she wandered to the doorway and gazed listlessly around her chambers.

She remembered how William had hidden in her room last night, and her heart leapt, her gaze shifting to the shadows near the window. Empty, of course. If only he were there tonight, hiding, waiting for her. She would not send him away.

Chapter 14

Rose spent another day healing in the village. The new healing technique William had taught her proved to be extremely helpful. She'd not understood the possibilities then, but now she realized that being able to feel the ailment as well as see it told her more than color alone. She'd held out hope last night that William would come to her on the pretext of returning her box, but he had not. In the morning she'd found it on the floor outside her chambers, and when she'd gone down to the quay, Jamie had been waiting for her, apparently determined to be the only man she spent time with today.

It wasn't long, however, before he began to complain that he was hungry and that his feet hurt. Though she gently suggested a number of times that he return to Lochlaire, he refused to go without her, fixing her with a wounded and accusatory stare, as if his discomfort was entirely her fault.

"I just have one more patient," Rose assured him as she hurried along the dirt path.

Jamie trudged glumly behind her, not touching her or even offering to help her carry her things. Earlier he'd grabbed her and tried to kiss her—only to thrust her away in disgust. Her clothes were stained with blood and other fluids. He'd kept his distance the remainder of the day.

"Can you not see them tomorrow?" Jamie asked, a slight whine to his voice. "We've missed dinner."

Rose gritted her teeth, tamping down the urge to snap at him. She was tired and achy, too. She'd reset a dislocated joint earlier, and it had been a great exertion. Her shoulders and arms ached from the strain.

"Here." From her bag, Rose dug a roll wrapped in cloth and offered it to him. He took it hesitantly but didn't eat it, eyeing it as if it, too, was covered with blood and sweat.

Inside the next cottage, Rose was delighted to find that the patient had an abscess. Delighted because in the past, it had often been difficult to determine whether a lump was a tumorous growth or a festering. But now, she could *feel* it. Removing a tumor could be tricky, and it didn't always fix the problem. An abscess was a simple matter of draining, flushing, stitching, and applying a poultice. Since it was in a rather sensitive area—the patient's groin—she was forced to ask her betrothed for aid.

Jamie held the man's leg for her, and when she finally allowed him to release it, he rushed outside and vomited. After instructing her patient how to care for his healing abscess, lest it fester again, she joined Jamie outside. He huddled on a bench beside the cottage door, his head in his hands.

She sat beside him. "Are you all right?" She pushed back the blond hair falling over his brow and pressed her palm to his clammy forehead.

He shrank from her touch, an unmistakable expression of disgust on his face, and scooted further down the bench, away from her. "You will stop this . . . *healing* when we are wed."

Rose dropped her hand, wondering if she should be offended by his reaction to her touch, but all she truly felt was relief. Just the day before, he'd been anxious to bed her. It appeared that would no longer be a concern. But then again, she meant to marry him, didn't she? She did not want her husband to be repulsed by her.

"Why should I stop?" she said. "I'm a healer. It's what I do."

"When we marry you'll be a wife. The MacPherson's lady." When she didn't respond, he straightened, giving her a pointed look.

She opened her palm in a placating gesture. "Someone must heal the people on your lands—"

"We already have a healer."

"I'm better."

He raised a brow. "How very modest of you."

Rose shrugged. "It's true. Besides, my mother always—"

"Your mother was burned alive. She is of no matter to us."

Rose stiffened. "She matters to me. She was a great lady who helped all who needed it. I don't care how she died. I can only hope to live a life as rich as hers."

Jamie groaned and rolled his eyes. "Let's speak of this later."

Rose stood, angry now. "I want to discuss this now. Let's return to Lochlaire and discuss it over dinner. I'm starving."

Jamie sighed and stood heavily. "I do not think I can eat." He looked down his nose at her, nostrils pinched. "You do intend to bathe, don't you?"

"Of course," Rose said, her cheeks hot.

He sniffed disdainfully and started for the loch. Rose followed, embarrassed as she'd never been before. She glanced down at herself, noting the stains all over her clothes. She'd never cared before; neither had anyone else who knew her. Her cheeks burned hotter with suppressed anger.

Before they reached the small dock, she noticed a skiff rowing frantically across the water.

"Miss Rose!" a lad called as she was untying a boat. "Wait, Miss Rose!"

Rose's heart tripped, wondering what had set the lad in such a frenzy. *Her father.* She waited on the shore until the prow hit the dock.

"Get in, hurry! Tira is having her wean!"

Rose closed her eyes in relief. Jamie gave her a puzzled look, and Rose said, "My uncle's wife is in labor."

They clambered into the boat. With Jamie taking a set of oars, they moved swiftly through the water. When they entered the castle's cavernous water entrance, Rose's gaze was immediately drawn to the man waiting for her quayside. William. Her heart stumbled at the unexpected sight of him, large and grim, a lone sentinel on the quay. He watched their approach, his hands folded behind his back, aloof. A shadow warrior, so alone in his self-inflicted exile. A lump rose in her throat. He would leave after Tira gave birth, and she would never see him again. Jamie would certainly never allow contact with him.

"What is *he* doing here?" Jamie muttered, pulling on the oars with renewed force. His eyes narrowed on the lone figure, and his jaw jutted pugnaciously.

"He has agreed to assist me with Tira."

Jamie snorted. "That's woman's work."

"Aye, unless you're a gifted healer," Rose said, her lips pursed together tartly. "Though I can deliver weans and mend many wounds, I cannot stop all the blood from draining out of a woman after—"

"Very well, I ken your meaning." There was a slightly green pallor to his skin, and his rowing had slackened considerably. It had never occurred to Rose that her husband-to-be would be so squeamish. She tried not to feel scornful about it but couldn't help remembering how William had healed others, oblivious of blood and sickness.

Jamie pulled in the oars as the boat slid the rest of the way to the quay. William descended the steps to help her from the skiff but retreated when Jamie hauled her roughly out of the boat.

"Easy, lad," William said when Rose winced from Jamie's hold on her arm. "She's not a Lachaber ax for you to be tossing about."

Jamie thrust her behind him. "You dare speak to me, scabbit bastard?"

William stood several steps above them. He stared down at Jamie, his expression mildly amused. "Scabbit? Mayhap. But no bastard. I assure you, my parents were married."

"It's not a legal marriage if one of the parties is a pig."

William's eyes narrowed, and his hand went to his dirk hilt.

"Och, need you a knife? Can you not just touch me and give me the plague, Wizard?"

"Jamie!" Rose found his jealousy no more endearing than his weak stomach. She darted out from behind him and climbed to the step above him. "You said you wouldn't fight."

"I promised not to kill him. I never said I wouldna speak my mind."

"Those sounded like fighting words to me," Rose said. She turned to William and gave him a pleading look.

He resheathed the dirk he'd pulled halfway from the scabbard at his waist. He held Jamie's gaze over her head for another moment before looking down at her. "Come," he said. "Tira asks for you."

Rose followed him through the castle, Jamie trailing behind. They climbed three flights of stairs to the remote apartments at the top of the west tower. From the landing, they could hear the screaming inside.

"Uh . . . Rose?"

Rose turned to find Jamie hanging back on the steps. Tira screamed again and he grimaced, head sinking down into his shoulders.

"I think I'll wait here for you, on the steps . . ." Tira shrieked again, as if someone tried to murder her. Jamie swallowed. "Except further down."

"Birthings can take a long time," Rose cautioned. "I might be in there twelve hours or more. Why don't you find some dinner and get some rest?"

Jamie's gazed fixed on William and his lips curled. He said, with more strength in his voice, "I'll wait on the stairs."

Rose sighed. "Very well." At least he wouldn't be in the birthing room, fighting with William. He looked her up and down, as if considering whether he wanted to kiss her, then settled for a pat on her shoulder before retreating down the steps.

Rose turned back toward the door. William leaned against the frame, watching her. "You must be near to swooning from such a passionate courting."

Rose glared at him. "I've been healing all day. I look hideous. No one would want to touch me."

He laughed and shook his head. Before she could ask him what was so amusing, the door opened and Tira's maid glared out at them. Hilda was a stout, sour-faced woman who made certain Tira obeyed every edict Roderick set forth regarding her pregnancy. After losing two wives to childbirth, Roderick was taking no chances. Tira hadn't left the tower room in two months.

Hilda did not allow William entrance until he moved aside slightly, giving the maid a view of Rose. Hilda fluttered a hand over her ample bosom and threw the door wide. "You're finally here!"

When William started to follow Rose inside, Hilda blocked his way. "The master says I admit no one except him or Miss Rose."

Rose patted her comfortingly. "Worry not. Lord Strathwick is a skilled healer."

But Hilda did not look convinced. Her brows lowered and her thick lips pursed together in a flat line, but she let him pass.

Tira sat up in bed, her belly huge beneath the sheet. Her face was ruddy with pain, and damp hair clung to her temples. She glanced from Rose to William anxiously, her brows raised in worry.

"Good morn," William said. "May I?" He indicated the stool beside her bed.

She nodded hesitantly. Long chestnut hair flowed over the snowy linen of her night rail and onto the bedding. Her skin was mildly scarred from smallpox, but it glowed with health, and her teeth were straight and white. She was a handsome woman, older than Rose by some years, a widow when Roderick had met her. She appeared downright robust to Rose—fully capable of delivering multiple weans with no harm to herself. Unfortunately, appearances were often deceiving.

After Rose made the introductions, she passed her hands quickly over Tira, assuring herself of her aunt's and the wean's health. Both mother and child were well. Rose placed her hands on Tira's belly and found that the baby still had not turned.

The muscles contracted, bulging hard, and Tira gasped and cried out. Rose looked up at William. "The baby is still breech."

"Can she give birth that way?" He looked uneasy, no doubt remembering Deidra's disastrous birth.

"She'll have to," Rose said, comforted by William's presence. The last breech birth she'd attended had been fatal for both mother and child.

"What does that mean? Am I going to die?" Tira cried, gritting her teeth against the pain. "It's a monster, isn't it? It's too big! Oh, God!"

Hilda stood over the bed, her brow puckered in confusion. "It canna come until the master is here."

Rose raised an amused brow. "That is of no concern to the babe—I vow it. He cares not at all whether his father is present or not. Besides, Uncle Roderick should not be present in the birthing room."

Hilda's gaze flew to William. "Then make him leave!"

"He's a healer. We may have need of him if aught goes wrong."

Tira moaned on the bed. "Oh God, Oh God! *Get it out!*"

William murmured soothingly to her.

"We need sheets," Rose said to the maid. "And while you're fetching them, see if you can find my uncle."

As Hilda left, Tira cried after her, "You must find him!" She clutched William's arm as another contraction gripped her. When Rose moved to the bedside, Tira grabbed at her sleeve. "Rose, please. If he's not here, I will die."

Rose hushed her, stroking her hand gently over Tira's damp hair. "Fash not, I've delivered many weans, and Lord Strathwick will not let you or your child die."

William met her gaze grimly. He could not promise that, of course; he could promise only that one would live, but there was no reason to tell Tira that.

"No!" Tira cried, thrashing about on the bed. "You don't understand—it will *kill* me! He put it in there—it's unnatural! It's a monster! You *must* find my husband!"

She screamed, gripping her stomach. After the contraction passed, William came to stand beside Rose. "What does she mean? A monster?"

"She's mad from the pain," Rose murmured.

He took her elbow and led her farther away from the bed. His expression was grave. "Which one, Rose? If it comes down to it, which one do I save?"

Rose's belly clenched. She could not make such a choice. "Let us pray the choice doesn't have to be made."

She tried to return to the bed. He held fast to her elbow. "Prayers aren't good enough. Which one? I have to know—for when it happens, there will be no time for debate."

Rose pressed her hand to her mouth and shook her head. "I know not! Pray you, wait until Hilda returns with my uncle. I cannot make this choice."

"Very well." He rubbed a hand across the black-and-silver stubble on his chin, eyeing Tira pensively. "If both mother and child are in danger . . . there *is* a way to save them both."

She clasped his arm hopefully. "Really? What is it?"

He gave her a long, fathomless look. "We'll cross that bridge if we come to it, aye? Let's hope we do not."

He returned to the bedside. Rose frowned at him for a moment longer, wondering what he could mean, then resumed her preparations.

Hilda returned with no news of Roderick. "I know not where he is. He did not even tell us he was leaving Lochlaire this morn. We sent for him when Tira began having pains. No one could find him. No one knows where he went."

Rose sighed heavily. This news only distressed her patient more, and she began raving again. Hilda wrung her hands. William's gaze urged Rose to make a decision but she could not, so she looked away, avoiding direct conversation with him. He'd said there might be a way to save both. That was her choice.

She gestured to the maid. "Help me get these soiled sheets off the bed."

Rose and Hilda stripped the bed while William lifted the pregnant woman as if she weighed nothing, heedless of the mess her sopping, blood-streaked shift had become. Rose and Hilda padded the mattress with a thick oiled skin and many layers of sheets. They'd been anticipating the birth for weeks now and had changed to a mattress stuffed with heather, so that when it was ruined, it would be no great loss. William laid her down, then built the fire back up as they changed Tira's shift and wiped her down with a cool cloth.

Tira cried and moaned, declaring over and over again that she would die without her husband's assistance, that the child was a monster. Rose knew very little about her aunt. Though she'd tended her the last few months of her pregnancy, Tira was a quiet, withdrawn woman, not inclined to gossip or idle conversation. She'd never seemed afraid of Roderick, and he positively doted on her. It was all very curious. Rose had seen women who, in the throes of birth pain, said many bizarre things. Afterward they barely remembered saying them.

The rapid progression of the labor was somewhat alarming. Rose had successfully delivered breech babies before, but loss of life was the more common scenario—for both mother and child. It really depended on the size of the baby and the size of the mother. Judging by the size of Tira's belly, Rose estimated that the baby was an exceptionally large one. Tira was not a tiny woman, but Rose still had some concerns as to whether she could easily pass such a large infant. She checked her several times and finally began applying hot compresses to help her expand.

William sat near the head of the bed, talking softly to Tira, while Hilda and Rose worked. She overheard William assuring Tira that her child was no monster but a gift, and of course Roderick put it in her belly—that's the way it worked. She cried and argued incoherently with him. William kept sending Rose worried looks. She tried to reassure him with her eyes that Tira's ravings were naught but nonsense uttered in some form by all women in labor.

Tira jerked forward suddenly and cried in a hoarse voice, "The monster is here!"

Rose looked down. A foot appeared.

"It's here," Rose hissed, silencing everyone but Tira. She pressed Tira's thighs further apart, speaking soothingly to her and urging her to push. Tira screamed and moaned, and Rose distinctly heard her beg William to kill the baby when it was born. Rose straightened from between Tira's legs to meet William's troubled gaze. He was holding up admirably amongst all the screaming and blood. She'd seen seasoned warriors faint dead away when presented with a wife's birthing—which was one of the reasons Rose never allowed men in the room. She had enough to worry about without head wounds added in. But William appeared entirely unaffected.

Rose urged Tira to keep pushing. On and on. The fire blazed and the room sweltered. Rose quickly removed her bodice and sleeves, tossing them somewhere behind her. Her shift clung to her skin and legs, her hair stuck to her face. Long moments passed, and only the wean's legs and pelvis had emerged. Exhausted, Tira whimpered that she couldn't push anymore, that it was killing her.

Rose passed her hands over the baby periodically, and when finally the abdomen slid out, the baby's color began to fade. The cord was pulled tight against the torso. Rose put a finger to it. The pulse fluttered weakly.

"Something is wrong," she said.

"Can you feel it?" William asked, beside her now. Tira had become oblivious in her pain, no longer aware of the others in the room with her.

Rose summoned the magic again, as he'd taught her, sending it down her arms. She'd seen the dark mass at the baby's neck, and now she felt it, thick and spongy, circling the baby's throat.

"The cord is wrapped around the neck. The position is strangling him."

"Can you pull him out?" William asked, touching a small, pale foot lying motionless against the sheets.

Rose's breath shuddered in and out of her chest as she slid her fingers into the birth canal, searching for the chin. "No—I can't find his chin." Her muscles trembled from the strain of supporting the substantial child on her forearm. "If I pull him out now, I could kill him."

William's hands were on her shoulders. "He will die anyway if you don't. I'm here. Pull him out."

"No. If I hurt his neck or head, he could die instantly. You told me you couldn't bring back the dead." Tira screamed again. Another hard contraction squeezed Rose's fingers.

"Pull her to the edge of the bed," Rose ordered, her voice frantic. "Now—do it!"

William gripped Tira's thighs and pulled her down so that the child's body dangled over the edge, supported by Rose's left hand and forearm.

An arm slid out, and Rose felt the chin. "I got it!" she cried triumphantly, lifting. The mouth was free, and indeed, the cord was wrapped tightly about the baby's neck. Rose quickly slipped her fingers in further, locating the other arm and freeing it. Then she grasped the feet with her right hand and flipped the baby up and back, freeing the head and laying him neatly on his mother's belly.

He wasn't breathing. He was limp and unresponsive, even after the cord was unwrapped from his neck. She cleared the mouth and nose, but still nothing. William took the baby from her and held it in his arms. Rose's heart pounded in her ears as she looked from his face to the child. A moment later, he thrust the baby back at her and went down on one knee.

A jolt of panic went through her when he collapsed further onto all fours. The baby still hadn't cried, but his dark eyes stared at her now, and they were full of life. Rose snatched a towel and lay the baby on a table. She massaged his feet and back until his shrill, angry cry rang through the room. Her shoulders slumped, profound relief shuddering through her. When Hilda appeared beside her, she turned over care of the infant to the maid.

Tira still moaned on the bed, and William was on the floor. Rose knelt beside him, pushing a lock of silvered black hair off his forehead. "You did it," she whispered, her throat tight, nearly overcome by what he was capable of.

But there was no time to become emotional. There was still work to be done.

Rose said William's name several more times, but he remained unresponsive. She lifted an eyelid and only saw whites. His pulse was weak and fluttery. When she passed her hands over him, she saw dark splotches near his head and chest, but his sapphire-blue color pulsed, healing him.

She managed to drag him closer to the fire and covered him with a blanket. She returned to her patient.

"You have a son, Tira—but you already knew that." Alan MacDonell had determined that months ago. Hilda brought the clean, swaddled child to the bedside, holding him out for Tira's inspection.

"He's a braw laddy," Rose said, returning to the end of the bed. "And certainly no monster."

Tira didn't respond or try to hold the child. Her face was pale, her eyes listless. Rose's lips compressed, and she glanced at William. The choice had been made; now it was up to her to save Tira. Throat tight, she set to massaging Tira's abdomen. She moaned pitifully as Rose worked, past the time when the pain should have eased. There was a great deal of blood, and it wasn't stopping. It had been a very large child and a difficult birth. Rose had been afraid something like this would happen. She gazed over at William again. What had he said? *If both mother and child are in danger . . . there is a way to save them both.* But *damn it* he was insensible now, unable to save anyone but himself.

She tried to stanch the bleeding, packing Tira with linens and giving her an infusion, but the sheets just turned crimson. Eventually, Tira grew unresponsive, and her skin became white and pasty, her pulse weak, her breathing shallow.

Rose crossed to the fireplace and knelt beside William. "William? She's dying, and I know not what to do. Can you hear me?"

His eyelids fluttered, then drifted upward. He gazed at her for a moment. "Heal her."

A small, frustrated sob escaped Rose. "I *can't*. I need you."

He swallowed and said, his voice weak and thready, "I told you . . . you don't need me."

"But I do. I can't do what you do."

"Aye, you can."

Rose shook her head, her vision blurring. "I can't!"

His hand slid from beneath the blanket and gripped her wrist. "Remember Wallace. You can do it." His hold on her wrist slackened, and his eyes drifted shut.

"William, I can't!" But he could not hear her any longer.

Rose straightened and returned to the bed. She stared helplessly down at her dying patient for several minutes. She did not believe she could do what he did. But they both saw the light. They both felt the ailments. She'd possessed the ability to feel them all along and had not known it. Could it be he spoke true?

She lowered herself onto the stool by the bedside and closed her eyes, summoning the magic. She had used it repeatedly this evening and it was stubborn at first, refusing to gather, but finally it obeyed. She saw it in her chest, a dark ball of light. She opened her eyes. Tira's pale pink light flickered, fading, blackness and streaks of dark red centered in her abdomen. Rose placed her hands there, against Tira's skin. She remembered that when William had healed Wallace, he'd sent his light into the man, then had drawn the ailment out. Rose sent the magic down her arms to her hands, then further, and she gasped, nearly losing it when her color spread outward from her fingers, into Tira's belly, circling the blackness. Then she called it back.

It happened so quickly that she was not prepared for the pain. She opened her mouth to cry out but made no sound. She toppled off her stool and lay on the floor, trying desperately to curl herself around the deep, stabbing pain in her belly. Her stomach revolted and gray specks danced before her eyes, but still she could not call out. Before the blackness engulfed her, she heard Tira's voice, panicked and confused . . . and *strong*. "Rose? What happened? What's wrong?"

Chapter 15

❧⟨∞⟩❧

Rose did not know how much time had passed, trapped in this nightmare from which she could not wake. Agony gripped her body, so intense that she had no control over her own thoughts or movements. Her sisters came and went from the room. And though Rose was aware of all that went on around her, she was nearly insensible from the pain. She was dying. She had no idea how she'd come to be in her own chambers, but she did remember the vomiting and dry heaves. Something was cutting her in two, killing her body. If she lived through this torture, she would surely never bear children.

Shouting and arguing roused her from the swirling tempest of misery. She heard her uncle in the distance once, yelling obscenities, and someone else—Drake?— demanding to see her. Isobel sat on the bed, wiping a cool cloth over Rose's brow. Rose raised a hand, impossibly heavy, pushing through mud.

"I want to see him." Her voice was a mere breath.

Isobel frowned and leaned close.

"I want to see him. Drake."

Isobel nodded and straightened, looking over her shoulder. Rose was relieved, as she couldn't speak any louder. It hurt too much. Speaking hurt, as if it vibrated through her, ripping at her womb. Everything hurt, even breathing.

Isobel left her side, and Rose soon heard her sister's voice raised with the other angry voices. Seconds later Drake was beside her.

He knelt close, his face creased with worry. "What happened?"

"William?"

"He is alive. But sleeps deeply and cannot be woken."

"He saved my nephew . . . born dead."

"Then he tried to save your aunt?"

Rose tried to shake her head but only turned it slightly against the pillow. "No . . . I saved her."

Drake's brow furrowed as he stared at her. "You?"

"Aye, William told me I could . . . and he was right."

He glanced at someone behind him and murmured, "She doesn't know."

"What? I don't know what?"

He straightened, turning away from her and speaking to Isobel in a soft, urgent undertone that Rose could not understand. Both stole worried glances at her throughout. Rose wanted to demand that they tell her what the problem was, but the pain was too great, washing over her in nauseating waves. She closed her eyes and groaned, trying to curl harder into herself. Someone jammed a rolled-up blanket into her stomach, and she clutched at it, pressing it hard into her gut.

"Here, drink this," said a soft voice beside her.

Gillian's cool hand slid beneath her neck, lifting and pressing a cup to her lips. Rose drank, recognizing the scents and flavor—valerian and willow bark. Good. She wanted to sleep.

When she woke next, the room was dim and quiet, except for the crackle and pop of the fire. She sat up in bed, her hand to her empty belly. It was sore and achy, but the pain was bearable. A head popped up beside her bed—wiry gray fur and a long snout. Broc, Gillian's deerhound. He snorted and gave a short bark.

Gillian sat in a chair near the fire. She set her sewing aside and came to the bed. "You are awake! How do you feel?"

"Better . . . how is William?"

Gillian handed Rose a cup of herbed wine. "Lord Strathwick? I know not."

Rose drank deeply, then said, "I need to see him."

"Can you eat?" Gillian asked.

Rose nodded, her belly rumbling hollowly.

"I will get you some dinner and check on Lord Strathwick. You lay here and rest, aye? You've been very ill. Broc will look after you."

Upon hearing his name, the deerhound sat up and whined softly, licking frantically at his mistress's hand. She scratched his head and ordered him to stay. He obeyed, though he watched her longingly as she left, fidgeting as if restraining himself from bounding after her. When the door shut, he lay back down.

Rose felt better after washing and combing her hair, and changing into a clean shift. She wanted to check on Tira and the baby. The thought of Tira sent a surge of dizzying excitement through her. She'd done it. She was a healer, just like William. She could hardly believe it, except she knew it to be true. She sat heavily on the bed, stunned to finally understand how William suffered when he healed. He'd been doing this for years. And now she truly understood what he'd said to her on the battlements. He would not put himself in a position of having to choose between wife and child again. He could not save both. If not for Rose's presence, Tira would have died.

The waves of wonder and awe that washed through her left her weak and tearful. She was giving thanks to God for this gift when the door opened. She expected Gillian with her dinner, so she was surprised to see William's broad shoulders filling the doorway. He gazed at her for a long while, his expression grave.

She could not speak at first, could only stare back at him, overwhelmed by what they had done. Together. Finally she said, "You knew. You knew and didn't tell me."

He left the door open and crossed the room. "I suspected." He took the stool beside the bed, sitting opposite her, their knees nearly touching. He didn't look at her. "I didn't wish to curse you to a life such as mine."

She let out an incredulous breath. "How can it be a curse? Tira *and* her child are alive. They both would have died, otherwise." She looked down at her own hands, then added, "There is no need for choices anymore, William. There's two of us now."

He took her hands in his; they were warm and strong, and she felt his touch to the pit of her belly.

"Rose, listen to me carefully."

His voice was so somber that she looked up quickly, searching his face. Something was wrong.

"Tira is dead."

It felt as if someone kicked Rose in the stomach. "Tha-that's impossible. I healed her. I felt it—I *heard* her. She spoke to me, after. And what about how ill I was? That's exactly what happens when you do it. Why would I suffer with her pain if I didn't heal her?"

He released one of her hands to rub his fingers over his whiskered jaw, then he pushed them through his hair. There was a significant new sprinkling of silver-gray at his temples. "I know not. I don't understand. You suffered a great deal. Your sisters told me about it. MacPherson and your uncle told me, too, when accusing me of attacking you with witchcraft."

"What?" Rose tried to stand, but he pulled her back to the bed by the hand. "You saved his son! How dare he accuse you of anything."

The look on his face tore at her heart. He was resigned to the thankless injustice of it. This was his life. "I'll fash on that later. For now, I want you to tell me what happened when you tried to heal Tira."

Tried. A weight settled in her heart. There was not two of them now. Nothing had changed. And yet she'd been so certain she'd succeeded. If Tira had died anyway, why had Rose suffered with her affliction? It made no sense.

"I . . . don't know. It was like always . . . then I sent the magic into her and called it back. When it came . . . it hurt so I couldn't breathe or think. Then Tira—who had been at death's door and not even opened her eyes—she spoke to me, asked me what happened!" Rose shook her head, tears blurring her vision. "I just don't understand how I could have failed!"

The blue eyes that gazed back at her were grim and disappointed. "I don't either." He put a hand to the side of her head and stroked her hair, his gaze dark and intense as it moved over her face.

Rose wanted to give in to him, to lean into his arms, sink into his kiss, but nothing had changed. She sighed, subtly moving her head so he dropped his hand. "I need to speak with my uncle and check on the baby. Then I must look in on my father."

He nodded, still solemn and thoughtful. "I'll go with you."

She eschewed the hand he offered, standing under her own power and wrapping her arisaid around her shoulders. They were at the door when Gillian returned with the tray, protesting that Rose couldn't leave until she'd eaten. Rose took an oatcake and promised to eat the rest later.

On the way to Roderick's apartments, William said, "You are still vexed with me."

Rose looked at him, surprised. "I'm not. I'm just . . . sad, about many things. We have a truce, remember? I agreed to it."

"That pleases me, as I know you can hold a grudge."

"That's not true. I don't hold grudges."

"Really? Hm . . ."

When he didn't elaborate further, she stopped on the curve of the staircase, turning so she looked down on him several steps below her. He gazed up at her inquiringly.

"Why do you think I hold grudges?"

"Because you're still so angry at your father about what happened on Skye."

"Wouldn't you be?"

He climbed a step, bringing them closer together. "Oh, aye, I would, but at the one who caused the injury. Your father didn't even know."

"He knew I was unhappy and still he made me stay."

"A witch he may be, but I don't think he's a seer like Dame Isobel. How was he to know why you were unhappy? Most lads and lassies are unhappy when sent away from their families."

Rose pulled her arisaid closer around her. "I tried to run away."

He smiled slightly. "Aye, you also came to fetch the wizard of Strathwick alone, disguised as a lad. Such acts are in your nature, methinks, and indicate naught more than an indomitable will."

Her hands fisted into the wool. "What are you saying? That I have no reason to be angry?"

"Nay, nay—you have every reason to be. But at the man responsible."

Her jaw clenched, hands tightening in the soft wool. "He's dead."

"Ah." He said it on a breath as he leaned his shoulder against the wall, a world of understanding in the single sound. He stared down at the steps between them, his mouth flat and hard.

"What does that mean?"

"The object of your ire is dead. So you've found another."

Something twisted hard in Rose's chest, and when she spoke, her voice was brittle. "You don't understand."

"I do, Rose." He looked up at her from beneath thick

black lashes. "I think you should tell your father instead of letting it fester."

She shook her head. "No, no, no. He's dying. I cannot let him die thinking I hate him."

"So you seek to heal him at any cost." Again his voice was rife with sudden comprehension that she found distressing. He couldn't understand. He thought he did, but no one truly understood.

"Aye! But you don't understand. I should have told him—it's my fault! If I'd told him long ago, it wouldn't have gone on. If I hadn't been so stupid and scared. I have to tell him or—or—"

"Or what?" He watched her intently.

She put her hands to the sides of her head, fingers curling into her hair. "I know not."

"It won't happen again. It *can't* happen again. You're a woman now, a strong, clever one." He climbed a step so they were nearly eye to eye. He took her hands and pulled them away from her face. "If the man who did this to you were still alive, I would kill him—after breaking every bone in his body—then maybe healing him so I could do it again. *Then* I'd kill him."

Rose put her arms around his neck and buried her face in his shoulder. His arms came around her waist, holding her close. She loved him. It rose inside her, sweet and piercing. She hugged him tighter. She'd thought that maybe she'd fallen in love with him the first time she'd met him, when he'd pretended to be a groom, but she was certain of it now. She wanted to tell him how she felt but couldn't place that burden on him. He'd made his position clear. If she carried their relationship any further, she'd suffer the consequences in silence. She thought that perhaps she was willing, just to be with him.

Heart pounding madly, she pulled back, looking into his eyes, letting him see that she wanted him. She slid her fingers into the soft hair at his nape, memorizing the silken slide of his hair, the lambent sapphire of his eyes, the austere line of his mouth, the mouth that could be so soft and warm. . . .

She knew the moment he understood what she was about. His breathing grew uneven, his gaze falling to her mouth as his throat worked. His fingers flexed into her waist. She leaned forward, holding his face, the scrape of whiskers against her palms, and she kissed him. His mouth opened beneath hers, warm and sweet and full of promise.

Approaching footsteps echoed in the stairwell. Rose pulled away from him. His fingers clung to her arisaid for a moment, his expression thunderous with frustration, then he let her go. His mouth curved into a sardonic smile and he gestured for her to precede him.

Rose hurried up the stairs again, her heart still racing, her body flushed with anticipation, the sensation of his fingers on her waist still burning. When she reached the landing, she turned to find a frowning Jamie appear behind them.

His suspicious gaze darted from Rose to William as the three of them stood on the landing. "I didn't hear you on the stairs until just a second ago."

William arched a brow. "Well, obviously we were there."

"Aye, but the countess said you'd left a few moments before I arrived at your chambers—not *seconds* before.

Besides . . . I would have seen you leaving. What were you doing on the stairs?"

Rose's heart beat furiously against her ribs, now with fear of discovery. She had no intention of marrying Jamie, but neither would she be marrying William. Jamie hated him enough without adding cuckold to the list of crimes. And if she did indulge in an indiscretion with the Wizard of the North, she had every intention of keeping it discreet.

"I'm coming to see my uncle and nephew. What do you think I was doing?"

He again looked from William to Rose, his expression skeptical, then he moved forward, taking Rose's elbow and pulling her to the door, his body a barrier between her and William. As he pounded on the door, Rose said, "I'm feeling much better now, thank you for asking."

The look he sent her was part irritation, part embarrassment. "Forgive . . . I'm pleased your ailment has passed." The door opened as he glanced at William over his shoulder. "So it was not the wizard's curse that struck you down?"

Rose's laugh was tinged with contempt. "How absurd! Who said such a thing?"

Roderick stood in the doorway. "Rose!" He seemed surprised to see her there. His gaze darted to Jamie, then behind them to William. "What are you doing here? You shouldn't be out of bed."

"I'm fine." Rose peered around him into the room. It was strangely empty, at least what she could see of it; the furnishings and rugs were gone. Tira's carved and padded chair was usually evident from the doorway. The small table that held her silver bell and embroidery basket was gone, too.

"Can we come in?"

Her uncle hesitated. He'd not opened the door all the way, and now he stepped out of the room, closing the door behind him. "Not now. Liam is sleeping."

"Liam?" Rose said. "Is that what you named him?"

He nodded solemnly. "Aye, Liam Roderick."

She touched her uncle's arm. "I'm so sorry about Aunt Tira."

Roderick took her hand and squeezed it. "Fash not, lass. I ken you did all you could. She's in a better place now."

"What happened?" she asked. "After the birth? I thought Tira was fine. She even spoke to me. What happened?"

He shook his head sadly. "Same thing that killed my other wives, it seems. All the bleeding. Hilda told me what a difficult birth it was. She went on and on about what a fine midwife you are, Rose, saving Liam's life. She said I could've lost them both, but you—"

"Uncle Roderick?" Rose interrupted, perturbed by the way truth kept twisting. "There's been a misunderstanding. *I* didn't save Liam. He was not breathing when I finally delivered him. Lord Strathwick healed him . . . that's why he collapsed afterward. Healing is . . . traumatic."

Roderick went very still. Though he didn't move a muscle, his gaze lifted to look at the man standing behind Jamie and Rose.

"He healed the wean, you say?" Jamie said, his voice rife with skepticism.

She slanted Jamie an irritated look. "Aye—I was there. I saw it. So was Hilda. Ask her."

Roderick's arms were crossed over his chest, and he brought one hand up to rub over his copper-stubbled mouth. "No, Hilda saw nothing. She thinks you did all."

"Then why would William collapse?"

"You collapsed, too," Roderick pointed out.

"Did you just address him familiar?" Jamie cried, his square jaw bulging. "William, it is now? What *were* you doing on the stairs, aye?"

"Nothing," Rose said, exasperated. "We are friends."

"Friends," he sneered. "I will not take your seconds, Wizard—and you, wench, will not speak to me in that tone."

William had him against the wall, forearm to his throat, eyes narrowed threateningly. "You are the one whose tone begs explanation."

Jamie tried to shrug him off, his teeth bared. "Unhand me!"

William shoved his arm harder into Jamie's throat until he made a choking noise. William's voice was calm when he spoke. "Rose has been patient with you, and you've been naught but rude. There is great friendship between Rose and me. Nothing more. You doubt her honor again and we shall meet somewhere dark and alone."

He released Jamie and stepped back. The younger man's face reddened with fury, and his hand gripped his dirk hilt. Rose looked between the two glowering men, wide-eyed and stunned from what had just happened. Jamie looked at Roderick, then his scornful gaze fell on Rose before returning to William. "This isn't over, Wizard—not by far."

He stalked to the stairs. At the top step he turned, fixing Rose with a hateful glare. "The betrothal is off!"

Rose resisted the urge to cry *Good riddance* at his retreating back. She turned back to her uncle with a heavy sigh.

He leaned against the door, arms crossed over his chest and copper brows hiked to his hairline. "Well!"

William sighed. "If he wasn't my enemy before—"

"Oh, aye," Roderick said. "He is now. The MacKays and the MacPhersons will be feuding in earnest after this, I'll wager."

"Will you talk to him?" Rose asked her uncle. "He promised me he would not fight with William at Lochlaire, but I think all promises are off now. Make him leave?"

Roderick nodded. "I'll do what I can . . . but you never did say why you collapsed, if he's the one doing the healing." He nodded to William with his chin.

Rose placed a hand on her uncle's arm. "That's what I wanted to tell you. I'm like William. He sees the colors, too—only he can use them to heal. And I discovered . . . or *thought* I discovered"—disappointment constricted her throat again—"that I could, too. Aunt Tira *was* dying. I did as William showed me and took it into myself. I suffered with her pain. And I heard her, Uncle Roderick. She spoke to me . . . I was so sure I succeeded." Her shoulders slumped.

Her uncle stared at her, plucking at his bottom lip with his fingers, the whites of his eyes showing.

"Forgive me," Rose said, realizing her clumsiness. "You're mourning her, and I stand here twisting a knife in the wound."

"It's . . . fine." He turned partially away, his gaze darting from William to Rose. "I . . . need to rest, I think." He disappeared into his chambers and latched the door.

Rose turned to stare dejectedly up at William. "I should have stayed in bed."

William stared at the door, his brow furrowed. "Your uncle wasn't very happy to discover you can heal."

"Why should he be? He probably doesn't even believe me. Tira's dead, after all. I'm the only one who believes she survived." Rose shook her head, confusion warring with all she'd heard. "But I vow, William, I heard her and she was well, not dying, her voice strong. What could have happened?"

"*I* believe you." He placed his hands on her shoulders, his gaze earnest. "And I know not what happened, but you *must* stop addressing me familiar."

"You asked me to."

He smiled wryly. "I know. It was unwise of me."

"I don't care. You're leaving anyway, aren't you? I will call you William until you leave, if it pleases you."

"It doesn't please me for you to make an enemy of MacPherson."

Rose gazed up at him, her heart in her eyes. "I wasn't going to marry him anyway."

He did not reply to that; he only stared down into her eyes, his mouth a hard line. He did not appear pleased by her revelation.

She took a step closer to him so that mere inches separated their bodies. "Did you mean what you said before? That there was nothing more than friendship between us?"

He dropped his hands from her shoulders and took a step back. "A pathetic lie, and you know it."

She walked around him, her arm and hand brushing his, her little finger twining with his as she passed. He lifted his hand to extend the tingling contact of their skin. At the stairs she turned and looked back at him over her shoulder. He still stood before the door, staring after her. The darkness in his eyes was unmistakable. Lust.

She smiled. "Come to my chambers, tonight—after midnight."

And she left, before he could refuse.

In her father's chambers, Rose was pleased to see that Conan was not on the bed. But as she crossed the room, she spotted the small dog on the rug beside the bed. She gave Hagan a cross look.

"What did I tell you?"

The Irishman shrugged. "Fash not. Alan cannot get him to jump on the bed. We've been trying, but the dog has developed a sudden aversion to it or his master."

Rose harrumphed, still displeased the guard continued to disobey her. "I'll be taking Conan with me when I leave this time."

Her father was awake and seemed well. His color was good, and he sat propped against pillows, rather than sunk down and barely able to hold up his head. They talked some about Roderick's son and Tira's death, then Rose told him what had happened with Jamie.

"He said the betrothal is off."

Alan considered her silently. "You don't seem terribly upset."

Rose shrugged. "I'm not, though I worry he will seek revenge."

"I thought you loved him."

Rose rolled her eyes. "I never said I *loved* him. I had fond memories and his letters were sweet. In truth, I cannot believe he wrote them now, at least not with me in mind. He finds me repulsive."

"Oh, leave off!" her father said, incredulous. "That's the daftest thing I've ever heard."

"Well, it's true. He came down to the village when I was healing and bocked after I drained an abscess. Then he acted as if I had the plague and wouldn't touch me. The only reason he wanted me at all was because of Lord Strathwick."

Alan stroked his thick gray beard. "Because he thinks the wizard fancies you?"

"Aye. He didn't want Strathwick to have anything that was *his*."

Alan studied her, his expression guarded.

"Why do you look at me so?" she asked.

"Is there any basis to MacPherson's jealousy?"

Rose blinked serenely at her father. "No."

He didn't look convinced; his eyes narrowed slightly, then he sighed. Rose continued to be impressed by the improvement in him and hoped it was due to the protective spell she and her sisters had placed on him. If it was witchcraft that ailed him, the spell would protect him until they discovered the culprit.

"Did you have nightmares last night?" she asked, passing her hands over him. His color was still weak but stronger than it had been the last time she'd checked.

He shook his head, then reached his hand out to her, palm up. Rose placed her hand in his.

"I wish you wouldn't take so much on yourself. I'm an old man—"

"You're not—"

"And old men have to die sometime. Let it go, love. You've done all you can. What more can you do? Move on. Marry a man of your choosing. What about this Strathwick fellow?"

"I just told you there was nothing between us but friendship. And you're not going to die. Look how long you've hung on. Soon Sir Philip will be back with Sir Donnan, and he will remove the curse. All will be well."

"Will it? Is that all that troubles you, love? My illness? Or is it something more that shadows your eyes when you look at me?"

Rose averted her gaze, fixing it on the silver terrier curled on the rug and staring unblinkingly at her. Sometimes Alan MacDonell saw too much.

"Talk to me, Rose."

And suddenly she wanted to. It pressed at her chest, wanting out, but she bit back the words, refusing to burden a sick man, knowing that telling him now and seeing the pain it caused him would only make her feel worse.

"There is nothing, Da . . . except . . . would it make you terribly angry if I never wed?"

He blinked at her, surprised. "But I thought you wanted to."

"I did . . . maybe I still do. But let's not do it this way— rushing a wedding because you think you're dying."

"But I want you looked after when I'm gone."

"I will be. I have two wonderful brothers-in-law who will let no harm befall me. And there is always Hagan."

"I'll protect her," the Irishman promised. He was a constant, silent presence in the room. Often Rose forgot he was there.

"I know you will," Alan said. He sighed unhappily. "But I'd like to see her with a family." His troubled gaze turned back to Rose. "You work so hard, Rose. You seem so unhappy."

"I'm not," she assured him emphatically. "I vow it. I love healing . . . and Jamie told me he didn't want me to do it anymore once we were wed. I don't want a husband like that."

Alan sighed again, still squeezing her hand. "We'll talk more on this later, aye? Let me think about it."

They spoke of other things until his eyelids began to droop. Then Rose gathered Conan under her arm and left, closing the door softly behind her.

Chapter 16

❧❧❧

William paced restlessly around the small chamber, his gaze continuously straying to the hour candle. Not yet midnight. Drake sprawled on the bed watching William with a knowing smile, a goblet of wine in his hand. Deidra slept at the foot of the bed.

"Why don't you go to sleep?" William asked irritably.

"I'm not tired." When William shot him a narrow gaze, Drake added, "I thought I might visit that bonny scullery maid—"

"Nay, you must stay here tonight."

Drake propped himself up on an elbow, black brows raised. "Really? Why? Do you mean to say that *you* won't be here? Have you an assignation?"

"It's not an assignation . . . not really."

"Then what is it?" William did not respond, so Drake pressed, "Is your 'not really an assignation' with Rose?"

William went to the window and stared out at the moon. "I should not go."

"Jesus God. Aye, you should! Go! I pray you."

William glowered at his brother for a moment over his shoulder before returning his attention to the open window. He shouldn't go. He knew what would happen, and it was wrong. She might not marry MacPherson, but she would eventually marry someone. He couldn't ruin her. But God, did he want to. He would go to her but to tell her that they should not. He closed his eyes and rubbed his lids with thumb and forefinger. An unlikelier scenario he could not imagine. If he went to her chambers, he would bed her.

Behind him he heard Drake leave the bed. "She told me she could heal, just like you."

"Aye, I thought she could. But the woman is dead."

"Why then was she so ill? It's just like you."

William shrugged. "I know. It makes little sense."

"Perhaps she just needs more tutelage. You're the only one who can teach her—but you can't do that at Strathwick unless she's there, too."

William gritted his teeth. "I've told you—"

"Aye, you have, but that was before, and though I didn't like it, at least I understood it. There's no sense to this. She's like you, Will . . . it's as if the two of you were somehow meant to meet and be together."

William turned to give his brother a mocking look. "How very sentimental of you."

"I know!" Drake drained his wine goblet. "You're making me soft, so I pray you, stop being an ass and go to the woman. You've been in a foul humor since MacPherson arrived. You say you can't have her but you won't leave her be—and worse, you act like a baited bear, growling at everyone."

William grunted. "I haven't been growling."

Drake made a rude noise. "Aye, you have, and I'm

damn sick of it. Go to her. There's two of you now—no more choices, aye?"

Wasn't that what she'd said to him? *There is no need for choices anymore. There's two of us now.* Though her words gave him hope, Tira was still dead, and that scared the hell out of him. But he found, as he stared out the window, that returning to Strathwick and resuming his empty life frightened him more.

"If I lose her . . . like Amber . . . I don't think I can bear it." His jaw hardened. He stared down at his hand fisted on the stone sill. "I love her."

"If you love her, you have to go."

William glanced back at the hour candle. It was time. Drake looked at the candle, too, then back at William expectantly. "*Go*, man—get out of here!"

William left, trying to ignore his brother's gloating. He paused outside the door. The corridor was deserted, and most of the torches had been extinguished. He passed no one on his way, and when he finally arrived, he did not waste time knocking. He let himself in and latched the door behind him.

He scanned the room. Rose was nowhere in sight, though a small terrier sat in the middle of the bed, a pink ribbon in its long, silvery hair. Then he saw her. She appeared in the doorway of an adjoining room.

"You came," she said.

"Aye." His blood quickened just to look at her. Her hair hung loose over her shoulders, a gleaming curtain of auburn satin. She wore only a night rail, elaborately embroidered at the neck and hem, the sleeves heavy with lace.

At the sight of her, all the things he'd wanted to say dissolved into lust. Later, he would remember, but for now . . . He crossed the room to where she stood. The fragrance of herbs wafted around her, coming from the dark room behind her.

Rose had been afraid he wouldn't come, but now that he was here, she could not think of what to do or say. She'd been so bold on the stairs, when it had just been an idea. The reality of his presence in her room held her immobile. She gazed up into his eyes, her throat tight with anticipation.

Then he touched her hair, his fingers twining in it, pushing it over her shoulder.

"Do you know why I'm here?"

She nodded.

His gaze burned through her, made her knees weak. "I don't think you do. I'm here because I didn't have any other choice."

She blinked up at him. "You didn't have to come if you didn't want."

"It's not about wanting anymore. Before, I was afraid of having to choose . . . but it's out of my hands now. I choose you."

What was he saying? She was afraid to ask. Her hands came up, curling into the snowy linen of his shirt. She whispered his name, pulling him down to kiss her. His mouth met hers in a searing kiss that deepened immediately, his tongue exploring, then demanding. He tasted rich and forbidding. Instant fire raced across her senses, leaving her breathless with want. She twined her arms around his neck, savoring his mouth, eager to finish what they'd begun on the battlements. He pressed her back, but there was nothing there but the open door. They stumbled backward, into the dark and fragrant room. The small of her back bumped into the table. His hands slid to her waist and lifted her, setting her on the table. Rose carelessly pushed her instruments and books aside, and some of them fell to the ground.

"That's better," he said, his voice rough as he moved between her welcoming thighs. He was so warm and big. She pulled him into her, hooking her calf behind his leg as he set his mouth on hers again. Her heart beat thick and painful, her body alive everywhere he touched her. She felt faint from his mouth, kissing and kissing her until all will and thought dissipated into sweet sensation.

He touched her through her shift, his palms sliding sensuously over ribs and breasts before fumbling with the ties and finally ripping them. The shift slipped from her shoulders. She pulled at the ties on his shirt until he shrugged out of it and his chest was bared to her. She brushed the warm curve of muscle and smooth skin with her fingertips. He made a soft, rough sound and drove her head back in another kiss, long and hot, as he pressed himself hard between her thighs. He pushed her night rail up, stroking her thighs, so all that separated them was the wool of his trews, sparking a melting, urgent pain at her center. Her breath caught and her hips rolled hard into him, wanting more.

He murmured her name as he rained fervent kisses over her eyes and nose and cheeks. His hands roved over the bare skin of her shoulders and back. She shuddered against him, trying to press closer, to reclaim his mouth on hers, but he'd moved lower, licking and sucking at her neck as his hands slid around to her breasts.

Her head fell back, her hands threading through his hair as the tip of his tongue played with her nipple. Her breath hitched, the heat swirling through her, urgent now. She pressed his head closer. He complied with her silent request and drew deep on her nipple. Pleasure speared to her core. She arched into him with a breathless cry. He lavished more attention on her breasts, until she moaned her need, her hands working at his belt until it fell to the floor with a thump.

He caught her wrists when she tried to unlace his trews. Thwarted at her task, she gazed up at him hungrily. His eyes blazed his desire. So why did he stop her? She pulled her hand away and stroked her palm against the hard bulge. He groaned and pressed his forehead against hers, his hands gripping her shoulders.

"Not here," he said. His hands spanned her waist to lift her off the table.

"Aye, right here," she whispered, and when she pulled at the ties again, he let her, his chest straining, sweat gleaming on the hard, tense muscles of his shoulders. It was perfect here, a longed-for moment with the man she loved, imprinted forever in this dark, fragrant room, surrounded by the comforting scents of bittersweet and mallow, horehound and lavender.

She rubbed her hand over him until his body shuddered and he made a raw, wordless sound in his chest. His mouth sought hers again, hands sliding beneath her shift, touching the damp curls between her thighs. She jerked at the sudden contact, the bliss of it nearly blinding her. His wicked fingers stroked and probed until she thought she'd die from the desperate throbbing. Her breath came in little pants. She wanted him inside her. She pressed her palm hard against his erection and he grew wild, pulling her hard against his chest. Rose's thighs gripped him as she moved her hips against him, urging him to take her, to fill her, to complete her.

The head of him pushed against her damp curls and her breath caught, exquisite need spiraling through her, the promise of sweet oblivion, and she wanted more. She moved again so the tip of him pressed against her entrance. But he held back, the muscles all along his arms and shoulders bunched with strain.

"God, Rose . . ."

"Please," she whispered. Then she took his earlobe between her teeth. He tasted good, salt and spice, and she wanted all of him. He shuddered violently but still didn't move—his hands braced against the table's edge, as if holding himself back, ready to push away, but arrested in the moment.

"Our first time shouldn't be like this." His breath blew hot against her neck.

"Aye, it should be just like this," she whispered in his ear. "I'm no innocent, William—I know what I want and I want this."

He made a harsh sound behind his gritted teeth, then the fine thread of his control snapped and he pressed into her.

She cried his name on an exhalation as he entered her, the sweetness of it already pulsing through her. His hands moved beneath her knees, lifting them higher over his hips before sliding under her buttocks so she could take him deeper.

He kissed her hard as he drove into her again and again, touching something deep, sending pleasure beating through her, swelling tighter. She thought her heart would burst from it as she moved with him, her breath burning her throat. She tore her mouth away as her crisis was wrenched from her, wave after wave flowing over her.

"Oh God, Rose . . ." His voice was raw. He ground his hips into hers, his teeth sinking into the tender skin of her neck as deep tremors racked him. Rose held him tightly to her until the desperate passion began to fade.

His forehead pressed into her shoulder and his hands still gripped her thighs. Their sweat mingled where their bodies touched. The sound of his breathing was loud in her ear, and then his hands tightened on her. He swore— a vile word that caused her to wince.

He swore again, pulling gingerly away from her and yanking his trews closed. He ran a hand through his damp hair.

She felt exposed suddenly and pushed her night rail down, sliding off the table. The top hung around her waist and she pulled it up, holding it closed with her hand to hide her nakedness. She felt cold and weak and uncertain. She could feel the remnants of their passion between her thighs, and her stomach took a sharp dip at the knowledge it could result in a child. She shouldn't hope for it, but she did.

He covered his face with his hands, his shoulders rising and falling heavily. Finally he turned to her, dropping his hands to his sides. "I'm sorry, Rose . . . Jesus God, I know not what I was thinking . . . I wasn't thinking . . . ruled by my god damned cock."

Rose stared at him, her bafflement growing. "What do you mean? It's what I wanted. It's why I asked you to come to me."

He waved a hand at her, his face tight with remorse. "I should have been gentle . . . after . . . well, *after*. God damn it." He stalked from the little room, full of self-recrimination again, and Rose understood. Immediately her eyes burned and her throat tightened. She hurried after him.

"William! It's not what you think."

When he turned to stare at her, hands on hips, she raised her brows and sighed. "I'd not meant to tell you this way. I meant to tell you before to fash not on ruining me—that I'd already been ruined."

He rubbed a hard hand over his eyes as if he couldn't bear to look at her. "Aye, I know. The MacLeans."

"Well, aye, but not how you're thinking. Fagan MacLean . . . did things to me, aye, things that make me sick and angry still . . . but not *that*. It was his son, Donald, and I was a willing party. It was three years ago . . . I was seventeen." He stared at her now, and it was she who had to look away, sick with shame. "I don't know why I did it . . . I suppose I thought I loved him at the time . . . and I wanted him to love me back."

He touched her chin, lifting her face so she looked at him. "That is not why a man loves a woman." Her neck and cheeks burned, and she tried to pull her chin away. He held her firm. "It's not why I love you."

Her gaze caught in his. She was so surprised to hear

the words from him. Her heart swelled with happiness. She had hoped he felt as she did, but she hadn't believed he'd ever admit it—to her or himself.

"And I love you," she said. "I wanted to be with you tonight before you leave here forever, but I didn't think you'd come to me just to talk."

He pulled her hard against his chest, wrapping his arms around her. She hugged him back. He buried his face in her hair, his voice muffled. "God, Rose, I would have come just to talk to you. Whatever you wanted."

She closed her eyes, inhaling the warm scent of his skin. "Really?"

"I don't know. I can't seem to keep my hands off you, so maybe not."

She laughed softly. "I'm glad. I want your hands on me."

She led him to the bed and tried to run the dog off, but Conan only retreated to the foot, his shiny black eyes watching them. Rose pulled William down beside her, and he held her close. He made love to her again, slowly this time, touching her everywhere and whispering words of love. Afterwards Rose relaxed in the strength of his arms and let everything slip away, all her cares and worries. She wanted to lie like this forever.

She thought he'd fallen asleep until he asked, "Tell me about your years on Skye."

Still held fast in his embrace, Rose stared blankly into the dimness of the room. "There is little to tell. I apprenticed under Crisdean Beaton until he died. I ran away once . . . my father sent me back, and I was Fagan MacLean's healer until he died." It was a sterile, emotionless account, and she knew it would not satisfy him.

"Fagan is who mistreated you?" he asked.

"Aye."

He propped himself on his elbow to gaze down at her. "Why did you never tell anyone?"

Rose bit the inside of her lip and averted her eyes, embarrassed suddenly at her own foolishness.

He caressed her bare arm and shoulder as he gently prodded, "How did he threaten you, Rose?"

"He . . . used to make me touch him . . . he told me it was Crisdean's orders, that I was to learn about the male body. This went on for some time before I told Crisdean that I thought I'd learned everything there was to know about it and I'd like to stop the lessons. He was surprised, and that's when I knew he didn't know. Not that he cared. He didn't like me at first anyway— thought women should stick to midwifing." She shuddered, swallowing a wave of revulsion. "After that, I told Fagan I wouldn't do it anymore. He said if I stopped or ever told anyone else, he would have my sisters and I burned as witches . . . I didn't realize then that we were all hidden and he didn't know where they were. I also didn't know how much my father paid him each year for my maintenance—most of which I did not see, either." She closed her eyes and shook her head. "I was so stupid . . . he couldn't touch my sisters, and he'd never have given up the yearly payments from my father. I wasn't thinking."

"Jesus, Rose, you were a child whose mother had just been burned alive. He was a god dammed filthy bastard for saying those things. It's no wonder you said nothing."

Rose opened her eyes. His face was hard and angry as

he stared down at her. Angry for her. She said, "But I did tell . . . eventually. I told his wife."

His breathing paused. "Aye? What happened then?"

She snorted bitterly. "She called me a liar and a whore. Told me I made her sick and she'd throw me out with nothing if I kept spreading such lies." William's muscles tensed beneath her face and hands. "But she believed me. I didn't realize it at the time, though I do now. She must have said something to him because he never made me touch him again after that, and he treated me with pure loathing. If not for Crisdean and the money, I think she might have had me burned." Her jaw clenched as she remembered it all. How Fagan would yell at her and call her names and throw things at her as she tended him when he grew ill. "I took care of him until he died."

"Why?" William said on an incredulous breath.

Her heart cankered at the ugly memory. "Because I caught him trying to use a servant lass as he did me. She was nine. After that I would let no one else tend him."

William rolled over, pushing her back on the bed and looking into her face. "You have naught to be ashamed of, Rose."

She stared up at him, tears tracking the sides of her face. She touched the wetness, surprised to find she'd been crying for some time. She'd never told anyone before. She'd been filled with shame and twisted fury. William was the only one who knew now, and he was not disgusted with her.

"And I think you should tell your father," he said, his expression grave. "You will be angry with him until you do. And if he dies, you might never stop being angry. Tell him."

She caught her bottom lip with her teeth. Maybe he was right, but she didn't know if she could. She tried to imagine telling her father what she'd just told William, and her mind shied away, afraid.

"I will think about it," she said carefully.

That seemed to satisfy him. He pressed a kiss to her forehead. "I should go," he murmured against her skin, "before someone discovers us." But he made no move to leave. He continued to cradle her, his lips pressed to her temple.

"No." Rose slid her arms around his neck and held him fast. "I don't care. Stay with me tonight."

He hesitated a moment, then sank back into the mattress beside her. She turned into his arms, snuggling deeper, content as she'd never been before and feeling a bit guilty for her happiness. With her father still so ill, it seemed wrong for her to be lying here, lazing in her lover's arms. But what else could they do but wait for Sir Philip to return with Sir Donnan? As she was drifting to sleep, Conan crept up between them, as close as he could get, and settled between their knees.

Jamie MacPherson slumped against the table in his chambers, his head thick and sluggish with whisky. Someone tapped at the door, and Jamie's man opened it. There was some murmuring, then the scrape of a stool.

With great effort, he raised his head, squinting at his guest. It was the uncle.

"What do you want?" Jamie's speech was slurred. He cleared his throat and made himself sit up straighter, though he still felt himself swaying gently.

The usually jovial uncle was very grave. "I want to make amends afore you leave in the morn. Your quarrel is with Rose and Strathwick, not with me. I will soon be chieftain of the Glen Laire MacKays, and I want no feud with the MacPhersons."

"Too late."

"Is it?"

Jamie tried to fasten his gaze on him, but the red-haired man swam in and out of focus. "What mean you?"

Roderick considered him. "What if I can give you your revenge?"

Jamie's brows drew together in confusion.

"The wizard and his family. I want him dead, too—"

"Why do you want him dead?"

"Because he killed my wife."

Jamie scratched at his head. This conversation wasn't making sense. "I thought she died in childbirth."

Roderick leaned forward, blue eyes fierce. "Rose told me she was alive after Liam's birth, so Strathwick must have killed her. I have been to the next village, right outside the glen. There is a witchpricker there. I have told him a witch has come to Glen Laire. The villagers had suspected something of the sort, as their oats were struck with a plague, so hearing a traveling witchpricker was near, they asked him to root out the witch. I hinted to the elders that if they take care of the witch, we will make sure they are well supplied with oats through the winter."

Jamie felt as if he were underwater, the uncle's words not quite penetrating his mind, his body swaying in the thick current.

"You want me to give them oats?"

The uncle's jaw hardened, and he looked skyward for a moment. "Try to follow. You will have your revenge on Strathwick. He is with Rose now, in her bed."

Black fury shot through Jamie, and he tried to stand, stumbling and falling against the table. "That blackguard! The whore!"

The uncle was beside him, his hand on Jamie's shoulder, urging him back down on his stool.

"Save it. Save the hate. Use it. He will have to leave her sometime. Your task is to make certain he and his daughter make it to the next village and into the hands of the witchpricker."

Jamie nodded, his fury clearing away some of the drunken fog. "Witchpricker. Next village."

"Good. Rest now. I have someone watching her chambers. I will alert you when he leaves."

William woke with a start, gasping for air. Something sat on his chest, crushing him. He could not move at first, but with a great effort he thrust his arm out. Nothing was there. He found himself swiping frantically at naught but air. He propped himself up on his arm, panting. A nightmare. Nothing more.

When his heart slowed, he put his hand on the woman sleeping beside him. In the gray predawn light he could make out the curve of her cheek, the sweep of lashes. He was not sorry about what they'd done. He wanted her with him always. He only hoped she wouldn't find more unhappiness at Strathwick.

He yawned so wide that his jaw cracked. He was surprised by how tired he was. His limbs felt leaden. He started to sink back into the bed when he thought of his daughter. He should be in his chambers when she woke. He dragged himself from the bed, dislodging the dog sleeping between them. It resettled itself against Rose's belly. He found his clothes and dressed slowly, lethargically, finally pulling his shirt over his head and looping his sword belt over his shoulder, too tired to actually buckle it on.

He returned to the bed and leaned over it, pressing a kiss to Rose's closed eyelid. "I'll be back," he whispered, but she did not wake.

The castle was silent, and when he arrived at his chambers he slipped in, heedful not to wake his brother and daughter. The room was completely dark. He wondered who'd let the fire die. He felt his way to the shutters and pulled them open, then lit a candle. He was turning toward the bed when he noticed something on his wrist. He pulled his sleeve up. A dark bruise in the shape of a star mottled the inside of his forearm. He frowned at it for several moments, then pressed on it. Touching it caused him no discomfort. He never bruised—and besides, he couldn't remember when he'd hit his arm. He turned to the bed, still puzzled.

Drake was asleep, buried under mounds of blankets. William crept to the bed to check on his daughter. She still slept at the end, beneath a plaid. As he watched, she twitched, then writhed, her face contorting.

"Deidra." He touched her cheek.

Her face was flushed and damp with sweat. She began to retch violently, her eyes rolled back in her head.

"Drake!" William barked. "Get me the chamber pot!"

But his brother didn't move. William swore and lifted his daughter into his arms. She began to cough and choke, her face turning an alarming shade of purple. William checked her color to see if he could heal her, but his examination showed nothing amiss, except a weakening of her color.

He clutched her to his chest, frantic. She was so small and frail. Her entire body jerked and spasmed with each heave, bringing nothing up. Her eyes sprang open, and she wheezed, gasping and gagging and clawing at her throat. She was dying.

William was vaguely aware that he alternately prayed under his breath and pleaded with his brother to help. He lay Deidra on the bed and forced her mouth wider, but he could see nothing in her throat. His heart stuttered as she continued to gag and make soundless noises as if she were choking, her eyes bulging and bloodshot. Her back arched, and her heels dug into the mattress. William thrust a finger down her throat, searching for the obstruction. He felt something stiff and narrow. He grasped it and quickly yanked it out.

It was a damp feather. Deidra immediately went limp, her head rolling to the side. He lowered his head beside hers, and relief washed over him when he felt her soft, warm breath against his cheek. She had choked on a feather. It made no sense. He should have seen and felt the feather in her throat when he'd examined her with his magic. And besides that, how the hell did a sleeping child manage to get a feather stuck in her throat? . . . *Witchcraft.*

He went to Drake and tried to shake him awake, but

his brother was as unresponsive as Deidra. Fingers of panic clutched at William's chest. He was afraid to leave them, and yet this was no ailment. This was black magic. A warning.

Fear had temporarily staved off his lassitude, but he felt it returning, weighing down his limbs. He didn't have time for weakness. He threw open the door, searching for a servant, someone to send to fetch Rose to him, but the corridor was deserted. He started to return to the bed, leaving the door open, when he spotted a piece of parchment on the floor just outside the door. It was sealed with a blob of black wax with no mark.

He picked it up, peering up and down the corridor again. After checking on his brother and Deidra and finding them the same, he broke the seal.

Your brother will wake at dawn. Your daughter will be released from the curse when you are clear of Glen Laire's mountains. Be quit from Lochlaire within an hour of dawn, and speak to no one, or your daughter will bock up pins until she bleeds to death. I wonder if you can heal that.

William read the letter over and over again, then looked at the star-shaped bruise on his arm. The task he'd sent Sir Philip on was futile. The witch was here at Lochlaire—and he had to leave or let his daughter die. He thought of Rose, waking and finding him gone. He closed his eyes, crumpling the parchment in his fists. Finally he dropped it onto the bed, staring at the open window. The gray of predawn burned off into the pink light of daybreak. Drake groaned, rubbing his hand over his face and pushing himself up to sitting. He groaned again, dropping his head into his hands.

"My head aches like someone spent the night hammering on it. I didn't drink that much."

William tossed him the letter.

Drake read it quickly. His brow furrowed, then his gaze shot to the window. "Who the hell—"

"Never mind that," William said. "Gather our things. We must be gone from here or Deidra dies."

Chapter 17

❧

The wizard watched from the battlements as the skiff containing Strathwick, his brother, and the unconscious witch-child rowed across the loch. Perfect. He left the battlements and returned to the hall. It was deserted. By now the Irishman would be too sick to notice anyone coming or going. Everything was progressing as planned.

He slipped into Alan MacDonell's chambers and was greeted by the sound of Hagan retching violently and groaning behind the painted screen across the room. Conan was gone of course, courtesy of Rose. That had *not* been part of his plan, but it was of no consequence.

He paused to make certain Alan still slept. He was motionless on the bed, oblivious to his guard's infirmity. It had been most difficult to get Hagan to ingest the purgative without somehow implicating himself in it. The guard had become even more diligent since Strathwick had suggested witchcraft. Irritation pricked at him. That had been another small rut he'd not planned for. No one had seriously suspected witchcraft until the wizard of the North had arrived. Now Isobel was determined to touch every damn thing in the castle, and Gillian hunted daily for ghosts. He might have made a mistake somewhere; he'd been arrogant before, secure in their trust. If he did not end this now, he would be discovered.

He crossed the room quickly, grabbing a pillow off the end of the bed. He stared down at Alan's sleeping face. So many years he'd languished under Alan's shadow, watching him pass up opportunities to expand the wealth and power of the Glen Laire MacDonells. No more.

He pressed the pillow over the sleeping man's face. Alan reacted immediately and with more strength than the man had anticipated. He threw his weight onto the pillow and lay there until Alan stopped struggling. He removed the pillow. Alan's mouth hung open, his eyes slitted and glazed.

"No more," the man whispered, triumph beating in his chest.

Then he noticed Alan's beard. It sparkled faintly in the firelight, as did the blankets covering him. He frowned, leaning closer—but there was no time to investigate. The sound of vomiting stopped abruptly, and all that could be heard was heavy breathing.

"Alan?" the Irishman called, his voice suspicious.

The man sprinted quietly to the door, taking the pillow with him; he couldn't chance Isobel touching it and seeing everything, and he had no time to place a spell.

"Who's there?" Hagan called, alarm in his voice.

The man slipped out of the room, relieved the hall was still deserted, then hurried to the safety of his chambers, where he waited for someone to bring him the news that the chieftain of the Glen Laire MacDonells was finally dead.

*   *   *

Rose cracked her eyes open. Her head throbbed and her mouth was as dry as straw. It took her a moment to remember all that had occurred. The first memories to assault her were disjointed images from a nightmare but unlike any she'd had before. A creature with horns and batlike wings—a small dragon, perhaps—had sat on her chest. She'd tried to throw it off but had been unable to move, paralyzed as it had sucked the life from her.

Even as she tried to recall the dream it dissipated, replaced by the memory that she had not spent the night alone. Warmth spread through her at those recollections. She turned her head. The pillow beside her was empty. She smoothed her hand over the bed where he had lain, her muscles protesting. Where was he? She wanted to jump out of bed and find him, but she was so very tired that she just lay there, thinking of him, a satisfied smile pulling at her lips.

The morning sun streamed through her open window. She sighed and pushed herself to sitting. Her head spun. Conan rested at the end of the bed, tongue lolling from his mouth. She had no clothes. A shiver rattled her teeth. She was reaching for her torn shift when she noticed that her shoulders were black and blue.

She gasped, holding her arms out to get a better view. Both shoulders and the tops of her forearms were covered with bizarre bruises. Bizarre but not unfamiliar. They were just like her father's bruises. A half moon, a horseshoe. She pressed her fingers to them but felt no pain.

There was a knock on the door. Before she opened her mouth, the door burst open. Rose pulled her shift over her head, covering herself. Isobel stood in the doorway, her hair wild, her face streaked with tears.

"Come quick, Rose! It's Da! The wizard has murdered him!"

Rose sprang to her feet, trying to push the lethargy away, though it still dragged at her. "Dead? No!" She ran down the stairs and through the corridors as if struggling through honey, her breath sawing painfully in her chest and throat. She burst into her father's crowded chambers. Hagan Irish sat by the fire, his head in his big hands and his shoulders shaking with broken sobs. Roderick sat in a chair beside the bed, his son Liam asleep in his wet nurse's arms behind him. Gillian and the earl embraced each other near the bed, and Stephen sat on the bedside, his head bowed. Rose pushed past them all.

"Oh, God, oh God, no," she muttered, forcibly pushing Stephen aside. She touched her father's cheek. It was pale and cool but not the pallor of death. She leaned close to him so her cheek was against his mouth. No breath. She called her magic to her, holding her hands over his body. Roderick grasped her shoulders, murmuring soothing words to her and trying to draw her away.

"No!" she cried, struggling to throw him off but unable in her weakened state. "Wait! He's not dead!"

The room fell silent behind her. Only the sound of the crackling fire could be heard as Roderick's fingers dug into her shoulders. Abruptly, he released her.

"The protection spell," she murmured. "It saved him . . . kept him alive."

But not for much longer. Her father's pale green light had faded to almost nothing, a mere pulsing hue, barely discernable, each pulse further and further apart. His heartbeat. It was slowing, stopping. There was something around his head, a gray film, similar to what she'd seen around Liam's head when the cord had suffocated him, as if the brain were dying.

"Someone get William!" she cried. "Now!"

"We can't," Gillian said beside her, a soft hand on her arm. "He's gone. He left the castle this morning at dawn . . . We believe someone poisoned Hagan. Uncle Roderick saw Strathwick leave Father's room . . . and Hagan was ill this morn. He heard someone in here, and when he came to check on Da . . . this is how he found him."

"Gone." The word rushed out of Rose on a harsh breath. He left? What had he been doing in her father's chambers? She looked back down at her father. He was dying before her eyes. She had no time to worry about William now. She would think of that later.

Rose put her failure with Tira out of her mind and placed her hands over her father's head. She shoved back the lassitude threatening to overcome her and called on her magic as William had taught her. It built inside her, swirling in her chest, a blue sphere, stronger than ever before. Hands were on her again, voices telling her to let him go, it was over, he was dead.

"Leave off!" she shouted, and the hands fell away.

She sent the magic down her arms, into her father. It swirled around the gray film, encircling it, and then she called it back. It rushed up inside her, cutting off her air, blackening her vision. She flailed her arms and felt someone catch her as she fell.

She was in the water of her dream, sinking down and down, except she fought it, struggling to rise to the top, struggling to suck in air. Something pressed over her mouth, smothering her with each inhalation.

"Da! Da!" she could hear herself calling as if from far away.

"Rose? What's wrong with Rose? What happened?" It was her father. Someone gripped her hand, and she felt the blackness, like a dam breaking, trying to flow out of her.

She wrenched her hand away and let the cold black water close over her.

It had taken them the better part of the morning, but by noon, William and Drake emerged on the south side of the narrow mountain pass, Glen Laire behind them. William found a shallow cave, built a fire, and waited.

The longer he waited, the angrier he became. He sat on a flat stone, head in hands, and went through the list of possible suspects. He came back to one person repeatedly. Roderick. Sir Philip was also a possibility, as he inherited if anything happened to Roderick or his son, but Sir Philip wasn't even at Lochlaire, so he could not have written the letter William had found outside his door.

Whoever wrote the letter was not following their end of the bargain. Deidra did not wake. She did not vomit up pins either. Several agonizing hours passed with no change. Finally William stood.

"I'm going back."

"Wait," Drake said, panicked. "What about Deidra? What am I to do if she starts bocking up pins?"

William shook his head, his heart like a stone in his chest. "I know not. *I* cannot even help her if that happens. That's why I have to go back. The only person who can release her is there, in Lochlaire."

Drake didn't protest anymore, but he looked sick with worry. "Be safe, brother."

They clasped hands. "If I don't come back . . ." He looked at his daughter's slack face, his throat and chest constricting. "I *will* come back."

William mounted his horse and left the cave, following the narrow ledge until he reached the mountain pass. He kept a hard hand on the reins as his fear and anger transmitted themselves to his horse. She shook her head, trying repeatedly to dart dangerously forward. At the pass a path led away from the glen, twining down the mountain, obscured in places by sharp boulders and scrub. William turned into the pass, then reined in sharply.

His way was blocked, filled steep wall to steep wall with mounted men, and at the center was Jamie MacPherson. William forced himself not to look back along the cliff to where his daughter and brother hid; he did not want to give their location away.

MacPherson spurred his horse forward, reining in when he came before William. "Where've you been hiding, Wizard?"

William calculated his chances of getting past the men and was not comforted by the odds. "This is between you and me, MacPherson. I'll fight you—just keep your men out of it."

MacPherson smiled. His eyes were bloodshot, and a day's growth of golden stubble glinted on his chin and jaw.

"I'm not interested in a fight anymore, Wizard. You've an engagement with a witchpricker who's verra interested in your magic."

William pulled on his horse's reins, turning it on its hocks to flee down the southern path. He drove his heels into the horse's side just as pain pierced his shoulder. He grabbed it; an arrow haft jutted out. White-hot agony splintered through his arm and chest, but he was still moving, his horse picking her way down the path. He heard the others behind him, following, and wrapped the reins around his hand.

"No!" MacPherson shouted at someone behind him. "No more—I want him alive."

William urged his horse faster, but it wasn't fast enough. He heard a horse closing in on him, then a fist struck out at him, to knock him from his saddle. William grabbed it with his good arm, yanking MacPherson from his horse. The other man snatched at him, and they both went down amid hooves and stones. William fell hard on his wounded shoulder, breaking the arrow haft and jamming the head deeper into his shoulder.

He rolled away, blinded with pain. Hands were on him, yanking him to his feet, twisting his arms behind him.

MacPherson stood before him, grinning malevolently. "Look what we found." He grabbed William's hair and forced him to look up the path. Sweat stung his eyes. He blinked rapidly, clearing his vision. Several of MacPherson's men descended the path on foot, one carrying Deidra, still unconscious, in his arms, two others shoving Drake in front of them.

William pulled at his bindings. "Let them go! They're not witches. You have me, what need you with them?"

"Och, I've heard different, Wizard. I've heard the child is a witch. And as for your brother." MacPherson looked away from William to Drake, who was being shoved roughly down the path. He stumbled and fell to one knee. MacPherson drew his dag from the saddle holster and aimed it at Drake's head.

"Heal this, Wizard."

"No!" William yelled, lurching forward. As the gun discharged, he slammed his forehead into MacPherson's nose. There was a liquid crack. It was enough to throw off MacPherson's aim, but the bullet took Drake in the chest. William watched his brother go down, blood staining his plaid.

"Drake!" William roared, surging forward as hands pulled him back.

MacPherson swung around, blood streaming from his nose, his mouth twisted with fury. "You'll pay for that one, Wizard."

He slammed the hilt of his dag into William's head again and again until he saw nothing else.

"Da!" Rose woke abruptly, the memories of the past few days flooding her the moment she opened her eyes.

"Aye, aye, I'm here."

She looked around, her mouth agape when she saw her father sitting in a chair beside her bed. "Da . . . you're out of bed!"

"Aye, that I am, thanks to you." He looked frail and tired, swaddled in a plaid, but he was here, *in her room*.

She couldn't speak. Her mouth opened and closed, and her vision blurred, but nothing came out. Finally she crumpled forward over her knees, face buried in her hands, and wept. Months of despair flowed out of her, hiccuping sobs gripping her weakened body. Her father was out of bed. He was not dead, like Tira. Every time she thought of his lifeless body and the blackness that had overcome her, she cried harder.

Her father murmured soothing words, distressed by her tears, so after a time Rose marshaled her emotions. She rubbed her hands across her eyes and gave her father an apologetic smile. "Forgive . . . but I had lost hope . . . and here you are, out of bed." Her voice caught, tears threatening to overcome her again.

"Well, don't get too excited. Lord Kincreag and Hagan must take some of the credit, as they practically carried me. But I'm here and it's been months since I left that bed. And it's because of you." He gazed at her, shaking his head in wonder. "Your mum always said to me that you were the strongest of us all. It's not that I didn't believe, love, because I did. I saw it in you every time I looked at you and spoke to you, the iron will. But I didn't understand what she meant. I do now."

Rose stared down at the blanket. "I would never have known what I was capable of if not for William—I mean Lord Strathwick." She shot her father an anxious look. His expression remained gentle and understanding. "He saw it in me and taught me."

"I don't believe he tried to murder me," Alan said. "But I don't know what happened. I was sleeping, then I couldn't breathe. The next thing I remember I was awake, feeling better than I have in months, and you were on the floor beside my bed." He shook his head, his brows drawing together in remembered grief. "Whatever happened, Strathwick was not responsible, of that I'm certain. Hagan wanted to send a man after him, to bring him back for questioning, but I refused. I told them to let him go."

Rose smiled sadly. "Thank you . . . and you're right. He could not have done it."

Her father studied her silently for several moments, then he said, "You love him, aye?"

Rose nodded, another annoying tear escaping to slide down her nose. She swiped it away.

"Then I will send someone after him, to fetch him back to us so he can marry you!"

Rose shook her head. "He knows I love him. He won't marry me. He can't."

"What?" Her father's thick gray brows drew together with indignation. "Is he already married?"

"No . . . he lost his first wife in childbirth . . . but he saved his daughter. He's afraid to go through that again, to be forced to choose, so he pushes people away. In the end, he pushed me away, too. I thought he'd changed his mind . . . but I suppose it just frightened him more." She dashed away her tears and gave her father a tremulous smile. "It's fine . . . I'll always love him, but I understand him, too. Better now than I ever did before."

Her father gazed at her sadly, obviously wanting to give her what she desired. But only William could do that. Perhaps she would write him a letter, tell him how she'd healed her father. Maybe then he would truly believe that he wasn't alone.

The door opened, and a servant bustled in with a tray topped with a steaming bowl of stew and a slab of bread. She set it on the table beside the bed and at a gesture from Alan, left discreetly.

"Here, eat something." He waved to the tray.

Rose's belly rumbled in response to the rich fragrances of beef and rosemary, and she took the stew gratefully.

"I hope you will use this gift wisely," her father said, watching her steadily as she ate.

"What do you mean?"

He leaned forward and reached out his thin, bony hand as if he wanted to touch her. He slumped back and instead touched his own hair, near his forehead. "Your hair . . . it's turning white."

Rose set the stew aside and fingered her hair, pulling a hank of it in front of her. A large quantity of silvery white sprinkled the lock in her hand. She clasped it in both hands, her heart swelling, as if it were some connection to William.

"This healing," her father continued, "is a great effort for you . . . and appears to age you. You cannot heal everyone. Do not try. You are a fine healer without the magic. Only use it when absolutely necessary and for those truly worthy."

Rose nodded, still staring down at the hair in her hand. Her mind turned back to William and the night they'd spent together. Thinking of him was like a hole in her heart, hollow and aching. But he'd said he loved her, and she'd believed him. She still believed him. She remembered what else he'd said to her. *I think you should tell your father. You will be angry with him until you do—and if he dies, you may never stop being angry. Tell him.*

"Da?" she said uncertainly, plaiting the hair in her fingers, eyes focused on her mindless task, not seeing it. "There is something I wish to ask you."

"Aye?" He sounded tired.

She should let him rest, not burden him with more worries. He was not fully recovered. She might have saved him from the latest attack, but there was still a witch trying to murder him. She began to turn those thoughts in her mind. If Sir Donnan wasn't here, then how—

No! Tell him! It was William's voice in her mind, and it strengthened her.

"I know why you sent us away twelve years ago. I didn't understand when I was young, and I was angry—"

Her father chuckled ruefully. "Don't I remember! You would rail at me every time I came to visit at you, begging me to take you home. And then running away!" He looked skyward and shook his head. He was smiling when he looked back at her. His smile faded when she didn't return it.

"Aye, I ran away. And you sent me back. Why?"

He blinked, seemingly at a loss, then said, "It's what your mother wanted, for you to learn from Crisdean Beaton. And you did, did you not? He wrote me what a fine healer you'd become."

Rose sighed, abandoning the plait and staring down at the blanket again. This was harder than she'd thought it would be. "Aye, I learned a great deal from Crisdean. It's just . . ." She closed her eyes. "It's . . . it's nothing. Forget I mentioned it." *Coward.*

"I don't think I can, love. Ever since you've returned

from Skye you've had shadows in your eyes. I thought it was because of my illness and your inability to heal me, but I see it's something else. Tell me what ails you, Rose, and mayhap I can make it better."

She shook her head, eyes still closed tightly. "No, I was wrong. Nothing will make it better . . . except forgetting, trying to put it from my mind."

He was silent for a long moment, then said, "You're scaring me—and me an old sick man. Tell me. Now." When she didn't answer, he said, "You aren't too old to take over my knee."

Rose gave a snort of laughter at that, and when she looked up at him, his gray brows were raised nearly to his hairline.

"Tell me. Why did you run away?"

"It was the MacLean . . . he made me do things—and he said if I told he would have me and my sisters burned for witchcraft. So I *couldn't* tell you. But you knew I hated it there." Her voice shook suddenly, thick with emotion. "You *knew* and still you made me stay."

Her father did not say anything for a long time; he kept his gaze steady on her. Then it fell away, until he stared at the ground. "What things did he make you do?"

Shame flushed her cheeks. She shut her eyes, her lips pursed tighter. She didn't want to say, not out loud. She'd said it already to William, but this was her *father*. She didn't know if she could. It was too vile.

"Tell me, Rose." His voice rose to a command.

"Things only a wife should do. Or a whore." After a long, heavy silence, she said, "That's what he did. Made me into his whore when I was eight years old."

Her father said nothing. He only stared at her, and as he did, his skin seemed to pale. His throat worked, and his eyes grew bright. He closed his eyes and pressed a white-knuckled fist to his mouth.

When he finally spoke, his voice was rough with emotion. "If he wasn't already dead—"

"You'd kill him. I know."

She looked away from his wounded expression, wishing she'd said nothing. She'd finally told him, and she didn't feel any better. If anything, she felt worse. She heard movement, and then the bed dipped slightly. Her father put his arm around her shoulders and pulled her close. Rose let him, pressing her face against the plaid covering his bony shoulder.

"Forgive me, lass, for being so blind and stupid."

Like a dam breaking in her heart, the tears came then, burning her eyes. "I should have told you! I shouldn't have been so stupid and believed him!"

Her father shook her slightly. "No! It's my fault. I knew Fagan MacLean was not a kind man, but I never guessed he'd touch you—whom I was paying him to protect. I'm the stupid one. Can you ever forgive me?"

Rose nodded, wiping her eyes. "Aye, I think I can."

So this is what it feels like to be just like everyone else. Utterly helpless.

William sat on the floor of a grimy cellar—a dirt hole dug in the ground for storing turnips and onions and apples . . . and apparently witches. His daughter lay across his lap, her head against his shoulder. She had finally awakened a few hours ago. After her initial fright, she'd grown silent. Speaking to the rats, probably. William didn't ask. He now wished she'd stayed unconscious. No child should be put through what was in store for them, but especially not *his* child. He didn't know if he could bear it; he was twisted in knots just thinking of it and being so damn helpless to do anything.

It seemed ironic that it should end this way. He'd been so arrogant, setting himself above everyone else, refusing to take the chances and risks that others took every day—that Rose took. And now here he was, all three of the people he'd let into his heart lost to him. Drake bleeding to death on the mountainside. His daughter held for witchcraft. Rose at the mercy of her uncle. And he was useless to them, just like everyone else.

And he was a fool, too. But it was too late to do anything about that.

Deidra stirred against his shoulder. "Someone is coming."

He didn't know how she knew—the vermin, most likely—because he heard nothing.

"Who did you tell that you can speak to animals, Squirrel?"

Deidra's curls brushed his shoulder as she shook her head. "No one, Da. I promised."

William sighed, impatient. "You *must* have told someone. How else did MacPherson know?" Unless Rose had told him. *No. She would never.* But his stomach felt strange and queasy, and his chest tightened.

"I know not! But the red-haired man—he already knew. He told me so."

Roderick.

Cold fury settled over him. "When did he tell you?"

"In the stable. He wanted to show me something, but Moireach warned me. *He's* the one the animals fear—the bad man. He uses them—kills some of them for black magic, puts demons in others. They all hate him."

William closed his eyes, the irony of it all making his mouth curve grimly. All along his daughter had held the answers, and he'd never thought to ask her. And she'd never thought to tell him, too worried about burdening him.

A shaft of light flooded the cellar, and a rope ladder rolled down until it hit the dirt.

William stood, setting Deidra on her feet and taking her hand. A bearded face thrust through the hole. "Get up here. Now!"

"Stay behind me," William murmured, grabbing the coarse hemp and climbing. He hoped no one would think to check his arrow wound, as it was nearly healed. Such a miracle would surely be construed as the devil's work.

When he was clear of the hole, he stood to the side until Deidra was out, too. They both squinted in the bright sunlight as villagers grabbed them, thrusting them along before them. William held Deidra's hand, keeping her close.

They were pushed into a cottage. The door shut behind them. William scanned the interior, his gaze fixating on a table covered with instruments of torture. A selection of wooden mallets. A "spider," a sharp iron fork used to tear flesh from the body. Phallus-shaped irons rested beside it for heating and inserting into various orifices. The turcas, a set of pinchers for ripping out finger-nails, lay clean and gleaming next to the irons. Needles to be driven into the nailless fingertips were stuck in a cushion next to the turcas. Beside them lay the penni-winks. The last tool on the table was the thumbscrews—a vise used to crush the bones in the thumb, similar to the penniwinks. A rope was looped over the side of the chair, for thrawing the skin from the head.

William swallowed hard, his hand tightening on his daughter's, his gaze lighting on a tall, thin man in black robes. He was not a Highlander. He wasn't even local.

"Good day, my lord Strathwick." He looked down his long, sharp nose at Deidra, his lips wrinkling slightly. "I am Luthias Forsyth, former witch-finder to the king. I trust you are well rested and ready for our first session?" He spoke pleasantly, as though this were a social call rather than a prelude to torture.

William's guts clenched. They were in serious trouble.

Chapter 18

❧⸎❧

Luthias Forsyth stared at the witches before him. A tall, brawny man—a Highland chief—and a child. He sighed. Force was not allowed to induce children to talk. And children were the easiest to question. But there were rules in place, and Luthias always followed them, even when he didn't agree with them. A village elder stood at his shoulder, whispering advice to him. Luthias silenced him with a look.

He would extract the information from the prisoner in his own manner. In Edinburgh, he'd spent time in the king's service as a witchpricker. Since the commission of 1592, which gave individuals the power to try and execute witches, he'd found his services in great demand across the country. But he'd never agreed with the kirk's commission. Common men could now try witches and burn them. God had called on him to leave Edinburgh and travel through the country, offering his services—for a fee—to any village in need of an experienced witchpricker.

A man of his vast experience certainly didn't need a village rustic interfering in his work, telling him how to induce a witch to talk. The interrogation of witches should only be undertaken by a professional such as himself. There were steps to be followed. Witches never acted as you expected them to. The only thing they could be counted on to do was lie.

The wizard continued to stare at him, his face expressionless, the child hiding behind his legs. He was a formidable man, tall and muscular. Though his inky black hair was liberally salted with gray, he was neither old nor feeble. Luthias would need muscle to conduct this interrogation.

Luthias removed his soft wool cloak, hanging it on a wooden peg. He smoothed his hands over his thinning hair and palmed the front of his robe. Eyes closed, he took deep, soothing breaths. One must always be calm and in control of one's faculties when confronting one of Satan's minions. They had such power.

He motioned to the burly villagers serving as guards. They brought the wizard to the table and forced him to sit. He did not appear frightened as he looked Luthias over curiously. The bold perusal sent a flash of anger through him that he fought to stifle. The devil was insolent and sought to intimidate him. This was nothing new. It was only the beginning of yet another battle between Luthias and the devil. It was God's will. God permitted evil—though he did not wish it—for the perfecting of the universe.

And Luthias was God's tool, just as the instruments of torture were merely Luthias's tools for achieving his ends. It was a hierarchy that Luthias rejoiced to be a part of.

The wizard spoke. "Why are you keeping a child prisoner?" His arm encircled the child, holding her to his side. "She has done nothing."

Luthias did not answer. He poured a measure of witch broth from the flagon on the table and offered it to the wizard. "Prithee, drink."

The wizard peered into the cup as though it were poison. "What is it?"

"It is the witch broth."

"Witch broth?"

"Aye, it was made from the gathered ashes of a witch after she was burnt at the stake. It will prevent you from casting a spell upon me during our session. Go on. Drink up."

The wizard would not take the cup from him. When Luthias pressed it at him, he swiped hard, knocking the cup from Luthias's hand and spilling the precious brew in the dirt. He glowered, completely unrepentant, as if Luthias were beneath contempt. Furious heat suffused Luthias's face. "I think me this session will be long and tedious."

"Let the child go. She is innocent."

"That is not what I was told. I was informed she communed with animals."

The wizard's expression gave away nothing. Luthias scrutinized the wizard and his witch-child. Perhaps he could make use of the wizard's concern for the child.

"Mayhap I will release her. If you cooperate."

The wizard's jaw bulged. "Verra well."

Luthias withdrew the parchment from his robes. He unfolded it. "William MacKay of Strathwick," he said, looking at the wizard over the top of the parchment, "it says here that you cure all manner of sickness."

Strathwick nodded, his eyes hard, implacable.

"How is it you came by these miraculous powers?"

"It is merely a knowledge of plants and herbs. Nothing more."

Luthias sneered. "The Lord cures our bodies through fasting and prayers, not through weeds." He studied Strathwick's impassive face. "That is the papist way of things. Be you a heretic as well as a witch?"

"Is there a difference in the eyes of men such as yourself?"

Luthias gritted his teeth and decided on the direct approach. "Who seduced you into witchcraft?"

"No one. I'm not a witch. Just a healer."

"What of the MacDonells of Glen Laire? I hear that is a nest of witches and that is from whence you came. Tell me which of the MacDonells are the devil's minions."

"There are no others. Not even this child. Only me, and I'm all yours."

The rapid scratching of the scribe's quill against parchment as he recorded the questioning filled the long silence that followed. Luthias glared accusingly at Strathwick. The wizard only returned the stare. Emotionless.

Luthias sighed and moved to the table where his instruments were laid out neatly. The sharp steel prongs of the spider gleamed in the torchlight. His hand hesitated over it, then passed on to the turcas. He longed to rip Strathwick's fingernails off with it. To make him scream. To see if tears would fall from his stoic eyes. He had read many treatises on witchcraft that said witches did not cry, but he'd found that not to be so. Some said it was saliva they smeared on their cheeks, not true tears. But Luthias had seen them weep. He liked when they wept. That's when Satan lost his hold on them and the truth poured out. When he was doing God's work.

He glanced at Strathwick, who watched warily. The skin of his neck was red. *Ah, not so devoid of emotion after all.* He feared Luthias's methods of encouraging him to talk. The witch-child peeked out from behind her father's shoulder. Or perhaps he only feared for the child? Time to find out.

He decided on the penniwinks. He motioned to the guards. Eagerly, they rushed forward to restrain Strathwick, pushing the child back against the far wall. Luthias guided Strathwick's hand inside the iron glove, then secured it. The wizard allowed this, unresisting. He chose the smaller wooden mallet. The larger one was for the boots.

"Now," he said, smiling. "I will repeat my question. What witches reside in Glen Laire?"

Strathwick shook his head as if he hadn't any idea what Luthias could possibly be referring to. So calm, so composed.

Luthias brought the mallet down hard, driving a wedge into Strathwick's finger. He heard the bone snap, and blood spurted onto the table. The child shrieked. A righteous fire flared through him. He felt drunk from it. Strathwick inhaled sharply through his nose, his jaw rigid, but he made no other sound. Luthias brought the mallet down again and again, punctuating each blow with a question. And every time the wizard's answer was the same.

The child cried through it all. "Da! Make him stop! Make him stop!"

"I'm fine, Squirrel," Strathwick said, his voice tight, his baleful gaze fixed on Luthias.

Luthias started to bring the mallet down again but paused. Strathwick had braced himself for the blow and was clearly irritated to be kept in suspense of the pain. Luthias regarded his subject thoughtfully. The man's hand was a bloody useless lump. If he were to live—which he would not, of course—it would have to be amputated. His face was lined with pain, and his hair was damp with sweat, but he'd not made a single sound of pain beyond harsh breathing throughout. This wizard was powerful. He would not crack.

Luthias set the bloodstained mallet aside. "Come here . . . Squirrel is your name?" What a stupid name for a child. But fitting for one who communes with animals.

The child looked at her father with enormous blue eyes. A pretty child, with glossy black curls, plump cheeks, and sinfully long black lashes. A daughter of Eve; the first deserters of Divine Law, as St. Clement called them. In a few years she would bespell grown men to evil.

"What do you want with her?" the wizard asked, his voice rough with pain.

"If you will not talk, perhaps she will."

When the child would not come, Luthias snatched her wrist, dragging her from where she hid behind her father's chair. She dug in her heels, and the wizard began to bellow, trying to stand, though the villagers and the penniewinks held him fast.

"I'll talk," he said, his voice cracking with pain and defeat. "Just leave her alone."

*   *   *

After Rose dressed, took her father back to his room, and gave Hagan explicit instructions on caring for him—the Irishman seemed rather in awe of her now and more inclined to listen—she went in search of Hilda. Rose was doing her utmost not to dwell on William and his desertion, so she turned her mind to Tira. What had gone wrong? She thought that perhaps she'd been mistaken: Perhaps she *hadn't* heard the woman's voice. It still did not explain why she'd suffered with her aunt's pain, but still, maybe she hadn't truly healed her.

But now she knew that was not true. So what had happened? Hilda had been the only other person present at the birth, and despite what she'd told Roderick, Rose wanted to question the woman herself. There was also the nagging question of what had happened to her father. Everyone had concluded that he'd been attacked because Hagan had heard someone and William had been seen leaving her father's chambers. But Rose did not credit this. She assumed her father had been attacked because of the gray film she'd seen around his brain. The only other time she'd seen such a thing had been when delivering Liam. Suffocation. There had been no marks on her father's neck to indicate a strangling, but he'd been feeble from his illness. A pillow pressed over his face would have done the job just as well.

Sir Philip still had not returned with Sir Donnan, but William had indicated he might have an accomplice within Lochlaire. Hilda had already been at Lochlaire when Rose had arrived, but only for a few months— Uncle Roderick had engaged her services when Tira had become pregnant, which was about the same time Alan MacDonell had fallen ill.

Even if Hilda did work for Sir Donnan, it did not explain why she would kill Tira. Perhaps the servant fancied herself in love with Uncle Roderick—he was a comely man, after all—and was ridding herself of the competition? It seemed a rather far-fetched theory, but then people did strange things for love. There was no limit to what she would do to protect William.

Rose knocked at the door to her uncle's tower apartments. When no one answered, she tried the door and found it open.

"Uncle Roderick? Hilda?" She stepped into the room. There was still no answer. The chamber was dimly lit with two candles and a dying fire. The scent of dried blood and incense hung thick in the air. Rose was immediately struck by how bare the room was, as if all signs of her aunt had been obliterated. She wandered about the room, looking for something, anything that would indicate Tira had inhabited these apartments—her sewing, her needles, her clothes, her comb—*anything*. But it was all gone, even the chair she'd sat on. Why would Roderick dispose of her things, and so quickly? The answer came to Rose with sudden, startling clarity. Because of Isobel. Isobel could touch objects and uncover all manner of information.

This opened up new, more sinister possibilities. Uncle Roderick? A witch? She remembered the things Tira had screamed during her labor. *It will kill me! He put it in there—it's unnatural! It's a monster!* Could it be that Tira knew something and could not be allowed to live? Her heart beating erratically, Rose returned to the door and shut it, then began methodically searching the room, opening cabinets, pushing aside the Turkey rugs to tap on the floorboards. Nothing. She went to the bedchamber and found that door locked.

Her hands shook as she located a stiletto blade of her uncle's and picked the lock. Where was Uncle Roderick? What would he do if he found her in here, rifling through his things? She felt time slipping away, and yet she had to find something, some proof of this if anyone was to believe her. She wasn't even certain *she* believed it.

The bedchamber was elaborately appointed, the bed piled high with furs and velvet coverlets trimmed in gold. Thick Turkey carpets covered the floor and walls. The ceiling was carved and painted with gold and red paint. As if he were already the chieftain.

Rose circled the room, searching everything. When again she found nothing, she moved the carpets aside and tapped the floorboards with a cane she'd found. She finally found what she searched for—a hollow knock. She knelt, sliding the stiletto in and around the sides of the floorboard. It pried up easily.

She fetched a candle and held it over the dark recess. Several dark shapes rested inside the hole. One item at a time, she removed the paraphernalia. A wand made of black glass, a small black bowl, smooth and gleaming like ebony. Inside the bowl rested scores of pins and three rusty nails. Also inside the recess were a small ivory casket and two lumps of dirty wax pierced through with long pins.

Rose studied the wax lumps uneasily. Both contained embedded objects—hair, fingernails, and other unidentifiable things—and a rusty substance streaked them. Blood. Hair protruded from the tops of the wax. One was a wad of black hair, as if gathered from a comb, and the other, a dark auburn tuft streaked with gray, clearly cut with shears. Both effigies were anatomically correct—one with a phallus, and the other, the black-haired one, with breasts. Rose noted on closer inspection that on the auburn one, nail parings had been placed along the base, as toenails.

She stared down at them in horrified revulsion, understanding what she held in her hands. Dark magic. Effigies her uncle used in his spells. The auburn one must be her father. Who was the black-haired one? She fingered the strands. Too long to be William or Drake; both wore their hair short. Both effigies had long pins piercing them. Rose was frozen with indecision, uncertain what to do with them. Instinct urged her to destroy them, but she feared that anything she did to them would harm the persons they represented in some manner she couldn't begin to imagine.

She peered under the floorboards again and saw something else—a dark rectangle. She drew out a black leather book. The pages were sewn in, and the scrawl was Gaelic. Roderick's grimoire. Rose paged through the dark spells with growing horror, stopping at one for summoning demon incubus to set on a victim—to suck the life from them. A loose page fluttered to the floor. The paper was different—not parchment but smooth vellum, the corner torn. She unfolded it with trembling hands and immediately recognized her mother's handwriting. The first line read, *I think Roderick is not all he seems . . .*

Rose heard movement in the next room. Quickly she replaced the objects in the recess, slid the floorboard in place, and covered it with the carpet. She kicked the cane away and hid the stiletto behind her back just as the door to the bedchamber opened.

It was her uncle, stunned into immobility at finding her in his bedchamber. His gaze immediately went to the floor, then darted back up to her eyes. He held his son swaddled in his arms. Liam cried weakly, a strange, warbling cry that raised the hair on Rose's neck and arms. What was it? Was it a child? Or some product of black magic?

"What are you doing in here?" her uncle asked, scanning the room, eyes narrowed, looking for anything out of place. *Murderer.* Rose saw him with new eyes. *Greedy, scheming, evil, out to ruin her life.*

"I was looking for Hilda."

"Why?"

"Because she was there when I delivered Liam. I thought she might be able to tell more about what happened after I healed Tira."

"She left after Tira died."

Rose's heart stuttered. "Left?"

His eyes were flat, his face expressionless. "Aye. I didna need her any longer and sent her away."

"Who is taking care of Liam?"

Roderick gazed down at his son. A small, pale fist waved from the swaddling. "He has a wet nurse. She's in the kitchens right now. Not that it matters . . . he's dying."

The urge to cross the room and pull back the swaddling to examine the child herself was strong, but Rose did not trust her uncle anymore, and besides, she hid a knife behind her back.

"What is wrong with him?" she asked.

"I know not . . . I thought Strathwick healed him." When he looked up at her, his face was hard, full of accusation and betrayal. "This is proof he's a charlatan."

"No. What he saved the baby from was strangulation. Liam was suffocated by the cord. Whatever ails him now developed later and can probably still be healed."

Roderick regarded her for a long moment. "You're no charlatan. I saw how you . . . resurrected Alan."

"I didn't resurrect him. He wasn't dead."

Her uncle's eyes glinted, but he made no reply to that. His gaze swept the room again, then he looked her up and down. "What are you hiding behind your back?"

Rose's fingers clenched around the stiletto's hilt. "Nothing."

"If you were looking for Hilda, why were you in my bedchamber with the door closed?"

Rose could think of no good answer to that. "Th-the door was closed?"

He gave her a reproachful look, then gazed back down at his son. "Will you heal him, Rose?"

She looked from her uncle to the bundle in his arms. "Perhaps . . . though I cannot now."

"Why?"

"Because I take on the illness, you saw that. And I cannot do that now. I must remain strong."

"Why?"

"Someone is trying to kill my father."

As she spoke, she heard the soft tapping of toenails, and Conan's black nose appeared from behind Roderick's legs. Rose's free hand went to her shoulder, remembering the marks that had been there, bruises, just like her father's, present after a night spent with Conan in her bed. And now that she thought back, one of the dogs Roderick had given his brother had always been present when her father had had the nightmares. And when the bruises had appeared, Alan had always felt worse, weaker, more feeble. Just as Rose had been nearly overcome with lethargy. The incubus.

Rose gripped the stiletto hilt tighter, her heart fluttering madly with fear. She knew too much, and she was fairly certain her uncle was aware of it. Tira and Hilda likely had known too much, too—and one was dead, the other had disappeared. And what of William? She had been upset and hurt at his abrupt departure, but she'd refused to examine it, like so many other things in her life, putting her mind to other tasks instead. But had he departed voluntarily? Whom did the other wax lump represent?

"Why did Lord Strathwick leave?"

Roderick shook his head slowly. "I know not."

"I think you do." Rose crossed the room until she stood in front of her uncle. She looked down at Liam. He seemed shrunken, smaller than he'd been when she'd delivered him. His pinched face had a bluish cast. He squalled suddenly, an odd, quavering cry.

Rose called on her magic, passing her hand over the infant. His color was a pale, wavering orange, like fading sunlight. The area around his chest was black and twisted, writhing like serpents. Rose glanced up at her uncle. What *was* Liam? A product of dark magic? Had Tira's ravings been more than labor pain?

"I can heal this," she said.

Roderick's copper brows raised with hope, and he held the child out to her. Rose did not take him.

"I will heal him. But not unless you tell me why Strathwick left and where he is now. Then you will take Liam and leave Lochlaire. Forever."

He stared at her for a long moment, a mask falling down over his face. He moved away from her, crossing to the bed and laying Liam in the center of it. Rose clenched her fist around the stiletto, certain she would soon be forced to use it.

He turned away from the bed and faced her. "Why would you be wanting me to leave, lass?" He came toward her, hands unencumbered, his pace unhurried.

Rose backed away, toward the door leading to the privy chamber. "Don't come any closer." She brought the knife out in front of her, brandishing it at him.

His pace did not let up. "You've been meddling about." He tapped his foot on the rug where she'd found his magic paraphernalia. "And you think you understand things, but you do not."

Rose continued backing away, clutching the blade with both hands. "I understand you're a murderer! You had my mother murdered because she knew what you are. You're trying to murder my father. You murdered Tira and probably Hilda. You disposed of all their things so Isobel cannot discover the truth."

His eyes widened. "You *are* clever. Too clever."

He came at her fast. Rose stabbed at him, but he caught her wrist, twisting it and swiping her legs from beneath her. She fell hard onto one hip and knee, her arm wrenching awkwardly in his grasp. Her fingers sprang open, and the stiletto clattered to the floor.

"There," he said pleasantly, pulling her to her feet. "I dislike talking to someone who is threatening me." He shoved her back into the bedchamber. "I will bargain with you but not at knifepoint. You heal my son, and I will tell you where Strathwick is."

Rose looked to the bed, where Liam made soft whimpering noises. Healing the child would incapacitate her, leave her at her uncle's mercy. He knew this, of course.

"I won't heal him here. I must have someone present."

He gave her a patronizing smile. "I don't think so. You agree to heal him now, and I will give you my word that you will recover in safety. I will also tell you about Strathwick."

Rose's palms sweat. Her heart hammered in her ears. She would not leave this room alive, whether she healed his son or not. He would not tell her all of these things if he planned to let her live.

"I suggest you accept my offer. Strathwick's time is running out."

Rose's heart leapt. *William*. What had Roderick done to him? Suddenly nothing else mattered.

"Very well." Rose's heart calmed as a course of action opened to her, one that she would never have considered before but was vital now. One her uncle would never suspect her of considering, or being capable of.

Rose crossed to the bed and stared down at the frail child. "What is he?"

"He's a wean, of course." Roderick sounded mildly offended. "You speak of the nonsense Tira spouted? He's no monster. I used spells to help her conceive and ensure it was a son—but nothing more."

Rose arched a brow. "Spells? No one guessed you were witch. Have you always been? Plotting and hiding?"

"Not always. My mother had a gift for spellcraft and taught me. I was not much interested until she died, until I watched Alan inherit what should be mine. My mother was noble—his was a common chieftain's daughter. My mother's dowry enriched the MacDonells." His lips curled in a sneer. "It all should have been mine. Lillian should have been mine."

Rose shook with fury. He had deceived them all for so long. She'd trusted him, never once suspected. And if she died here, no one else would suspect him and he would eventually succeed in murdering her father.

Roderick raised his brows expectantly. "Shall we get on with it? Even now your beloved Strathwick could be dying."

Rose climbed onto the bed beside Liam. She wanted to be certain her uncle would have to get close to her to retrieve his son after she healed him. "Tell me now, before I do it. Where is William?"

"No. I'll tell you after."

She slammed her fist into the bed. "Damn it! That's not fair."

"Not fair? My only child is dying. I have waited and planned and taught myself magic for years. Everything rolled along smoothly. Alan wasted away. You latched onto the idea of the Wizard of the North like a dog to a bone, refusing to give it up. The more I warned against it, the more determined you became. He was just what I'd hoped for, a charlatan—the kind whose remedies do more harm than good. He was perfect. But now you've ruined everything. I'd never guessed you could do more than see colors. I'd never thought such a thing possible."

Rose's pulse raced as she grew afraid again. He would not be saying these things to her if he didn't mean to kill her. And he knew she was no fool. They were both playing games, and they both knew it. Rose feared she couldn't win this one. Roderick was clever enough to have hidden the fact that he was a wizard for years.

"Tell me where William is or I won't do it." Her voice shook with fear and determination.

He apparently saw that she meant it, because he sighed. "Very well. I'll tell you. He's in the village south of Glen Laire, the same one that lynched and burned your mother a dozen years ago. I happened to meet up with a witch-finder I'd met once in Edinburgh. He travels the country now, offering his services to communities in need. I sent them Strathwick—with the aid of your betrothed, of course. I doubt he's actually been burned yet. Mr. Forsyth is a thorough man. No doubt he's torturing the truth out of your beloved."

Rose's limbs went weak with fear. She put her hand to her mouth and shook her head. "He harmed no one. How could you?"

"How could I not? He was the perfect person on

whom to place the blame of Alan's death. But that is ruined now, too, as Alan is still very much alive." His face hardened in sudden fury. "Everything is ruined, and now my son is dying."

Rose didn't think she could carry this charade out to the end. They both knew he would kill her—and yet if she didn't heal Liam, she didn't stand a chance. He could easily overpower her. Using her witchcraft was her only hope. William's only hope.

She put her hands on Liam and called on her magic. It swirled up inside her, warm and pulsing. She sent it down her arms to her hands. It embraced the blackness around Liam's heart, only this time the ailment didn't leave as readily as her father's and Tira's had. It struggled to keep its hold on the heart. Her mouth opened in shock and pain. She redoubled her effort, commanding it to return. With the sudden force of a door unjamming, it rushed into her, slamming into her chest and stealing her breath.

Liam let out a lusty scream, balled fists raised to the heavens. His color strengthened until he nearly glowed a rich copper-orange. Rose collapsed onto the bed. Her heart squeezed painfully in her chest, and every heartbeat ripped through her, excruciating to breathe. She could not move or speak; she could only stare mutely at the carved wooden canopy above, fighting for her next breath. And then the next. And the next.

Her uncle picked up Liam from where he screamed beside her. Her vision shimmered red with pain. She willed her arms to move, to grab him, but she had no command of her own limbs. He murmured to the child and moved away. Rose did not know how long she lay there, or where her uncle went, but suddenly he was beside her again, staring down at her.

"You *are* a great healer," he said, his voice soft with awe. "Like Finian the leper. That's why it grieves me so to have to do this."

"You promised," she said, her voice a breathy croak. A vise crushed her chest. Speaking made her head swim. Pinpoints of light danced at the edges of her vision.

"I know," he said, sounding disappointed. "But we both knew I was lying. You played the game and you lost. I will tell Alan that you followed your wizard lover and were attacked by broken men. We will all mourn you. *I* will mourn you." He placed a fatherly hand on her hair, looking down at her with sadness and regret.

Rose closed her eyes, wishing she could smite him somehow through her head, but it didn't work that way. She tried to lift her arms to grab him, but they were leaden.

"You were my favorite, you know. It was my idea to send you and your sisters away all those years ago. You were right, before. I *was* the one who set the villagers on your mother. I feared what I did to Lillian would have consequences I didn't anticipate or want, so I urged Alan to send you to safety. I cursed Lillian's ring and gave it to Gillian. I feared your mother's spirit would attempt to contact her. And you wouldn't believe the trouble I've gone to, removing items or placing shielding spells on objects so Isobel remains ignorant. I couldn't bear to hurt any of you, but I needed you here, back at Lochlaire.

I'd long meant for Alan to die of a wasting illness, and I needed witnesses, others to vouch that no poison or other foul means had been involved. I thought my lovely nieces would never suspect me, that they loved me as I loved them." He took Rose's face between his hands and stared at her, begging her to understand. "I never wanted to harm any of you. Do you understand? I loved you all as if you were mine."

Rose wished she could spit in his face. As it was she could only stare at him with all the loathing in her heart. He had killed their mother, cursed Gillian, was slowly murdering their father, had given William to a witch-crazed mob, and now he planned to murder her. He loved no one but himself.

He disappeared from her line of vision. Rose's breath came in small, painful gasps. Tears wet her hair at her temples. She was going to die, and Roderick would win. William would burn. *William.*

He was back, a large pillow between his hands. "I am sorry, Rose," he said, as the pillow came down, blocking his face from her vision. She couldn't scream, couldn't breathe as the linen pressed into her mouth and nose, stealing away what little breath she'd been capable of.

Grab him! Do it! She forced her arms to move. Pain tore through her, but she had him. She clutched the arms pressing the pillow over her face, and felt the blackness rush eagerly out of her. He tried to throw her hands off, but she clung to him as her strength returned. He cried out. She bucked frantically, throwing her uncle and the pillow off.

She slid onto the floor but quickly regained her feet, turning in a stance of readiness. There was no need to fight. Her uncle lay across the bed, motionless except for his eyes, blinking as he stared at the wooden canopy, occasionally twitching his fingers. She knew what he felt. The crushing pain made it impossible to move or speak. She stared down at him, devoid of even pity.

"I'm not sorry," she said and left him there.

Chapter 19

William sat in the cellar alone. He did not know where his daughter was. He did not know what would happen when they came for him again. He opened and closed his hand—mangled the day before, now mended and whole. This would not go well for him. He kept it wrapped in the bloodstained bandage, hoping no one decided to check on it.

He tensed as the racket started up again—screaming, strange animal noises. He stared at the narrow slats of sunlight streaming between the boards covering his hole. What was happening up there? He was afraid to contemplate it. Something odd had been going on since sometime in the night. It had started with food being dropped into his hole. Two loaves of fresh crusty bread, a large chunk of meat, five apples, a bag of nuts, a sausage, a hot cooked eel, and an onion. Much better fare than any prisoner deserved—and all of it strangely damp but edible after William brushed the dirt off.

Then the screaming had started. At first it had been some far-off screams he'd paid no mind to, but soon they'd drawn closer, punctuated with squawking ducks, bleating sheep, and, near his hole, a savagely growling dog that had soon been silenced by someone beating it. It had whimpered in pain for some time near his hole before it had either died or been removed. Then later there had been a pounding above him that had set the earth shaking. Dirt had crumbled from the walls and ceiling of his hole, and he'd feared he would be buried alive. A stampede.

Whatever was happening in the world above, it kept the villagers sufficiently occupied to forget about him for a very long time. He'd had plenty of time to think and worry. He'd given the witchpricker one name. Roderick MacDonell. He'd vowed he knew of no other MacDonell witches, and the witchpricker had seemed to believe him. He'd taken Deidra and sent William back to the cellar, presumably so they could verify his story, or take Roderick into custody. . . . Who knew? William couldn't fathom what might happen. His only hope was that if he had to burn, Roderick would burn with him.

The hole in the ceiling opened. "Will? Are you down there?"

William shielded his eyes. "Bloody Christ—Drake? Is that you?"

"Wait—I'll get something to lower down to you."

"Drake?" But there was no answer. He closed his eyes, profound relief washing over him in waves. His brother was not dead. If Drake was alive and able to rescue him, it meant one thing—Rose was behind this. His heart contracted with painful fear and longing. He should have known she'd not sit by complacently, waiting for her father to die.

A wooden ladder was lowered down to him a few

minutes later. William climbed out of the hole, squinting the whole while. As soon as he was clear of the hole, his brother grabbed him and embraced him hard. William clasped him back, his eyes so dazzled by the sunlight that he could hardly see.

"Deidra—where is she?"

"Down this way, we think. Come on."

And he raced off. William jogged after him, blinking at the sights around him in disbelief. It looked as if a storm had hit the village. The debris-littered streets were devoid of people, the cottages shut up tight, shutters closed fast.

"What happened?" William asked.

"I know not," Drake called over his shoulder.

At the far end of the village a small group gathered before a cottage—the same cottage where he had previously been tortured. Animals surrounded the cottage— ducks, sheep, horses, cows. All lounging. William's gaze was immediately drawn to the red-haired woman leaning heavily against a balding blond man, also in contemplation of the cottage.

"Rose!" William called.

She turned her head toward him. It was Wallace who held her. She took several steps toward him, then he caught her up in his arms. He embraced her as tightly as he dared, knowing she suffered from Drake's wound. "You did it, Rose," he whispered into her hair.

She clung to him, her breath warm on his neck. "Thank God you're alive." Her voice cracked with emotion. "I feared we were too late."

"We have a bit of a problem," the earl of Kincreag

interrupted. William released Rose reluctantly, keeping an arm around her to support her. She leaned heavily against him.

The earl nodded to the cottage. "Have a look."

William left Rose and went to the open door of the cottage, passing through the mob of loitering animals. They took scant notice of him.

The interior of the cottage was dim, but his eyes adjusted quickly. The witchpricker sat on a bench, Deidra beside him. He looked much different than he had the last time William had seen him. His face was pale, and his sparse gray hair was sticking up in tufts about his head. His fine black robes were torn and filthy. He held a dirk to Deidra's neck, his wild gray eyes fixed on something in the far shadows. William turned his head, peering into the dark, and took an involuntary step back at the sight that greeted him.

Three wolves sat in a line, tongues lolling from their mouths, staring at Luthias Forsyth. They seemed to be smiling, daring him to do something with the dirk.

"Make her call them off!" Luthias cried. Sweat trickled down his temples.

Deidra gave William a worried look. "I'm sorry I told, Da, but I was afraid he'd hurt me."

"It's all right, Squirrel." William took in the terrified witchpricker, the animals crowded around the cottage, and the waiting wolves. Something strange and sick and proud turned in his chest. "What happened here? Did you ask the animals for help?"

She nodded hesitantly. "He says he'll kill me if the wolves come near. But I think he'll kill me if I make them go away. You, too. The one I sent to guard you was killed." Her bottom lip wobbled, and her eyes filled with tears.

His daughter. Jesus God. She'd set the animals on the village and had probably kept them both alive long enough for Rose and Drake to arrive with reinforcements. He'd not understood. He'd thought he'd understood. *Communing with animals.* They surrounded her, protected her, did her bidding. They'd brought him food, and at least one had been killed for it. It made him weak to think of what she was capable of and how others would perceive this act.

"Where are the villagers?" William asked.

"They ran," Luthias said, lip curling. "They deserted me. I know not where."

"Da," Deidra said, a whimper in her voice, her eyes bright. "I want to go home."

One of the wolves fidgeted and whined. The witchpricker's eyes widened.

"Mr. Forsyth, if she sends the wolves away, will you put down the dirk and release her?"

The witchpricker looked at him incredulously. "Are you mad? This is a dangerous witch. It is not in my authority to question a child, even if she is a witch, but it is in the king's. He will be most interested to make her acquaintance."

"I'm sorry to hear that." William unwrapped the bloodstained linen from his hand, exposing a perfectly functional hand.

The witchpricker gasped, his gaze darting to William's other hand, as if this might be a trick and he'd find the other the mangled mess. William held them both up for his inspection.

"How is this possible? Your hand was ruined."

"Aye, I know. Do you understand, Mr. Forsyth, what you're dealing with? Let the child go or you will not leave here alive."

The witchpricker's thin throat worked, his Adam's apple bobbing. "I will not stop my fight against the enemy, against *God*'s enemies, until there is no more breath in my body. Satan will not prevail so long as I live!"

Splendid. Perhaps it was better if the man was dead. Then he couldn't run to the king or regroup the villagers to lynch them all.

William felt someone beside him and looked down. Rose had joined him, leaning heavily against the door-frame.

She touched his arm and gazed up at him with worried eyes. "Jamie MacPherson is coming."

William stepped away from the door to look. MacPherson rode up the street with a handful of men, looking about him with the same bewilderment William had felt. When he saw Kincreag, then Drake, his gaze cut to William and Rose. His nose was a swollen, misshapen mess, the skin around it mottled purple and black.

He pulled his dag out and trained it on William. "Who did you kill, aye?" The gun barrel stabbed the air at Drake before leveling on William again. "Who did you kill to save him?" His voice was thick and nasal.

"Put the gun away, MacPherson," Lord Kincreag said, annoyed.

"Stay out of this, my lord—"

The earl stepped forward, his black eyes narrowed with anger. "I'm in it, MacPherson. Now put the gun away before I make you verra sorry."

MacPherson pointed the dag at Kincreag. "No! The bastard killed my father and dammit, he will pay!" He dismounted, gun aimed at William again. "You will fight me, Wizard, just like we agreed."

William held out his hands, placating. "I don't want to fight you, MacPherson." He had other worries right now—his daughter in the hands of a zealous witch-pricker was primary.

"Not your decision." MacPherson closed the distance between them until the barrel of his dag nearly touched William's forehead. His lips pulled back from his teeth, his eyes wild. "I wonder, if I shot you here, could you heal yourself?"

William said nothing. His heart beat swiftly and his muscles tensed, waiting for MacPherson to make a move.

MacPherson pressed the barrel into William's forehead. "I'll make certain you're dead, Wizard. I'll cut off your head and burn it."

"Leave off!" Rose cried, pushing away from the doorframe and coming to stand between them. She put her hands on MacPherson's arm, trying to force it down. "You were a child when your father was killed and William was acting on his chief's orders—"

MacPherson's hand shot out, striking Rose across the face and sending her reeling back into the stones of the cottage. Black fury surged through William. He grabbed Jamie's arm, wrenching it down. The dag discharged harmlessly into the dirt.

MacPherson pulled a dirk from his boot and slashed. William moved back but not soon enough. It slashed across his belly, slicing through plaid and shirt and into his skin. Before he could react, the wolves from the cottage flew out the door and attacked MacPherson, snarling and ripping. He screamed, trying to beat them off, but there were too many.

"No, Deidra!" William bellowed. "Make them stop!"

"I can't!" she cried. "They don't want to!"

He whirled toward his daughter. "Make them!"

Tears streaked her face, and the witchpricker was such a shade of white that William thought that soon they would have no worries about him—he would faint.

Deidra's brow furrowed, as if she were in deep concentration. Abruptly, the wolves left MacPherson and docilely returned to the cottage, resuming their place before Deidra and the witchpricker, muzzles glistening with fresh blood.

Rose knelt beside MacPherson, who lay motionless on the ground. William dropped down beside her. The lad was covered with blood, his throat ravaged, but he was still alive, his eyes wide and staring, the breath laboring out of him. Blood pulsed from his throat and foamed at his lips as he tried to speak.

Rose met William's eyes and shook her head slightly. "You cannot. He wants you dead. He'll kill you as soon as you heal him."

"I must. I *owe* him." Besides, Deidra was responsible, and William had to set things right before he taught his daughter control.

With great reluctance, he set his hands on the dying man.

*   *   *

Rose watched, her heart in her throat, as William healed Jamie MacPherson. When he fell back, his hand to his throat, Rose rushed to his side, pulling his head into her lap and shielding him with her body. Her own shoulder ached with a deep pain from healing Drake, but she was functional. Though seriously wounded, Drake had not been near death when they'd found him on the mountainside.

Jamie pushed himself up, his hands to his throat, blinking in confusion. His nose was even healed, perfect and aquiline again.

"Stay away from him!" Rose yelled, clutching William closer. The earl and his men surrounded them, protecting William, but she still feared Jamie would somehow harm him.

Jamie said nothing for a long while, staring at Rose and William, his expression odd. Then his gaze moved to the doorway of the cottage. The witchpricker stood there, no longer holding a dirk to Deidra's throat. His hand was still on her shoulder, though. The child looked up at the witchpricker. When his eyes remained fixed on Rose and William, she broke away, throwing herself on her father's inert form.

"I'm sorry, Da! I'm sorry!" she cried, clutching him, burying her face in his bloodied plaid.

William was unable to speak. He put a hand on his daughter's head before his eyes closed.

"Is he dead?" Jamie asked, staring down at William with narrowed eyes.

Rose feared the same, and her fingers sought the

pulse in his neck. "No," she said, relieved. She smoothed the silvered black hair from his forehead and pressed her lips to his fevered skin.

Jamie stood, his hand still gripping his neck. He looked at the wolves. They'd left the cottage and were nosing through a nearby midden pile. He turned his troubled gaze on Deidra, then back to William. He gingerly fingered his nose. He seemed bewildered and afraid. Finally his gaze met Rose's.

After a long moment he nodded, as if in some internal conversation with himself, and turned away. He mounted his horse, gestured to his men, and rode out of the village.

Rose heard footsteps beside her and looked up to see the witchpricker. He frowned down at William for a long time, then crouched suddenly, his tattered black robes pooling on the ground around him. He studied William's face closely.

"There is no evil in what he does," Rose said softly, holding him tighter to her breast. "He is a healer."

"But the child—"

"Is a child."

His thin gray brows arched. "She nearly killed a man. He would be dead if not for Lord Strathwick."

"I did not see her do anything," Lord Kincreag said. "You had a knife to her throat. I know the king doesn't allow such tactics in the questioning of children."

The witchpricker glanced up at the earl, unimpressed but seeing the truth in his words. He had violated the king's edict. He rubbed a thin-fingered hand over his mouth, eyeing Deidra, who still lay on her father's chest.

Under the witchpricker's intense stare, she turned her head away and hunched her shoulders.

The witchpricker stood. "Let us hope our paths do not cross again." He strode into the cottage and shut the door.

Rose let out the breath she'd been holding. She looked up at Drake and the earl. "Let's get out of here before he changes his mind."

Roderick MacDonell passed from life two days later. He never regained his power of speech, but unfortunately for Gillian, in death he was exceedingly vocal. He pursued her through corridors and into her bed at night. The earl lamented that she refused to even kiss her own husband with her dead uncle looking on.

Rose stood on the quay, embracing her sister warmly as she and the earl prepared to leave. "Forgive me, Rose," Gillian said, "but I cannot stay. He is so angry. Forebye, Father is doing so well, I feel no guilt."

"But what about us?"

Gillian lifted her shoulders helplessly. "He's a ghost— and a new one. He can do nothing. No one has even seen him but me. We will return in a month or so, and by then mayhap he'll tire of haunting this place and be ready to move on."

The earl took his wife's hand to lead her down the steps. "We'll send word if we cannot return within the month," he said. "I have great hope that the king will consider my counsel."

Rose did, too. He and Gillian were traveling to Edinburgh to petition the king to rescind his witch-hunting commission and return the jurisdiction for trying witches to the king and privy council only. He planned to use the near lynching of William and Deidra as evidence that the commission had been grossly abused.

Rose said her good-byes and returned to her father's chambers. It had been nearly a fortnight since Roderick had attempted to murder him, and his recovery was nothing short of miraculous. But, of course, it wasn't sufficient for him.

Rose found Hagan fighting to get him back in bed.

"Da!" she cried, rushing to Hagan's aid. "I told you, you must take it slowly."

"I feel fine," he said, brows drawn together crossly. "I will never regain my strength if I must lay in bed eating broth."

Though Rose pressed on his shoulder, urging him to sit, he resisted—with considerable strength. He was eating a great deal more than broth, and she was pleased to see his face filling out again. The graying beard had been trimmed, and his green eyes were clear and lively.

Conan barked and ran in circles, excited to see his master out of bed. With Roderick's death, his spells had lost their power. Conan was free of the dark magic that had bound him, and he was no longer content to lie around. Isobel had been spending a great deal of time in Roderick's chambers, trying to discover more about their uncle and what he'd done. She'd managed to unravel the spell he'd used on the wax effigies, and they were destroyed, much to everyone's relief. Sir Philip had returned with news that Sir Donnan had passed away nearly a year prior.

Rose and her father were still debating the benefits of bed rest when Deidra and William arrived with Liam and his nurse. William bounced the solemn wean while Deidra made faces and noises, causing Liam to emit strange moans that seemed to signal pleasure. Alan's eyes lit up at the sight of his nephew. Despite the pain of his brother's deception, he held none of it against the baby. He was overjoyed to finally have an heir to raise and train.

While Rose was distracted at the sight of William, Alan slipped out of bed and took the baby, thus making it impossible for Rose to force him back into the bed.

She sighed. "Very well. But you are not to overexert yourself."

He ignored her, gently bobbling his nephew while Deidra showed Alan the little gowns and hats the wet nurse had made for him. Rose's father exclaimed over each item as if it were a priceless treasure. Though Rose and William had not yet wed, Alan was already enjoying his role as Deidra's grandfather. He asked her to bring him a different animal every day to converse with, and Deidra was happy to oblige.

Rose turned her attention back to William and found him gazing at her oddly, a slightly bemused look on his face. She'd caught him looking at her so several times over the past few days. When she questioned him about it, he only shook his head, refusing to reveal his thoughts. She raised impatient brows at him, and this time he inclined his head. She followed, leaving her father with Hagan and Deidra.

She led him to her chambers, where they could have

some privacy. They had not made love again since the first time, and every touch and look from him set her body aflame in anticipation of their impending wedding night. The banns had been posted the past two Sundays and would be announced the third and final time tomorrow. They were to be married immediately afterward.

Inside her chambers, with the door closed, he pulled her close and kissed her. She sank into the warmth of his mouth, twining her arms around his neck. He pulled away too soon, his fingers threading through the hair at her temple, pulling it free of her braid and rubbing it between his fingers. It was streaked with dozens of snowy white strands.

"You've been healing," he said reproachfully.

Rose shrugged. "Nothing much. Just some burns in the kitchen, and Cook cut himself." Rose curled her hand into a fist at the memory of that. It had been a most horrific wound. Cook would have been forced to retire his ladle if she had not mended him.

"Prithee return to conventional healing if that suffices—and surely kitchen burns and cuts aren't a matter of life and death."

Rose made a face at him. "You find me ugly with white hair?"

He slid his hand over her head, cupping her neck. "Never. I just . . . fash for you."

"Why?"

He took a deep breath. "Because I don't know what it means, how it works. I sometimes wonder if every time I heal someone it . . . subtracts time from my life. And the gray hair . . . maybe I lost a day for every gray hair." He touched her white hairs again, his throat working as he swallowed hard. "Before . . . it didn't matter. The sooner, the better. But now . . . now everything has changed."

Rose pressed herself against his chest. His arms came around her, and he lay his cheek atop her head.

When she could speak again, she said, "Then I must needs heal more, so I can catch up to you, aye?" She reached up, sifting her fingers through black and silver silk. "For you have lost many more days than I have."

"Do not speak so. No more healing for you—at least for another year or so."

Rose pulled back to frown at him. "Why?"

He looked down, his gaze resting on her belly. "Because our child needs all of your strength."

Rose gasped, mouth agape. "How can you tell? I've barely missed my courses. How do you know?"

His mouth curved into a bemused smile. "Because I see him. His color is different from yours."

Rose's hand went to her belly, joy filling her. She had never been able to see her own color—but of course he could, and if there was life inside her, he would see that.

"What color is he?"

"Green, like sage."

She arched a brow at him. "How do you know it's a boy?"

He lifted a shoulder. "I don't." He covered her hand with his, pressing it into her belly. He kissed her again, his mouth warm and urgent, and Rose thought it impossible to love someone more. Just a month ago she'd never expected to be so happy. But she knew it wasn't over. They still had Strathwick to return to, and life was different there.

Later that night, after Deidra had fallen asleep, they stood on the battlements together, gazing across the water to the flickering lights of the village. William's arms were warm and heavy around her shoulders. She pressed closer, her hand on the hard muscles of his belly, thinking still of how to make peace with the people of Strathwick. She pulled away suddenly and fixed William with a determined stare.

He raised a brow at her sudden animation.

"You must tell Allister that he is your brother."

Both brows raised. "That's not a good idea, methinks."

"It is. It's perfect."

He laughed without humor. "If you think he hates me now, just wait and see how he reacts to discovering we're brothers—if he even believes me." He shook his head firmly. "Nay. *That* is not the answer."

"*It is.* How can he condemn you when he shares your blood?"

He shook his head again, grim. "That won't matter to him."

"It would if he, too, was a witch."

William narrowed his eyes thoughtfully. "I don't know for certain that he is."

"You said he never sickens and healed miraculously from a serious wound. I didn't know *I* could heal until you showed me. Mayhap he doesn't either. Wouldn't it be better to make an enemy into an ally? To at least try?"

He raised a shoulder, still dubious. "It's a good thought, but I doubt he'll volunteer for lessons."

Rose arched a brow at him. "Make him. Hold him prisoner." When he opened his mouth incredulously, she placed a finger against it. "It will keep him out of trouble, aye?"

He gazed down at her for a long moment, sapphire eyes slowly turning molten. Rose recognized the look, and her body answered eagerly, a melting warmth spreading through her limbs. He pushed her back against the wall, insinuating his knee between her thighs. "Perhaps. What if he still refuses?"

Rose smiled up at him, sliding her hands over the hard muscles of his chest. "I'll make sure he doesn't. Recall you that we have Betty? His wife. Methinks that's what the fuss is really about."

He looked at her in astonishment and pleasure. "God's bones, but you're a schemer. How did I ever manage without you?"

"I know not," she murmured, pulling his mouth to hers and making it clear he would never be forced to blunder along without her again.

Epilogue

To my loving father, Alan MacDonell,

It is with great regret that I write to inform you we are unable to join you in the festivities at Lochlaire this Christmas. As you know I am expecting a child in the spring, and this prohibits travel. William wishes me to inform you that all is well with the child, so you have naught to fash on. Deidra sends her love and informs me that Conan does as well. He understands your sudden aversion to dogs. He wishes you to know he has found a comfortable home with new friends. I have some happy news and an exciting tale to share when we are finally together again. But for now I will say Drake has finally married! It was a surprise to us as well, but the lady took his heart by storm. It was a rather troublesome affair, as she was betrothed to someone else, and it involved kidnapping—but rest assured, all is well now! Her name is Ceara, and we are indeed blessed to have her join our family.

Your last letter brought such welcome tidings! Isobel and Sir Philip have been blessed with a son, and Lord Kincreag was successful in his petition to the king. No news is more welcome in Strathwick than this! Let us hope this is cause for Mr. Forsyth to retire from the witchpricking business! We are well pleased to hear Liam is already walking. He is surely a gift to be praised and a most amazing lad. Methinks he is a MacDonell indeed.

Please accept our humble thanks for your generous gifts. We pray God gives you health and preserves you many more Christmases and that soon we will all be together again. Please accept the gift we send with goodwill. You know we at Strathwick are not as wealthy, but William thought it meet to ask his brother, Allister, to make you this chair. His skill in woodworking is exceptional, I'm sure you'll agree, and with the pillow Betty (Allister's wife) and I embroidered, it will be a splendid place to take your rest before the fire in the evenings.

With the remembrance of my humble duty unto you, I humbly take my leave and rest,

Your dutiful and obedient daughter,
Rose MacDonell, Lady Strathwick
From the House of Strathwick xx December
The year of our Lord 1597

Don't miss the first two novels in Jen Holling's sexy *MacDonell Brides Trilogy!*

My Wicked HIGHLANDER

When Sir Philip Kilpatrick is sent to deliver the beautiful Isobel MacDonell to her noble betrothed, he doesn't know that she is a witch. Isobel fears that he will discover the truth, but she longs to help him uncover the secret that has tortured him for more than a decade. She charms her way into his heart, but if she uses her second sight to solve the mystery of Philip's past, will it destroy them both?

My Devilish SCOTSMAN

After his betrothal to the eldest MacDonell sister is broken, Nicholas Lyon, Earl Kincreag, wants nothing more to do with the MacDonell girls. But when he is offered another daughter, Gillian—whom he'd secretly preferred all along—Nicholas reluctantly accepts. Now Gillian hears strange voices and sees specters inside the Kincreag castle and fears there may be more to the rumors of her devil earl than she'd ever wanted to believe.

Available from

POCKET BOOKS
A Division of Simon & Schuster
A VIACOM COMPANY

www.simonsayslove.com

12871

FINALLY A WEBSITE YOU CAN GET *PASSIONATE* ABOUT...

Visit
www.SimonSaysLove.com
for the latest information
about Romance from Pocket Books!

READING SUGGESTIONS

LATEST RELEASES

AUTHOR APPEARANCES

ONLINE CHATS WITH YOUR
FAVORITE WRITERS

SPECIAL OFFERS

AND MUCH, MUCH MORE!

11912